Mary Larkin was born in Belfast and, after forty happy years there, now lives in the north-east of England. She is married with three sons.

For more information about the author and her books, visit www.marylarkin.co.uk

SUSPICIOUS MINDS

Mary Larkin

SPHERE

First published in Great Britain in 2010 by Sphere
This paperback edition published in 2011 by Sphere

A CIP catalogue record for this book
is available from the British Library.

ISBN 978-0-7515-4348-3

Typeset in Sabon by Palimpsest Book Production Limited,
Falkirk, Stirlingshire
Printed and bound in Great Britain by
Clays Ltd, St Ives plc

Sphere
An imprint of
Little, Brown Book Group
100 Victoria Embankment
London EC4Y 0DY

An Hachette UK Company
www.hachette.co.uk

www.littlebrown.co.uk

I dedicate this book to Theresa for her guidance along the way.

Acknowledgements

To Celia Levett, my sincere gratitude for her editorial input.

To Sue McDowell, for just being there in my hour of need.

To my son, Con, my grateful thanks for his unselfish help with any computer problems I encountered during the course of this book.

Author's Note

The geographical areas portrayed in *Suspicious Minds* actually exist, and any historical events referred to in the course of the story are, to the best of my knowledge, authentic.

However, I wish to emphasise that the story is fictional; all characters are fictitious and any resemblance to real persons, living or dead, is purely coincidental.

Belfast

Early 1960s

1

Her body tensed when she heard the key rattle in the front-door lock. Head tilted, Maura Brady listened with bated breath to her husband's progress along the hall. Her lip curled with contempt as she pictured him checking himself in the hall mirror for any tell-tale signs that would betray his infidelity: that he had been with another woman. She wanted to rush out and confront him, ask if he thought her a bloody eejit or something, but she didn't dare. What if that was what he wanted? A confrontation! An excuse to end it all.

After what seemed like ages but in fact was only a few moments, he came through to the kitchen, a look of contrition on his face, apologies dripping easily from his lips. With a glance at the wall clock as if he didn't know the time he said, 'Is that the time it is? Oh I am sorry I'm late, love.'

His whole demeanour was so innocent, so casual, even, that her blood boiled with such an anger that it was almost tangible. Afraid of the repercussions should she turn round and face him, she remained standing at the sink, gripping the edge tightly to control her nerves and gazing blindly out at the garden she so lovingly tended each day, all the while trying to quell the rage bubbling within her. She didn't dare look at him in case her temper erupted. She wouldn't be responsible for the consequences, should that happen, and that could be the beginning of the end of their marriage. Why did he risk taking chances like this? Acting as if nothing out of the ordinary was going on? Surely he must have some shred of feeling for her, no matter how small.

When he had been dumped, by the love of his life, some years back, Maura had caught him on the rebound and had given up everything to try to mend this man's heartache. She had thought she had succeeded. Now, after all the effort she'd put into making a go of their marriage, she wasn't going to stand idly by and take any old nonsense from him. Whilst she had always known he could never love her the way he had loved the beautiful Evelyn, surely loyalty wasn't too much to ask? But then again, what if he had no choice in the matter?

4

What if this other woman had such a strong hold on him that he couldn't escape her clutches even if he wanted to? What then? Could she risk making a big issue of it or should she let the affair run its course and hope for the best? Blinking furiously to hold back the threatening tears, and with lips that trembled, she said abruptly, 'Your dinner's ruined!'

He frowned, his eyes boring into her unresponsive back, gauging her mood, willing her to turn and face him. When she didn't, he shrugged indifferently. 'Don't worry, love. It doesn't matter. I had a sandwich earlier on. Where's Danny?'

Without so much as a glance towards him she said bitterly, 'In bed! Where else would he be at this time of night? He was asking for his daddy, wanted you to read him a story. I'm sure in his own childish mind he's wondering what's wrong. He can't understand why you don't read bedtime stories to him any more.' She blinked furiously, warning herself not to give him the satisfaction of seeing her cry. 'He'll be wondering what's wrong, the way you're acting lately, so he will. He's fretting over it. Probably in his own childish way he's worrying that he's done something awful to upset you. You know the way his wee mind works. Anyway, what kept you to this hour?'

Adam Brady tentatively approached his wife, and putting his arms round her waist, he nuzzled his face in her soft auburn hair, teasing it away from the nape of her neck and planting soft kisses there. She trembled at his touch. He was ashamed of himself for cheating on this good woman who meant everything to him, but, to his everlasting shame, he couldn't help himself. He'd managed to convince himself that what Maura didn't know wouldn't hurt her and he certainly hadn't expected his affair, if one could even call it an affair, with the lovely, devious Evelyn Matthews, to last. A kiss now and again when she needed comforting. Big deal! She had caused him enough heartache once before and he had no doubt that she would do so again should somebody more exciting come along. Meanwhile . . . God forgive him, he found the lure of that woman so overpowering it was almost hypnotic, so that at times he could hardly breathe in her presence.

Maura stiffened in his arms, wanting to retch, as a whiff of perfume assailed her nostrils. That was one thing he couldn't get rid of in a hurry. That tantalising whiff of expensive perfume was what had first aroused the worm of suspicion, now twisting away in her stomach, that he was having an affair. Swallowing the bile that rose in her throat, she roughly pushed herself away from the sink and out of his embrace, and wrenched open the oven door with unnecessary force. With hands that shook, she grabbed a tea towel and lifted a covered plate from the centre shelf. Curbing the desire to throw it at him, she thumped it down on the table and removing the cover stood for a long moment, staring at the food as if trying to figure out what it was. Only when she was sure she was in control of her voice did she repeat, 'Well, it's after eight! What kept you? You should have been home ages ago.' This time she saw the casual lift of his shoulders and wanted to scream and lash out at him in frustration.

He looked defiantly down his nose at her and asked irritably, 'I don't understand . . . Is anything wrong? What's up with you? Why the sudden interest? Well, if you must know, we were packing up for the day when the boss asked me to go across to the Antrim Road, have a look at a garden there and see if it was worth landscaping.'

The lies dripped easily off his tongue, but he found it difficult to make eye contact with his wife. Pulling a chair away from the table, he sat down. There was something different about Maura tonight. His mind balked as a thought struck him. Surely she didn't suspect anything? He almost smiled at the absurdity of the idea. Of course she didn't. How could she? He would never intentionally hurt her, so he was very careful that his work colleagues never found out that he and Evelyn Matthews had once been lovers.

Maura sat opposite him, arms resting on the

table, fingers drumming an impatient tattoo, and for the first time since he'd come home she looked him full in the face. With a great effort he managed an expression of complete innocence, as if butter wouldn't melt in his mouth, as he gazed back at her. She wasn't fooled! Liar! Adulterer! her mind screamed. Did he think she was some kind of imbecile?

She gestured towards his plate of steak and kidney pie that she had lovingly prepared. It covered half the plate, with boiled potatoes, roasted carrot and parsnip arranged alongside it. Two hours ago it had been a lovely appetising meal; now it was a congealed mess. 'Well, was it?'

Again that look of naivety as he blinked at her in bewilderment. 'Was it what?'

'The garden!' she jeered. Did the fool think she was enquiring after the sordid details of his love life? 'What else? Was it worth the journey to the other side of the lough?'

'Oh! Yes. Yes, as a matter of fact it was,' he was honestly able to assure her.

He had indeed, a few weeks ago, been sent over to make up an estimate for restoring large gardens that had gone to pot through years of neglect. Being able to speak truthfully gave his confidence a boost. Straightening himself in the chair he looked her straight in the eye as he continued, 'The house has been lying empty for some time. It's one of those big houses on the Antrim Road near the top of Serpentine Road with a wonderful view of the lough. You'd love it! Those gardens must have at one time been very beautiful, but they need a complete facelift now. The bushes and shrubs have been left to fend for themselves and certainly need a good pruning back, while the flower beds are in a shocking state, covered in weeds. Some of the wild animals up in Bellevue Zoo wouldn't look out of place there, it's like a bloody jungle. So, as you can imagine, there's quite a lot of work to be done, and I'll probably be over there a lot more for the next month or so.'

He was relieved to be setting up an alibi for some time to come. He could answer her truthfully about the gardens. The expansive grounds around the house where Evelyn Matthews and her husband lived were well laid out, even if they were over-grown, but as he had just explained, they needed a lot of expert attention to bring them back to their former glory. And who else would Evelyn want to do the work but Gallagher Nursery Centre, Holywood? She had told them that Adam was an acquaintance from way back and could he possibly be the one to come over, as she preferred to deal with people she knew, whom she could trust, as she put it, rather than a complete stranger. That was three weeks ago. The first time, he had arrived at her door in all innocence, not knowing who or what to expect. From that fateful day on, his world had turned upside down as he became hopelessly embroiled in the physical attraction she held for him.

Maura watched him push his food aimlessly around his plate. 'Eat that up,' she warned curtly. 'It cost good money. And as you are well aware, we can't afford to squander any.'

His lips tightened and without another word he stabbed a cube of steak and sticking it in his mouth slowly chewed on it. He wasn't in the least bit hungry. How could he possibly be, when Evelyn had been bringing out sandwiches and titbits all day long to him and his young helper? What on earth was he going to do? He couldn't go on like this. He'd have to tell Maura about Evelyn. Perhaps she would understand and they could come to some kind of arrangement. After all, she knew what Evelyn had meant to him in the past. As he mused, he skewered a piece of kidney and pushed it into his mouth. Now he was being daft. What kind of arrangement? Did he really think she would say, 'Oh! That's OK. Go ahead, sweetheart. Have your fling. Get her out of your system once and for all.'

But he *had* warned her that this might happen, he righteously reminded himself. Maura couldn't say he hadn't. He had told her that if Evelyn ever came back, he wouldn't be accountable for his actions, and she had been willing to take that chance. That had been some years back when Evelyn had dumped him and in his grief he had turned to Maura for comfort, seeking forgetfulness in her arms.

His wife watched him struggle with the pie. Good God, you'd think it was poisoned the way he was picking at it. Now there was an idea. Perhaps next time, it would be chicken and mushroom pie and the mushrooms might just be of the poisonous variety. How's about a nice chicken and Death Cap pie, darling, or maybe a lovely Destroying Angels casserole, she thought viciously. Pushing the chair away from the table, she hurried from the kitchen before she made a complete fool of herself by breaking down in front of him.

Later, they washed and dried the dishes in silence, then settled down in separate chairs for what was left of the evening to watch TV. The happy, easy, contented nature of their relationship was missing lately and time passed slowly. The tension was like a taut wire between them. A romantic thriller was on the screen but Maura, lost in the depths of despair, watched it and yet didn't see any of it. She had a feeling that things were coming to a head. It was dreadful. How would she be able to bear it? Adam sat gazing down at the *Belfast Telegraph* spread out on his lap and when he at last lifted his head and looked at her she saw only misery reflected in his eyes. To her horror she actually felt the urge to jump up, take him in her arms and console him. God, what way was her mind working? This man was cheating on her and she wanted to embrace him and ease his misery? What about her hurt and pain? She really must be losing her marbles, she thought bitterly.

Panic gripped her and, afraid she would give in to her impulses, she surged to her feet in a rush, muttering, 'I can't get interested in this film. I'm away out for a breath of fresh air.' Before she could say something they might both regret, she grabbed her coat and practically flew from the house.

Adam stared after her, at a loss for words. What on earth had got into her? Then horror drove everything else from his mind. Surely his wife didn't know that Evelyn Matthews was back in town? Could she possibly? That would certainly be enough to send her ballistic.

April had lived up to its name, with plenty of light showers, but May had been bright and warm. The past couple of days had been pleasant with a hot sun drying all beneath it. People had taken advantage of the good weather to mow their lawns and generally tidy up their gardens. Tonight it was calm and warm, with a clear starry sky and the smell of freshly mown grass permeating the air. Walking down past the yacht club to the beach, Maura strolled slowly along the seafront, sick at heart. The light sea breeze cooled her hot cheeks and she took long, deep breaths of its briny fragrance to calm her nerves. How would she be able to keep up this pretence that all was well between them? She'd try. God knows she'd try, but would she succeed? She feared that she was nearing the end of her tether and fighting a losing battle.

She loved living in her beautiful house here in County Down. However, with her son, Danny, to consider, if her marriage broke up she would have to move away from Holywood and return across to the other side of the lough, to Greencastle on the Antrim coast. What else could she do? Would it ever come to that? She hoped and prayed not.

At first she had tried to ignore all the signs that her husband was seeing another woman; she couldn't believe or, subconsciously, didn't want to believe what her heart and senses were telling her. Their beautiful son was just approaching his third birthday. To her their marriage had seemed perfect, every woman's dream. She had been content with her lot. Had she become too complacent? Did Adam regret having to marry her? No! She couldn't believe that, not for one single moment. The passion and fulfilment were still there. Well, they had been there until a few weeks ago. What had driven her husband into another woman's arms?

13

Was something lacking in their marriage? One would have thought that he had learned his lesson when Evelyn Matthews had jilted him. It had nearly been the finish of him, when some years back the beautiful blonde Evelyn had handed him back his engagement ring and run off with a man old enough to be her grandfather. A very rich grandfather at that, absolutely rolling in it. The shock of it had sent him reeling into the depths of despair and, in his grief, he had turned to Maura for solace.

Thank God, Evelyn was living down in County Cork these days, otherwise Maura wouldn't stand a snowball's chance in hell of holding on to her husband. He had been besotted with Evelyn, but Maura had felt comparatively safe and secure in the knowledge that her love rival was far away at the other end of the country. She couldn't comprehend how, after the way Evelyn had treated him, Adam would carry on with yet another woman. You'd think he'd have learned his lesson. 'Once bitten, twice shy,' as the saying goes.

Maura couldn't believe that he was risking all they had going for them, by seeing someone else. She had thought that he was happy enough with his life. How could she have been so blind? Still, all the signs were there for her to see . . . and smell. One didn't have to be a brain surgeon to recognise them.

* * *

14

Adam worked for two brothers, Benny and George Gallagher, who owned the Nursery Centre in Holywood. They had built up a successful business more or less from scratch and now employed a substantial workforce. Adam had been one of their first trainees straight from school and had quickly progressed through the horticultural ranks to contracts manager, driving from site to site, supervising the work and making sure that everything was going according to plan. When the brothers had heard that he was getting married, they had offered him a house close to the nursery for a nominal rent and had helped out with renovations to the building: an extension built on to the back of the house, with a bathroom and a bedroom above.

Maura and Adam had worked hard in their spare time, painting and wallpapering and putting up shelves and building cupboards. No effort was too great. The room above the bathroom was turned into a lovely nursery for the arrival of Danny and the house was fast becoming the home of Maura's dreams. Her little palace. And now this.

Her heart quailed as a sudden thought assailed her. It was a tied house that went with the job. If they split up she would have no option but to move out. Fear gathered in a tight lump in her chest. Surely Adam wouldn't consider moving his new love into their beautiful home? Dear God, surely he wouldn't be that cruel. Would he? What if this other woman insisted they live here in Holywood? What then? How would she be able to bear the humiliation? Besides, if Adam moved in with this woman, the Gallaghers would claim back the house for one of their other married employees. After all, business was business and sentiment wouldn't enter into it.

Stopping at the sea wall, she leaned against it and gazed out over Belfast Lough. In the hazy light she could just pick out Greencastle across the water where she had been born and bred. The lough was a lazy, heaving swell of silver-crested wavelets that lapped gently on the shingle. So tranquil and serene. She stood there for almost half an hour until suddenly, and for no reason, the quietness unnerved her. Becoming aware of her loneliness, she huddled inside her coat and clamped her arms across her chest as if for warmth. Reluctantly she retraced her steps, determining in her mind that she'd fight tooth and nail to hold on to her man. Meanwhile, she'd bide her time and see how things worked out.

The house was silent when she got back; no sign of her husband. He must have retired for the night. Perhaps, afraid that she would expect him to perform in bed, he would feign sleep? Well, she'd give him plenty of time to drop off. The very thought of him touching her, with the scent of another woman still clinging to him, was repulsive. She would be unable to respond and might even lash out at him in anger.

Having made a cup of tea, she sat by the dying embers of the fire brooding over her uncertain future. A half-hour dragged by. Unable to put bedtime off any longer, she rinsed the cup and checked the windows and doors. As she made her way slowly upstairs, a dread settled on her. She sincerely hoped that Adam would be asleep. Small talk would be a pain and her nerves were in too brittle a state at the moment to pretend that all was hunky-dory with her. He was a better actor than she was, that was for sure. But then he'd certainly had plenty of practice lately.

The nursery door was always kept ajar in case Danny woke up during the night. Now she quietly pushed it open further to look in on the boy before going to her own room. Danny lay on his back in the big cot, arms and legs outstretched. On the single bed, bought when the child had restless nights cutting his teeth and couldn't be left alone, lay Adam, his arm spanning the dividing space, clutching his son's hand. Both were fast asleep. She stood by the cot gazing down on her son, then gently pulled the covers up over the child. He stirred but didn't waken. Her husband didn't budge. He was out to the world. She grimaced. Anyone looking at him would think he hadn't one iota of guilt on his conscience, not a care in the world. Was it all in her mind? No! Of course not. He was carrying on with another woman. Of that she was sure.

Maura stood for some moments examining his handsome features. It was a strong face. Straight nose, wide sensitive lips and a chin with a cleft that Kirk Douglas would be proud of. Adam had already removed his shoes. Fetching a spare blanket she covered him, before tiptoeing from the room, quietly closing the door after her.

She surmised that Danny must have cried out in his sleep and Adam had, as was usual, lain with him for a while until he had settled down. Normally, she would have awakened Adam to come to his own bed, but not tonight. Tonight she could do without his company and attentions, thank you. Not that he was bothering her much in bed lately. Probably saving all his energy for his fancy woman.

She sat in front of the small utility dressing table, brushing her long hair, in contemplation, for many minutes. She had inherited her mother's thick auburn mane and was proud of it. How she missed her mother and wished she was here to confide in. Joan Craig had died of TB when her daughter was twelve years old. Maura and her father had become very close. Indeed, she had made it her life's ambition to look after him.

Up until the time she had confessed to him that she was pregnant, Davey Craig had thought the world of her, the model daughter who could do no wrong. He was scandalised at her news and blamed himself for not persuading her to go out more often, mix with people her own age.

To be fair, he *had* tried to get her to go out and about more. With her father's approval, she and Francie Murphy had struck up an acquaintance. Then, one night when she was out for a drink at the Railway bar with Francie and her father, she had been introduced to Adam Brady, who was in the company of one of Davey's regular fellow drinkers. She had been drawn by the sadness he'd been unable to hide. It was written all over his face for all the world to see. Shortly after that first meeting they had started dating on a regular basis. Her father hadn't been too happy about the relationship. Knowing all about Adam being jilted, he had thought Maura was wasting her time going out with him and could only get hurt in the long run. Sometime later when she had confessed to being pregnant by Adam he couldn't believe it; he was devastated and had ranted and raved at her for being so stupid. He couldn't face the shame of it, thinking he had failed in her upbringing, and in the end he had told her to pack her bags and get out. 'Go to your lover, see if he'll take you in,' he yelled at her as she had rushed to her bedroom to pack what she would need for the night.

There had been no reasoning with him. In desperation she had turned to her Aunt Hilda who lived on the Whitewell Road, sure of her sympathy. Hilda was one of life's timid creatures who wouldn't hurt a fly and was forever apologetic no matter who was in the wrong. As Maura had expected, her aunt had indeed taken her in that night and in her own timorous way had tried to comfort her. However, she was obviously embarrassed when she heard about her pregnancy and who the culprit was, and said she was sorry for Maura's distress. Hilda had told her that, as much as she would like to have her, Maura couldn't stay indefinitely, not with her own two young girls in the house. She had pointed out that her husband would surely object. It would set a bad example for their daughters when her pregnancy started to show, she told Maura as nicely as possible, trying not to hurt her feelings. How could they explain it to two inquisitive young minds? What with her not being married and all that?

Maura, agreeing with her aunt, told her not to be so apologetic and not to worry herself on her account. As a last resort she had reluctantly been forced to tell Adam of her plight. He had never once expressed any love for her and she didn't know how he would react, but she was at her wits' end with nowhere else to turn. He didn't bat an eyelid at the news. 'We'll get married,' he had said without compunction, and the past few years had been the happiest of her life.

Twisting her hair in a knot, she skewered it on top of her head and, reaching for a jar of Astral cream, proceeded to massage it into her face. Her skin was silky smooth and without a blemish. She examined her features. Small tilted nose, eyes wide spaced, but a pleasing deep-green colour. Not too bad really, but in comparison with Evelyn Matthews she must surely seem what people might describe as somewhat plain. But then again, looks weren't everything, and she *had* given Adam a son!

With a sigh she removed the surplus cream from her face and kneeling by the bedside asked God to guide her in keeping her marriage from crumbling around her. As she lay on the bed that had always brought her so much pleasure and comfort, she thought back to the beginning and once again thanked God that Evelyn Matthews was living far away in Cork. Perhaps this new woman wouldn't have as strong a hold on Adam. Hopefully, she was just a passing fancy. She would try to be patient, give him plenty of rope either to hang or to rescue himself. She prayed it would be the latter. In this happier frame of mind she lapsed into a shallow sleep.

* * *

21

After a restless night, Maura slept in. She woke to find Danny cuddled up beside her and Adam placing a cup of tea and a round of toast on the bedside table. He was already dressed for work.

She struggled to sit up, trying not to disturb Danny. 'You should have wakened me. What about *your* breakfast?'

'I've already eaten. It's only half seven. You may as well take a lie-in when you're getting the chance.' He bent forward and gave her a peck on the cheek. 'See you tonight.'

'Will you be late?' She watched him closely and detected a flustered look sweep across his face before he had time to compose himself.

'I don't know. You know how it is with gardens, Maura. I can't just up and leave in the middle of a job. I'll try not to be too late, OK? See ya then.'

With a deep sigh she reached for the cup. She had a feeling he would be late again and already dreaded the stilted conversation they would have when he did return. All the joy had suddenly gone out of her life. She didn't know what to do, how to handle the situation for the best. If only she had someone to confide in. Get someone else's opinion and weigh up all the options. Burying her head in the pillow, she cried long and sore until little fingers pulling at her hair brought her back to her senses. Wiping the tears from her face with the corner of the bed sheet, she pulled

Danny into her arms and smothered his small face with kisses.

'Let's get you some breakfast, love, and later we'll take the bus into Bangor and buy you some new shoes. Won't that be nice? Those wee feet of yours are growing so fast I can't keep up with them.'

Big blue eyes so like his father's examined her face, then he smiled and nodded his head. Maura was sometimes surprised at the perception of her young son. He seemed to understand every word she uttered, more than was creditable for a child of his age. She'd have to be more careful what she said in front of him and make a better job of concealing her unhappiness.

2

Evelyn Matthews sat with long legs curled under her on the window seat of her spacious and elegant lounge looking out over the grounds of her enviable home. Built high up on the Antrim Road, it had the most spectacular view over Belfast Lough. The gardens, sprawled around the house, were a wonderful display, with multicoloured flowers struggling for survival among an entanglement of weeds and nettles. A glorious mass of disarray, it was also an avid gardener's nightmare. Capability Brown would have turned in his grave at the state of it. It was in dire need of expert attention to bring it back to its original splendour, something Evelyn had already set in motion. Beyond the rear gardens a panoramic landscape stretched out before her, right down to Greencastle and the lough shimmering in the distance, separating the County Antrim and Down coastlines. A magnificent view to behold.

She felt a smugness creep over her, surveying these beautiful surroundings. Greencastle was the village where she had been born and reared. She had certainly done well for herself since then, thank you, and was very proud of all she had accomplished in such a short time for a mere Greencastle lass. The man she had chosen to run off with some years ago had been much, much older than herself, but he had been very wealthy and she had wanted for nothing. He had been kind, considerate and easily pleased. In her own way she had grown to love him as the father she had never known. Her only regret was the loss of Adam Brady, the handsome, dynamic young man she had once planned to marry. She hugged herself with glee. Now, with a little manipulation on her part, Adam was back in her life and, furthermore, she sensed that he still cared for her.

At the time of her marriage to Charles, Greencastle had been rocked by the scandal. She couldn't understand why; what were they all up in arms for? After all, Charles Matthews had been a widower for many years. Granted, he was a successful businessman and although his only son was now running the business, Charles still held the reins and called all the shots. Since his marriage to Evelyn he had ruled his enterprise from the comfort of his own home. His first marriage had been a happy one, but after the death of his wife he had been very lonely and had become a bit of a recluse. Friends had tried to get him interested in other women, but no one had ever held his attention for very long.

Until that day he first set eyes on Evelyn Delaney in the perfume department of Robinson & Cleaver on Donegall Place where she worked. He had been completely bowled over by her fresh young beauty and vibrant personality. To the amusement of her fellow assistants, he had come back time and time again buying numerous perfumes as an excuse to talk to her. If Evelyn was busy, no one else was allowed to serve him. He graciously declined their assistance and waited patiently until Evelyn was free to attend him.

Obviously getting on in years, Charles was still a striking figure, standing at least six feet tall, his back straight as a ramrod, with longish white hair and an aristocratic, almost imperious face. Always immaculately dressed, he wore one black kid glove on his left hand in which he carried the other glove. Had he worn a tailed coat and top hat he could have fitted the description of one of the Victorian gentry in a Dickens novel.

The girls had called him her sugar grandaddy and had teased her mercilessly about him.

Embarrassed by the spectacle he was making of himself, Evelyn had confided in Adam Brady, her fiancé, about this kind old gentleman. Secure in the strong love bond they shared, he had laughingly warned her to go easy on the old boy and not do anything that might bring on a heart attack. But on the other hand, he had warned her not to get carried away with herself and let her head be turned by this man's apparent wealth, never dreaming for an instant that such a thing was ever likely to happen. Not to his Evelyn.

When it became obvious to Evelyn that Charles Matthews' intentions for her were indeed very serious and honourable, and fully aware that there might be serious adverse consequences, she had nevertheless encouraged him, just to see how far he was willing to go, she assured herself. There was no way she would ever consider having anything to do with a man in his twilight years, no matter how kind and generous he was. She truly believed that a well-heeled man like Charles Matthews would soon tire of her and move on to pastures new.

But no! As time passed it became apparent that he really was besotted with her and that his intentions were indeed deadly serious and honourable. Confident that she would be able to talk Adam round to her way of thinking, she had led Charles on, until, sure of his response, she had made it quite clear that, yes, she did like him; she liked him a lot, in fact, but would settle for nothing less than marriage. Their complete courtship had been conducted in public over the perfume counter in Robinson & Cleaver, causing many a curious glance from both customers and staff, or in the Carlton Rooms on Wellington Place where she had dined with him on a number of occasions during her lunch break.

From the outset she had made it crystal clear that there would be no hanky-panky going on between them! She had no intentions of being an old man's bit on the side, to be used and discarded like an old coat as and when it suited him. No, it had to be all or nothing. To her surprise, he had quickly come round to her way of thinking. The only stipulation he had made was that they be married quietly and without any fuss. Because of their age difference he didn't want the wedding to be turned into a spectacle, setting idle tongues wagging and elbows nudging. Evelyn was only too happy to fall in with these plans. Her unmarried mother had died in childbirth and she had never known her father. The aunt who reared her had died a few years back, so a quiet wedding suited her just fine. The banns were called and six weeks later they were married quietly in St Mary's Church in Greencastle.

She was still very much in love with Adam Brady and couldn't understand why he couldn't see things her way. As far as she was concerned, that had been the only fly in the ointment. Her love for Adam had been all-consuming, but the lure of all that money, and the life of luxury and comfort it afforded, had given her the courage to jilt him. After all, she convinced herself, they were all the same under the blankets. But nothing had prepared her for such a contradiction to the old adage. Charles could never hold a candle to Adam Brady's finely tuned, muscular body and, even in the dark and under the blankets, the difference was indisputable. But then again, it had seemed a small price to pay for all the luxury and wealth that Charles provided, and he was so easily pleased.

Of course, the fact that Charles's son David and daughter-in-law Rose hadn't been too happy about the marriage was putting it mildly, to say the least. They were furious and had been very outspoken about Evelyn, called her a conniving gold-digger and a whore, David telling his father to catch himself on, that he was cradle-snatching and needed his head seeing to. Incensed by these snide and hurtful remarks, Charles had decided to take his young bride away from all this malicious talk and speculation, and set about looking for somewhere far away. Money was no object and, leaving his son in control of the business while he househunted, they had eventually settled in County Cork at the extreme south of Ireland.

At the time she had urged Charles to sell the house and sever all connections with Belfast, dreading the idea of coming back to visit and bumping into Adam Brady whom she missed more than she had ever dreamed possible. When she had told Adam of her intention to marry Charles, she had hoped to have her cake and eat it, explaining that nothing need change between them, that they could meet on the quiet and carry on as before. After all, she pointed out, Charles was an old man and couldn't live much longer. She knew that she stood to inherit quite a large slice of her husband's estate and then they would be rich and fancy free to go and do as they pleased. She had it all figured out.

She recalled the day she had told Adam of her plans to marry Charles. He had been outraged. At first he'd thought that she was pulling his leg, had laughed at the very idea and had chided her for her wit. She remembered the horrified look on his face when the penny dropped, convinced at last that she was deadly serious. A man for whom veracity meant everything, he quickly scorned the idea that she had the audacity to think that he would even consider having an old man's plaything on the side. In a sense the man she loved had dumped *her*. Knowing that he was devastated and hurt, she had begged and pleaded with him, convinced she could bring his mind round to her way of thinking, but in vain. She later heard through the grapevine that he was dating Maura Craig. A short time later he had married her on the rebound. Evelyn couldn't believe it. Maura Craig? An old school friend of hers! How could he do that to *me*?

Now she was glad that Charles had decided to keep the house. When he'd had a stroke four months ago he had asked to be taken home and she had been only too willing to comply with his wishes. Although much older than her, Charles had been such good company and because of his great wealth they had been well accepted into the upper-crust circles of the Cork aristocracy. They had bought a cottage in Bantry overlooking the bay and, while she sometimes yearned for Adam, her life had been contented and happy enough – until Charles had had the stroke. With him now practically bedridden and the doctors holding out little hope for a full recovery, she had thought that, here on the Antrim Road, close to his family and friends, life would be more bearable for him and certainly a lot easier for her!

Since their marriage, Charles had devoted most of his time to his young wife. Although still the company chairman, his son was very much the boss at the moment and, confident that his father would never return to Belfast, David had enjoyed the experience of his elevated position in the firm. But Charles was still the owner.

They had been home a month now, but his son and daughter-in-law had yet to put in an appearance. David continued to conduct any business over the phone or by post as he had done when his father had been living in Cork, ignoring hints that Charles would like him to call in and see him, even if it was only a flying visit to bring him up to scratch with the company's affairs.

Not that Evelyn cared one bit if the arrogant swine never set foot in the house again, but she knew Charles was pining for his son and was very depressed at his continued absence. A few of Charles's old friends had dropped by to see him since his return and she had been dismayed at their attitude towards her husband. It was as if they thought he had one foot in the grave already and were offering their prior condolences. Though he hid it well, she sensed that Charles was of the same line of thought and this depressed him further.

Even though he was paralysed down one side and his speech was slightly impaired, the doctor had explained to her that Charles's constitution was in great shape. With the right kind of therapy, he would surely improve still more and could live for some years to come. With this in mind, all the necessary remedial equipment was purchased and installed in one of the many spare rooms and a professional therapist, Gordon Baxter, was employed. The room looked like a mini-gymnasium with a weight machine, exercise bicycle, treadmill and rowing machine. Gordon Baxter came in three mornings a week. After a spell of intense therapy and light exercise on the treadmill to start with, the doctor assured Evelyn that her husband was responding quite favourably. Evelyn would join her husband during these sessions to give him inspiration whilst herself using every piece of apparatus to keep her figure in peak condition. Charles was beginning to enjoy the exercises and was now doing short stints on the bicycle as well as the treadmill.

Nurse Morrison coming into the room brought Evelyn out of her reverie. Gracefully unwinding her long length from the window seat, she went to meet her.

'My husband was very restless during the night. Is anything wrong, nurse?' she asked anxiously.

The nurse brushed the air with a hand and assured her quietly, 'No worse than usual, he's just a bit tired. I hope he's not overdoing it on those exercise machines.'

'No! No, Gordon's always in attendance to supervise everything he does. At the moment he uses just the treadmill and bicycle, and only for about ten minutes at a time.'

'That's good to hear. Gordon certainly knows his work.'

Nurse Linda Morrison had moved to Greencastle a year earlier as part-time district nurse to the local doctors' surgery in neighbouring Whitehouse, and she came well recommended. When Evelyn made some tentative enquiries about hiring a private nurse, her attention had been directed to Linda. When Evelyn had approached Linda, she was only too glad of the extra money to attend to Charles.

Gossip had been rife at the time and Linda's neighbours had made it their business to let her know of Evelyn's past. Yes indeed, she had been informed just who Charles and Evelyn Matthews were and the scandal they had caused with their carry-on.

'Imagine him at his age in life. You'd think he'd know better and catch himself on. And as for her, that trollop, she should have gotten a good kick up the arse to bring her to her senses. But there again, we all know she married him for his money, don't we? And as for that poor Adam Brady, as nice a man as you're likely to meet. Did you know they were engaged? I'll bet you didn't. That hussy, for that's all she is, almost left the lad standing at the altar rails with his two arms the one length, so she did.' And so it went, on and on. They didn't pull their punches in their character assassination of Charles and Evelyn. The couple's arrival back in the area had reactivated the gossip of the past and set scurrilous tongues wagging again.

Linda was well aware of the circumstances of Mr and Mrs Matthews, not that she thought it any big deal and it was certainly none of her business. Mrs Matthews wasn't the first young girl who married for the luxury that money could afford, and she most certainly wouldn't be the last. Some lived to regret it, others thrived and, as far as Linda could make out, Mrs Matthews was one of the lucky ones. And she did show genuine concern over her husband's welfare, which spoke volumes in itself.

'Charles is ready for his breakfast now,' she continued, shrugging into her coat and preparing to leave. She came early mornings to wash and dress Charles and prepare him for the day ahead, returning early evenings to prepare him for bed. Now she offered, 'I could call in this afternoon if you like. We could perhaps move one of those big comfortable armchairs close to the window and settle him there. Let him admire that beautiful view. The days must drag for you here on your own all day long with him.'

'No, that won't be necessary, Linda, thank you. I can manage all right. Let's wait till the weather gets a bit warmer and he can sit out on the balcony. The therapy seems to be working wonders on him, strengthening his limbs. The doctor is quite pleased with his progress and is convinced he will soon be able to move about more freely of his own volition.

Wouldn't it be better to leave things as they are for a while? Not upset the apple cart?'

'I suppose you're right. I'll see you this evening as usual.'

Now that she had Adam Brady eating out of her hand again, Evelyn wanted her afternoons free from any unnecessary interruptions when he came to attend to the gardens. A slight smile of anticipation curved her lips as she thought of what *other things* she hoped he might eventually attend to.

Assuming the smile was a parting gesture from her employer, Linda Morrison smiled kindly in return. No matter what the villagers thought of her, in Linda's opinion this was a brave young woman. Regardless of age difference she was in love with her husband and happy to spend her lonely days caring for him.

'Well, remember now, you've only to let me know if you need a break and want me to come in the afternoons. I'll be only too happy to fit you in.'

'Thank you, Linda, you're very kind. I'll bear it in mind.' Evelyn had been gently guiding her through the hall as they talked. Now she opened the front door and ushered her out. 'Good morning, Linda.'

'Good morning, Mrs Matthews.'

Closing the door, Evelyn leaned back, her head against the cool hard wood for a time, eyes closed in contemplation, before going to prepare her husband's breakfast. Linda Morrison was right in her assumption. She did find the days long and lonely but the future looked brighter now that Adam Brady was back on the scene.

As he ate breakfast that morning, Adam gave a lot of thought to the situation he now found himself embroiled in. Evelyn Matthews had lured him to her home with the intention of rekindling the fierce passion they had once shared. He had been shocked when she had answered the door to him that morning three weeks ago. A vision in a soft blue cashmere sweater that moulded high breasts and heightened the cornflower blue of her eyes, hair a shining halo around her head, had smiled and eagerly greeted him. He had thought for a moment he was hallucinating. Wasn't she supposed to be living far away in County Cork?

He had been ill prepared for the shock and, in a stupor, had found himself blindly following the vision indoors. In his bemused state he had allowed himself to be led by the arm, through the hall and into the spacious lounge. When she turned to face him, and stood, wide eyes pleading and lips parted invitingly, it was the most natural thing in the world to gather her to him and savage the lips she offered, the full sensual lips that still haunted his dreams. The remembered contours of her body clung to his for some moments and he wallowed in the delight of crushing her close. Their bodies were meant for each other. He hadn't realised just how much he had missed her, and for some moments forgot everything but the renewed delight of her body against his.

Very much aware of the turmoil she was generating, she whispered against his lips, 'I've missed you, Adam.' Burrowing her head against his chest, she lamented, 'You'll never know how much I've missed you.'

Like a slap in the face, these words brought him to his senses. He could very well imagine how she felt. Hadn't he felt the same? He thrust her roughly from him. What on earth was he thinking? This woman had hurt him beyond measure and here he was fawning all over her as if nothing had happened. 'Too bad,' he snarled bitterly. 'You made your choice. What are you doing back here, anyway?'

'I live here now. This is my home.'

'So the old man kicked the bucket, eh? He didn't last very long. Was it worth it? Did he leave you all his money? Are you the lady of the manor now?' he sneered.

'No! No, my husband's not dead, but he *is* very ill and wanted to come back home to be near his family and friends.' Pleased to have caught him off guard, and already aware by his response to her advances that he was still attracted to her, she moved close again. 'Have you missed me, Adam?' she purred.

Of course he had missed her, but he must never show how much. Ignoring the question, he made for the door. 'Look, I've been sent over here to do a job and that's what I'm going to do. Now just show me round the grounds and then I'll be on my bike,' he snapped over his shoulder.

Confident that she could change his mind, she meekly shadowed him as he walked around the gardens, stopping here and there, pointing out the changes necessary and the work it would entail. Adam was very conscious of her presence as she trailed closely behind him. Her nearness and the delicate fragrance of that recalled perfume was driving him to distraction. Angry at the effect her presence was having on him, he silently vowed that he would send over two other men to do the work here. And by the state of the place there would be an awful lot to be done. At another time and place the state of these grounds would have excited him, got his adrenalin flowing. He would have seen it as a challenge to his talents and would have asked the boss if he could attend to the restoration work himself. This was something he occasionally did to keep his hand in, and these gardens certainly made him eager to get stuck in, but Evelyn's ever beguiling presence was undermining his thought process and he needed to get away from her. Get things back in perspective.

Putting the finishing touches to the details he had roughly sketched out for reconstruction, he headed for the van, anxious to go before his emotions got the better of him. As he turned to speak to her, she managed to look vulnerable, but he knew she was putting on a big act for his benefit. Tapping his biro against his clipboard to get her attention, he said, 'I'll go over these with the boss, and send you out a design and typed-up estimate. You can let me know one way or the other. OK? Good day, Mrs Matthews.' He headed for his van.

She bustled along beside him until she was forced to grab hold of his arm to halt his hasty retreat. 'You'll have to come back inside and talk me through what you intend doing, Adam. I don't fully understand all that horticulture jargon. My husband will be expecting me to explain everything to him, like names of plants and shrubs, and the cost, and things like that,' she whimpered, putting on another of her attention-seeking acts. 'What am I supposed to tell him?'

'As I've already said, when I get a proper estimate and specification typed up for you, it'll tell you everything you need to know. On the other hand, if your husband's available now, I can talk him through it, go over everything so's there's no misunderstanding,' he said sarcastically, knowing full well he'd a better chance of finding a snowball in hell than of ever meeting Charles Matthews.

She hesitated. The two men in her life had never met. Charles wouldn't recognise Adam. It could do no harm, she supposed. 'Yes, why not? That's a good idea, Adam. It's always better to speak face to face, I think. Come in and meet my husband.'

Taken unawares, Adam shrugged his broad shoulders and reluctantly followed her indoors. In the hall she paused.

'Look, you must understand that Charles is bedridden, so go easy on him, OK?' Glad that she had already told her husband that she was arranging for the gardens to be restored, she said, 'This way, please.' Without much more ado she threw back her head with an air of authority and ascended the stairs with slow, elegant steps.

Adam hesitated for some moments at the foot of the wide staircase, watching the sensuous sway of her hips. What was she up to now? Was this another one of her tricks? She paused on the landing and waited. Hesitantly he climbed the stairs and joined her.

In a low voice she chided him, 'Don't be so childish, Adam. I'm not going to seduce you, you know.' Canting her head in the direction of a door, 'My husband's in here.'

Crossing the landing, she opened the door and entered the room.

'I trust I'm not disturbing you, darling. There's someone here to see you. Would you like to come in, Mr Brady.'

The man propped up on an arrangement of pillows was not what Adam was expecting to see. He had pictured a decrepit old geriatric and was surprised to see instead a handsome, elderly gentleman with bright, intelligent blue eyes. He sat with hands clasped together on a colourful bedspread as if in meditation. At first glance his skin looked waxen, as if chalk had replaced the blood in his veins, but he was very much alert to his surroundings. Adam felt drawn to him and without further thought approached the bed, holding out his hand in greeting. 'I'm pleased to meet you, sir.'

With his strong right hand, Charles gripped the one offered and looked askance at his wife.

'Remember I told you I was going to have the gardens done over? Well, I wanted to surprise you. This is Adam Brady. He's a professional landscape gardener from Holywood. He's had a look over the grounds and has made up some sketches and an estimate for you to consider. While he goes over them with you, I'll bring up some tea.' She motioned to a chair by the bedside. 'Sit down, please, Mr Brady.' Bending over the bed, she rubbed her hand affectionately along her husband's arm and asked gently, 'Are you all right, Charles? Do you feel up to this?'

He nodded and with a reassuring squeeze on his arm she left the room.

Adam pulled his chair closer to the bed and spread out his sketch of the grounds. 'This is only a rough sketch, you understand. I intend getting you a proper layout and specification drawn up, but your wife wanted me to discuss it with you first, to see if you have any input to make. There's a lot of work involved, as I'm sure you realise?' Charles nodded his agreement and Adam continued, 'The gardens have obviously been allowed to go to pot for some time.'

'I know. We've been away a few years now and it was rather remiss of me not to have arranged for them to be looked after in our absence. Tell me what's required, young man.'

Adam inwardly sighed with relief. That this man had all his faculties about him was obvious. Although the paralysis seemed to have affected one side of his body, just a hint of a slur of the odd word impeded his speech. Adam set about explaining what was involved and the time estimated to complete the work

Evelyn entered the room carrying a tray and Adam hurried to relieve her of it. Avoiding eye contact, he placed it on a small table close to the bed. In the presence of Mr Matthews he felt real guilt; as if he were here under false pretences.

Evelyn poured a cup of tea and handed it to

43

Adam. When she reached for the other cup, which had a drinking spout, her husband waved her away. He liked this young man and didn't want the embarrassment of drinking from an 'invalid's' cup in front of him.

His eyes scanned the rough sketch. 'You seem to have just about covered everything. You obviously know what you're doing. When will you be able to start the work?' he enquired.

'Well, we haven't agreed on the price yet, but with your approval I can have two men out here next Monday, if that suits you, sir?'

'Monday will be fine.'

Evelyn gave a little start of surprise when he said he'd be sending out two men. This wasn't what she had envisaged. She wanted Adam to come alone.

'Surely it won't take *two* men?' she asked, quietly. 'Won't that be rather expensive?'

'Well, it certainly won't be cheap. There's a lot of work to be done, Mrs Matthews, so I'll allow for two men in the price. And even with two men working full time it will take roughly six weeks to complete and that doesn't allow for any wet time.'

'What in the name of heaven is *wet time*?' she enquired, feeling that she was losing a grip of the situation.

Her husband interrupted her. 'It's when all work stops due to heavy rain, my dear. It happens all the time in the building trade, as I should know from experience. And in Adam's position, to continue working in the rain would cause more damage than was good in the gardening trade.'

'I couldn't have put it any better myself.' Adam smiled. 'Look, I'll tell you what. Why don't I send you out a proper estimate and when you see the price and what you're getting for it, you and your husband can browse through it. Then, if everything's to your complete satisfaction, you can choose where you'd like us to start. It doesn't have to be all done in one visit, you know. We could do sections at a time. Go over it at your leisure and let me know what you want and what you can afford,' he said, tongue in cheek, knowing full well just what Evelyn had in mind.

'I still think that two men would be very costly,' she complained.

Charles was staring at his wife in amazement. This was a turn-up for the books. Evelyn had never worried about spending money before.

'Don't be silly, dear!' he admonished her with an affectionate smile before turning his attention to Adam. 'Money's no problem. Send me a proper copy of this sketch and an estimate. And remember, I want the best of everything. We'll discuss it in more detail when you come back. Meanwhile, please get your labour organised for a Monday start.'

Business settled, they discussed current affairs for a while, whilst they drank their tea. When Adam finished he rose to his feet and thanked Mrs Matthews for a lovely cup of tea, then offered his hand to Mr Matthews. 'It's been a pleasure meeting you and discussing business with you, sir.'

'Likewise, son.'

Evelyn led Adam back downstairs and out of the house in angry silence. Once outside she rounded on him and hissed, 'Did you have to go on about the costs? You know damned well we can afford anything you come up with. And I trust you were joking back there when you said you'd send two men to do the work,' she said curtly.

'No, I wasn't. It *will* take two men,' he argued, feeling a lot happier with this solution.

She gripped his arm. 'It will take one man even longer! Adam, please say you will come . . . alone.'

'I like your husband. It would be improper for me to work here.' He shrugged off her hold and climbing into the van fired up the engine. 'Besides, your husband's no fool. He'd soon twig to any shenanigans going on under his very nose. Goodbye, Evelyn, nice to have met you again.'

Before he could drive off she leaned into the van and planted her mouth over his. Immediately, he responded. Putting his hand on the back of her head he devoured her lips before pushing her away. 'I hope someone saw you do that and tells your

46

husband. He seems a fine, decent man and deserves better. Why can't you be content with your lot?'

'Are you?' she hissed. 'Eh, Adam? Are you content with Maura Craig? Can she satisfy you the way I did? Tell me,' she thrust out her chin defiantly, 'did she deliberately get pregnant so you'd have to marry her?'

'You're talking rubbish,' he said tersely and without another word was off down the drive.

Remembering his words, she glanced furtively around. Had anyone been spying on them? The house was well back off the road and had a high boundary hedge. No one could possibly see, but guilt made her nervous as she hurried inside. It wouldn't do to start tongues wagging now. David Matthews would just love to hear rumours like that, true or otherwise. He'd have a field day. Nevertheless, she intended to see Adam again, come hell or high water. Now that she knew he still had feelings for her, she intended resurrecting their relationship. If he didn't show up on Monday, she'd drive over to the nursery centre with some cock and bull story to get him back on the job. She smiled inwardly at her choice of words. She'd just have to be more careful how she went about it, was all.

3

For three days Adam had disciplined himself enough to stay away from the Antrim Road contract. It would have been wonderful to work there, he thought. He saw the restoration of those gardens as a challenge to his creative mind and would dearly have loved to do the work himself, suggesting to Mr Matthews ideas that had come to him later when away from Evelyn's disruptive presence, ideas that would enhance the gardens still further. But he had to deny himself that pleasure. It could be a bit dicey working there. The vibes that flowed between him and Evelyn were still too strong and tempting, and he needed to be on his best behaviour, summoning up all his reserves of self-restraint to keep himself out of her clutches.

Besides, he didn't do the donkey work any more. He travelled around from site to site in a supervisory capacity, making sure everything ran smoothly and according to plan. Therefore it would cause too much speculation if he were suddenly to get involved on one particular job, especially this one. He knew that he should be glad to have escaped Evelyn's clutches, but his heart was contrary and he felt a heavy desolation settle there at the thought of what might have been, had Charles Matthews not turned her head with the lure of his great wealth.

In his stead, he had programmed Steve Patton, the company's top landscape gardener, and Bobby Murray, his young apprentice, to do the work. On their return at the end of each day, when they reported in on their progress and ordered new plants for the next day, he had listened with bated breath to all their comments about the beautiful Mrs Matthews: how charming she was; the numerous cups of tea she had made for them; the witty comments she came out with. Oh yes, she certainly had them eating out of her hand.

He was ashamed of himself to find how disappointed he was that Evelyn had given up on him so easily and apparently was content letting Steve and young Bobby do the work he himself had so longed to do. Footloose and fancy-free, Steve Patton was quite handsome in a rugged sort of way, and it was obvious that he was smitten by the glamorous Mrs Matthews. And, by the sound of it, Evelyn was using her ample charms to great effect on him. Adam wondered whether it was all a big act put on for his benefit to arouse his jealousy. She would guess that she would be the topic of conversation when the men checked in each evening and knew Adam would be all ears listening to their exploits. Otherwise, why would she go to all the trouble to have this particular nursery centre in Holywood do the work when she could have gotten it done by the one in Glengormley, or even Whiteabbey, which were closer to home?

Perhaps he was wrong. Maybe she just needed someone to play up to her whims. Well, if she only knew it, he had been tempted! God knows how he had been tempted. It seemed he'd had a narrow escape there. So why then did he feel so cheated?

He made a determined effort to erase Evelyn Matthews from his mind. After all, it was better this way, he assured himself. He couldn't afford any complications that might arise if he didn't watch his step. He had to avoid the snare of Evelyn's inviting charms at all costs, not let her come between him and his family. With this in mind he devoted all his spare time to Maura and little Danny.

Since his visit to the house on the Antrim Road he had been uptight and distracted around his own home and was aware that as a result Maura was upset and fretting about him, wondering what was wrong, and whether she had unwittingly done or said something to bring this on. He set out to alleviate his wife's concern. The danger was past. Evelyn might as well still be at the other end of the country as far as he was concerned. She was totally out of reach. At least that's what he told himself. However, the spirit might be willing but the flesh is weak. In spite of all his good intentions and resolutions, the desire to see Evelyn and to be with her again increased daily until it became an unbearable obsession, like some incurable sickness eating away at him

He succeeded to some extent in his endeavours to please Maura, and harmony of a kind was restored at home. He was happy with Maura, no doubt about that. Until now, that is. She was a devoted wife and mother and he'd lived without Evelyn these past few years, so there was no reason why he shouldn't continue in this vein. Ah, but then a small niggling voice in his head reminded him that Evelyn had been unavailable, hadn't she? She had been far away in Cork! Not just across the lough, like a siren trying to lure him over.

On Thursday morning he was making out the invoices when he chanced to glance out the window and got the shock of his life. A bright red MG Midget sports car came whizzing through the gates of the nursery centre and skidded to a halt in front of the office block. Mesmerised, Adam watched as long, shapely legs, clad in sheerest nylon, emerged from the car and Evelyn Matthews stepped gracefully out on to the forecourt. Not an easy feat by any means as the car was quite low to the ground, but Evelyn managed to leave it in one smooth, fluid movement as if she had practised it to perfection. She stretched sensually as she slowly looked around, as if getting her bearings, but in fact calling attention to her high breasts and slim waist, before heading towards the office.

Near the entrance, Benny Gallagher sat gobsmacked watching her every move. As she approached the doors he quickly scrambled to his feet and, stretching to his full six-foot stature, straightened his tie, pulled in his stomach, smoothed down his unruly hair and, with a broad smile, went to greet her, obviously bowled over by her beauty. George also put in an appearance from one of the greenhouses, to stare and pay silent homage to this vision that had suddenly appeared before them. Like a true professional, Evelyn took it all in her stride. With a radiant smile and a flutter of long, thick, golden eyelashes, she introduced herself to Benny and George who had now hurried over to join his brother.

Heart thumping in his chest, Adam went slowly out to join them. His eyes swept in admiration over the immaculate car and dismay overwhelmed him as he realised that it must have passed his house to get here. Maura was always going on at him to get a car and would have been interested in this racy-looking machine, had she noticed it go by. Had it caught her attention and if so had she seen who was behind the wheel?

With a languid turn of her head, Evelyn switched her attention to Adam and when he met her eyes he detected mockery lurking in their depths. 'Ah, there you are, Adam. I was telling these two fine gentlemen that my husband was so disappointed that you wouldn't be doing the reconstruction of our gardens yourself,' she chided him gently. 'Charles was terribly impressed by you, you know. He could see that you knew what you were talking about, thought it would be a challenge to you. He was under the impression that you would be in charge.' Her words hung in the air as she looked from one to the other of them, and, knowing full well where authority lay, she smiled beguilingly at the brothers. 'Is it not possible for Adam to do the work himself? It would please my husband ever so much if he could.'

Benny frowned and looked askance at his site manager, bewildered. 'Well now, let's see if we can arrange something that'll be to everyone's benefit. You've got nothing of any great importance on your plate at the moment, have you, Adam?' he queried.

'I've got to go and look over those gardens in Comber tomorrow, Boss,' Adam reminded him. 'For that friend of yours, Mr Shields, remember? You know, the job you particularly want me to do?' Benny had been adamant that Adam had to be the one to attend to his friend's request and if possible do the work. No one else would do. Now Adam watched his boss wrestle with his conscience.

So much for friendship. There was no contest. Evelyn won hands down. 'Can't Steve do that job?' Benny suggested tentatively. 'We're not awfully busy at the moment. Do you not fancy keeping your hand in?'

Frustrated, Adam shrugged. He couldn't afford to make an issue of it, start an interrogation. But one thing he could do . . . He could bloody well make Evelyn wait! And he would do just that. 'Tell you what . . . I'll go over to the Comber job tomorrow as planned and have a look round the place, then I'll come back here and draw up an estimate for the job. If Mr Shields is satisfied with the price, Steve can start work there next week, if you're sure that's all right with you, Boss?' Benny nodded in agreement and Adam resignedly gave his attention to Evelyn. 'That will leave me free to work on your gardens, Mrs Matthews. Tell Mr Matthews that I'll be over first thing Monday morning, if that suits him.'

'I suppose it will have to. Charles will be so pleased. We'll look forward to seeing you bright and early, then.'

George, loath to let this gorgeous creature escape so soon, eagerly said, 'Can we interest you in a cup of tea or coffee, Mrs Matthews, or something cold perhaps?'

'That's very kind of you, Mr Gallagher, but no thanks. I must get back to my husband. I'm sure Adam has already told you that Charles is an invalid and needs a lot of care and attention.'

'No. No, he didn't. But that's very understandable. You must get back to your husband. Maybe another time perhaps.'

A sad smile played about her lips as she explained. 'Yes, poor Charles. That's why I want the garden made to look its best, so that he can sit outside when the weather's fine and enjoy the view. Thanks again for your kind offer, and as you said, maybe the next time I'm over this way.'

Sliding in behind the wheel of the car, she was well aware that a fair amount of nylon-clad flesh was exposed as her short skirt rode further up her thighs. She thought the brothers' eyes were about to pop out of their sockets at the exhibition and had difficulty concealing a little appreciative smile. With a final nonchalant lift of the hand in farewell, and a hooded look in Adam's direction, she fired the engine into a throaty roar. All three men watched avidly as the car turned and smoothly nosed its way back through the entrance gates.

Adam stood silent for some moments, praying inwardly that Maura would be too busy to notice the car pass by. At last, with a sigh, he brought his attention back to the present and was surprised to find the brothers eyeing him speculatively. His heart sank. Surely they hadn't sensed how he felt towards Evelyn? No! George was speaking.

'Wow! How come you never mentioned how glamorous Mrs Matthews was?' he asked with a nudge and a sly grin.

'And,' Benny butted in, 'why didn't you tell us her husband was an invalid?'

'Here . . . hold on a minute! When have I ever discussed a customer's family background with you, eh? I didn't know it was expected of me. Unless of course I thought there might be a cash-flow problem. And, believe me, money's not a problem where she's concerned. Her husband's loaded, so he is. Besides, you must have gathered how alluring she is. Isn't Steve forever drooling about her? He sickens me the way he goes on. I'll tell you something, though, he won't be too pleased to be taken off that job. Who's going to break the good news then?' He looked from one brother to the other.

Benny laughed delightedly. 'You're right there, son! Steve has gone on about her. But to see her in the flesh, and what flesh! Well, that's another matter. I guess that gorgeous creature cast a spell on me for a minute back there, and my brother as well. Eh, George? And you a confirmed bachelor into the bargain! There's not many like her in a dozen. No wonder Steve can't stop talking about her.'

George with a wag of the head agreed. 'She sure is some thoroughbred. You'd better watch your step there, lad. We don't want you to go falling under her spell or Maura will be after our blood.' He laughed.

Adam entered the house with trepidation that evening, expelling his breath in a slow sigh of relief when everything appeared normal. Obviously Maura hadn't noticed the car and who was driving it or she wouldn't be smiling tentatively at him, as if gauging his mood. No! She would be rearing up on her hind legs ready to pounce, giving him the rounds of the kitchen. He had been reprieved . . . again.

Ashamed that his wife was acting warily in his presence and swamped with guilt at the knowledge that from Monday onwards he would be seeing Evelyn Matthews on a daily basis, he was nevertheless excited at the prospect. He was extra-attentive towards his wife and young Danny over the weekend, incurring apprehensive glances from Maura who couldn't fathom the reason for his mood swings. Adam salved his conscience with the thought that he had tried to avoid working for Evelyn but Benny had decreed otherwise. And, after all, it was Benny who paid the weekly wages. Any objection he might raise against the decision would cause unnecessary speculation. It had been taken out of his hands entirely. One could only do one's best. He would just have to be careful and control his feelings, keeping things strictly on a business footing. Best to bring along company in the form of a helper. He surmised that Evelyn wouldn't be too pleased with this but who cared: she'd just have to grin and bear it.

Monday dawned bright and clear. The traffic was heavy at that time of the morning, so he lost some time going over Queen's Bridge and along Corporation Street towards the Shore Road. As he drove the van up Whitewell Road and along the winding Serpentine Road, Cave Hill appeared to loom close at hand. He knew from experience that rain was surely on its way and he would be forced to seek shelter at some time during the day. He recalled to mind the large shed at the Matthews' house where all the gardening equipment was stored and, turning to his companion, said, 'If it rains, don't you go tramping wet muddy boots into the house. There's a big garden shed where we can shelter.'

Jackie Flynn gaped at him in amazement. 'Steve said the woman didn't mind if we went into the house. He says she was always inviting him and wee Bobby in for cups of tea or coffee.'

'You'll do as I say. Mrs Matthews has enough on her plate with an invalid husband to attend to, without running around after us. Steve should have known better than to go tramping through that house.'

The wide double gates stood open and he turned in and drove up the long sloping drive. Observing a Hillman Minx car parked at the front of the house, he assumed Evelyn had a visitor and continued on round the back, expecting her to put in an appearance in due course. After they had unloaded the shrubs, plants and tools they'd brought with them, there was still no sign of her. Nor was there any movement in the rooms at the back of the house, so he walked round to the front door to let someone know they had arrived. He was anxious to get started before the rain came and wanted to get some shrubs planted in the soil.

'Wait here,' he said tersely, and left Jackie glowering after him.

The Hillman was still there, parked close to the house. Climbing the steps, he had the great brass knocker clasped firmly in his fist, ready to announce his arrival, when the door was suddenly yanked open, almost pulling him to his knees. Hastily letting go his grip on the knocker, he managed to regain his balance.

'Oops-a-daisy! Sorry, Adam, that was a close call. But there's no need to throw yourself at my feet. A curtsy would have sufficed.' Evelyn giggled, putting out a hand to steady him. She turned to her companion. 'Linda, this is the man who's come all the way from Holywood to transform these gardens for us. Adam, this is Nurse Linda Morrison. Linda helps me look after Charles.'

They eyed each other and exchanged nods. After a few perfunctory comments about the weather, Linda climbed into the Hillman and drove off. As she cruised along Antrim Road, and turned down Serpentine Road, the nurse found something niggling at the back of her mind but she couldn't put her finger on what was bothering her. Ah, well, if it was that important, it would come to her later.

Suddenly the penny dropped. *Adam!* Wasn't that the name of the man Mrs Matthews had once been engaged to, she mused? The one she'd jilted to marry Mr Matthews? The Adam she was thinking of had been a local lad, but Mrs Matthews had said that her gardener was from Holywood . . . Therefore it was most unlikely to be the same person, otherwise it would be highly improper of Mrs Matthews hiring him to work on her gardens. It was probably just a coincidence.

She had to deliver some medicine for young Thomas Devlin and, as she turned the car into the driveway on a bend further down Serpentine Road, she decided that she would try to find out whether Annie Devlin knew anything. Originally from Springfield Road, Annie had lived in the district for quite a few years. If anybody knew of any local scandal, Annie would. Her widowed mother had married a Greencastle man and now lived near the bottom of Whitewell Road, in the hub of the village, where gossip was just another aspect of life, something to stand on the corner and talk about for hours on end. Annie would surely know whether or not it was the same Adam.

The Devlin house was locked up and there seemed to be no one at home. Annie was probably down at the school with her two wee daughters, Linda surmised; she should have remembered that. Just as well Annie was out, for she was disgusted with herself. Imagine wanting to gossip about her patient and employer. She'd have to catch herself on and guard her idle tongue. Pushing the small package through the letter box, she bade herself mind her own business or she would soon find herself out of a very lucrative job.

Evelyn smiled happily at Adam. 'Come in, you naughty boy,' she chided him. 'Surely you didn't think I'd let you off the hook just like that, hmm?

Besides, it's true, Charles really was taken with your deep knowledge of gardening – only he called it horticulture. He couldn't understand why you hadn't come back. He was determined that you'd be the one to do the work here, so he sent me over to Holywood personally, to make some enquiries.' She gestured him inside but he remained on the steps. At his sceptical look, she added, with a laugh in her voice, 'Honest! He really did. Come inside . . . please.'

Still sceptical, he nodded down at his dirty boots. 'I can't come in. I've everything unloaded round the back. I just wanted to let you know we're here.' Her eyebrows rose questioningly. 'Young Jackie Flynn's with me. He's almost out of his time and needs some experience working a big garden from scratch. I'll go and make a start now before the rain comes and won't disturb you again unless it's absolutely necessary.'

Apprehensive, she gripped his arm. 'What do you mean? It's a beautiful morning. It won't rain. And you've someone with you?' She leaned closer and, eyes twinkling, said, 'You're having me on, aren't you? And you can disturb me any time you like. You know that, Adam. Your wish is my command. I've got to make Charles some breakfast now. He'll want to see you afterwards. OK?'

'That's fine by me. Will he want to see Jackie as well?'

She frowned her displeasure. 'It's true then. You really have someone with you?'

'It's true.' He smiled mockingly at her. 'I couldn't possibly do all the work on my own. It's against company procedure to work alone and it would take me ages to complete the job.' Not waiting for the expected reply, he turned abruptly and headed to where Jackie was waiting, throwing over his shoulder, 'And take my word for it, it will rain.'

Did she deliberately slam the door on him? He smiled inwardly and to rub it in started whistling 'April Showers'.

Adam and Jackie started on the bottom end of the long back garden that rose in a gentle slope towards Antrim Road. Steve and young Bobby had had the ground cleared and turned over ready for the new shrubs and, as he planted them, Adam couldn't help but smile as he recalled Steve's reaction at being taken off this job. That the man had been far from pleased was putting it mildly. In fact, he had taken it so badly he had stamped off in a nasty temper, which was unlike him. Usually, as far as Steve was concerned, one garden was like any other where work was concerned. He must have really taken a shine to Evelyn.

Tongue in cheek, Adam had questioned Bobby. 'What's wrong with him?'

The young lad had shrugged. 'Well now, he and

Mrs Matthews were getting on like a house on fire and then he was suddenly taken off the job. But sure she's a married woman, so what good would it have done him?' He was so straight-faced that, for the life of him, Adam couldn't tell whether the lad was naive or just stringing him along. Because of Bobby's tender years, he didn't pursue the matter further.

Completely engrossed in his work, Adam toiled steadily away for some hours and was surprised when Jackie glanced at his watch and told him it was almost twelve noon. Time they took a tea break. Hadn't Evelyn said that her husband would want to see him after he'd had his breakfast? Had she meant for Adam to come back to the house or wait for her summons? Deciding that he had better investigate, he wiped his hands on an old towel and walked up towards the house.

Jackie was hard on his heels. 'I need to go to the loo, Boss.'

When he had toured the grounds with Evelyn on his initial visit to see what had to be done, she had shown him a small washroom attached to the garden shed. He now pointed the young lad towards it, warning him not to go into the house.

There was no sign of life until Adam neared the kitchen window, when muted voices reached his ears.

He paused, then, quietly stepping on to the wide

64

veranda, cautiously peered through the slats on the venetian blind on the window. Evelyn was standing with her back to him and facing her was a tall man who was talking in a heated manner. Evelyn swiped her hand through the air as if dismissing what he was saying. Adam was poised, ready to interfere, as the man reached out and gripped her by the upper arms, and he watched enthralled as he pulled her roughly against him, their noses barely inches apart and, with an anguished gasp, appeared to snarl something into her face. Then with a tormented sound through clenched teeth, he threw her from him. Without further ado he turned on his heel and stormed from the room, quickly followed by a greatly agitated Evelyn, holding a clenched fist to her chest.

It was like watching a scene from a silent movie unfolding before him, with Evelyn as the leading lady and the tall stranger the villain. The only thing missing was the dramatic piano music. Quickly Adam scooted along the veranda and round the side of the house. Careful to stay out of sight, he watched for the man to emerge through the front door. He had to see the outcome of this ha'penny opera. Even as he peered warily round the corner of the house the heavy door was hauled open and the man, face blazing with anger, thumped across the veranda and down the wooden steps. Pausing at the bottom, he swung round, hands balled into fists, spitting specks of white, fluffy spittle, for a final word.

'You may have my father under your spell, you conniving witch, but you haven't fooled me for one second. He'll soon see through your charade and realise what a fool he's been. When he comes to his senses you'll be out of here on your sweet little ass, so fast your feet won't even touch the ground. You mark my words.'

'Don't hold your breath while you're waiting. Or . . . on the other hand . . . please do just that! Be my guest.'

Adam stood in awe, rooted to the spot. He'd never seen anyone so enraged as this man. There wasn't a vestige of colour in his face and his lips were now a hard, straight, angry line. In spite of the anger emanating from this stranger, Adam was aware that the man was at war with himself. It was so obvious that he desired Evelyn. It was written all over his face as if it were an open book. The fervid gaze, the tortured longing in his expression, the lust. His whole composure. Was he an ex-lover? Or another sucker she'd been stringing along?

Evelyn was obviously upset as she watched him storm off. Climbing into a Rover car and slamming the door none too quietly, he screeched away down the drive in a cloud of dust and gravel. She became aware of Adam in her peripheral vision and turning, gestured him forward with a little wave of her hand. 'Come inside. Charles will want to speak with you.'

Removing his boots, Adam left them outside on the step and followed her across the wide hall. 'Who was that when you're writing home?'

'That obnoxious piece of tripe – for want of a better description – is Charles's son. My husband hasn't bothered much about the business since his stroke. He'd lost all interest in everything. But now, thank God, his therapy is beginning to show signs of improving his mobility. Today, for the first time, he let me and Linda help settle him out on the balcony where he can look out over the lough. He was so pleased to be out in the fresh air, and to be doing something different for a change.' She slapped her hands against her hips in defeat. 'And now this. I was so happy to see him show an interest in something. I was thrilled when he asked me to fetch his business files for him to look over, thinking it would take his mind off other things. Afterwards he asked me to get David on the phone. He'd worked himself into such a tizzy I feared he would have another stroke. I tried to quieten him down, talk him out of it, but he insisted that he needed to have an urgent word with David. I brought the phone to him and he ordered his son to come over immediately. He must have found something amiss in those files, but he wouldn't tell

me anything, except to say it was about the business. And this is the outcome.'

The hurt on her face was almost palpable as she
flapped her hands aimlessly about in frustration.

'Now, according to David, his dad is changing
his will, and he's blaming it on me. I don't understand. Charles has already been more than generous
to me in his will. I'm not a greedy person. Why
should he change it now?'

Adam watched her through narrowed lids.
'Maybe he's cutting *you* out of the will.'

With a flash of blue eyes, she showed her exasperation. 'Huh! And you think David would worry
about that? Catch yourself on, Adam. He'd be over
the moon if that were the case. He'd have been
doing cartwheels out of here, not spitting fire and
brimstone as you must have observed. There was
no need for that kind of carry-on. He was acting
like a big spoiled brat.'

Still sceptical, he questioned her. 'Why was he
having a go at you just then?'

'Whatever went on between them up there,
David thinks I put Charles up to it. Imagine! Why
should I do a thing like that? I know as much
about the building trade as I do about brain surgery.
I wouldn't know where to start or what to do with
the firm, should anything happen to Charles. And
the best of it is, there's plenty of money for
everyone.'

She stood for some moments undecided.

'Look, Adam.' Still distraught, she nodded towards a door that led to the kitchen. 'You make yourself a cup of tea or coffee. I'm sure Charles must be upset after that performance, so I'd better go up and check on him and if he's still up to it, I'll take you up to him for that chat.'

'What about my helper, can I make him a cuppa as well?'

She gazed at him in dismay. 'Oh, God, I forgot about him. By all means, you make him something and I'll see you later.'

Adam gazed thoughtfully after her, at the long shapely legs and the natural sway of her hips. Was she really unaware that her stepson fancied her? He smiled to himself at the very idea: that this middle-aged man, who obviously had designs on her, was her stepson. But Evelyn was nobody's fool. She must have been aware of the man's feelings towards her. She might have, who knows, unconsciously led the poor guy on. She couldn't help how beautiful she was, or the magnetism she held for the opposite sex. Putting it simply, she was a walking dream. Even now his body was crying out for hers. He'd have to tread carefully round her, now that young Jackie was working with him.

Evelyn's expression clouded in bewilderment as she climbed the stairs. Why should Charles want to leave everything to her? What had brought on this sudden change of heart? Surely David must have gotten his wires crossed.

She shivered as she remembered the unashamed hatred etched on his face. He had always looked down on her with utter disdain, had even tried to make her look small and idiotic in the company of others. Charles – bless him – had soon put a stop to that nonsense and had warned his son in no uncertain terms to treat Evelyn with more respect or suffer the consequences.

Then today, she couldn't believe the lust she had witnessed burning deep in his eyes when he grabbed her; she had been startled by the intensity of it. Had she imagined it? Oh no . . . She recognised desire and unbridled lust when she saw it. If he did indeed fancy her, he had managed to hide it well over the past few years. But on reflection, his wife had always accompanied him whenever he had come to the house to discuss business matters with his father, before they had gone off to live in Cork. He had never at any time been alone with Evelyn, not until today, that is. Again she shivered with revulsion. David Matthews was one man she would never look sideways at, let alone take a fancy to. He was a right sickener!

Charles was slumped in his comfortable easy chair on the balcony and she rushed to his side.

His eyes were closed and his chin rested on his chest. 'Are you all right, love?'

He nodded but his eyes remained closed and his breathing was shallow. Pouring a glass of water from a carafe on a side table, she gently touched his shoulder.

'Here, take a sip of this, darling. Shall I fetch the doctor?' Her anxiety was so apparent you could almost touch it. 'Would you like to come inside and lie down?'

He opened his eyes and the heartache present there was such that she put a cupped hand over her mouth and gasped aloud. 'What's wrong, Charles? What has that son of yours done to upset you so badly?'

'Leave it for now, love. I'll tell you all about it later,' he said in an almost inaudible whisper. He sipped at the water. 'Give me one of my tablets, please. It won't be necessary to get the doctor out. I spend enough time in that bed as it is. I'll just rest out here for a while till I pull myself together, then I'll see that young gardener when he's finished for the day. OK?'

'Of course. Anything you say, love, but I could always tell him not to bother you today and you could talk to him tomorrow when you're feeling better. Are you warm enough?' He nodded as she tucked the woollen rug more closely around his legs. 'Try and get a wee nap, won't you? It'll do you good.'

71

He grabbed her hand and clung to it, then, with a sudden burst of emotion, pleaded, 'Thank you, love. Please don't ever leave me, sure you won't? I don't know what I'd do without you. You've been a rock for me.'

Placing a kiss on his forehead, she gently replied, 'Of course I won't! What on earth has that David fellow been putting into your head? He wants locking up, that one. But you can rest assured, whatever he's said, or done, I'll always be here for you.'

Adam carried two mugs of tea outside and joined Jackie sitting on the back veranda. With his hands clasped around his mug, he gazed out over Belfast Lough, his thoughts turning to his family. He pictured Maura across the water in Holywood, going about her daily chores, and cautioned himself that he'd have to be on his best behaviour. He knew his own make-up as well as what Evelyn was capable of. He was aware that he was taking one hell of a chance being here. Should Maura ever find out that Evelyn was back in town, and he was working here at her house, she'd go berserk! The very fact that he was keeping her in the dark about Evelyn's presence would make her all the more suspicious that something was going on behind her back. But so far it was strictly business, and he intended keeping it that way.

He glanced at his young helper, the unwitting chaperone he had brought along to save him from temptation, and lifted his mug in a silent salute.

With a confused smile, Jackie returned the salute. 'Cheers.'

Adam's eyes scanned the grounds stretching before him. He loved his work and couldn't wait to get his teeth into this job, itching to bring it all to fruition so that he could stand back and admire the end result: his own handiwork. It would take at least another four weeks, possibly more – depending on the weather – to complete the work. His wife rarely came over to Greencastle these days, only on the odd occasion to visit an old school friend, and he wondered whether he could get away with it. These gardens, after all, were a good distance from Greencastle, and he couldn't think of any reason why Maura should happen to pass by. Should he chance staying on here to finish the job?

He rose to his feet as Evelyn joined them. He could see how upset she was and said, 'Mrs Matthews, this is Jackie Flynn.'

'Nice to meet you, Jackie.'

'You too, mam.' Jackie touched his forelock with respect.

'You go on back to that plot we're working on and I'll join you in a minute, Jackie,' ordered Adam.

'Come back in ten minutes and I'll make you a bite to eat, son,' Evelyn contradicted.

73

Not knowing what to do, Jackie looked at his gaffer for permission. Adam nodded his consent and, with a big beam of delight, Jackie said, 'Thanks, missus.'

Once he was out of sight, Adam turned his attention to Evelyn. 'Is your husband all right?'

She nodded wearily and pointed upwards. 'He's asleep.' She sat down on the wicker chair beside his. They listened for a while and heard gentle snores coming from the balcony above them. 'Charles wants to speak with you before you go. He's in an awful state at the moment. God forgive that David fellow for causing his father such distress. He's already got enough physical pain to put up with, without his only son breaking his heart in the process.'

Adam drained his cup and setting it to one side moved to leave the veranda. She looked so pathetic sitting there that he had to get away before the urge to take her in his arms and comfort her became too unbearable. Glancing up at the sky, he said inanely, 'I'd better get some of those shrubs in before the weather changes.'

She inched to the edge of her chair and, putting her hands between her knees, pressed them together and looked entreatingly at him. 'Adam, don't leave me yet, please! Keep me company for a few minutes. Just till the lad comes back.' Tears silently ran unheeded down her cheeks. Without further thought of the danger ahead, he was on his knees before her. Cupping her face in his hands, he brushed the tears away with the pads of his thumbs, trying vainly to check the flood, but they gushed from a well of pain in which her whole being was submerged. The more he brushed the harder they fell.

'Hey, come on now,' he whispered. 'Don't let it get to you like this.' He delved into his pocket, glad that Maura always made sure that he carried a clean handkerchief. He thrust it into her hand.

She sniffed and scrubbed at her cheeks with it. 'I know you're right, but I'm scared. I'm at my wits' end. What will I do if anything happens to Charles? I'll have no one to turn to.'

'Look, you needn't worry yourself over David, your solicitor will look after all your affairs. He'll take care of things for you. That's what your husband's paying him for.' Still she sobbed. 'Listen! You'll manage all right. A beautiful woman like you?' He gave a derisive laugh. 'Men will be all over you like a rash; they'll be throwing themselves at you.'

She gave him a watery smile. 'But that's just it! I don't want other men. I've only ever loved you, Adam.' Thick eyelashes lifted as tear-drenched blue violets gazed forlornly at him. 'Did you mean what you said just now?'

He blinked in confusion. 'Did I mean what . . . ?'

'Do you still think me beautiful?'

'Ah, Evelyn . . . Of course I do. How could I think otherwise? You are so beautiful, my love. Evelyn . . .'

Her name came out on a sigh against her lips as he brushed them with his. Fleeting thoughts of Maura trespassed on his mind, only to be pushed aside. Then the rain came as Adam had predicted; just a shower, but when he glanced up at the gathering clouds it looked as if it was on for the rest of the afternoon. He rose to his feet and reached for Evelyn's hands, pulling her up into his arms.

'The lad will be back any minute now, Adam, thanks to that rain,' she said sadly, gently extricating herself from his embrace. 'I wish you hadn't brought him along. Anyway I promised I'd make him some sandwiches, so you'd better bring him into the kitchen when he gets back.'

When the door closed behind her, Adam gazed blindly at it. He couldn't believe that in the heat of the moment he had forgotten completely about Jackie, forgotten about Charles dozing above him, forgotten about his wife and young son going about their everyday business across the lough. Aware of it or not, Jackie really would have to chaperone him from now on. What kind of man was he turning into? He sure couldn't trust himself to be working here on his own.

Maura put the finishing touches to her make-up. Scrutinising herself critically in the mirror, she sighed. You're no oil painting, girl. But on the other hand, neither are you unattractive, she quickly reassured herself. She wasn't all that bad. If she were to put it in writing she would have labelled herself nice-looking. Think positive was her motto for the day, she decided, as she examined her reflected image. Finished with her self-criticism, she stood and turned this way and that, looking over her shoulder in the mirror. Her figure was quite good: narrow waist and nicely curved bust. Her hips on the other hand were just a little bit on the big side, although Adam had told her often enough that there was nothing wrong with them. She moved her head and was pleased when sunrays slanting through the bedroom window caught the auburn highlights. She was so proud of her hair; freshly shampooed, it fell to her shoulders in soft flowing waves.

Today she was going into Belfast city centre to meet her old school friend, Mary Moon. Maura had been living in Holywood, on the opposite side of Belfast Lough, since her marriage to Adam, which meant that the girls didn't see each other as much as they would have liked, so they made a point of meeting in the city centre for lunch when there was occasion to celebrate something. Tomorrow was one of those occasions. It was Mary's twenty-fifth birthday. Saturday was always such a busy day in Belfast that they had decided to meet today, Friday, instead.

Earlier that morning Maura had received a letter in the post from Joe Moon, Mary's husband. In it he explained that they were having a bit of a party in Conway's bar on Saturday night to celebrate Mary's birthday. Nothing great, he assured her, but he wanted it to be a surprise and he knew that his wife would be as pleased as Punch if Maura and Adam were to turn up. Remember Mary doesn't know anything about it, so don't let the cat out of the bag when you see her on Friday, he wrote. No need to get in touch, just come along Saturday night if you're free. Any time from eight onwards.

Not being much of a drinker, Adam wasn't all

that keen on socialising in pubs, but Maura was optimistic that she would be able to persuade him to come along with her. He had been so busy lately that it was a long time since they'd had a night out together. She had already made up her own mind that, with or without Adam, she intended to be at her best friend's do tomorrow night.

'Come on, Danny, my lovely wee boy, let's get your coat on. We're going to meet Emma and her mammy. Won't that be nice?'

The child was bursting with excitement: blue eyes aglow, small pearly teeth gleaming, as she strapped him into his Tansad pushchair. 'Emma! Emma, Mammy? Emma's dog too?'

'Yes, love, Emma. You like her, don't you? No, her dog won't be there. Brin must stay at home and guard the house. Make sure no bad men get in and steal Emma's toys while she's out.'

Danny's exuberance faded somewhat, so Maura promised, 'We'll go over and visit Emma at her home one day soon and you can play with Brin. You'll like that, won't you, sweetheart?'

He brightened up and nodded. 'Yes, Mammy.'

Maura checked her purse and put it in her shopping bag together with the gift she had bought for Mary. She intended giving her friend the birthday present today just in case there were any hitches and she was unable to get across to Conway's tomorrow night. Unlikely, but better to be safe than sorry. Pushing the pushchair outside she locked the front door and set off at a brisk pace down the road.

She was glad to be getting away from the confines of her home for the day. Lately, she had found herself spending too much time brooding, wondering what Adam was getting up to and who with, making herself absolutely miserable. It was tearing her apart, not knowing what to do, which way to turn. She had effectively cut herself off from her friends when she had married Adam Brady and moved across the lough to Holywood, but not for one minute had she regretted it. Their marriage was a happy one and she had had no complaints – that was, until these past few weeks.

As she passed the nursery centre on her way to the bus stop, she glanced up towards the office and, catching Benny's eye, waved to him. She wondered whereabouts Adam was working today. Probably over on the Antrim Road, she surmised. That job was taking a long time! It must be one hell of a big garden.

On the bus journey into Belfast she pondered on the change in her life. The past month had been awful for her, not knowing what was going on. It devastated Maura to watch her husband putting on a big act, pretending that all was well when obviously it wasn't. He must think her daft or something. But then, wasn't she indeed being daft for letting him get away with it from day one? The writing had been on the wall and she had chosen to ignore it. Was she being foolish not to confront him: bring it out into the open – clear the air once and for all, thrash it out and to hell with the consequences?

She sighed. No, she couldn't do that. She was too big a coward, too afraid of what the outcome would be of such a confrontation. What if this woman had such a hold on Adam that he chose to leave her and Danny? Pack his bags and go? She couldn't imagine him leaving his precious son, but stranger things did happen when a man's head was turned by a pretty girl. Then what would she do? How would she be able to bear it? The disgrace, the malicious gossip? Where would she go?

No! The more she thought about it, the more she convinced herself that she would be better off to sit it out, weather the storm. Be a coward, if that's what it took. Anything to save her marriage. Whatever happened, she decided she'd just have to grin and bear it.

She often wondered whether anyone else was aware of her husband's infidelity. Not here in Holywood, of course, but over in Greencastle where everybody had been aware of the scandal when Evelyn Matthews had jilted Adam. That had been the talk of the village for weeks. Except for this mystery woman; she would know, but that went without saying. Had this woman no conscience at all? Unless she was unaware that her lover was a married man with a young child. Or she was already married herself. Had Adam neglected to let her know of his marital status? Had she assumed that he was unattached, free to do as he pleased? Where was he meeting this woman? Not very likely in Greencastle where he was well known and there was a good chance that Maura might get to hear about his shenanigans.

No. If he had any sense at all, he'd steer well clear of Greencastle. Perhaps somewhere off the Antrim Road? There were numerous places along there, like the castle grounds, for instance, or Hazelwood, where they could meet in secret. Maybe they even met in the woman's own home whilst her husband was out at work. Maybe this, maybe that! All these maybes were doing her head in. She straightened up, suddenly struck by a thought. Maybe in the grounds of *her* house, the very house where Adam was working?

This thought stopped her in her tracks. If that were the case, he must be having one whale of a time, spending day after day with her. No wonder the job was taking so long. No, she chastised herself, Adam wouldn't do that to her. He wouldn't be so cruel. But how could she prove otherwise? At first she had thought it would peter out and she didn't want to know anything about the other woman, didn't want to put a face to her love rival, so she had made no attempt to look for any snippet of gossip from across the lough. But it was going on too long now, and womanly curiosity was getting the better of her. She now wanted to know who the competition was and what it looked like.

Would Mary Moon be able to enlighten her? If Mary was in the dark about the affair, Maura didn't want to whet her appetite, give her food for thought, as it were. If her friend twigged that something was afoot, that Maura was worried, she would soon wean the whole sorry tale from her. And the one thing Maura didn't want was pity. She would have to be very careful how she went about finding out whether or not Mary knew anything about Adam without arousing her curiosity. Of course, she realised that Mary, being Mary, would have great difficulty holding her tongue if there was the slightest hint of a scandal, so Maura would just have to let things take their natural course and all would be revealed in time. On the other hand, Mary wouldn't want to offend Maura and might just somehow manage to keep her lips zipped.

Leaving the bus at Oxford Street terminus, Maura came out of her musing and flashed a quick smile at the young man who lifted the pushchair from the well under the stairs and placed it on the pavement. He then swung Danny down beside it.

'Thank you very much.'

He gave her an appreciative glance and smiled in return. 'You're very welcome, love.'

Maura gazed after his retreating figure for some seconds. He had just made her day. It was heartening to know that a handsome fellow like that apparently found her attractive. Securing Danny in the Tansad, she continued towards the city centre, along Oxford Street to Ann Street, with a spring in her step.

Mary was already waiting on the corner at Cornmarket and came forward to greet her. The two women embraced and Maura said, 'Happy birthday.'

Mary grimaced. 'I can't believe I'm twenty-five. It seems like only yesterday when I first went to the dances. I remember thinking then that once you reached twenty-five you were over the hill, an old woman, and the next milestone was the old-age pension,' she lamented, shaking her head at the very idea.

'Tell me about it! Remember, I'm three months older than you. I know exactly how you feel.' The two children were struggling with outstretched arms to reach each other and Maura said, 'Look at them, they're so pleased to be together. It's too early for lunch. Shall we go for a quick cuppa and get them out of these pushchairs for a while to let off steam? We can get a bite to eat later, eh? Or are you in a hurry to get back to collect your daughter from school?'

'No, that's fine by me. I'm in no rush, Maura. Mam offered to pick up our Jenny today.'

'Right then, let's go over to that wee café on Rosemary Street that has plenty of room for these Tansads.' They walked up towards High Street and Maura continued, 'It really is great to see you, Mary. I've been looking forward to this outing for ages.'

'Me too. We really should do this more often, you know. I can't think of a reason why we don't.'

Maura could. Although Joe Moon had a well-paid job, he was tight-fisted and Mary was never flush where money was concerned.

High Street was crowded with shoppers so they concentrated on manoeuvring the pushchairs over the zebra crossing into Lombard Street in silence, until they arrived at their destination in Rosemary Street. Choosing a corner table, they sat Danny and Emma in chairs close to the wall where they could amuse themselves with the few toys their mothers had brought along to keep them from getting bored.

As they awaited their order, Maura reached into her bag, brought out a tiny parcel and thrust it across the table. 'Happy birthday, Mary,' she said again.

Mary sat wide-eyed with pleasure. 'Oh, you

85

shouldn't have, Maura.' She fingered the present tentatively.

'It's not much, mind. Just a wee token of friendship. But I think you'll like it all right.'

'Can I open it now?'

Maura laughed at her friend's eagerness. 'I'd be offended if you didn't,' she said with a fond smile.

Mary, as was her nature, painstakingly undid the wrapping paper; if she was careful, she would be able to use it again. Maura watched patiently. She herself would have vigorously ripped it off, but she was used to her friend's penny-pinching ways. Married to Joe Moon, how could she be otherwise? Nothing ever went to waste in the Moon household. Thrift was their middle name.

At last the paper was off, neatly folded and put carefully away in her handbag. Mary gazed down at the small, black box for some moments before lifting the lid. There were tears in her eyes when she looked up at Maura. She gently lifted out the gold cross and chain and held it across the back of her hand to catch the light. 'Not much?' she exclaimed. 'Oh, Maura, it's beautiful. I'll treasure it always. Thank you. Thank you very much.' She reached across and gave her friend a tight hug.

'I'm glad you like it.'

Maura knew that the gift was truly appreciated. To her knowledge the only jewellery Mary possessed was her wedding ring and a few other worthless pieces of cheap paste. Joe Moon was a tight git all right and he handled all their money matters. Maura remembered how shocked she had been to learn that her friend even handed over the wages she earned when working behind the bar in McVeigh's pub. Mary had been annoyed at Maura's scandalised expression and had said rather huffily that she preferred it that way. Joe gave her pocket money every week and that suited her just fine. He looked after their finances and Mary was happy with this arrangement, she insisted. That way, she didn't have to worry about paying the bills.

'I know it's not my birthday until tomorrow, but I'd love to wear it now, if you don't mind, Maura. Do you?'

'No, no, of course I don't mind. Go ahead.'

Mary held it against her throat and lifted the hair from the nape of her neck. 'Please fix it for me, Maura.'

Maura did so, fighting back the lump rising in her throat because her friend was obviously so overjoyed.

Mary confided, 'You know something, I don't think Joe remembers that it's my birthday tomorrow.'

'Oh, he'll remember all right. I'm sure you've thrown him more than a few hints. Eh?' Maura said slyly, as she nudged her with her elbow.

Embarrassed colour flooded Mary's face. 'You're

right! But he doesn't seem to have paid any attention to them. He hasn't said a word, not one word. And that's not like him. He usually makes mountains out of molehills when he has to spend money, no matter how little. You'd think we were living on the poverty line the way he sometimes gets on.'

'Never mind. I bet he'll have a lovely big bunch of flowers or something nice for you in the morning. Or he might even have something better in store for you. You'll just have to wait and see.'

'Huh! That'll be the day. But he had better remember,' Mary threatened. 'Or believe you me, there'll be blue murder if he doesn't.'

Their order arrived and conversation was shelved for a while as they tucked in.

The next couple of hours were spent dandering around Smithfield Market, in and out of all the second-hand stalls. Maura loved browsing around here; you never know what you might come across. She bought a vase that she was sure would one day increase in value, but Mary, careful as ever, managed to keep her money in her purse. They then went round the big stores along Royal Avenue, looking at and examining everything that caught their interest yet buying nothing, until the children became bored and cranky. The girls then decided it was time to get something to eat and made their way round to Ann Street to their favourite café.

Thrusting a menu at her friend, Maura said, 'Choose whatever you want, Mary. My treat today, remember. How's about a big juicy sirloin?'

'That's very kind of you, Maura. Thanks.' Mary spent some time perusing the menu and at last decided on her favourite meal, cod and chips. 'I know I'll enjoy the cod, whereas you can't always depend on the steak being tender enough, and I do hate tough meat, so I do. I think it's a waste of good money.'

'I know what you mean,' Maura agreed, choosing cod and chips as well. She also ordered bread and butter, a pot of tea, and lemonade and plates of chips for the children.

While waiting for their meals, Maura tried in vain to broach the subject that was a thorn in her side at present. She didn't know how to frame the words without confessing to Mary how worried she was. Mary, on the other hand, sat fingering her present and chattering about everything under the sun.

Everything, that is, except Evelyn Matthews. She had decided that Maura must surely know that Evelyn was back, and yet she hadn't mentioned it, not a single word about her. Mary decided that Maura must be too embarrassed, so held her counsel. If her friend didn't want to talk about it, she would respect her wishes.

With a great effort, Mary had managed to hold

her tongue until late afternoon when they were parting company, when she said tentatively, 'I'm sure you must already know . . .' Her voice trailed off.

Maura sighed. Here it comes, she thought. She was about to hear that there was talk about Adam and some woman. Please don't let it be anyone I know, she prayed silently. Smiling wryly, she said, 'OK, out with it, Mary. What must I already know?'

She managed to sound unconcerned and Mary's relief was paramount. She rolled her eyes to the skies and her words tumbled out in a rush. 'Thanks be to God! You do know then. Why didn't you say something? Here was me afraid to open my big mouth in case you would get upset. I told Joe you wouldn't be a bit annoyed, so I did. All that's in the past, I told him. It's history. After all, Adam Brady's married to Maura now and they have a lovely wee son. Why should Maura care one way or the other?'

Maura was now utterly confused. What was Mary talking about? They were on different wavelengths at the moment. 'Look, Mary, I haven't the foggiest idea what you're on about.'

Taken aback, Mary was quiet for some seconds, her eyes wide and questioning as she scanned Maura's face. Then she said flatly, 'You don't know, do you?'

'Know what, for God's sake? What are you talking about?'

Still Mary dithered and Maura lost her patience. 'Come on, out with it. And if you don't hurry up I'll miss my bus. What don't I know?' She was smarting to think that Joe Moon had offered advice about something concerning her welfare.

With a sigh Mary said, 'I wish I hadn't opened my big mouth now.' She reached for Maura's arm and squeezed it sympathetically. 'Evelyn's back in Greencastle. Well, not actually *in* Greencastle, but she *is* back.'

If Mary had smacked her on the face with her clenched fist, Maura couldn't have been more shocked. This was something she hadn't contemplated. Never in her wildest dreams. It had never, not once, entered her head that Evelyn Matthews might be back. Wasn't she living it up, playing lady of the manor down in Cork? Hadn't Maura thanked God that the woman she most feared was living so far away? Realising her jaw was sagging, she snapped it shut.

'Evelyn Matthews?' she croaked, unable to hide her distress. Her nerves were jumping like cold water hitting hot grease and the blood was draining so rapidly from her face that she might have severed a main artery. 'She's back?'

Mary could see that her friend was devastated and answered weakly, 'I'm sorry, Maura. I thought you must already know.'

'Don't be daft! How could I know? Eh? I hear

91

nothing, stuck away over there in Holywood. This is the first I've heard of it. How long? When did she get back?' The questions tumbled from her trembling lips and she looked as if she were about to pass out.

'I'm not sure. Some time ago, I think. You know how I do relief work behind the bar in McVeigh's? Well, the other night I overheard some of the regulars talking about her. Seems her husband had a stroke down in Cork and wanted to come home. That's all I know. Mind you, I haven't seen hide nor hair of her about the village. She must be keeping a low profile. Probably ashamed to show her face.'

Knowing she would miss her bus back home if she didn't get a move on, Maura nevertheless delayed, gripping Mary's arm, preventing her from boarding the number ten trolley-bus to the Whitewell Road. 'You knew about this all along and you never once mentioned it to me? We've been together for hours, for God's sake, and you never said a single word about it. How could you, Mary? I thought we were friends. Whereabouts is she living?' she forced herself to ask, although she thought she already knew the answer.

'Of course we're friends, Maura. You know I wouldn't do anything to hurt you. I was sure you already knew. Anyway, I believe she's living on the Antrim Road, not far from Serpentine Road somewhere. Look, Maura, I can get another bus in ten minutes, but if you don't hurry you'll miss your connection and you'll have to wait an hour at least for the next one and Danny will be bored stiff hanging around in that bus station.'

Coming to her senses, Maura gave herself a little shake. 'You're right, of course,' she replied tersely. 'See you soon.' And without so much as a backward glance, she hurried off in the direction of Oxford Street.

Mary's voice followed her. 'Thanks for the lovely present, Maura.'

She was furious with herself. Joe was right! Why was he always right? She should keep her big trap shut and mind her own business, that way she wouldn't get into any trouble. Now her friend was upset and it was all her fault. Upset? Devastated was more like it. She had never known Maura to lose her temper before. She was the one with the cool head on her shoulders, the one who was able to think things through first before venturing an opinion. Not like speak-first-and-think-afterwards Mary.

Her bus was pulling out of the bay as Maura rushed into the station with the pushchair. She waved frantically at the driver to hold on, and for one awful moment thought he was going to ignore her. She knew she would go nuts if she had to hang about here for another hour, given the state she was in. If she hadn't Danny to consider she wouldn't go home at all. Give Adam something to think about. With a look of annoyance the driver slowed to a halt beside her.

'Thank you. Thank you very much, driver.'

Her mouth paid lip service as she hurriedly released Danny and lifted him from the pushchair, but inwardly she fumed and vented her wrath on the driver. Some of them sickened her the way they got on. They acted as if they personally owned the bus instead of working for Ulster Transport. It was her, and folk like her, that kept these beggars in employment. She regretted this thought immediately. The drivers were only doing their jobs. She was the one in the wrong, not them. She thanked the young girl who sprang from her seat and lifted the Tansad aboard, leaving her free to dig out her return ticket.

The journey to Holywood was uneventful and Maura spent it trying to quell her temper. Danny was fretful and she devoted her attention to him, pointing out and naming articles advertised on passing billboards. Getting him to repeat the names, cigarettes, cars, or whatever, after her. She always did this when travelling. To her mind it was a great source of education and also helped pass the time. In spite of her best endeavours to keep her brain occupied, she felt physically sick in the pit of her stomach when thoughts of Adam's betrayal forced themselves into her tortured mind. Damn him! Damn him to hell for keeping this knowledge from her. She must be the laughing stock of Greencastle. There was now no chance of her going to Mary's wee do tomorrow night. No chance at all! How could she show her face there now?

The house was silent. She quickly opened the door, glad of the respite before facing her husband. Danny was tired and she managed to keep him awake for a while before feeding and bathing him, then settling him down for the night. While she did this she had space to think and decided to play dumb for a while longer, pretend she knew nothing of Evelyn Matthews being back. Lead Adam on; watch him make a fool of himself with his lies; get him to trip himself up. But in case a row erupted, she wanted Danny to be in his night's sleep. She didn't want to upset an innocent child listening to any bad-tempered words flying around.

Adam had told her that, since she was eating out today, she was not to worry about making him any dinner, saying he'd get something to eat before he came home. She recoiled inside now when she thought how grateful she had been of his consideration, when all along he had probably been glad of the excuse to spend more time with Evelyn Matthews. How she hated that name! That woman!

And most of all she hated her deceitful husband, Adam. She hated everything at the moment. She was inconsolable.

When at last he put in an appearance, her temper had cooled down considerably and her emotions were under control. He was not too late. In fact, if she didn't know the truth, she'd be so happy to see him home this early.

After his usual stop at the hall mirror to check himself, he came into the kitchen where she was doing the ironing and pecked at her cheek. 'Have a nice day, love?'

She managed not to recoil from the touch of his lips. 'Yes, it was very enjoyable.'

'Did Mary like her wee present, then?'

The faint smell of *that* expensive perfume clung to him, and brought bile to her throat. Lately when she'd smelled it, she'd assumed that he and *she* had been at it, picturing this unknown woman and Adam naked in bed together. Of course she knew there were innocent ways one could pick up the scent of perfume. But it was easy to forget such things. She had no trouble at all visualising them locked together in a passionate embrace and it drove her to distraction.

And now she had the added agony of being able to put a face to *her*. A beautiful one at that . . . and a beautiful body to go with it. Her heart wept at his deception and she longed to slam the hot iron into his smug face. See then if Evelyn would want him, looking like the Phantom of the Opera. Setting the iron down carefully, in case the temptation became too much, she turned and faced him.

He was immediately concerned when he saw how pale and drawn she looked, and reached out to comfort her. She eluded his arms by turning aside and pretending to sort through the clothes yet to be ironed. At a loss, he asked, 'What's wrong, love?' His gaze swung anxiously around the room and he voiced the fear that flooded him. 'Where's Danny? Is he all right?'

His show of concern was more than she could take. Afraid of giving the game away, she said, 'He's in bed. He was exhausted. And so am I for that matter.' She smiled wanly and rubbed her temples with her fingertips to try to relieve the pain in her head. She wasn't fabricating; her head really did throb. She wanted to spit out all the pent-up venom from her system, but instead she said curtly, 'I've been on the go all day and I've a splitting headache. But I enjoyed seeing Mary and being brought up to date on all the news. The latest *scandal*.' She put unnecessary emphasis on the last word.

Adam's face closed up. He walked slowly to the table and sat down, his fingers drumming a rat-a-tat-tat on its surface. Not knowing whether the villagers knew of Evelyn's return, he had dreaded coming home tonight, afraid Mary Moon would have filled his wife's ears with the latest gossip. But apparently not. Maura seemed OK. Just tired. Mary must surely have known that Evelyn was back, so why hadn't she said? For once in her life she must have held her tongue. If Mary had spilled the beans, Maura would have been on him like a ton of bricks before he even got a foot through the door.

'Who are they ridiculing now?' he asked sarcastically. 'You should know better than to listen to spiteful gossip, Maura.' Although convinced he was safe, he still sat on the edge of the chair with bated breath as he awaited her reply.

She actually noticed that he was holding his breath and she grinned inwardly. Let him worry and sweat a bit. Maybe if he holds it long enough he'll suffocate, she thought angrily. But she managed to say in a light voice, 'Oh, there wasn't any scandal worth talking about. Everybody seems to be living decent lives over there at the minute, but I did enjoy Mary's company. And what do you think? Joe Moon is throwing a wee do for Mary tomorrow night in Conway's bar. We've been invited over. I'll ask Beth Gallagher if she'll have Danny overnight so we won't have to hurry home. Won't that be great? It's a long time since we've had a night out together.'

Adam sat at the kitchen table and eyed his wife,

trying to think up an excuse for not going. 'I'll be working over the weekend,' he ventured.

'So what's new!' she snapped.

'It's all right for you, but I'll be tired and won't feel in the mood for going out socialising.'

'Yes, I've noticed how tired you've been recently.' She forced herself to sound concerned. 'Are you sure you're not overdoing it? To be truthful, I've been worried about you lately. You seem to have lost interest in everything. Maybe you should make an appointment to see Dr Givens for a check-up.'

'Don't be silly. It's just that some days are harder than others. It depends on whether I'm doing spadework or planting.'

She jumped at the opening right away. 'I thought you didn't do the donkey work any more since your last promotion?'

'I don't usually. But this is a big job. A lot of money's involved and Benny asked me to oblige.'

'Oh, I see.' More than you know, you slimy bastard, she thought. 'But I am telling the truth. I am worried about you. You're not even active in bed of late and that's not like you. Don't you feel well?' Or guilty, her mind ranted, or just shagged out; she thought that a more apt description for his condition. 'Is there something you're not telling me, Adam?'

'No! There's nothing wrong with my health,

Maura, if that's what you mean. No need for you to worry on that score.'

'You never want to go out any more. You know we need to get out and about now and again, while we're still young. You're working too hard, that's what. You know the old saying "All work and no play." I'm sure Benny will understand that you need a break. I'll throw him a hint tomorrow morning when I call in to ask if Beth can babysit. And I'll see if the hairdresser can fit me in while I'm at it. OK?'

Sensing that it would be foolish to start arguing about it and risk the wrath of the gods, Adam reluctantly gave his consent, but told her he would have a word with Benny himself and make the hairdressing appointment for her while he was at it. He didn't want Benny in all innocence to go shooting his mouth off about the glamorous Mrs Matthews.

Maura nodded with a satisfied grin, knowing full well that she had won the first round. Just let him stew until round two when she really went for the knockout. He'll not know what hit him when I mention Evelyn Matthews' name. I can't wait to see the look on his face, she thought with a malicious glint in her eye.

5

Saturday dawned bright and dry with a pale sun promising a warm day ahead. Maura spent the morning cleaning with unnecessary energy and tidying up round the house, spurred on by dark thoughts. She always worked harder when in a mood, and the house was shipshape in no time at all. Still uptight at Adam's attempts to get her to change her mind about going to Mary Moon's party, she had been adamant that she would go, with or without him. Now, she didn't particularly want to go, dreading what she might be walking herself into, but his very reluctance had only served to fuel her anger and determination. She had decided that she would go and face the music, get it all out in the open, find out what he was so afraid of. Adam had, with bad grace, eventually capitulated and spent the rest of the evening sulking and watching TV in strained silence, punctuated by the odd curt remark.

Before he left the house that morning she had reminded her husband to ask Benny to phone home and find out whether his wife, Beth, would be able to babysit for them, and to try to get Maura an appointment with her hairdresser. Now that she had set her mind on going, it would be awful if Beth couldn't look after Danny for the evening. It was about time that they had a telephone installed. That was one of the drawbacks of living so close to work. If Adam was off work but was needed in an emergency, one of the apprentices was sent to their house post-haste, so Adam had argued that there was no need for the expense of a phone and she had gone along with him. Why did she always agree with him? One of these days she'd put her foot down, just for the hell of it, and say *no* for a change.

She fretted while she worked, one eye on the clock, until Benny sent one of the young lads down to assure her that his wife would be only too happy to babysit and that she would pick Danny up about twelve to leave Maura free to get ready for her big night out. The lad also told her that Adam said the hairdresser was booked out but she could squeeze her in at four-thirty. As Maura had antici-pated, Beth had offered to keep Danny overnight until Adam picked him up on Sunday morning. Now to go through her sparse wardrobe and see whether she could find something suitable for Mary's party.

Shortly before noon Beth arrived. Opening the door, Maura ushered her into the living room. 'Thank you, Beth. I'm obliged to you. It's lovely out now, isn't it?'

Beth agreed. 'It is a beautiful day. There's a lot of heat in that sun.'

'Shall I put the kettle on for a quick cuppa?'

'Have you time? I don't want to hold you back. I can still remember how long it took me to get ready when I was going somewhere special. Of course I wasn't as attractive as you, so I had to work harder on my appearance.' Beth patted her ample frame and confessed, 'Thank God I'm past that stage now. I can tell you, it's a relief not having to watch those sexy young things make a play for my husband when my back's turned.'

'You always look lovely, so you do,' Maura chided her.

This was true. Although a little on the plump side, at fifty-five Beth Gallagher could still turn a few heads when she was all spruced up for an evening out.

'And I'm sure Benny never gave you any cause for concern. He's a good family man.'

'Don't be too sure of that, my dear. All men need watching at some time or other. They have to be kept on a short leash. Very few can say no when it's handed to them on a plate.'

Maura went still for a moment. Was there a hidden agenda in those words? Was Beth trying to warn her? Her friend appeared completely indifferent. Maura decided there wasn't any innuendo intended so she continued, 'Still, I imagine Benny would be one of those who could and would say *no* if the temptation presented itself. And I have plenty of time for a good old natter, so I have,' Maura stressed. 'The hairdresser can't take me until half four, so I've stacks of time to take a bath and decide what to wear. Go on, have a cuppa.'

'Oh, all right, then.' Beth smiled and gave in gracefully. 'You've twisted my arm.'

'Tea or coffee?'

'Coffee, please.'

Beth followed her into the kitchen where a delighted Danny scrambled up from where he was playing with his toys to launch himself at her.

Scooping him up into her arms, Beth hugged him close. 'Oh, you're a lovely, lovely boy. How would you like to come out with me and we'll go to the shops and I'll buy you some sweeties, love? And then I'll take you home with me for a while. You like staying in my house, don't you? And do you know what? We're looking after our neighbours' beautiful wee puppy while they're on holiday. You'll love it.'

Big blue eyes glowing with happiness, he darted towards Maura. 'Mammy too?'

Beth threw Maura a sad look. 'See! That's what happens when he hasn't seen me for ages. He's only being cautious. Really, Maura, you and Adam should go out more often. You've no excuse. I'll always babysit for you. You know that! Even on short notice like today, if I possibly can, I'll take Danny. Mark my words, once another baby comes along you'll be tied down. You'll regret not getting out while you had the opportunity.'

Maura gave her an appeasing smile. 'I know, and I'm sorry about the short notice, Beth. I really do appreciate you looking after Danny. You see, it's my best friend's birthday today and yesterday I received a letter in the post inviting me over to Greencastle to a bit of a do in the local pub. Adam tried to cry off when I told him last night, but for once I put my foot down and told him I'd go on my own if necessary, so he's consented to come along with me. He's working late most nights and every weekend at the moment. That's why we never get out much lately,' she lamented sadly.

Beth nodded sympathetically and sat down at the table. Delving into her shopping bag she took out a small banana. Maura had difficulty getting Danny to eat any kind of fruit, so every chance

Beth got she brought along a piece of fruit and blackmailed the child into eating it. Peeling back the skin, she said, 'Here you are, son, if you eat this all up, you can pick whichever kind of sweets you like when we get to the shops.' Beth called it the Gallagher psychology, and it never failed.

Danny's reluctant little fingers closed around the banana and he looked at it as if it were some curiosity to be immediately discarded, screwing up his small nose with distaste. Then he ventured a tentative nibble. Turning it round in his hand he gave it a further examination and must have decided it wasn't so bad after all as he started to eat it. Probably knowing from experience that the women would be busy talking while they drank their coffee, he headed back to his abandoned toys.

Beth watched him fondly. Then, giving Maura a satisfied 'See what I can do' wink, she lifted the cup of coffee Maura had placed in front of her. With elbows resting on the table she held the cup in both hands and blew on it to give herself time to think. Beth was well aware of the glamorous Mrs Matthews. Benny had been full of her when he got in that night and had laughingly related to her how upset Steve Patton had been to be taken off the job. It seemed that the Matthewses had particularly asked for Adam to do the work, and when big money was involved the customer was always right. He called the shots. It had been on the tip of her tongue to tease Maura about Adam spending so much time working for this bombshell when intuition cautioned her that such remarks might not, at this moment, be welcome, so she held her counsel and chose another topic to talk about.

'What do you intend wearing tonight, my dear?'

'Well now, that's something I'd like your advice on, Beth. I haven't got much of a wardrobe to choose from, I'm afraid. It's either those black trousers and that sweater I wore to your house at Christmas, or, you know, my blue dress with the plunging neckline, but you may not think it suitable for a pub. Unfortunately they're the best I've got. What do you think?'

'The trousers and sweater every time. You look lovely in them. That green sweater is the exact colour of your eyes, Maura. But then, you would look lovely in anything.'

'Hmm, I wish you meant it.'

Putting down her cup, Beth straightened in her chair and looked sternly at Maura. 'I'll have you know that I mean every word of it.' Maura's mouth twisted in a wry smile of disagreement and Beth rolled her eyes. 'Come on now. You must know how attractive you are. What's got into you, girl?'

Maura looked into the eyes of this kind woman who had taken her under her wing when she had first come to live in Holywood, and had a great urge to pour out all her worries and fears, but she quickly curbed the temptation. That would never do. It would be wonderful to have a confidante, a shoulder to cry on, but she was too ashamed to pour out her sorry tale of woe, not wanting to lose Beth's respect. What would she think if she knew about Maura's past? How could she bring herself to admit that Adam had married her on the rebound when she had fallen pregnant to him? Beth would assume that she had led him on, that she had been the seductress, but it hadn't been like that. It hadn't been like that at all! She had fallen in love with Adam. He had been so grief-stricken that she'd offered him all the solace she could muster, though she hadn't set out to get pregnant. It had just happened. Nevertheless, she felt cheap. Knowing that Adam was in love with someone else at that time, she felt that she had pressurised him into marriage. Was she now to suffer for it because Evelyn Matthews had returned?

Stifling the impulse to confess, she smiled brightly. 'Maybe it's because I suddenly feel old and jaded. I see very little of Adam lately, you know. We're like ships passing in the night. It'll do us good to get out tonight. Thanks for having Danny.'

Beth's heart sank. Maura might be putting on an Oscar-winning performance for her benefit, but Beth wasn't fooled for one minute. She could sense that her young friend was desperately unhappy. Surely Adam wasn't stupid enough to have his head turned by another woman. Especially a sultry blonde, by all accounts, and a married one at that. That would be courting trouble. There was certainly no idle talk flying about at the nursery centre, no rumours of an affair. In her opinion, Adam and Maura were ideally matched, and she would have sworn that they were very happy together. Especially as they had a delightfully bright son to consider.

Besides, she would have heard if there had been any talk being bandied about . . . or would she? She paused, suddenly unsure. Benny usually confided in her, but perhaps her husband was turning a blind eye, hoping it would all blow over. He wouldn't want to lose his best worker and, like Beth, he was very fond of Maura. Hiding her fears, she chatted about local affairs for a while, then, eventually, draining her cup, she rose from the table.

'That was lovely, thank you, my dear.' Putting her arms around this young girl who was more like a daughter to her, she hugged her tight, offering her silent comfort. 'You see and enjoy yourself tonight and you can tell me all about it the next time you're over.' She gave her a little shake. 'Do you hear me? That's an order! I'll go now and let you get on with it; take a long luxurious bath. Convince yourself how lovely you are. Come on,

Danny, let's get you ready and go see the puppy. His name is Finn. You'll love him.' Danny immediately jumped to attention and Beth flashed a glance at Maura. 'I love having him, you know. He's such a good child.'

As she hurried home from the hairdresser's, Maura felt slightly apprehensive. Wanting a more fashionable image with which to face the local clique over in Conway's tonight, she had decided to have her hair cut short. Now she wasn't sure that it suited her. Her neck felt cold and bare and her head much lighter. The staff in the salon had told her that she looked fantastic, but then they would say that. They'd hardly say, 'What a mess,' and go into a fit of the giggles.

She stood in front of the hall mirror for some moments, eyes closed, afraid of what she might see there. She needn't have worried; she turned her head this way and that, shaking it gently so the light reflected the highlights. She was delighted with the result. Here in the confines of her own home she could see that her thick, auburn hair did look very chic indeed. It was cut in the latest fashion, shaped close to her head in a shining bob, the sides hugging her face, emphasising her high cheekbones and small straight nose, and accentuating the fine symmetry of her features. *She* liked it and that was all that mattered. It made her look younger, yet sophisticated. But . . . would Adam like it? He was forever admiring her long tresses, liked threading his fingers through them when making love. For a minute she pictured Evelyn's silvery-blonde locks and wondered whether she still wore her hair long. Did Adam's fingers comb through her hair now?

She shivered in trepidation as fear gripped her heart. Was she wise going over to Conway's tonight? Would they all be pitying her? Whispering among themselves at her daring to show her face now that Evelyn was back?

She was glad that her dad drank across the road in McVeigh's pub. At least she wouldn't have to face him. See that smug 'I told you so' look on his face. It was over a year since she had last clapped eyes on him. Although he was proud of his grandson, he couldn't hide his disappointment in his daughter, and she was so hurt by his attitude that she stayed away from his house. After all, she wasn't the first woman to fall from grace and Adam *had* done the decent thing and married her. In reality, it had been a nine-day wonder, but not as far as her dad was concerned. Now the past was back to haunt her, resurrected by Evelyn's return to the district.

With a final pat to her shiny mop, she dragged herself away from the mirror. Enough of these morbid thoughts. Straightening to attention, she went to prepare a light meal for Adam. He should be home shortly. He'd promised to be back before six, and God help him if he tried to cry off at the last minute.

She would wring his bloody neck!

They would be taking a taxi to Greencastle and back in case he went over the drink limit, so Adam left the company van parked up at the nursery centre. His feet dragged and his thoughts were in turmoil as he walked the short distance to his home. He dreaded the evening ahead. There was no doubt in his mind that Evelyn's return would have been the talk of the village, but she had already been back a couple of months. It was old news; surely it would have played itself out by now. Would anyone mention her tonight, he wondered? He shook his head in frustration. With him and Maura arriving over for Mary's party, how could it be otherwise? The tongues were bound to start wagging as soon as they put in an appearance, and how would Maura react to any criticism directed at them? At least no one was aware that he was working up at Evelyn's house and for that he was grateful. He would just have to play it by ear and hope that everyone would mind their own business for a change and enjoy the party.

Taking a deep breath in an effort to relax and

appear to be in a carefree mood, he entered the house and passed along the hall without as much as a sideways glance in the mirror. There was no need for his daily ritual in front of it. He'd worked hard all day planting a variety of shrubs and rose bushes and hadn't had either the time or the inclination to indulge Evelyn. Because of this he hadn't got anywhere close enough to her to have to worry about lipstick smudges or the scent of perfume. Besides, these tantalising kisses were beginning to bore him. What use were they when they didn't lead to anything more exciting? To be truthful, he hadn't tried very hard to win Evelyn round. Let her sweat. He had been too preoccupied with what might happen tonight if the cat got out of the bag. With a great effort, he plastered what he hoped would pass for a smile on his face and pushed open the kitchen door.

'My, but it's quiet in here without His Nibs.' His eyes swept round the room. 'And tidy too,' he chuckled. 'You must have been hard at it today.'

Maura eyed him closely and decided his smile was too tense to be sincere. He was troubled. Not a good sign for the evening ahead. 'But we wouldn't be without him, would we?' she asked tentatively.

She was so curt, Adam was quick to assure her. 'Of course we wouldn't! That goes without saying.' His eyes took in her shining bob. 'Hey, what's with the new hairstyle? What brought this on?'

'Do you like it?' She held her breath with anticipation.

'Hmm, very nice. Very nice indeed.' He examined her head closely and nodded his approval. 'Yes. It suits you, makes you look like a wee teenager.'

Appreciating his praise, she relaxed. He made to peck her cheek but she turned her head away. She was fed up with his pecks. One would think he'd forgotten how to kiss properly. But then wasn't he getting what he wanted elsewhere, so why waste time putting on a show at home.

'I just fried an egg and a few rashers of bacon for you. There's sure to be a buffet laid on at the party.' Remembering Joe Moon's phobia of spending money, she added apprehensively, 'At least, I hope there will be.'

Adam knew the road her thoughts were taking and smiled wryly. 'Even Joe wouldn't dare have a wee do without laying on something to eat. For one thing, Mary wouldn't let him get away with it. She'd put him to shame. But you can be sure of one thing, he won't be buying any drink. Deep pockets and short arms, that's Joe. He'll expect everyone to buy their own drink and his too if he can wangle it.' He nodded at the table. 'But what about you? Aren't you having anything to tide you over?'

'I had a bite earlier. While you're eating, I'll go and get ready. Leave the bathroom free for you. OK?'

Adam nodded. 'I've a taxi ordered for eight o'clock.'

He usually enjoyed a good old fry-up, but this evening the bacon and egg tasted like sawdust as he nibbled at them. He was aware that Maura was a bundle of nerves and he was so apprehensive that his stomach knotted like a clenched fist. His throat muscles refused to function properly and he had difficulty getting the food down. He really did feel quite ill. If only he could persuade Maura into having a nice quiet night in, but he knew she wouldn't hear tell of it. She was hell-bent on going to Mary Moon's party. He didn't know what had gotten into her. She usually avoided visiting Greencastle on account of her father's stance towards him. He stopped chewing, mouth wide open. Unless . . . Bloody hell, she couldn't possibly know. Could she? Would she go over if she knew Evelyn was back? Did she intend to show up and make a public spectacle of him? And could he blame her if she did?

Pushing away from the table, he picked up his plate and scraped the remains of the half-eaten meal into the bin. He couldn't stomach another bite.

It was half eight when the taxi pulled up outside Conway's bar on the Shore Road. They had travelled over in companionable silence. While Adam

115

paid the driver, Maura crossed the pavement and entered the pub. The public bar was on her right and she cautiously put her head round the door to have a look. Immediately, a hail of friendly welcomes were thrown in her direction. She laughingly returned the greetings and, with a wave and a nod, backed out towards the stairs. Adam wasn't so lucky. He was called into the bar and, with an apologetic look and a shrug, left her waiting at the foot of the stairs. She paused for some moments and when Adam didn't return she slowly climbed the stairs to the lounge; raised voices and laughter grew louder as she neared the top.

A glance downward told her that Adam was still in the bar when she reached the landing. She hesitated, but just for a few seconds, then tossing her head back, she pushed open the door to the lounge where ladies accompanied their men for a quiet drink. Tonight, however, it was packed and anything but quiet. Conway's was a popular venue and always got a good crowd in on Saturday nights, but tonight it was bursting at the seams. Joe was a regular drinker here so all the other regulars would have been invited to join him for Mary's birthday party, as well as the family members and friends especially invited along.

Maura might as well have been invisible for no one paid her any attention whatsoever; they were too involved in their own individual cliques, laughing and talking with loud voices, trying to be heard over the surrounding clamour. Her eyes swept over the sea of happy faces and shock coursed through her when she saw the familiar figure of her father seated at a corner table. What was he doing here of all places and tonight of all nights? Had McVeigh's burned down during the night and no one had bothered to tell her? Then his companion lifted his head and gazed straight into her eyes. At once guilt consumed her.

It was her old flame, Francie Murphy. How come he had this extraordinary knack of making her feel small every time their paths crossed? She had never made him any promises. Still, she had been dating him before Adam came on the scene and she guessed that his intentions had been serious. Well, he should have told her so and maybe she wouldn't have become attracted to Adam Brady in the first place.

Francie leaned towards her father, muttered something to him and started to rise from his chair. At that moment Mary Moon saw her and swooped across the room, obscuring Francie's view. When Maura next looked over he had sat down again but he was still watching her intently. Her father sat with bowed head.

'Maura! Joe said you might get over tonight. I'm so glad you could make it.' Mary's eyes darted towards the door. 'Isn't Adam with you?'

'Oh, he'll be along shortly. Someone nabbed him down in the bar. He'll be here . . .'

Adam's arm came around her waist and he pulled her close. 'Now! I'm here now. Hello, Mary.' He gave Mary a peck on the cheek. 'Happy birthday. Sorry about that,' he whispered for his wife's ears only. 'I couldn't get away from Billy McDowell.'

'Thanks, Adam. I'm all excited, so I am. I was just saying to Maura yesterday that I thought Joe had forgotten all about my birthday, but she knew all along that he was planning this surprise and never said a word.' She gave Maura a reproachful look, then suddenly noticing the new hairdo went into raptures over it. 'Oh, your hair's gorgeous, Maura,' she enthused, 'absolutely beautiful. Come over here where I can get a better look at it. We've kept two seats in case you could make it.'

Mary tugged at her friend's arm and led her to a table in the opposite corner from where her dad and Francie sat. Maura chose the chair with her back to them and sat down.

Mary, jubilant that Joe had managed to arrange this party without her knowledge, was in her element. She was bubbling over with excitement. Excusing herself, she went from table to table making everyone feel welcome and thanking those who had given her presents. When she returned to their table and sat down beside her again, she spoke softly to Maura, patting her on the arm as if to hold her attention.

'I'm sorry about yesterday. Are you all right?'

'Of course I am. That's all water under the bridge now. As you said yourself, why should I worry? You took me unawares, that's all. I didn't know she was back.'

Mary squeezed her arm. 'You look great. Just great! Like a film star,' she said enviously. 'That hairdo really suits you.' Leaning closer, she confided in a whisper, 'Your dad would like a word with you, Maura. Any time at all, he says, before you go home.'

Maura turned, looked across the room and, catching Davey's eye, nodded. She relayed the message to Adam, adding, 'I'll go over now. I don't suppose you'll come with me and pass yourself?'

Her husband dithered. He was in two minds what to do. So far Evelyn Matthews' name hadn't been mentioned up here in the lounge. Down in the bar the men had got a few sly digs in and he had parried their questions by pleading ignorance, saying that he hadn't a clue what they were going on about. But what if Davey Craig knew and wanted to talk to his daughter about it? If Adam was present, harsh words might be bandied about, possibly resulting in a fracas, whereas if Maura went alone, Davey would probably talk to her in confidence, keep it low-key, as it were. Davey wouldn't want to start a barney here at Mary Moon's party.

Adam nodded towards the bar where they were queueing to be served. 'Look, I'll go join that lot and get the drinks in while you have a chat with your old man, OK?'

He was rewarded with a disgusted look. 'Suit yourself!' Maura rose to her feet and sidled her way between tables across the crowded floor.

Francie was already on his feet, asking people to move along the upholstered bench where they were sitting against the wall, to make room for her. Maura knew most of the crowd and, thanking them with a nod and a smile, slipped into the space made beside her father.

Francie remained standing. 'I'll get you a drink, Maura. Give you a chance to talk to your da in private. Is it still Pernod and lime?'

'Yes, thank you, Francie.'

'Ice?' She nodded and he said, 'I'll leave you to it, then.'

Glad that they were in a corner and thus had some privacy, Maura turned to her father. He was looking at her, eyes full of pity. 'You're enjoying this, aren't you?' she hissed furiously.

Davey's hand reached out and gently patted her arm where it rested on the table. 'Hold on now. You're jumping the gun, girl.' His voice was low and for that she was grateful. She hoped he'd keep it that way when he started to berate her, as he was very likely to. Davey was eyeing her, a quizzical look on his face. 'You do know she's back, don't you?'

'Yes.' She sighed. 'And you don't have to remind me that you said this would happen. Is that why you're here tonight? To gloat? To say "I told you so"?'

Davey shook his head sadly. 'Don't go on like that, Maura. It doesn't become you. I'm here because Francie asked me to. He works with Joe Moon, remember, and Joe invited him here tonight and extended the invitation to me as well.'

She grimaced. 'I'm sorry. I'd forgotten about that.'

Pacified, Davey relaxed and confessed, 'I'm worried about you, daughter, that's what. What will you do now?'

Bewildered, she questioned him. 'What do you mean, what will I do?'

His eyes widened in consternation. 'Well, surely you're not just going to turn a blind eye to what's going on,' he exclaimed. 'You'll be the laughing stock of the village if you do.'

Hiding her confusion, she asked, 'Turn a blind eye to what?'

Davey was slowly losing his temper but still managed to keep his voice to a whisper. 'The bloody antics of themins up in that big house. I bet he hasn't told you that the whore's back. Has he? What a carry-on. I'd love to wring his bloody neck, the way he's treating you.'

Maura's heart sank. So it *was* Evelyn's house that Adam was working at. Pride gave her a nonplussed expression. 'Adam's working there, is all. They want their gardens landscaped and that's what he does for a living, in case you've forgotten. He has to go where he's sent. And anyway, what proof have you got to think there's anything going on between them?'

'Why else do you think he's working there? If he had an ounce of respect for you at all, he'd be avoiding her like the plague. I remember you were putty in his hands when he seduced you, and now he's taking you for a mug. Wise up, girl, and don't try to tell me he's not getting his leg over up there. Why else would he go there, and her husband bedridden into the bargain? They're making a fool of him too. Poor old sod.'

Tight-lipped, Maura leaned closer still and glowered at him, but still managed to keep her voice down. She didn't want everybody gaping at her, pitying her. This was neither the time nor the place to start her da off on his ranting and raving. 'I'll have you know that I trust Adam! But thanks for the warning, Da.' She made to rise but his hand on her arm held her down.

'Listen, daughter, I'm sorry. I didn't mean to upset

you. I asked you over to tell you how sorry I am. I know I've been an old fool, and I miss you, I really do miss you, and I want to get to know that wee grandson of mine. He's a fine wee fellah. Will you please bring him over to see me now and again?'

She nodded her agreement. She would have agreed to anything to get away from him and his hurtful insinuations. 'All right, I'll do that. But you're wrong, Da. Adam would never be unfaithful to me. I trust him.'

She rose unsteadily from the table. His softly spoken parting words just reached her. 'There you go then.'

Her eyes sought Adam as she made her way towards the door. He still stood at the bar and was deep in conversation, totally unaware of her. She was through the door, on her way to the cloakroom, when Francie caught sight of her. Undecided, he eyed the Pernod and lime he was carrying, then followed her out.

'Maura, shall I leave this on your table or will you be going back to your dad's table?'

She took the glass from him and gratefully downed half the contents in one swallow. 'Thanks, Francie, I needed that.'

His eyes scanned her pale face. 'Are you all right? I told Davey not to mention Evelyn . . . but obviously he did. Did you not know about her being back?'

'It seems that the wife is always last to find out.' She grimaced and confessed, 'You know, I always thought that was a load of old rubbish – that the wife must be blind if she didn't guess what was going on behind her back. But now I know it's all too true, that she *is* the last to know.' Tears threatened, and she blinked furiously to hold them back.

'Do you want to powder your nose and I'll take you home?' he asked gently.

'Oh, no! Definitely not. Give that lot,' her head jerked towards the lounge, 'something else to gloat over? Besides, although I didn't know until yesterday that she was back, I do know that Adam has a job to do, and he would never be disloyal to me on that score. He probably didn't want me to worry and that's why he didn't tell me.' She only hoped that she didn't have to eat these words. She downed the rest of the Pernod and handed him the glass. 'Thanks for that. I'll see you later, Francie.'

In the cloakroom, Maura locked herself in a cubicle and fought for self-control. She sat with eyes shut tight and fists clenched. She was almost frantic with anxiety as she sat jiggling her knees. She must not disgrace herself by breaking down out there of all places. To be truthful, no one seemed to be bothered about her. They were all enjoying themselves too much to notice her misery. She was just another number among the happy revellers. It would be tomorrow when the rumours would be rife, and then she would be well away from the gossipmongers, safely back on the other side of the lough, and it wouldn't matter in the slightest what they thought or said. After all, what she couldn't hear, couldn't harm her. Meanwhile, whilst she was here she just had to keep her cool, smile at everybody as if everything was tickety-boo and she hadn't a care in the world.

Someone entered the cloakroom and went into the other cubicle. She waited until they left, before venturing out to the handbasin. She must compose herself, put on a brave smile, get back in there and act as if she were none the wiser. God, would she be able to pull it off? She had her doubts. The outer door opened again and Maura prepared to put on a show in front of the mirror. She smiled brightly at the reflection of the young woman who came through it.

Glad it wasn't anyone she knew, she said, 'Hello! It's very hot in there tonight, isn't it?' She glanced at her reflection in the mirror and almost collapsed at the sight of her image. She looked like death warmed up. 'This heat's getting to me.'

Linda Morrison looked at her with some concern. 'Are you all right, love?'

'I'm OK! Just a bit squeamish. My tummy's upset.' Maura gave a harsh laugh. 'And they haven't even served the food yet. I had a prawn sandwich earlier today,' she lied. 'Seafood doesn't agree with me. But I couldn't resist it. You know how it is.'

Linda looked relieved. 'For a minute there I thought that maybe you might be pregnant and in some kind of discomfort. I pictured myself sending for an ambulance.'

'Good gracious, no! What makes you think that?' Maura's hands instinctively went to her flat stomach. What was this woman talking about?

She looked so scandalised, Linda was quick to apologise. 'Never mind me, dear. I'm a nurse and my imagination runs away with me at times. But you don't look too good, you know. If you get any worse during the night, get the doctor out.' She thrust out her hand. 'I'm Linda Morrison, the district nurse. I haven't seen you around these parts.'

Wishing that she could skulk off somewhere quiet to lick her wounds, Maura clasped the proffered hand. 'Pleased to meet you. I live over in Holywood. Mary Moon and I are old friends, and Joe invited me and my husband over for the party. I have heard your name mentioned though. I'm Maura Brady.'

A wide smile split Linda's face. 'Oh, I think I've met your husband. Is he a gardener by any chance and does he work for the Matthewses on the Antrim

126

Road? You see, I help look after Mr Matthews. He's a grand old man for his age.'

The flicker of hope that still lived within Maura was finally extinguished. At least she could pretend to this woman that she knew he was working there. 'It's a small world, isn't it? Yes, that's my Adam. They're old friends, you know.' Against her better judgement, she asked, 'Is Evelyn still as beautiful as ever?'

'Oh, she is a very beautiful woman all right.'

Maura dried her hands and prepared to leave. 'Nice to have met you.'

Linda stared for some moments in consternation as the door closed on Maura Brady. So it *was* the same Adam. The very one Mrs Matthews had jilted. And that poor girl looked as if she had just found out about it. Linda's heart went out to her. As far as she knew it was all open and above board up there, but then they would be very careful to keep their affair – if there was one, she hastily reminded herself – very discreet. And anyway, she chided herself, it was none of her business what they did.

6

A tumult of emotions argued for precedence within her: anger, anguish, desolation, as she hovered by the lounge door, trying to will herself to go back inside. The very thought of having to face everyone proved too much for her and she felt physically sick in the pit of her stomach. She imagined that all eyes would be focused on her and if anyone spoke, she'd probably start blubbering and make a spectacle of herself. She mustn't disgrace herself in that way, by letting everybody know the hurt she felt. How she wished that she had stayed at home or that her dad had kept his big trap shut and she was still living in ignorance of her husband's infidelity. Seeing a shadow coming towards the frosted-glass window in the lounge door, she panicked and blundered blindly down the stairs, glad to get outside without encountering anyone she knew.

Although it was June, at this late hour there was a slight nip in the air, and without her coat she shivered in the sharp night air. What to do, that was the question. Clamping her arms across her chest as if to hold in the warmth, she scurried along Shore Road. Hesitating at the junction with Whitewell Road, she gazed longingly up it. If only she could go to her Aunt Hilda who lived further up the road, she would have a shoulder to cry on, someone to talk to. But she didn't want Hilda to witness how distressed she was. Besides, Adam would worry if she didn't get back to the lounge. And what about that! Why should she worry what Adam thought, her mind ranted? This mess is all his doing.

Her eye lighted on the phone booth on the far side of the road, outside Stewart's Cash Stores, and her relief came out on a sob. There was the answer to her plight staring her in the face. Silly fool! Why hadn't she thought of it sooner? She would go over, phone for a taxi and go straight home. There was money in the house so she could pay the driver when she got there. That's what she'd do. Leave Adam to make her excuses, let him stew in his own juices for a change. Serve him right if they started whispering and nudging each other as they watched the antics of him running round looking for his wife. He'd be infuriated.

This thought heartened her and her feet brought her to the edge of the kerb, before her tortured mind sent the message to her brain that she had no change for the phone. She had left her handbag on the table when going to talk to her father. Frustration brought tears to her eyes but she blinked furiously to contain them. Somehow or other she had to compose herself, go back to the pub and face the music if necessary. She had no other option. And she must not break down in tears in front of everyone and cause further speculation. That would be the final straw; the shame would send her round the bend. She battled to retain her self-control. Another thing she had forgotten: she had nothing to repair her make-up with. If only I had grabbed my handbag, she lamented, I could be on my way home by now.

As she stood there steeped in self-pity, she felt an arm slung across her shoulders making her jump with fright. Her nerves now completely shattered, she was pulled close to a muscular body. Gratefully she snuggled against the recognised warmth of a comforting shape; Adam must have followed her out. He'd be able to put everything right with her. Wouldn't he? But her sensitive nostrils soon told her that the spicy aftershave, although familiar, wasn't the brand Adam used. Suddenly alarmed, she tried to push herself away and looked up into the concerned face of Francie Murphy.

He resisted her efforts to struggle free and forcefully drew her up Whitewell Road and into the alleyway at the side of the church hall. 'Be still!' he ordered, releasing his hold, but keeping a wary eye on her in case she tried to bolt. 'Here.' Shrugging out of his jacket, he wrapped it round her shoulders, then gently gathered her close again.

She sniffed and he urged, 'And for heaven's sake don't cry! Do you hear me? You're going back in there, so you won't want to make a mess of that beautiful face of yours. The alternative is to let me drive you home. I've only had one pint, so it'll be safe enough for me to drive. Just say the word.' She remained silent, lost in a world of despair. Cheek against her hair, he said, 'Well, what's it to be?'

To give herself a brief respite while she considered his proposal, she shrugged away from him and made a feeble effort to return his jacket. 'Here, take this back. You'll catch cold in that thin shirt.'

If she did as he asked and let him, of all people, drive her home, Adam would be incensed. Francie had had the gumption to upbraid Adam when he had learned that Maura was pregnant, accusing him of taking advantage of her when she was infatuated with him, and they had almost come to blows over it. It had annoyed her greatly at the time and she had told Francie to keep his nose out of her affairs. She had made her bed and she must lie on it, she had said. He had never bothered her since, but she knew that all hell would be let loose if she went off with him now, and God alone knew where it would all end. In her vulnerable state, anything might happen. If Adam ever needed an excuse to leave her, she would be playing right into his hands.

Francie stilled the hands that were trying to remove his coat by holding them in his large fists. 'Catch cold? A healthy big lump like me? You've got to be joking. Catch yourself on, Maura.' He was glad to see her relax and the threat of tears subside. 'Just say the word . . . what do you want to do?'

'I don't know,' she wailed, against his chest. 'How can I face that crowd again, eh? The very idea terrifies me.'

He released her hands and cupped her face, forcing her head up. 'Look at me, Maura!' Thick wet lashes lifted and eyes like emeralds gazed into his. He had always thought her beautiful. Why, oh why, hadn't he told her so all those years ago? From their school days he had always looked at her in awe, had been delighted when he had worked up the courage to ask her out and she had said yes. Hoping to marry her, he had respected her so much that he had never once put a foot wrong, only to lose her to Adam Brady, who used her to assuage his loss of another woman. Why hadn't

Francie stood up for his principles and fought back? Because his pride was hurt. After that he had kept his distance and hadn't spoken to Maura since, fool that he was.

He was overwhelmed to have her once more in his arms where, in his opinion, she belonged. He could almost hear his heart thudding against his ribs, as he held her. Him and his hurt pride, he ranted inwardly. What had he been thinking of? He should never have let Adam Brady waltz off with her. How could he have been so daft? He should at least have tried to win her back but he'd let pride rule his heart and a lot of good that had done him.

Pushing his own woes aside, he gave her a gentle shake. 'You're overreacting, you know. Look at it this way. No one in Conway's has said anything – except your dad – to annoy you, have they?' She gave this some thought, and at her nod of confirmation, he continued, 'There you go then, what are you worried about? Even if someone does make a snide remark, you should be more than able to deal with it, but I don't think that's likely to happen. They're not a bad crowd in there, so just take it easy and everything will work out fine, you'll see. There, are you OK now?' Again she nodded but a sob trembled on her lips. His arms tightened round her and he said, 'Good. Now I want you to take a deep breath and let it out slowly.' She grimaced, as if deriding him, but obeyed. 'Now, do it again.' To her surprise she felt the tension ease from her body and her anxiety subside somewhat. Chucking her under the chin, he admonished her, 'See? I'm not just a pretty face.'

However, her nearness was proving too much for him and he felt his passion rising. It was so long ago since those idyllic months when they had gone out on dates, and he had built his hopes on her returning his love. When his face lowered towards hers she didn't object and he claimed her lips. The comfort of his arms and the feel of lips soft and gentle on hers were a balm to her hurt pride and she returned the kiss. With a great effort, without releasing her completely, he distanced himself.

'Feel any better?' Confused and feeling guilty at her actions, Maura nevertheless nodded and he went on, 'Good. Now remember you are a lovely woman and Adam Brady would be a fool to leave you, especially for the likes of Evelyn Matthews. He needs his head examined, so he does. Now let's get you back to the pub, before we call attention to ourselves; then they would have something to talk about.' He smiled.

They left the comforting shadows and made their way round the corner and along Shore Road without incident. If some of Francie's mates they met along the way were tempted to tease him, as to what he was doing walking with his ex-girlfriend at this time of night, one look at his set face and the withering look he gave them soon curbed their tongues and they passed by with non-committal smiles and goodnights.

Outside Conway's, he relieved her of his jacket. She gazed up at him and he could see her resolve faltering. 'How do I look?' she asked fearfully.

'Beautiful, as always, and you'd better remember that. Right now, chin up, best foot forward and let's get you back into the fray.'

They climbed the stairs together, his hand on her arm offering silent solace and support. At the door to the ladies' room, Maura whispered, 'I'll nip in here first and you go on in. Wouldn't do to start tongues wagging by us going back in together.'

'I don't know about that.' Francie nodded sagely. 'It might be just what Adam Brady needs to buck himself up. But if that's what you want . . . Is it?' She dithered and he added, 'You can still change your mind, you know, and I'll take you home.'

A sad shake of the head. 'I've no other choice, Francie, but thanks all the same.'

Inside the ladies' room, the face that returned her gaze in the mirror now told a different tale. She was still a little bit pale and wan, but there was composure there now, not dread; a glint in her eyes of an awareness that she was still attractive and desirable, if not to Adam any more, then at least to other men. Wonderful what a long, tender kiss could do to one's ego. Francie Murphy had unconsciously restored her self-esteem and for that she was grateful. The memory of that kiss brought much needed colour to her face and she felt ready for battle, if need be.

As she left the ladies' room, Adam was coming through the door of the lounge. He scowled at her. 'What on earth kept you? I was coming to look for you.'

'I was talking to Francie Murphy.'

Adam grunted in disbelief. 'What! In there? You're joking, aren't you?'

'Don't be daft. As a matter of fact, we went for a dander up Whitewell Road.' That covered her should anyone mention seeing them.

'Indeed! And what's he sniffing around you for? He still fancies you, you know. The slimy bastard. Stay away from him,' he warned.

Still wrapped in the warmth of Francie's kiss, she agreed smugly. 'Yes, I know. And there is nothing whatsoever slimy about him. I must say it gives me a nice warm feeling to know that someone still wants me. It was kind of you though, breaking off that interesting conversation with Tommy Magilp long enough to worry about me,' she added slyly.

Guilt reddened his face and he gruffly apologised. 'Sorry about that. I got carried away. We were talking about the Linfield match. Can you believe it, Bangor stuffing the Blues three-nil.'

She nodded her head. 'Ah! That explains your neglectfulness.'

If it hadn't been football it would have been something else, she thought sadly. When they did go out together she was used to being left on her own while Adam lorded about, acting the big fellah and getting in rounds for his old cronies.

Head poised high, she now paused to gain his full attention and, looking him straight in the eye for greater effect, said quietly, 'Why didn't you tell me Evelyn Matthews was back?'

Her abrupt question took him completely off guard, bringing him up short. He blustered and tried to turn the tables. 'I suppose that's what your da wanted to talk to you about, eh? Trust him to stick his nose in where it's not wanted.'

A finger poked sharply into his chest. 'Don't you dare criticise my dad. You've been working on the Antrim Road, and doing God knows what else for weeks now, and not one word about Evelyn Matthews. Why not, eh? Guilty conscience or something? Surely you weren't dumb enough to think I would never find out?'

He at least had the grace to look sheepish and, looking over his shoulder to see if anybody was listening, said, 'I was waiting for the right moment.'

'Huh! Right moment, my ass. From what I hear,

137

she's been back weeks. But we'll talk about it when we get home. As for now, let's go back in and put on a big act for our friends. You should be able to get away with it. You've had enough practice this past few weeks and I've been the unwitting stooge. You should be on the bloody stage, so you should. You could give Richard Burton a run for his money. So let's get in and keep up the pretence.'

She made to pass him but he gripped her arm. 'I think we should go home now. You can't go in there, the mood you're in.' He gave her a gentle push away from the door. 'You go on downstairs, I'll fetch your handbag and we'll call for a taxi outside.'

She wrenched her arm free, obviously insulted by his remarks. 'You've got to be joking. And spoil a perfectly good double act?' she said sarcastically. 'We'll be the star turn. We'll knock 'em out, so we will. Let's get the show on the road.' Her adrenalin was now pumping as she brushed roughly past him and flounced into the lounge.

In her absence, tables that had been previously covered with white cloths had been unsheathed and people were helping themselves from the delicious array of food. She went to join them, Adam hard on her heels, when they encountered the nurse she'd met in the cloakroom, and who had now stopped to talk to her husband.

Maura lingered to hear what she had to say and Adam was forced to introduce her.

'I've already met your wife earlier on in the toilets,' Linda confided. She smiled at Maura. 'You're looking much better now. I'll not keep you. That grub's lovely and it is fast disappearing.'

Linda moved on and Adam said tentatively, 'So that's how you know about Evelyn.'

'No. I've already known for days. Linda thought I looked ill and was concerned I might be threatening a miscarriage.'

Adam couldn't keep the shock from his voice. 'Are you . . . pregnant, I mean?'

'Why, would it worry you if I were? Would it interfere with your plans, whatever they may happen to be?'

Adam glowered at her. 'Look, leave it for now. Let's get something to eat. All this bickering's given me an appetite.'

Sunday morning arrived with a reddish-pink-washed horizon under pale-blue skies. Seagulls kicked up a screeching racket on the nearby shore as they fought over bits of food. Bright sunlight blazed through the window. It was the sunbeams dancing across the room and bathing the bed that aroused Maura. She groaned at the pain that announced itself to her brain with the first flicker of her eyelids. It pounded like a hammer behind her eyes, making her huddle under the bedclothes, away from the cruel dazzling light. Who had opened the blinds? After some moments of confused thought, she ventured to peep from under the blankets only to gape in amazement. What on earth was she doing in Danny's room? And where was Danny? Memory, like a splash of cold water on her face, came rushing back, heightening the pain and making her cringe with humiliation.

She whimpered with embarrassment as recollections of the previous evening slowly returned. Whether or not it was her defiant attitude towards Adam, she'd never know, but other than her father, no one in the lounge had mentioned Evelyn Matthews' name, at least not within earshot. Throwing caution to the wind, Maura had been the life and soul of the party. Knowing she had a pleasant singing voice, she hadn't been shy when called upon and even sang a couple of duets with Mary Moon. It helped her pretend that she hadn't a worry in the world. She had, however, downed more than a few Pernods at an alarming rate – to give her Dutch courage – watched over by an anxious Adam.

Joe Moon hadn't stinted on the food line and had surprised everybody by putting on a great spread of pork pies, sausage rolls, chicken pieces, et cetera. There was also a large birthday cake to follow, everything cooked and baked that day by the local home bakery. The appetising food helped keep Maura reasonably sober. At the end of the evening she had gone over to say goodnight to her father, and Francie had quietly congratulated her with an admiring, 'Well done, Maura.' His praise had raised her spirits and she made her farewells with a happy-go-lucky attitude, kissing one and all and hoping Adam noticed how she lingered longer with Francie.

Thanking Mary and Joe for a lovely evening, she told Mary that they must definitely meet up more often, so that she could be kept up to date with all the local gossip. This was said with a scornful glance in Adam's direction and she smiled at his red-faced discomfort. Back home she had left her husband to pay the taxi driver and stumbled upstairs, disdainfully scorning the marital bed in favour of the single one in the nursery. She must have passed out because that was the last thing she remembered.

Holding her forehead, she gingerly swung her legs off the bed and attempted to stand. The effort proved too much. The floor came up to meet her and the room started to spin. She felt as if she were caught in a whirlpool and sank slowly down again, clutching her head, afraid it might explode with the effort. When she next ventured to open her eyes, she gazed in anger at her crumpled finery of the night before. She must have been really drunk to fall asleep fully clothed, jewellery and all. Vague pictures raced before her eyes, of Adam trying to cajole her into removing her clothes; of herself lashing out at him, accusing him of wanting to use her. With a bad-tempered grunt he had left her to it. Mortification blocked out any further memories. Oh, to disgrace herself like that. She writhed with humiliation at the memory.

She was small now, huddled on the edge of the bed, arms embracing her body, rocking herself. It seemed like ages before she could focus on the small dial of her watch. Ten past eight, and not a sound coming from the house. Had her husband slipped out early to avoid the threatened showdown? What genuine excuse could he possibly offer for his betrayal? Would she ever be able to trust him again?

Dragging herself from the bed, she tottered from the room and along the landing. As she passed the main bedroom, the door was ajar and she cast a furtive glance inside. Shock brought her to a standstill and she slowly retraced her steps to gaze in disbelief. The coverlet was smooth as a millpond, not a crease to be seen. The bedroom was empty and the bed obviously hadn't been slept in. Where had Adam spent the night?

No matter where or who he had spent it with, she didn't want him to find her in this state. She was in no condition for a slanging match. Firmly clutching the banister, she timidly descended the stairs and reached the sanctuary of the bathroom without catching sight of Adam.

After a cold shower, which took her breath away but lessened the stupor that had enveloped her, she was dressed and sitting at the kitchen table, hands clasping her third cup of strong coffee. She had swallowed two aspirins, trying to ease the Pernod-fuelled hangover. She looked fixedly at Adam when he at last came in through the back door.

He acknowledged her appearance with a nod of approval. 'I didn't expect you to be up yet.'

Not hiding her repugnance, she said, 'And why not?'

'Because you were legless last night.'

Ignoring his sarky remark, she parried, 'Where've you been?'

Sagging against the worktop, he asked reasonably, 'Where do you think I'd be at this early hour on a Sunday morning?'

Her mind wasn't functioning properly but she realised that he must be in the right or he wouldn't sound so confident. Where could he have been? She eyed him with contempt and blurted out the thought foremost in her mind. 'With *her*, I suppose.'

'Oh, for heaven's sake, catch yourself on, Maura. I was at eight o'clock Mass. I knew you wouldn't be in any fit state to go, so I went on my own.'

He took the frying pan out of the cupboard and thumped it on the stove. 'Do you want a fry?'

She managed to hide her relief; how could she have forgotten that it was Sunday morning? But that didn't explain the bed not being slept in. 'Are you joking? I don't know how you can even think of eating. The very thought of food turns my guts, makes me want to throw up.'

Placing his hands on the table, he leaned across and looked at her intently. 'Because I wasn't sloshed last night. That's why a fry-up appeals to me. But you . . . you made a right spectacle of yourself.'

'Did I? Did I really?' she wailed, horrified at the thought.

Seeing how upset she was, he relented some. 'Well, you weren't completely out of it, but I have never known you to down so many Pernods. You may not have been plastered but you were well oiled. I kept expecting you to fall flat on your face.'

Her head in her hands, she groaned, 'I'll never drink that stuff again.' He reached across to touch her but she cringed away. 'Your bed hasn't been slept in,' she accused.

'I'm surprised you noticed.'

'So you thought you could get back before I awoke? Was that your plan?'

'I didn't have a plan. As I've already said, I went to eight o'clock Mass. I've plenty of witnesses. If you don't believe me, ask your friend Agnes McCormick. I walked back with her and she was wondering where you were.'

'And where were you before that? Where did you spend the night?' she ground out through

144

clenched teeth. If he had spent the night with Evelyn Matthews, that would be the final straw. Their marriage was out the window, over and done with, kaput.

'I slept on the settee, as you'll see if you care to check. The blanket and pillow should still be there.'

'Oh . . .'

He returned to the stove. 'Now, do you want that fry or not?'

Pushing herself away from the table, she headed for the door. 'No, thank you,' she snapped and, remembering to favour her splitting headache, gently closed the door behind her.

Adam gazed bleakly at it for some moments. What was to become of them? Discovering he had lost his appetite, he put the pan away, reached for his jacket and quietly left the house. It was too early to collect his son from Beth's, but he needed space to think. He'd go for a walk along the seafront. The cool breeze coming off the water and the sharp tang of brine on his lips always had a soothing effect on him.

The sun was now high in the sky. Taking off his jacket, he slung it over his shoulder and lifted his face to the warm rays. He flailed about in his mind for a solution to his problem. Would he be able to convince Maura that he hadn't crossed the line of decency where Evelyn was concerned, except for a few kisses? Unlikely! Once they started thrashing it out, he knew that, innocent or not, he'd never be able to convince his wife that he had never slept with Evelyn.

He sat on a rock, elbows on his knees, chin resting in his hands, and gazed out over the calm waters. This was a beautiful spot to live. Maura loved Holywood, but lately she had been restless, longing for the company of her old friends. It all seemed so hopeless. Charles Matthews was a kind and considerate man. Adam could see him giving Evelyn plenty of scope if she were discreet. And who could she be more discreet with than her gardener? Shades of *Lady Chatterley's Lover*, the book he had borrowed from Steve. It had whetted his curiosity because of all the publicity, good and bad, it had received in the media as well as having been banned by the Church. Him being Mellors, he mused wryly. Not that he would ever chance it, not in a million years. His marriage was already teetering on the brink and he hadn't even done anything to warrant it.

From the secluded spot at her upstairs window, Maura stood with conflicting emotions, watching Adam move out of sight. She realised that if there was to be any hope of them salvaging their marriage, they would have to sit down and have a good, honest, heart-to-heart talk, thrash things out like two sensible adults. But was she ready for this? What if Adam wanted to continue working on the Antrim Road job? Would she be able to live with the knowledge that he was seeing Evelyn Matthews every day?

When she talked to that nurse Linda Somebody-or-Other in the ladies' room last night, she had said that Mrs Matthews was indeed very lovely. Maura shook her head in desperation. No, she couldn't bear the thought of Adam working every day in close proximity with Evelyn Matthews. She just couldn't live with it. He'd have to send someone else over to finish the work or she would have to move out of her lovely home. There were no two ways about it. But first she would have to be sure she had somewhere to go, if the worst came to the worst.

7

Monday morning! After a night that she had again elected to spend, miserable and lonely, in the nursery, Maura lay listening to the sounds coming from the kitchen below as Adam prepared breakfast for himself. Was she daft? If she had condescended to share their bed last night, in its intimacy Adam might have convinced her that she had nothing to fear, that everything would be all right. She very much doubted it, not while Evelyn Matthews was still in the frame.

She had sobbed her heart out late into the night and her throat was parched and sore. She willed him to bring a cup of tea up to her but was not surprised when he left the house without so much as a shout of farewell. After all, hadn't she ignored him earlier when Adam had looked in on them before going downstairs? She had feigned sleep and with crossed fingers had willed Danny not to wake up. The child obliged and for some seconds Adam watched her intently, then gently closed the door as if believing she was still asleep . . . as if he were that green.

Sunday afternoon had passed quietly with hardly a word spoken between them. Even Danny was quieter than usual, opting to play outside in his tent with his imaginary friends. Indoors, at meal-times, when he was chattering away, they had made an effort to join in his childish banter but the child wasn't fooled; even his young mind must have sensed that all was not well. Wolfing down his food, he had returned to his playthings, taking pleasure in his imaginary world where everybody was happy, smiling and friendly. Maura wished she had an imaginary place to escape to of her own.

At eight o'clock Adam had bathed the boy, put him to bed and read him a story. That had taken longer than usual; Adam was obviously avoiding a tête-à-tête with his wife. Maura, on the other hand, was content to let him have this time with his son. It would probably be the last time he would do so, for some time at least, unless he came downstairs in a different frame of mind. She had given her husband every opportunity during the day, dropping subtle hints in their conversation that he could have taken advantage of, had he

149

wanted to, but he had made no attempt to try to explain things to her, to try to sort out the problem that was tearing them apart, and she couldn't stand it any more. Her nerves were raw and stretched to breaking point and she wanted to lash out at him, but Danny's presence helped her control her temper.

Not being the bravest of women, Maura didn't want to force a confrontation with Adam. It would look as if she was grovelling, and she'd had enough of his evasive ways, of falling in with his every wish without complaint. Last night she had come to a decision and today she was going to carry it out. She intended going to Greencastle to ask her father whether she and Danny could come over and live in his house. This was something she dreaded doing. Never in her wildest dreams had she imagined it would ever come to this. Her father had such a sharp tongue, and in her fragile state she couldn't bear to be on the receiving end of its sometimes cruel accusations. But she had no choice in the matter. She couldn't stay in this house another day longer.

Later Maura examined herself in the mirror. Not wanting to appear the downtrodden housewife, she had spent a lot of unnecessary time getting ready. She was glad now that she had gone over the top and got her hair styled, regardless of the cost. It clung to her head like a silk cap and was so easy to manage that she couldn't imagine why she had been so reluctant to part with her long tresses. Of course, hindsight is always a wonderful thing and it would be too costly to keep it styled like this, but she would certainly give it a go.

She wore black trousers with a red, waist-length jacket, over a plain white cotton top. Carefully applied make-up made her more sophisticated-looking than usual. Not that her father would be impressed, or even notice for that matter. He didn't like any kind of cosmetics, calling them the devil's tools, used to lure men into sin. But she needed to feel good in herself and to do so had paid more attention than was required to her overall appearance. Now as she stood before the mirror she smiled at her reflection. Yes, she was very satisfied with the result of her cosmetic labour.

Why did this have to happen to her? She dreaded what lay ahead of her. Should she feign ignorance for a while and hope things would sort themselves out? She liked the idea. The temptation was so great that she thought she had found the solution to her immediate situation, but just as quickly as the idea had formed she pushed it fiercely from her mind. No! She'd end up in Purdysburn if she started thinking like that. Well, that would solve everybody's problems. With her in a mental home there would be no holding Adam back. He'd have a free rein to make his play for Evelyn.

Danny was calling out to her. Pushing self-pity aside, she went to join her son. Gathering him close, she hugged him fiercely. 'What do you think, love? We're going to visit your grandad. Won't that be lovely?'

The child's forehead wrinkled with bewilderment, as well it might. With a pang of regret, Maura realised that he probably didn't remember her dad; it had been many a long month since they had last visited Davey Craig, which went to prove that she was the wrongdoer. If she had paid no attention to her father's attitude and insisted he get to know his grandson, in spite of how he felt about her marriage to Adam, all this would never have happened. She would have known about Evelyn Matthews' return from day one and would have put her foot down right away before the bitch got her claws into her husband. Would it have made any difference? Recalling how desolate and bereft Adam had been when Evelyn Matthews had dumped him, how he still sometimes cried out her name in his sleep, she didn't think so.

Maura sat passively on the journey into Belfast city centre, automatically talking to Danny about the posters that flashed past pasted on gable walls and billboards, her mind elsewhere. When she boarded the number ten bus on Royal Avenue on the second half of her journey to Greencastle, she grew fretful. Her father had appeared to have mellowed somewhat towards her on Saturday night, but was his concern genuine, or was it the drink doing the talking?

She got off the bus at the bottom of the Whitewell Road. Danny had dozed off and she had great difficulty struggling with him whilst trying to open out the Tansad. Jimmy the butcher noticed her plight through the shop window and hurried out to assist her.

'Thanks, Jimmy. How are you?'

'I'm very well. Business is booming, thank God.'

'I'm glad to hear that.'

Jimmy was aware of the gossip and with a sympathetic pat on the shoulder said, 'Better get back to my work. See you around, Maura.'

At last Danny was strapped in his pushchair and talking softly to him she reminded him who they were going to visit, then crossed the Shore Road and headed towards her father's house. She approached it with some apprehension, her nerves a tight ball in her stomach. Catch yourself on, girl, she chastised herself. This is your da you're going to see, not some monster. He won't bite you. She laughed softly to herself as she muttered, well, I hope not.

At the door she drew in a deep breath and her eyes widened with surprise as she scanned the front of the house. Her da was certainly looking after the place. The paintwork was freshly applied, she could still detect the faint pungent smell of it, and bright white nets hung at the windows. He must have changed his ways. Those curtains were a different pattern from the ones that hung there previously and looked more expensive. Davey Craig was not the kind of man to spend money on silly things like decorating when there was no reward to be gained from it. Oh no, he believed in keeping the place clean and tidy but found it against his religion to squander money where decorating was concerned, expecting things to last for ever. What had changed him, she wondered?

All the same, this was all good news to her. Was he expecting her to come back to the fold and was this work done to encourage her to stay if she did come back? Perhaps he might even have an indoor toilet fitted now. That would be such a relief. She dreaded Danny having to use an outside lavatory, especially during the cold, dark nights. The child would find living here such a big upheaval as it was, without having that to contend with. Still, it hadn't done her any harm in her younger days. Her mind scuttled ahead. Maybe her da had had a bathroom built on out the back. Now she was being ridiculous. Davey Craig spending all that money? Not that he couldn't afford it. He'd had a nasty accident at work in the mill some years ago and hurt his back. The company had settled out of court, awarding him a tidy sum and a three-day-a-week job doing light work. He wasn't short of a bob or two.

Her hand was poised, ready to grasp the knocker, when, before she could knock, the door opened. A pair of large brown eyes looked at her inquiringly and a pleasant voice said, 'Hello, can I help you?'

Maura gave the woman a confused smile. Surely her da hadn't moved house without letting her know? 'I've come to see Mr Craig?' she said cautiously. 'He does still live here, doesn't he?'

A slight nod indicated agreement, leaving Maura more confused than ever. The smile slid from her face and she said in a nervous voice, 'I'm his daughter. Can I come in, please?' and made to step into the hallway.

A frown knotted the stranger's brows and the big brown eyes weren't so friendly now, as she stood resolutely blocking Maura's entrance. 'He's not here at the moment. You'll have to come back later.'

Words failed Maura. 'I beg your pardon?' she managed to splutter.

'I said he's not here at the minute, therefore I can't let you in. How do I know you're his daughter? I'm afraid you'll have to come back later.' The door was closed in Maura's face with a decisive click.

Maura stared at it dumbfounded, her mouth hanging open. Who on earth was this woman and just who the hell did she think she was, closing her father's door in Maura's face? There was a familiar look about her, but Maura couldn't remember ever having met her. Snapping her mouth shut, she stood undecided. What to do? What was her next move? Bang on the door and demand entry?

On the other side of the door, the woman stood clamping her clenched fist against her lips, ears cocked, listening, until she heard the sound of the pushchair being wheeled away before returning to the kitchen. Now she'd done it! What had brought the girl here, just when she and Davey were getting on so well? One thing was for sure. If he found out he would never forgive her for turning his own child away from his front door. She sighed. She'd cross that bridge when she came to it, convince him that she hadn't believed the girl was his daughter. After all, he never spoke of her, so why should she believe that the caller was who she said she was? She could have been anybody. Meanwhile she fervently wished the girl would go back to wherever she belonged. Leave them in peace and let her get on with cementing her relationship with Davey.

Pushing the Tansad slowly away from her father's house towards the zebra crossing, Maura crossed over and headed back towards Whitewell Road. She had decided to pay her Aunt Hilda a visit, find out who this mystery woman was and how the land lay. If anyone knew, it would be Aunt Hilda. Wrapped up in her thoughts, she accidentally bumped the Tansad into a man coming out of the bookie's, studying a betting slip whilst crossing her path.

With a smothered curse he glared at her. Then, recognising her, he quickly apologised and acknowledged her with a wry smile. 'Maura Craig! Long time no see. I must say, you're looking well. How are you?'

Maura smiled back at Jimmy Nolan. 'I'm not too bad, Jimmy. How's about yourself, have you and Bridie tied the knot yet?'

'Ach, sure you know me, Maura, couldn't be better, and no, we haven't got married yet. But one day we'll take the plunge . . .'

He hesitated. 'Hmm, are you looking for your da, by any chance?'

'Well, as a matter of fact, I am.' She nodded towards the bookie's shop. 'Is he in there?'

'He certainly is, I was talking to him just now. Hold on and I'll nip back in and tell him you're here.'

Thanking him, Maura walked along to the newsagent's and read the For Sale notices in the shop window while she waited.

A few minutes later Jimmy came out, followed by Davey Craig. With a farewell wave of his hand Jimmy moved on down the road.

'Is anything wrong?' A worried frown bunched Davey's heavy brows as he hastened to his daughter's side and Maura quickly reassured him.

'No, no! Remember I told you I'd bring Danny over to visit you? Well here we are.' She shrugged her shoulders and gave him a broad smile.

He looked baffled and she didn't blame him. The way things were between them lately he'd every right to be suspicious.

'So why didn't you use your key to get into the house and wait for me there?'

'Well, I thought I'd be polite and knock first but some strange woman answered the door and told me to come back later.'

His face stretched with amazement and then comprehension set in. 'Oh . . . I see.'

He had forgotten all about Cassie being in the house. Would she have had the good sense to leave once the coast was clear? He doubted it. She didn't agree with these clandestine meetings, wanted everything to be open and above board. To walk out with him openly for all to see.

Realising that his grandson was watching him wide-eyed, he hunkered down beside the pushchair and gave him all his attention. 'Hello, Danny. Don't you recognise your auld grandad?'

Danny smiled and glanced fleetingly at Maura for guidance. She prompted him. 'Say hello to your grandad, Danny.'

'Hello, Grandad,' he said in a little sing-song voice.

'Let's get back to the house, Maura, and I'll make us a nice wee cup of tea. OK?'

She nodded and together they crossed the road. At the door Davey hesitated, then taking a key from his pocket opened the door and ushered Maura and the pushchair through the hall and into the kitchen. The mystery woman emerged slowly from the scullery and silently stood, eyes fixed on him. Smiling wryly, Davey made the introductions.

'Maura, this is Cassie Hamilton . . . Cassie, this is my daughter, Maura.'

Cassie held out her hand and Maura clasped it limply before dropping it. Cassie knew when she was being slighted and, grimacing, she apologised. 'I'm sorry I turned you away earlier on. But you can't be too careful nowadays. You know how it is?'

I bet you're sorry, Maura thought, and tongue in cheek agreed. 'You're right, you can't be careful enough.' As if anyone would try to get into a house under false pretences in this quiet village, where everybody knew everyone else and their business.

'Cassie comes in some days to do for me, Maura. I don't know what I'd do without her. She's a gem.'

'That's very kind of her, I'm sure.'

'Oh, it's not all kindness.' Cassie was quick to intervene. 'It's my job. I get well paid for it.' Her voice was tight with anger. She was fuming that Davey was making her out to be his skivvy. The hired help.

Pretending not to hear, Maura removed her jacket and hung it on the rack near the door. Danny was tugging at her trouser leg and plaintively struggling to get out of his restraining harness. Whispering words of reassurance she released him and he immediately made a beeline for the door to the cubbyhole under the stairs. He re-emerged smiling from ear to ear and hugging a fire engine.

Maura praised him. 'Clever boy! You do remember being here, don't you, love?'

'Yes, Mammy.' He disappeared again and returning with a toy tractor settled down in front of the fireplace to play with the toys.

Maura watched Cassie Hamilton beat a hasty retreat back to the scullery and sank down into her father's comfortable old armchair. There was something about Cassie that kept niggling at Maura. She had a strange feeling that she had met her somewhere before, but for the life of her she couldn't place where or when. Her father with an apologetic smile followed Cassie into the scullery.

Maura turned her attention to the interior of

the house. Not many changes here in the kitchen, but it was spotless. The lino shone and the square rug in front of the Devon grate was well brushed. Definitely not her father's work. Who was this mysterious woman? Did she just come in to clean for Davey, or was there more to it than met the eye?

Maura sat up straight as this thought struck her like a bolt from the blue. Surely her da wasn't cohabiting with Cassie? No, Maura was sure that Mary Moon would have enlightened her about a scandal of such enormity. But then again, would Mary know? Perhaps it was all kept very hush-hush and being the 'hired help' was a front for her real reason for being in this house. Maura had been so completely out of touch with things in Greencastle this past year or so that she hadn't a clue what was going on any more. She rejected these thoughts. Not her da. No way! Out of touch or not, Maura was sure she would have heard something on the grapevine.

The couple returned to the kitchen and, with an abrupt nod in Maura's direction, Cassie lifted her coat from the rack and quietly left the house. To get time to gather his wits together, Davey swept his grandson up in two large hands and held him aloft.

'So you found your toys, eh? My, but you're a clever boy.'

He pretended to drop the child and Danny's eyes nearly popped out of his head with fear, but when he was thrown up and caught again he giggled with delight and yelled for more.

Davey obliged, then lowered the giggling boy down into his arms and looked at Maura, undecided. An uneasy silence fell on the room. Lowering his grandson gently to the floor, he at last said, 'I'll make us that cup of tea. Would you have some juice, Danny?'

With a beaming smile, Danny said, 'Yes, Grandad.'

Rising to her feet, Maura offered, 'I'll make it, Da.'

'No, you sit there. I won't be too long.'

Danny followed his grandad into the scullery and Maura heard the child's giggles as her dad entertained him. She sat in a dither. This was so unexpected and she now wasn't sure how to proceed. Who was this woman and would she throw a spanner in Maura's carefully laid plan? Her dad had obviously been embarrassed when he had introduced them. She decided to let him set the theme of the conversation and see where it led to. When he returned with a laden tray, she silently pulled forward a small table to set it on.

Davy asked, 'Will you do mother?'

'Why not, I've done it for years on end,' Maura reminded him. 'Or have you forgotten?'

She poured two cups of tea and, handing one

to her father, offered him the plate of biscuits. He selected a digestive. Danny took a shortbread. Leaning back in her chair, Maura clasped the cup in her hands and eyed her father over the rim.

'Aren't you having something to eat?' he asked tentatively. 'I could make you a ham sandwich if you'd prefer it to them biscuits.'

'It's OK, Da, I'm not hungry.' She was sick with nerves and eating was the last thing on her mind at the minute, but she managed to put on a calm front. If her father was serious about this woman, what was Maura to do and, most of all, where would she go? Who else would take her in?

Davey smiled down at the boy sitting at his feet and patted his head. 'It's good of you to bring the lad over, love.'

'I said I would, remember?'

'I know . . . Still, I wish you'd let me know in advance, I'd have been more prepared. I might even have baked a cake.'

She smiled wryly at his corny joke and broke her vow to let him set the theme of the conversation. 'You mean that woman wouldn't have been in the house on her own had I warned you I was coming? I must say I was surprised when she opened the door and that's putting it mildly. I thought you'd moved out without letting me know. She looks very familiar, though, but I don't recognise her. Is she from around these parts?'

Davey's cheeks tinted a little. 'Just someone who does for me now and again. You know, does a wee bit of cleaning and dusting round the house.'

Does she indeed, Maura thought cynically. 'What a relief. For a moment there I thought she might be living here with you.'

He thrust out his chin. 'Oh, no, nothing like that, I can promise you,' he replied rather too quickly.

'Like what?' she kept at him.

'Like what you're insinuating.' Davey's voice was a growl in his throat now.

Maura urged herself to back off. She didn't want to upset her father. Hadn't she come here to ask a favour of him, not start a war? 'So how did you meet her then?' she persisted.

Davey drew a deep breath. 'Look . . . she's new to the village. I met her in McVeigh's one night with her daughter, who, by the way, is now the district nurse, and her son-in-law. They got one of those houses over on Graymount estate some time ago and when Cassie's husband passed away she came to live with them. Here endeth the lesson.' He smiled coyly.

Maura gave a sudden outburst of laughter and her father looked askance at her. 'That's why she looked so familiar,' she explained. 'I've met her daughter, Linda, that's her name, isn't it?' At his surprised nod she continued, 'On Saturday night at Mary Moon's party . . . remember? They are very alike.'

He nodded in acknowledgement. 'Ah, yes, I remember now. Linda and her husband were indeed in Conway's on Saturday night. And you're right, she does resemble her mother.' Davey leaned towards his daughter. 'Now tell me, what *really* brought you here, Maura?'

Maura hesitated, not knowing how to put it, then took the plunge. 'I came over to ask you if I could come back here and stay for a while. Me and Danny.'

'So, you and Adam have split up. Is that what you're telling me?'

'No. He doesn't know I'm here. It was just a thought. I've been distracted, you know, with all this talk about Evelyn Matthews. I need some space to figure things out.'

'Well, I'm glad you've come to your senses at last, girl. Of course you can come back here, stay as long as you like.'

Maura sighed deeply. 'I'm not so sure now, Da. Perhaps I should stick it out and see what happens. Who knows, maybe Adam will come to his senses.'

Davey made tut-tutting sounds with his tongue. 'And you'd forgive that mealy-mouthed twat? Catch yourself on. Don't let him walk all over you, Maura. You always were putty in that git's hands. Come back home. I admit that I let you down

165

badly when I should have been there for you, but I was mortified back then. I couldn't stand the shame of what you did. Now I know better. I should have swallowed my pride, been more supportive about you getting pregnant . . . even if it was out of wedlock.'

'Da, I know you don't like him, but even if you hadn't put me out of the house I would still have married Adam. He was a tower of strength when I told him that I was expecting his baby. There were no recriminations whatsoever.'

'But that's my whole point. If he loved you he shouldn't have made you pregnant in the first place. He should have done the decent thing and put a ring on your finger first.'

'Da, it takes two, you know. People get carried away in the heat of the moment. I won't let you lay all the blame on Adam.'

'OK. Now tell me this, do you trust him working up there with *her*?'

Maura secretly crossed her fingers. 'Yes, Da, I do. After all, it's his job. He can't just stop working because Evelyn Matthews owns the property.'

'He shouldn't have gone there to begin with. I'm sure he's not the only gardener in that nursery place. Can't they get someone else to finish the job?'

Not for the world could Maura ever admit that Adam had refused to do just that. 'No. It's an important contract that could lead to more work on this side of the lough, so Benny Gallagher sent his best man. And that best man is Adam.'

'Well then, I'll borrow Francie's van and come fetch you and your belongings back here. OK?'

Maura contemplated for some minutes. Should she leave the house, just like that, without warning Adam first?

Davey watched her expression change with mixed emotions as she fought with her thoughts, and wasn't surprised when she at last shook her head.

'No, Da. So long as I'm sure that I'm welcome back here, I can go home in an easier frame of mind. I'll have it out with Adam. See what way he takes it. Is that all right with you?'

'I suppose it'll have to be. Are you sure I can't change your mind?'

'No. It will be better this way, Da.'

'All right. If you can get word to me I'll come as soon as possible. Now, tell me about life across the water.'

'You should have come and seen for yourself, Da. I was so disappointed when you didn't come to Danny's christening.'

Davey sighed. 'I know. I was a foolish, stubborn old man. I let my pride rule my heart. I can only say I'm very sorry. Can you ever forgive me, pet?'

'I can, but Adam . . . Well, that's another matter.'

'I don't give a . . .' He paused and, with a wary look in Danny's direction, changed his words. 'I couldn't give a tinker's cuss about Adam Brady. My only concern is for you and Danny.'

'Dad . . .'

'Look, Maura, let's leave Adam out of it for the minute, OK? Tell me about your friends and what it's like over there.'

The next couple of hours passed quickly and Davey asked her to stay for tea. Thinking of going home to an empty house, Maura wasn't too hard to coax but agreed only if he allowed her to prepare the meal whilst he kept his grandson occupied. She was pleasantly surprised to find the fridge well stocked, but remembering Cassie she realised that this would probably be her doing, the woman's touch. It looked as if she had her feet well and truly planted under the table, no matter what her father implied.

Davey had arranged to meet a couple of mates in the pub for a darts match, so shortly before seven o'clock she cleared up and they left the house together. Maura insisted that her father mustn't be late and watched him enter the pub before heading along to the bus stop outside Grogan's shop, still unsure what she intended doing.

She had shooed her dad on into the pub, saying that she could manage on her own. Now she regretted this decision. The Shore Road was very busy at this time of day. At the bus stop she struggled to keep a strong hold on Danny and close the Tansad at the same time. An elbow gently nudged her to one side. Francie Murphy folded the pushchair and stood looking intently at her.

'Have you and Davey made it up then?'

'No, but we're getting there and I did promise I'd bring Danny to see him, and I did. We've just spent a most enjoyable afternoon together. And there's going to be some changes made. From now on I intend for my son to get to know his grandfather better, not see him once in a blue moon.'

Setting the pushchair at his feet, Francie moved closer and holding her by the upper arms gave her a little shake. 'Good on you, girl. Now listen, don't you take any lip from anybody. If you need me, I'll be here for you. Understand?'

Unwittingly, she swayed towards him and she looked so forlorn that he leaned down and gently touched his lips to hers. She clung on until the trolley-bus drew into the kerb and stopped. In a bemused state she pulled away from Francie. Silently he helped her and the child aboard and watched as the bus moved off.

He was crossing over to go up Whitewell Road when a man driving a van that had stopped to give way to the Shore Road traffic caught his eye. The malevolence in his stare brought Francie to an abrupt halt on the edge of the kerb. Adam

Brady lifted his hand in a scornful wave in his direction and, with teeth bared in a sneer, accelerated off in the direction of Belfast.

For some moments Francie stood rooted to the spot. Had Adam Brady seen him kiss Maura? He probably hadn't. Still, for her sake he hoped not. Adam's look had been one of pure venom, his face screwed up in a twisted mask of undiluted hatred. He'd be thinking all sorts of the wrong kind. Francie thought that he had probably dropped Maura in it. Why couldn't he have kept his hands to himself? Maura Brady was not for him even if he did still love her.

She was a married woman, for heaven's sake.

8

In a seething temper Adam gripped the steering wheel so hard that his knuckles shone white as he followed the trolley-bus along the Shore Road. Eventually he was able to overtake it when it stopped to pick up passengers at Donegall Park Avenue. His fury knew no bounds. How dare Francie Murphy kiss his wife like that. How dare he! And out in the open for all to see. Something for the Greencastle gossips to chew over.

This thought startled him and made him examine his conscience. Would it have been all right if it had been done in secret where no one could witness them? Where he was unlikely to hear about it, and thus not be upset like this? Just so long as no one saw them in the act: was that all that mattered? The fact that Francie Murphy was kissing her openly surely meant it was just a farewell peck, a kiss between old friends. Neither of them was stupid enough to behave like that in public. They wouldn't want to call unnecessary attention to themselves.

That's how it must have been, he mused. As far as he could see she wasn't showing any signs of objecting and Maura wasn't one to fuel idle gossip. She would have soon put Murphy in his place if he was chancing his arm with her. So it must have been just a farewell kiss after all, nothing to worry about.

On the other hand, was he deluding himself? Did Maura not care for him any more? She certainly appeared to be lapping it up. No doubt about it, she was enjoying it. Limp and passive, she'd looked like a puppet in Francie Murphy's hands and him pulling all the strings.

Adam suddenly remembered that he was not alone. Had young Jackie seen the spectacle Maura was making of herself? A sideways glance at the lad's face convinced Adam that he hadn't noticed anything untoward and he breathed a sigh of relief. The lad must have been looking the other way . . . or was in his usual daydream.

What was his wife doing here anyway? She certainly hadn't mentioned that she would be visiting Greencastle today. But then they weren't on speaking terms lately. And hadn't he slipped out after breakfast to avoid talking to her? He had been glad that she had pretended to be asleep and happy to postpone yet another interrogation. On previous occasions, to leave the house without clearing the air would have been unthinkable. They always made up their differences before parting.

He silently mocked himself. To think that today of all days, he had been making every effort, in vain, as it turned out, to leave the Antrim Road job early. But, as if she had guessed his intention, Evelyn had kept putting obstacles in his way. Perhaps she had read his mind and was deploying silly delaying tactics. He had sincerely hoped that he would be able to convince his wife that he must see this job through to the finish, and then he would never see Evelyn again. But would he? Could he bear not ever seeing her again? He would certainly give it his best shot. Meanwhile he must convince Maura that it was *her* he loved and she had nothing to worry about. It had come like a kick in the teeth seeing his wife carrying on like that with her old flame. But then, was he letting jealousy override his common sense? He sighed; he had a nerve to point the finger when his wife must be out of her mind with worry over Evelyn and him.

What to do? Should he turn a blind eye or speak out? He would be giving Maura more scope for recriminations and fault-finding if he questioned her about kissing Francie Murphy. He already knew how much at fault he was and he couldn't bear to listen to her whine on and on. White-knuckled, he suddenly twisted the steering wheel and swerved round a parked car at Fortwilliam Park, bringing a startled glance and loud protests from his companion.

'Hey, Boss. Take it easy, for heaven's sake. Are you in a rush to get into the cemetery?'

Lost in his vile thoughts, Adam had again completely forgotten that he wasn't alone in the van. 'Sorry, son. I'm in a hurry home tonight and I got a bit carried away.'

'Thank God for that. I thought for a minute there you had a death wish and were going to take me with you.'

Adam flashed a wry smile at him and easing his foot off the accelerator continued at a modest speed until he reached the nursery, where he dropped Jackie Flynn off. Handing over the day's worksheet for him to pass on to Benny, with a screech of wheels he drove off in a cloud of dust as if the devil himself was after him, leaving Jackie staring open-mouthed after him. What on earth had gotten into Adam? He was usually such a careful driver.

Maura was surprised to find Adam home before her. He had the table set and stood at the stove stirring something in a saucepan, with the kettle on the boil. She met his eyes, a suspicious frown on her brow, and nodded towards the stove.

'What brought this on?'

'I managed to get away a bit early and thought I'd surprise you. But wouldn't you know, it back-fired. You're home late. Still, I did get the tea started.' He paused, giving her time for an explanation as to why she was late. But it wasn't forth-coming; she was still staring at him blankly. 'Where's Danny?'

'Asleep in the hall. He has already eaten and he's in his night's sleep. I'll put him up in a minute when I get his cot ready.'

Adam's voice followed her up the stairs 'Would you like some scrambled eggs and toast?'

'No, thank you. Just look after yourself, I've already eaten.' Her voice was curt; she sensed that there was something behind all this but couldn't fathom what. By the look on Adam's face it didn't look too good.

A few minutes later she was back down, and going into the hall she released the sleeping child from his harness and carried him through to the kitchen. Eggs ready, Adam had removed the saucepan from the stove and was watching her every move with intense interest.

Still uneasy, she tried to find out what was playing on his mind. 'Is anything wrong?' Her eyes

175

ranged over him and she gasped. 'Has there been an accident? Has anyone been hurt?'

'No. Nothing like that. Everything's fine. What about you?'

'Me?'

'Yes, you. What have you been doing with yourself today?'

Still she gaped at him uncomprehending. 'I've been visiting my dad. Now give my head peace while I put Danny to bed. He's no lightweight, you know.'

'Here . . . I'm sorry, let me carry him up.'

She was already on the stairs and threw over her shoulder sarcastically, 'Never mind. I'm almost there.'

Adam put the scrambled eggs on the toast and carried the plate to the table. He must be on the wrong track. Maura hadn't looked in the least guilty. It must have just been a friendly peck after all. It was as well he hadn't started throwing accusations at her.

As she put Danny's pyjamas on and settled him down for the night, Maura cast her mind back over the events of the day. Was her da having an affair? It was hard to take in. As far as she was aware he had never so much as looked at another woman since her mother died. But he was still a comparatively young man and at times he must be lonely living on his own. Why wouldn't he court a woman given half a chance? There was nothing to stop him and it certainly wouldn't be a crime if he did. But if he was, she couldn't see herself living back in his house, not if that woman was to be a constant visitor. Hopefully, she hadn't already gotten her feet too far under the table.

And then there was Francie Murphy . . . He had certainly surprised her, kissing her like that! And she had to admit that she had enjoyed it, perhaps a bit too much for her own good. She had better be careful or Francie would be getting the wrong idea and that would never do. To be honest, she would be better off staying put here in Holywood, keeping out of temptation's way until Adam made his future plans clear. She would give him every opportunity to convince her that she had nothing to worry about over Evelyn Matthews and that she and Danny were his only concern. With this in mind, she quietly descended the stairs and sat across the table from him.

Elbows on the table, she rested her chin on her entwined fingers and contemplated her husband. 'How did your day go?'

'Interesting! Mr Matthews now wants a waterfall built and the way the back garden slopes down from the Antrim Road gives us plenty of scope for something spectacular. Jackie and I dug out the foundations today.'

'Will this job last much longer, do you think?'

He grimaced. 'It's hard to say, Maura. Charles Matthews has money to burn and he's always coming up with new ideas. I suppose it gives him something to think about. Takes his mind off his physical disability. And to tell you the truth I'm enjoying the work. Charles is a grand old gent, knows how things should be done and knows I'm capable of carrying out his wishes to the full. It will all be worth while when the job's finished. In fact it should look magnificent.'

Maura heard him out in silence. 'That doesn't sound very promising as far as our marriage is concerned.'

'Look, I give you my word, Evelyn and I aren't at it.' His arms spread wide with frustration. 'What more can I do or say to convince you, Maura? I swear I'm not messing around with her. Her husband never leaves the house, for heaven's sake. And most of the time he's resting out on the balcony overlooking the garden where I'm working. And people are in and out of the house most days. And another thing, young Jackie Flynn is by my side most of the time, like my guardian angel. You're the only girl for me and I'm not interested in any others.'

Maura sat taking this all in. If only she could believe him. But where there was a will there was a way. She couldn't believe that the perfume that sometimes clung to him was there by accident. She decided to be truthful and see how he reacted. 'That's all very well. As a matter of fact, I went over to Greencastle today to see if my da would allow me to stay with him until we get things sorted out here.'

He was about to shove a forkful of egg into his mouth but at her words he carefully set it down and scowled at her, lips tight with anger. 'You did what?'

She nodded slowly. 'You heard! And why not? Surely you understand that we can't go on as we are, not with that hussy always there between us.'

'I don't believe you.' He was on his feet now, both hands spread on the table and leaning forward into her face. 'You went over to Greencastle and discussed our private affairs with your father without a word to me? Why? Tell me why! Are you fed up living here with me? Don't you love me any more?'

'Of course I'm not fed up living here and of course I love you. How can you think otherwise? I'm not the one who's causing all this disruption. It's *you* and that bitch Matthews who's the cause.'

'Oh, but you are. You don't trust me. Other men work with their ex-girlfriends and their wives don't badger them. But at the first hitch in our marriage you're so insecure that you're threatening to run home to your father.'

'A hitch?' She tossed her head in scorn. 'More like a bloody bomb ready to go off, if you ask me.'

'Don't talk rubbish.'

'You listen to me, Adam Brady. I know how much you loved Evelyn Matthews before we got together. If I hadn't got pregnant would you have married me? Eh?' His face blanched and she hissed, 'I thought not. If you and her get back together again, what will become of me and Danny?'

'Trust me, Maura . . . it won't happen.'

'Please, Adam, I can't live with this uncertainty any more. Get someone else to finish the job. Surely that's not asking too much, is it?'

'I can't, Maura. You don't understand the predicament I'm in. Benny is depending on me to try to get some more orders over there. You know how big those gardens are along the Antrim Road and surrounding district, and a lot of them could do with a good facelift. I've seen them. We've put up boards advertising the nursery and Benny says I'm the most experienced person to deal with any enquiries on site. And he's right, I am. And people *are* showing interest and stopping to make enquiries.'

Maura pondered on these words but was far from being reassured. 'You mean if you get more orders over there, you could be working in Belfast most of the time?'

'No, no. Once the orders are established, Steve and the others will be able to do the work.'

Her brows bunched as she pondered over this. 'Why then wasn't Steve sent over in the first place to do the Matthews job? After all, you're the site manager. You don't normally do the donkey work.'

'Because they especially asked for me.' The moment the words were out, he knew he had put his foot in it.

'I don't believe it!' she exclaimed.

'Now, now, Maura. Don't let your imagination run away with you. This is the way it happened. Benny asked me to go over and make up an estimate for landscaping a garden.' He realised the cat was out of the bag and he might as well be truthful. 'You can imagine the shock I got. I nearly dropped dead on the spot when Evelyn opened the door. Believe me, I had no idea she lived there. And that's God's honest truth.'

Maura leaned back in her chair. 'Ah . . . I remember that time you were sent over to the Antrim Road. So she's been back as long as that, eh? And if I remember correctly, it was shortly afterwards that you started acting strange and that was the first inkling I got that you were involved with another woman. You came home most days smelling of expensive perfume. I suppose that was when you decided to do the work yourself.'

Adam sank back down and stared hard at the

181

egg on his plate as if expecting to see the answer stamped there. 'No! I did not. I did the estimate and when my tender was accepted I sent Steve over to start the job. Then Evelyn came to the nursery a few days later and said that Charles – that's her husband – wanted me personally to do the work. Benny was already so pleased to get the contract, knowing it could lead to more work across the lough, that he asked me if I fancied keeping my hand in.' He shrugged. 'What could I do? He pays the wages.'

Her voice was clipped with anger. 'Man, but Evelyn's playing you like a violin. You should have explained the situation to Benny there and then.'

'How could I? I didn't think you'd want everybody to know our private affairs.'

'Are you forgetting that half of Greencastle already knows about Evelyn Matthews dumping you, and me picking up the pieces, eh? We'll be the talk of Greencastle all over again. And let me tell you this, sweetheart, as from tomorrow, that's where I'll be living. The gossipmongers won't annoy me.'

'You will not! I forbid you to go.'

'You're not in any position to dictate to me, Adam Brady. And I *will* go, so don't you dare try to stop me.'

The argument swayed backwards and forwards for some time with neither gaining the upper hand.

She was determined that he hand the work over to someone else and he didn't want to do that as it might upset Benny.

Maura was glad she was able to hold back the tears until she reached the sanctuary of the nursery and threw herself down on the spare bed. What was to become of her and Danny, she hadn't the faintest idea. Should she try the age-old method of getting a man to change his mind – sharing the bed with him? No. Evelyn Matthews was too beautiful a rival to compete with and Maura was afraid of rejection. She knew it wouldn't be outright rejection, but she'd know if he was putting on an act. She would know and she couldn't risk the humiliation.

Maura rose early next morning and started packing Danny's clothes. She could hear Adam moving about downstairs but made no effort to join him. After all, he had been adamant that he must finish the job and she refused to stay in Holywood if he did. There was nothing more to talk about as all negotiations between them had reached a deadlock.

Locked in dark thoughts, she was unaware that he had come upstairs. His voice startled her and she swung round to face him.

'So you're going through with it then?'

'You forced it on me. You won't budge, so I'll

have to take the initiative. I'm sorry, but I have no other option.'

'Don't give me that! Is it Francie Murphy that's the attraction? Would you have stuck it out here if he hadn't been coming on to you?'

Colour rose in her cheeks and she glared at him. 'Don't you dare try putting the blame on me. I haven't done anything that I'm ashamed of.'

'Give over, Maura. I saw you.'

'What do you mean, you saw me?'

'At the bus stop.' Still she looked puzzled. Now confused, Adam prompted, 'Kissing Francie Murphy.'

Her jaw dropped, but instead of looking guilty, her eyes widened with amazement. 'You actually saw me waiting for the bus and you drove on? What kind of man are you, to leave your wife and young child facing a long journey home on two buses? It just shows how little you care. You sicken me. You're despicable, so you are.'

He grabbed her by the arm. 'I sicken you? How do you think I felt, seeing you make an exhibition of yourself on the Shore Road yesterday? I'm just glad young Jackie Flynn didn't notice. Besides, I didn't want to spoil your pleasure. You and Francie Murphy were slobbering all over each other and, worse still, my son was watching the two of you. What kind of an example is that to set a young child?'

Maura was stunned into silence, to think that

Adam had passed at that moment. 'You do tend to exaggerate. It was only a farewell peck.' She tugged her arm free from his hold. Knowing in her heart that it must have looked bad, she explained, 'He saw me struggling with the Tansad and stopped to help.'

'That was very gallant of him, but it didn't look like a farewell peck to me.'

'Well it was and don't you try to make something worse out of it.'

'Huh! If you kissed me like that now and again we wouldn't be at each other's throats all the time.'

She glared at him. 'I can't remember you wanting too many kisses lately. You actually seemed to be avoiding any chance of me kissing you. Besides, tell me, Adam, truthfully: can you picture me carrying on at a bus stop in broad daylight for all to see?'

Doubting his own eyes now, he dithered. Had jealousy tainted his vision? Had he jumped to the wrong conclusion? He doubted it. The kiss had been too intense. 'Perhaps you got carried away and forgot where you were! Did you spend the day with him?'

'No, I didn't. I've already explained to you why I was in Greencastle yesterday. I had just left my da's house to catch a bus home when he happened to be passing by and saw me struggling with the Tansad, so stopped to help. That's all.'

However, she was uneasy. She had enjoyed Francie's caress, but it had lasted only a few seconds, hadn't it? Yes! Luckily the bus had come along just then, putting a premature end to their antics. Convinced in herself that she had done no wrong, she retaliated, 'It seems to me that you were looking for an excuse to leave me standing there.' She tried to turn the tables on him. 'Was *she* in the van with you, by any chance?'

He threw his arms in the air in frustration. 'I give up. There's no reasoning with you, so do whatever you want. If you still insist on going, then there's nothing I can do to stop you, and there's no need to get word to your father. I'll come back about two and take you over myself. OK?'

He slammed the door behind him. She sank down at the table, buried her head in her arms and sobbed her heart out. She had handled that all wrong. Was there any way back for them? What could she possibly do to repair the damage she had already done?

9

Adam returned shortly before two o'clock. The van
had been cleared out and plastic sheets were spread
on the floor to protect Maura's bits and pieces. He
had hoped that she might change her mind but the
assortment of cartons and Danny's furniture ready
and waiting spoke silent volumes. Grim-faced and
with a brief nod in her direction, he started loading
the van. Most of the articles belonged to Danny:
cot, nursery furniture, toys and games. Maura
wanted familiar things around the child so that he
would feel more at home in his grandad's house.
Everything she would need, except clothes and
toiletries, was already in her old room at her father's
house. At least, she hoped they would still be there.
Surely her da wouldn't have allowed that woman
to take over *her* room! And why not? Why not

indeed? Her thoughts taunted her. He was a free man, with no ties whatsoever. Besides, there was the small room downstairs and if push came to shove she could use that.

Davey would be surprised to see her as she'd had no means of contacting him. Please God, don't let that woman be there, she prayed silently as she helped Adam arrange things in the van to prevent damage in transit.

Adam paused momentarily when he reached for the plastic baby bath Maura had dug out to bring along. He frowned down at it, then threw her a look of disgust as its implication sank in. She cringed inside as she realised that he had forgotten that her father's house didn't have a bathroom. Her chin lifted defiantly as she reminded herself that neither did thousands of other homes in Belfast, and she flashed him a withering glance. Just who did he think he was?

Danny sat wide-eyed, clutching his favourite teddy and chewing away at its ear, as all this was going on, his eyes following every movement his father made. Adam saw the frown that puckered his son's brow and wondered what was going on in the child's mind. What was he making of all this upheaval? It wasn't fair. It wasn't Danny's fault. But wasn't it always the innocent that suffered in cases like this? Heart-sore, he wished Evelyn had remained in Cork, then he wouldn't be in this predicament now.

At last everything was loaded, and they were ready to go. Adam helped his wife and Danny up into the cab, then climbed into the driver's seat. Anger was still a red-hot hard core burning deep within him and he cautioned himself to drive carefully. He couldn't believe this was happening. He should never have let it come to this. He loved Maura! But then . . . how did he feel about Evelyn? Deep in unhappy thought, he was surprised when they arrived in Greencastle so quickly. Not a word had been spoken throughout the journey. They were both engrossed in their own private hell. Even Danny, now deprived of his bear, had sat sucking his thumb in silence.

At Greencastle there was no sign of Cassie. Although Maura sensed that the house was empty, she decided not to take any chances and tentatively knocked on the door before using her key to get in. Everything was unloaded in silence, broken only by Adam wanting to know where Maura wanted things put, and Danny whimpering in bewilderment at the strangeness of it all. Maura could actually sense the aura of misery radiating from Adam but she couldn't bring herself to beg for him to put an end to his affair. Tentatively she offered him a cup of tea but he gruffly declined, saying he had to get back to work. He was in the hall, about to leave, when Davey came rushing along the road and, panting heavily, plunged through the front door. Obviously in pain, he stooped over, holding his back with one hand and gripping the door handle for support with the other.

'I couldn't believe my eyes when I saw the van outside the door. Why on earth didn't you let me know you were coming? I'd have taken the day off.' Still bent over and gasping for breath, Davey threw Maura an accusing glance.

Adam stood looking at him with disdain. He hated the thought of Maura and Danny living under the same roof as this surly man. Davey had never given him the chance to be part of his family, hadn't even tried to get to know him. Not that he cared, but it would have made things so much easier for Maura. After all, he didn't expect Davey to love him like a son, so why couldn't the man have made an effort, kept his big mouth shut and played along for the sake of his daughter's happiness?

Now Adam derided him. 'Catch yourself on, man! How could she? Eh? Maybe put a message in a bottle last night and throw it in the lough?'

When upright, Davey could give Adam an inch or two, and now in spite of the pain in his back he forced himself to straighten up to his full height in an endeavour to look threatening. 'Ha ha, very droll. But then you always did have the gift of the gab. You could even sell holy water to the Pope.

That's how you tricked my daughter into marriage, isn't it?'

'Da . . .' Appalled, Maura started towards her father ready to chastise him, but Adam's next words brought her up short.

'*Me?* Trick *her?*' he spluttered with exaggerated astonishment. 'I think you've got your wires crossed, Davey. I wasn't the one who got pregnant.'

He was immediately contrite for his stupid outburst. He didn't, for one second, believe that Maura had tricked him into a hasty marriage.

Adam lifted his son up in his arms and held him close to his chest. Danny clung to him. Over the child's head, Adam eyed Maura spitefully. 'Mind you, I'll want to see him as often as possible. We'll have to come to some arrangement. And the sooner the better.'

With a final hug and a kiss pressed into the child's curly hair, he set Danny gently down and left the house without a further glance at his wife. Danny made to follow him but Maura held him firmly by the hand. The boy writhed in her restraining hold as he strove to break free. Tears streamed down his face and he screamed, 'Daddy, no! Daddy, don't go! Daddy!' Adam's stride faltered at the child's plaintive cry as he watched him leave, but he carried on walking, his shoulders slumped in defeat.

Maura gazed after him dumbfounded. Did he really believe all this time that she had tricked him into marriage? Oh, but that hurt. How it hurt.

Davey was making a big fuss of his grandson, wiping his face dry and making an effort to take the boy's mind off his father's abrupt departure. He motioned for Maura to give him a hand and, heart aching, she joined them. Her thoughts were in a jumbled mess. Had she done the right thing? Where would it all end? No matter! Whatever way it panned out, Danny mustn't suffer, but if Adam chose Evelyn . . . How could it be otherwise?

The toys had been left downstairs for the child to play with, and once he was distracted by them, Maura turned to her father and said quietly, 'If it's all right with you, Da, I'll nip upstairs and move things around a bit so he will feel at home if he wakens during the night. OK?'

A comforting hand was pressed on her shoulder. 'That's fine by me, lass. In fact, I've run out of cigarettes. Will I take him with me and buy him a comic? You like the *Dandy*, don't you, Danny?'

Danny was already on his feet and grabbing Davey's hand tugged him towards the door. He loved looking at pictures of Desperate Dan and Korky the Cat. Maura nodded her consent. 'Be a good boy for your grandad, Danny. And don't buy him any sweets, Da,' she warned.

'Now she's being a spoilsport, isn't she, Danny?'

'I mean it, Da. I don't want him ending up with a mouth full of black, rotten stumps for teeth when he's no age.'

'OK! OK, I get the message. Come on, son.'

Davey winked at Maura as Danny led the way out without more ado and Maura thanked God that children were so adaptable.

She remained for some seconds staring blindly out the window on to the Shore Road. She would certainly miss the views from her window over in Holywood, but then, from her back bedroom here in this house, she would have a good view of both the County Down coastline and Holywood. In fact, with a good pair of binoculars she would probably be able to see her own house.

With a resigned shrug, she went upstairs to sort out her son's bits and pieces. Adam had put the cot up. She unpacked the bedding and got it ready for Danny's afternoon nap, setting his small table and Disney lamp close by. She was relieved to find the room just as she had left it: the bed stripped and the belongings she had left behind set out on the dresser. She unpacked and put the empty suitcase on top of the wardrobe. Fetching bedlinen from the ottoman in the big front bedroom, she made up the single bed. Still restless, she decided to get things ready for the evening meal and descended the stairs. She was glad that she had, some years ago, persuaded her father to get a fridge

193

and she now checked it to see what she could make for the evening meal. There was plenty to choose from. Seeing Cassie's influence at work here again, she resolved to find out if her da was serious about this woman. And if he was, what then?

She took out two pork chops and sausages ready to grill. Was one of the chops meant for Cassie? Tough luck if it was, she thought. Cassie would have to go elsewhere for her tea. Maura went out the back to the lean-to shed where her father stored the vegetables and cooking pots. To her surprise she found only a few potatoes and no vegetables. Cassie had slipped up there. But then, Maura mused, the woman probably waited until Monday, which was when Stewart's shop got their fresh stock in after the weekend rush. If Maura was correct in her assumption, then Cassie could arrive any time now with fresh vegetables. Maura decided that if she did come before her dad got back, she wouldn't answer the door. Let her father do all the explaining when he next saw the woman.

She was wrong in one assumption and right in the other: she didn't have to open the door. Cassie had her own key and let herself in. When she came through from the hall she paused, taken aback when she saw Maura. Then, with a slight nod of acknowledgement, she carried on into the scullery and set the shopping bag next to the draining board, throwing over her shoulder, 'Your father didn't mention anything about you coming here today.'

Maura had followed her and stood at the entrance to the narrow scullery.

'That's because he didn't know.'

'Oh, I see.'

'Why? Does it make any difference? Does he tell you everything that goes on between us?'

'No, not at all. If I can be of any assistance while you're here, let me know. I'll be only too happy to oblige.'

'That won't be necessary. And by the way, while I am here there will be no need for you to come in every day. I'll do the cooking and cleaning.'

'I'll wait until I hear that from Davey's lips, if you don't mind.' She glanced at her watch. 'Is he not home from work yet?'

'He is. He's taken his grandson down to Grogan's to buy him some comics.'

Cassie quickly unpacked the shopping bag. Stacking a few tins of peas, a packet of tea and some sugar up in the cupboard, with a nod at the vegetables she said, 'I'll leave you to take care of this lot. I want to catch up with Davey.' She turned to leave but Maura blocked her way.

Reaching for her purse, she asked, 'How much do we owe you?'

Sidling past her, Cassie said, 'Doesn't matter.

Davey will see to that. Good day to you.' Without a further glance, the woman gave a loud sniff and headed for the front door. She left the house just as Davey passed the window.

The door opened quickly and Danny came running in. Davey's voice followed him. 'In you go, son, and show your mammy your comics.' The door closed again.

From behind the heavy net curtains Maura watched her father and Cassie face each other on the pavement. Cassie was red faced and obviously angry. Davey looked as if he was pleading with her. Maura tried to lip-read but in vain; their body language was too volatile. They were having a right old barney out on the footpath. Leaving them to it, she went into the scullery and started sorting out the vegetables.

Davey was indeed pleading his case. 'Look, Cassie, I can understand you're upset. But I wasn't keeping you in the dark! I honestly didn't know Maura was coming here today.'

'Huh! And you expect me to believe that?'

'Yes! As a matter of fact I do. It's the God's honest truth.'

'And when will we see each other again, eh? And I don't mean in the pub. Where can we be alone together?' To keep her voice down, Cassie had resorted to hissing.

Davey looked at her in disgust. 'I'm surprised at you, Cassie. It's your companionship I want, your friendship. It's not just sex I'm after, ye know.'

Her mouth gaped in disbelief. 'Well then, why did you . . .' Her voice trailed off.

'Come on, Cassie. These things happen. It's not as if I seduced you. You're old enough to know what's going on. You were all for it!'

Cassie was fighting back the tears. 'I thought you cared. You've made a right fool of me, haven't you?'

'Of course I haven't. As a matter of fact I'm very fond of you, Cassie, but we're not a couple of spring chickens looking for marriage. We can still be friends. Can't we?'

Davey reached out his hand but she brushed it aside. 'You'll live to regret this, Davey Craig. You mark my words!'

She stormed off down the road and Davey stared bleakly after her. He'd had such hopes for them, but the return of his daughter had put paid to that little romantic fling. It really was a shame. They got on so well together. However, in the long run blood is thicker than water. He had let Maura down once before and had regretted it. He must never allow it to happen again.

Davey was very subdued when he at last came indoors. Maura watched him covertly for some

197

minutes whilst pretending to read the newspaper, willing him to talk to her. Then unable to bear the tension any longer, she said tentatively, 'Da, I have to know . . . Are you and that woman . . . you know . . .'

'No! You can put that idea out of your head right away, girl. And by the way, that woman's name is Cassie, as if you didn't know already. She's just a good friend. But mind you, I've been glad of her company and I will continue to see her.'

'That's good to know, Da. I hope I haven't spoiled things between you.'

'You've nothing to worry about. As I say, I'll still be seeing her, so I will,' he stated firmly.

'I'm glad for you,' Maura lied brightly. 'Look, it's a bit late, but still, I'll see if I can get Danny down for a while. A half-hour in bed does him a world of good, keeps him from getting cranky, so here's hoping. Come on, son, let's go upstairs and read your *Dandy* and then you can have a nice wee nap.'

After dinner, Danny scrambled down from his chair and came to stand by Maura, tugging at her skirt. 'Home, Mammy?'

Maura's breath caught in her throat and her mouth went dry as she cast about in her mind for an agreeable excuse. 'I thought we could stay with Grandad tonight, love. Maybe even for a couple of days. It will be like a wee holiday, so it will. We'll be able to walk down to the seaside.'

Wide-eyed, Danny stared at her. 'Daddy too?'

'No, Daddy has a big job to finish. I thought you and I would stay here for a wee while and maybe tomorrow we'll go and visit Emma. You'd like that, wouldn't you?'

But he was not to be put off. He gave it some thought, then said, 'We go home to Daddy tomorrow?'

Lifting him on to her knee, Maura clasped his little face in her hands. 'We'll have to wait and see if Daddy was able to finish the job he's doing.'

'Then home?' he insisted.

'I hope so, love . . . I hope so.'

She lifted big watery eyes to Davey who had risen from his chair at the table and was watching them intently. 'He'll soon settle down,' he mouthed at her. 'Just you wait and see.'

Maura didn't think it would be as easy as that. Danny idolised his father and vice versa. The future looked dismal for them. Hell roast Evelyn Matthews for coming back and causing all this disruption. But then, was it really all her fault? All Adam had to do was allocate the job to someone else and every-thing would have been hunky-dory, wouldn't it? She was beginning to doubt that things would ever be the same again, and a deep sadness settled on her.

10

Steeped in misery, Adam drove past Evelyn's house and continued along Antrim Road. The blood in his head pounded and he knew he couldn't face Evelyn at the moment. It had been bad enough leaving his son in tears without her probing the wound, even though her intentions would be sympathetic. Turning in at the entrance to Bellevue Zoo, he drove up the winding path, heading for the Floral Hall and Hazelwood beyond, still brooding over what had befallen him. How on earth had it all come about? His deceit! That's how. He should have been honest with Maura from the beginning, but it was asking too much to expect her to trust him now.

He became belligerent. I should have exerted my authority and ordered her to stay put. That's what!

After all, she was his wife. In spite of himself he smiled at the very idea of Maura submitting to him. It would have made her even more determined to leave him. Leaving the van in the zoo car park, he headed towards Hazelwood on the slopes of the Cave Hill. He needed some respite to think, to sort things out in his mind, examine all the options, if there were any available. This time of day there weren't many people about. Too late for mothers with their young tots; they would be collecting the bigger children from school. Too early for workers; most of them didn't stop until five or later. Passing the Floral Hall, he noticed an ice-cream van parked near by and realised he had skipped lunch.

He bought an ice-cream cone, commiserating with the vendor. 'Not much trade today then, by the looks of it.'

He gave Adam a broad grin and replied, 'You'd be surprised, sir. I was quite busy up until about an hour ago and then it dropped off. A lot of schoolchildren often gather here for ice cream or crisps or whatever, so it's worth hanging on a while longer till they've all gone home, then I'll shut up shop for the day.'

Bidding him the time of day, Adam headed along the winding dirt path. The warm sun filtered through the hazel bushes, caressing his face, and a gentle breeze ruffled his hair as he climbed higher up the hill. He felt the tension slowly ease from

201

his body. It was great to be up here away from all distractions.

Finding a secluded clearing, he stretched out on the long grass, his head resting on his hands, and lapped up the soothing peace of his surroundings. Tranquillity! Broken only by the sounds of the insistent humming of a large bumblebee as it flitted among the clover flowers and some songbirds that seemed to be in contention as to which one could produce the sweetest music. He could make out the unmistakable notes of a song thrush and definitely a blackbird too, possibly a robin, as well as other distant tweets and chirps he didn't recognise, Adam thought as he listened, captivated by the feathered chorus.

He needed to be alone. He hurt so deeply inside that it was like a sharp pain in his breast as he mourned the break-up of his marriage. And if Maura's father had anything to do with it, that's what would happen. Davey would be conspiring to keep Maura and Danny away from Adam. No doubt about that! Davey Craig hated his guts. Even so, why couldn't Maura give him the benefit of the doubt and trust him for a few short months until he finished his work on Antrim Road? But he already knew the answer: he had foolishly abused her trust.

Benny and George were so pleased at the interest being shown in the landscaping work he was doing on the Matthews' property, sure that it would bring in more work by the time it was finished. And the brothers were very good to Maura and him, especially Benny and his wife. There was no denying that. In fact, Maura should be only too glad to oblige Benny for a change, after all he and Beth had done for them. Why was she being so stubborn? Had he ever given her cause to doubt him before? Never! He had been a good husband and father.

It was all very well his wife saying he should delegate the work to Steve, but she didn't understand the ins and outs of it. It wasn't his decision to make. How would he be able to explain his change of heart to the brothers who were depending on him? Unknown to Maura, Adam was playing his cards close to his chest, doing all he could to make himself indispensable to the Gallaghers. Benny had often talked of opening a smaller branch on the outskirts of south Belfast and had hinted that Adam could take over the running of it. He would be his own boss. Now there was a strong possibility of that happening. If he played his cards right and the new centre flourished, who knows where it would lead. He might, in time, be offered a stake in the firm, a partnership even. The possibilities were enormous. He grimaced. Then he berated himself. And why not! Stranger things had happened. Was he kidding himself? He shrugged philosophically; it cost nothing to dream.

He lay there, spread out on the grass in the warm afternoon sun, and thought about what he should do. Soon the sleepless night and the bird chorus took their toll on him and he found it difficult to keep his eyes open, drifting into a troubled doze where he could see Danny running away in the distance but couldn't catch up with him. He was jolted out of his reverie by a little fox terrier dog sniffing around him. A quick glance at his watch showed him he had been asleep for almost an hour. He playfully cuffed the dog and it started barking at him as its owner came into view. Squinting against the bright sunlight, Adam recognised Joe Moon. Rising to his feet, he stood, feet apart, and with his hands on his hips he arched his back to dispel the stiffness. Grinning sheepishly, he confessed, 'I must have fallen asleep.'

Joe took in his tousled appearance and peered around suspiciously. 'You're lucky. It's lovely up here, so quiet and peaceful. I wish I could find time for a snooze in the woods. For me it's straight home from work and out to walk him.' He nodded towards the dog.

Guessing the path Joe's mind was taking and by the way he was furtively casting his eyes about as if expecting to find someone lurking in the bushes, Adam kept the smile on his face. 'Aye, it's a hard auld station, all right. And I don't really have the time to loiter about here any longer, no matter how nice it is. My mate will be wondering where I've got to. So it's back to the grindstone for me.'

He started off down the hill silently berating himself for letting Joe catch him in this situation. Looking back over his shoulder, he shouted, 'Enjoy your walk, Joe, and thank the dog for wakening me.'

So much for wanting space to think! All he had accomplished was a waste of good time, but at least he felt better for it: refreshed and more able to face Evelyn after his wee snooze.

Joe stood gazing after him, the look on his face one of grim satisfaction. He hadn't believed a single word Adam had uttered. Joe had hinted to Mary that he thought Adam Brady was playing away and it looked as if he was right. He was in his element. He couldn't wait to tell Mary where the illicit meetings were taking place. He frowned in thought. But then, where was Evelyn? Then he thought, she must have scampered off when she heard him coming. Adam would probably pick her up in the van on the way down. After a good look round, and sure that he had seen all there was to see, including the flattened patch of grass, Joe called the dog to heel.

'Time we headed home, Brin.'

He was happy, already embellishing in his mind the tale he would relate to his wife.

* * *

Evelyn must have been on the lookout for him, for when Adam drove in later that afternoon, she came out on to the veranda and waited for him to approach. Aware that young Jackie was also watching them covertly, Adam drew Evelyn back inside the house. There was sure to be talk and speculation about them and he didn't want to give Jackie fuel to add to the gossip. He would try to keep his affairs under wraps and well away from the other side of the lough for as long as possible.

'You were away a long time.' Evelyn was watching him closely, fear in her heart. Had Maura eventually persuaded him to give up on the job?

Adam nodded in agreement. 'I know, sorry about that.'

Jackie had stepped on to the veranda to wait and Adam asked, 'Have you finished round the back for today?' The lad nodded and Adam said, 'Good. I'll follow you round in a minute. I want to have another look at the waterfall site before we leave.'

With a nod Jackie trudged round the corner of the house on reluctant feet. Another look? Who was Adam trying to kid? Why, he hadn't been in work all afternoon. He'd left all the hard graft for him to do and now he was talking about going home? Jackie was aware that all was not as it should be and wondered what the heck was going on with Adam.

When he was out of earshot, Evelyn said impatiently, 'Leave? You've only just got here. Would you mind explaining yourself?'

He shrugged his shoulders. 'I know, but I can't talk about it now. I'll tell you everything tomorrow.'

'Did Maura cause a scene, then? Is that it?' she persisted.

Adam rushed to his wife's defence. 'No! Far from it. In fact, she was very dignified about it all. Her da was there of course, getting his oar in, and that didn't make things any easier. It was heart-breaking leaving Danny. He was in a right state, screaming after me.'

'I'm sorry to hear that.' A grunt was Adam's answer and she continued, 'Charles has been asking after you. He wants to speak with you before you go.'

'What did you tell him?'

'That you had gone back to the nursery for some more fertiliser.'

'Good. Will you tell him that I've been called away, on an urgent matter? I can't talk to anyone at the moment, the mood I'm in. Look, I'll head on home now and see you tomorrow. All right?'

Evelyn didn't like being thwarted and stood eyeing him, a steely glint in her eyes and a defiant tilt to her head. He locked eyes with her and in spite of herself she wavered. 'OK. I'll see you in the morning. Early, mind.'

He watched her enter the house and went to collect Jackie, glad he had the rest of the day to come to terms with his plight.

Maura also had a restless night and awoke late, still half asleep and with a throbbing headache, her eyes swollen and red. At first as she gazed around the room she was confused, unable to understand why she was in her old bedroom.

'Mammy.'

Danny's voice brought her upright and out of bed in a flash, causing her head to throb even harder. His face was tear-stained and guilt swamped her. Had he been crying long and she hadn't heard him? Sweeping him into her arms, she hugged him close, muttering endearments. What time was it anyway? A glance at the alarm clock on the bedside table told her it was ten past nine. Her father would already be at work; his hours were nine till three.

Quickly throwing on her dressing gown, she piloted Danny down the stairs and settled him on the settee, then gave him his favourite teddy. He clutched it to his chest and immediately the bear's ear was in his mouth, a sure indication of his anxiety. He silently looked at his mother with wide questioning eyes. She fell to her knees beside the settee and gathered him fiercely to her breast again. 'It's going to be all right, love.'

This was awful. How would she be able to cope?

Now he was sobbing again. 'I want my daddy.'

'I know, love. I know you do and you will see him soon. I promise.'

'When?'

'I'm not sure . . . but soon.'

Somewhat pacified, Danny whimpered, 'Wanna see Emma's doggy.'

Regret stabbed at her heart. Why had she mentioned Emma to him? She no more wanted to face Mary Moon than she did Evelyn Matthews. With a long-drawn-out sigh she replied, 'Yes, love, as soon as we get our breakfast we'll go see Emma.'

This was one promise she could at least keep. She had to meet Mary Moon eventually, so the sooner the better.

Maura had a feeling of apprehension as she pushed the Tansad towards Mary's new house on Graymount Crescent, wondering what bad news she would hear from her today.

When the door opened and Mary saw who was standing there, the surprise on her face was evidence to Maura that her friend hadn't heard about her coming back to her father's house.

'What brings you here?' Mary gasped; then pushing the door wider, she said, 'But don't just stand there, come inside for goodness' sake.'

Recalling Joe's revelations the night before, she was confused.

As Maura guided her pushchair into the hall, she said, 'What? I've been back at me da's nearly a whole day and you're telling me you haven't heard about it yet? My God, things are slowing down around here.'

'No, I never heard a single word, honest.' Danny was out of the Tansad and looking at Mary expectantly. 'You go on into the front room, Danny, Emma's in there. You too, Maura, while I put the teapot on. The place is a mess. I haven't had time to clear up yet. I'm just back from leaving Jenny down at school.'

Danny trotted off and Maura followed him, saying wryly, 'Your house is never a mess.' She watched Mary closely as she delivered her bad news. 'Adam and I have decided that we should spend some time apart to try to get things back to some kind of normality.'

'Does that mean . . . you've left him?'

Maura shrugged. 'My, you're sharp today, Mary. But that depends on how long we remain separated. I suppose it could come to that,' she confessed and looked away so that Mary wouldn't see the tears welling up.

'Ah, Maura, what will you do?'

'Well, me da says if it comes to the crunch, I can stop at his house indefinitely. But . . .' Pulling a chair out, Maura sat down at the table and lifted green eyes luminous with tears to meet her friend's. 'Do you know a woman called Cassie Hamilton?'

Aghast at the state her friend was in, Mary shook her head. 'No, I don't know her to speak to. I've seen her about, mind you. I think she lives in The Drive. Her daughter is the new health nurse down in Canavan's surgery but I've yet to meet Cassie. Linda, her daughter, is a lovely pleasant girl, so she is.'

Maura watched Mary closely. 'Yes, I know, I met her at your birthday party, remember? But her mother, now she's the fly in the ointment where I'm concerned. I get the impression this Cassie and me da are more than just good friends, if you get my drift.'

Mary's chin dropped a bit. 'I don't believe you. Surely not Davey Craig.' She shook her head and laughed at the idea. 'Never! Your father is too much of a gentleman as far as anything like that is concerned.' She stopped as if hit by an uneasy thought and finished hesitantly, 'All I can say is, if there is anything going on between them, they are being very secretive about it, because I haven't heard a word. Not even a whisper. But then, my Joe has joined the indoor bowling club and I don't get out as often these days. Still, he would have heard if anything was going on. You know yourself that men are like old women at times where anything like that is concerned.'

In spite of her own worries, Maura was intrigued. 'Why don't you get out any more, if you don't mind me asking?'

'Because Joe is all newly fangled with this bowling business and goes to practice in the hall at least once a week, sometimes twice. Then there's always a league match every week in the hall or at the opposition's hall. Some weeks I hardly see him at all.' With a flap of her hand she went on, 'Look, that's neither here nor there. Let's get back to your predicament, Maura. Surely you're not going to sit on your backside and let Lady Muck steal your husband, are you?'

Again that defeated shrug that tore at Mary's heart. 'I can only hope and pray that everything will turn out for the best, Mary.'

Danny wanted a wee, so Maura took him to the bathroom. Mary's mind was in turmoil as she cut and buttered slices of Veda bread and topped them off with Cheddar cheese. Surely no man in his right mind would be so callous as to rush his mistress up to Hazelwood to celebrate driving his wife out of her home? No, Joe must have got his wires crossed. He did that often enough. She decided not to mention anything about it to Maura.

As they sipped their tea, Mary brought her friend

up to date on other bits of gossip. When they had finished the snack, Maura suggested that they take the two children out for a walk, before returning to Mary's house for a cuppa.

'You're right! This weather's too good to be lounging about indoors. We'll take a walk up Serpentine Road on to the Antrim Road, eh, Maura?' Mary said gleefully. 'Have a wee look round. You never know what we'll find out.'

Maura was astounded at the direction of Mary's thoughts. 'No way. I'll not stoop so low as to spy on my husband.' She grimaced. 'Besides, I might find out something I'd rather not know.'

'So, no matter what, you'll still take him back?'

'I don't really think he's done anything wrong, so why court disaster?' She paused in thought. 'Tell you what, we'll go up Gray's Lane and along Antrim Road. OK?' That would take them well away from where she imagined Evelyn's house to be.

'Whatever you say. But if you ask me, you're too soft for your own good. Anyway, we'll take the dog with us, then Joe won't have to take him out until bedtime. That'll please him.'

'I'm not asking you, and I hope you'll refrain from talking about me to the local gossipmongers.'

'People don't mean any harm, you know that, Maura. They care for you. That's why I warned Joe to mind his own business last night.'

Maura was in like a shot. 'Why? What was he saying about me?'

Colour swamped Mary's face and she started stuttering. 'N-n-othing. He didn't say a word about you. Cross my heart and hope to die.' Maura hadn't been mentioned the night before, so Mary spoke with some confidence.

Maura mused about this for some moments, then said triumphantly, 'Then what did he say about Adam, eh? I'm right, aren't I? He said something about Adam, didn't he?'

In a quandary, Mary said virtuously, 'I promised not to repeat a word Joe said, to anyone, and that means you as well. I'm sorry, Maura.'

'Come on, Mary. Spit it out. You know I won't stop until I've wormed it out of you.'

They had been strapping the children into their pushchairs while they spoke and now Mary stood upright, hands on her hips. 'No! And that's final. So let's get out into the sunshine and enjoy ourselves.'

Maura let it go. She'd decided that she didn't want to hear any more bad news. She had more than enough to contend with already.

They made their way across Graymount Park and on to Gray's Lane, which was a narrow uphill road without footpaths and quite dangerous for pedestrians. It ran from Shore Road to Antrim Road, splitting Fortwilliam Golf Links into two unequal halves: eleven fairways on the left and seven on the right. There was little conversation between the women as they concentrated on pushing the Tansads uphill and keeping an ear cocked for the odd car that might suddenly appear round a bend in the road. At the top, breathless, they sat on a bench seat overlooking the golf links and Belfast Lough beyond while they regained their breath.

'That should burn up a few calories,' Mary exclaimed, panting.

'I hope it comes off my hips, I could do with a bit off there,' Maura gasped in reply.

Mary, who had lost a stone in weight after the birth of her second child, looked neat and trim in her slacks and top, but she was quick to reassure Maura, 'There's nothing wrong with your figure, you look fine, so you do. Shall we go over the road and call into St Gerard's? We could say a wee prayer and have a rest while we're at it before we go any further?'

Bewildered, Maura canted her head along the road to the right. 'Why not Hazelwood? The kids could play on the grass there with Brin.' At the sound of his name the dog strained frantically on his lead, barking excitedly. 'Besides, we couldn't possibly take the dog into church, now could we? In any case, he wouldn't know how to bless himself, let alone genuflect,' Maura joked.

Mary laughed at Maura's wit as she flailed about in her mind for an excuse to avoid going to Hazelwood without starting another argument, but Maura had already taken the initiative and was on the move.

'Come on, let's go,' Maura called out as she headed along the road, and without more ado a disgruntled Mary trudged after her.

At Hazelwood they chose a sheltered spot where the two children could run about chasing the dog without getting too hot. With a slight frown, Maura said, 'It's lovely here, isn't it? Very peaceful indeed. I can't understand why you were so reluctant to come.'

'No, I wasn't,' Mary blustered in denial. 'Whatever gave you that idea?'

With a sad shake of the head, Maura said, 'Forget I asked. I don't know who my friends are any more. Nobody seems to want to give me a straight answer to a straight question these days.'

'Don't say that! You know we're staunch friends, Maura. I just didn't want to make you feel any worse, so I didn't.'

'I couldn't feel any worse than I am now, believe me.'

With an exaggerated sigh, Mary admitted, 'Let's hope not. I heard this is where Adam and Evelyn come for their little trysts.'

To her surprise, Maura actually laughed out

216

loud. 'Don't be stupid. Adam would never dream of coming here. He'd be afraid of anyone seeing him. After all, he is a married man and he'd want to keep up appearances.' In her heart of hearts she wasn't sure of this but she hoped she was right. Surely he couldn't be so besotted with Evelyn that he would risk running into someone from Greencastle.

Relieved, Mary agreed with her. 'That's what I said to Joe.'

Maura's lips were a tight line. 'And just where did Joe dig up this bit of filth from?'

Offended, Mary tossed her head and said defiantly, 'He saw them.' She immediately regretted the words the moment they left her mouth.

'Joe actually saw them?' Maura gasped in horror. 'He actually saw my Adam and that harlot together, up here?'

'Well, yes and no! I gather he saw Adam and he was acting so embarrassed that Joe assumed that Evelyn must have heard him coming and slunk away somewhere to hide from him.'

'You mean, Joe saw Adam on his own and his mind immediately went into overdrive. He put two and two together and got five. Is that what you're saying?' Maura ground out betwcen clenched teeth. 'When did all this happen?'

'Yesterday.'

'Yesterday, Adam left me at my da's house at about

217

half three, and he had to go back to work and make up for lost time. Don't forget, he's not working on his own up there. He has a young lad with him, so he can't go gallivanting off when the notion takes him. When exactly did Joe see him, eh?'

'You think Joe was telling me lies about Adam, don't you?'

'No, I just want to get things straight in my own mind. Go on, convince me.'

'Well, he got a pass out of work early. The club had a bowling match last night and Joe was asked to play lead on one of the rinks. He took the dog out while I made his tea, so it would have been around five o'clock, maybe a little later. I didn't take much notice of the time.'

After some thought, Maura said, 'I can see Adam coming up here to get his head showered after the state Danny was in when he left us, but I can't imagine him collecting Evelyn Matthews on the way up. What excuse would they give her husband and young Jackie? And do you think for one minute that Jackie would be able to keep his mouth shut about Adam skiving off with her? You tell Joe he had better watch what he says, because if Adam or, indeed, Evelyn ever found out that he was spreading false rumours about them, they'd have him up for slander. You can be sure of that.'

Mary took offence. 'And what if he's telling the truth, what then? Have you considered that?

He certainly wouldn't be up for slander then, would he?'

'I know Adam Brady better than anyone and I'm certain he didn't leave his son in tears and rush to take Evelyn Matthews up here. I'd stake my life on it. Besides, her husband's an invalid. She can't leave him at the drop of a hat. He needs looking after twenty-four hours a day.' Maura was getting more and more agitated and turned away to hide her tears.

'Ah, Maura, I'm sorry. I didn't mean to upset you.'

'Huh! Well, you sure know how to make a girl's day.'

Giving her friend's arm a sympathetic pat, she whispered, 'Maura, I really am sorry. I'll never learn to keep my big mouth shut.'

Maura drew a deep breath. 'Look, let's forget all about my affairs for the day and try to enjoy ourselves, eh?'

Time passed slowly after that and they made desultory conversation, keeping away from any topic that might cause further tensions. They played catch the ball and hide-and-seek with the children, until Maura was glad when Mary mentioned that she needed to get a move on to collect Jenny from school.

Maura immediately hailed Danny. 'Come on, son, it's time to go and get Jenny.'

219

Danny loved Emma's big sister and came running, plying his mother with questions. As she strapped him into the pushchair, Maura thanked God for giving her this bundle of joy. Without him she'd be lost, not knowing which way to turn. With him to look after, she had direction. Come hell or high water, she would survive. He was her salvation no matter what happened. Mother and son, they depended on each other.

11

To avoid further unsolicited confidences, Maura talked about everything under the sun and yet nothing, all the way back down Gray's Lane to the Star of the Sea primary school on the Shore Road. With a flap of the hand she airily pushed away Mary's excuses and apologies as inconsequential. After all, her friend couldn't help being married to a wimp like Joe who just thrived on spreading gossip about other people's shortcomings.

Mary trudged along unhappily beside her, justifying herself in her own mind. God knows, but she hadn't meant her friend any harm. Who would have thought that Maura would react like that? Hadn't she already left Adam because of Evelyn Matthews? In future she'd keep her big trap shut and leave others to be harbingers of bad news.

Inwardly, Maura fumed. By now the whole of Greencastle would know. The worst of it was that Maura didn't believe a single word of it, but others would. They'd lap it up. No doubt about it! Adam had been in such a state when he left Danny and her that she could see him needing some time alone to pull himself together, and the quiet and peace of Hazelwood was the ideal place for that. Not one to wear his heart on his sleeve, he'd want to regain control of his emotions before returning to work. Furthermore, Evelyn Matthews wouldn't stoop so low as to go up there with him; she liked her comfort too much. She knew when she was well off, so why rock the boat?

Annie Devlin, with young Thomas in his pushchair, was waiting by the entrance gates at the foot of the driveway that led up to the school. She joined the two girls for a chat. 'Hi, Mary. Nice to see you, Maura. Are you over on a wee visit to your dad?'

Mary was relieved to see Annie; it got her off the hook for a while. Maura had been ranting on and on, all the way back, like some eejit. For a while there, she had been quite worried about her friend's state of mind.

Now Maura gave Annie a defiant stare, as if to say, 'Don't *you* start,' then, realising that Annie was the quiet private type who kept very much to herself and had probably not heard any gossip about her return, she allowed warmth to colour her tone of voice. 'Yes, I'm staying with me da for a few days, Annie.'

Annie leaned over the Tansad and admired Danny. 'He's a lovely wee boy, so he is.' She ruffled his hair. 'Aren't you just lovely, Danny?' she asked.

He smiled and with childish simplicity said, 'Yes.' They all laughed.

'You're very lucky,' Annie said wistfully.

Maura bent over Annie's son, who was a few years older than Danny. Thomas, who had been injured at birth, was retarded and unable to walk properly. 'Hi, Thomas.' He gave her a big grin and squinted up at her. He was such a pleasant child, it was a shame. 'How's he doing, Annie?' she asked softly, for Annie's ears only.

Knowing Maura's concern was genuine, Annie answered truthfully, 'He's coming along all right. Sean and I are very pleased at the progress he's making.' Normally she would just say he was fine and change the subject.

A bell rang out, followed by a horde of yelling children waving sheets of paper and racing down the drive from school, which put an end to the conversation. After exclaiming over their offspring's paintings and enquiring about the star stuck to Jenny's jumper, the three women started off along the Shore Road, the children running ahead. Rachel and Rebecca Devlin were lovely girls and Maura, who had not seen them for some time, commented on their good looks, receiving a big smile from Annie. When they arrived at the bottom of Whitewell Road, Maura slowed down and, saying her farewells, left the other two to go on up the road while she went into the butcher's shop near the corner.

Mary, disappointed that Maura obviously wasn't coming home with her for coffee as planned, immediately voiced her displeasure. 'You said you'd come up for a cuppa,' she exclaimed, but Maura was adamant that she had some shopping to do before going home. Mary stared angrily at her retreating back as Maura entered the butcher's shop, before turning back to Annie.

With a wry grimace Annie said, 'I thought you two were a bit stilted when you arrived at the school. Sorry if I interrupted anything.'

'Oh, it's all right, Annie. I think I upset her, that's why. You see . . .'

Contrary to what Maura might think, Annie was only too aware of the rumours flying around Greencastle; she just didn't believe in lending voice to them. McVeigh's and Conway's bars were rife with whispers about the alleged antics of Adam Brady. Annie's husband Sean and her brother George drank in the bars on Saturday nights and Annie had heard all about the muckraking, as she called it. She could well believe that it was blown out of all proportion. People who didn't mean any harm could unwittingly be so callous at the expense of others. Now she held up her hand to stop Mary's explanations.

'Sorry, Mary, but I don't want to know, thank you. I've had enough trouble caused by malicious rumours to last me a lifetime and, believe me, I wouldn't wish it on my worst enemy.'

They continued on up the Whitewell Road in silence, each involved in a separate misery, Mary wondering how she could make amends with Maura and Annie plagued by her own worries. Her half-brother George was seeing Josie, a girl of ill repute who lived in Whiteabbey, and Annie's mother was trying to put a stop to it. But George really doted on the girl and God knew where it would all end. And, of course, all this was fuelled by malicious hearsay.

In Campbell's butcher's shop, Patsy came forward to serve Maura. There was never any malice in his words. The type of person that people called 'always the same', he always had some jokey remarks to make about the latest rumours, or the weather, or the gee-gees, but not today. Not when it was about someone he respected, and he'd always had a soft spot for Maura Craig. He greeted her in a friendly fashion.

'Hi, Maura, I heard you were back.' No beating

about the bush with Patsy; straight in. 'I'm sorry to hear about your trouble.' He paused in sympathy for a moment then, that out of the way, said, 'What can I do for you, love?'

Taking the words in the way they were intended, Maura replied, 'Thanks, Patsy. Have you any point end of the rump?'

He glanced at the window display and then touched the side of his nose in a knowing way. Going into the cold room at the back of the shop, he came back with a large joint of meat. Throwing it on to the chopping block, he winked at her. Carving knife poised over the point end, he said, 'How much do you want, Maura?'

'Two nice thick slices, please, Patsy. I'll also have a pound of braising steak.' She had vegetables in the house and would do the braising steak today, saving the rump, which looked succulent, for tomorrow's dinner.

He weighed the rump steak and told her the price. 'Is that too much, Maura? I can take a bit off if you like,' he queried.

'That's fine, Patsy. Me dad deserves a treat for putting up with me.' Maura took a five-pound note from her purse and gave it to him.

He wrapped up the meat and gave her the change. 'There you go, love.'

'Thanks, Patsy.'

'I hope things work out for you.'

226

Recognising his sincerity, she grimaced and said, 'Thanks, Patsy. Bye!'

As she came out of the butcher's, Maura spied her father some distance down the Shore Road and hurried across to his house. Cassie was with him, and Maura wanted to avoid speaking to her. Davey was surprised to see his daughter at that time of day. Cassie had expected to come into an empty house to sort out how things stood between them now that Maura was back. But he could see that wasn't about to happen and, by the look on his daughter's face, he knew Maura thought the same.

Maura sensed her da's surprise and thought it no wonder. The night before, she had told him that she would visit Mary Moon today and would probably be home late. She had said that he was to wait and she would make the tea when she got back. So of course he thought he had plenty of time for a 'clear the air' chat with Cassie. Davey could see by his daughter's demeanour that something had happened, which was probably why she was back so early.

Pretending not to notice them, Maura opened the door and going inside closed it after her. Danny was asleep in the pushchair. She unbuckled him and laid him gently on the sofa. Catching sight of herself in the wall mirror, Maura recoiled in shock at her image. Her face was pallid and drawn, her eyes shadowed and lifeless. She looked all washed out, as if she had aged ten years since her arrival back in Greencastle. That certainly wasn't a face to encourage any man home. What would she be like if she had to remain here any length of time? An old hag, that's what! Not that Greencastle was to blame for her appearance, not by a long shot. It was the shame of how Adam was behaving that was getting on top of her. They must be the talk of the district. This was all his fault. She still loved Adam, but how could she ever find it in her heart to forgive him?

She sighed with relief when her father came into the house on his own. She couldn't bear to make small talk with that woman just now.

'I'll start the dinner, Da. It'll take about an hour if you want to nip out to the pub for a while.' She wanted to say, 'That will give you enough time to talk with your friend,' but she resisted the temptation. What if he was after an excuse to invite Cassie in? Better to pretend that she hadn't noticed them.

Fully aware of the situation, Davey said gently, 'Are you all right, love?'

A big artificial smile stretched her lips. 'I'm fine, Da. Couldn't be better.'

'Sure?'

She nodded, turning away so she could remove the smile that was such a strain.

Davey knew she was far from fine, but decided

to give her a chance to pull herself together before he tried to glean from her what had happened to cause her so much distress. Touching Danny gently on the head, he said, 'Then I'll nip over to the bookie's. I won't be too long.'

Hating herself for spying on him, Maura watched from behind the nets. Cassie was indeed loitering out on the pavement. Davey joined her and they headed back down the road, arms linked, heads close together in serious conversation.

Maura put the braising steak, chopped carrots, parsnips and onions in a casserole dish and added gravy mix and herbs. Placing the dish in the oven, she prepared the potatoes and left them in a pot on a low light to simmer. Now she could take a break and try to relax. Danny was well into his afternoon nap so she decided to shampoo her hair and have a good wash down. In her da's house this used to be quite a chore, but he'd had an electric immersion heater installed over the sink and at a flick of a switch this heated the water very quickly. Fetching towel, flannel, soap and shampoo, she barred herself in the scullery and set about her ablutions.

Washed, dried and dressed, with the potatoes bubbling away on the stove, and a delicious aroma from the oven permeating the air, she was sitting on a chair towelling her hair when her father came back.

'Win any money then?' she greeted him. He looked askance at her and she could see that he hadn't the foggiest idea what she was talking about. She prompted him. 'At the bookie's? You said you were going over there, remember?' She could almost hear the penny drop.

'Ach no,' he blustered. 'I bumped into Cassie and we went for a dander down to the beach instead.'

Tongue in cheek, she nodded, accepting his excuse. 'The dinner will be ready shortly.'

'No hurry.' He made a big show of sniffing the air. 'It certainly smells nice. It's making my tummy rumble.'

Davey watched as she towelled her hair and then brushed it into shape. The damp hair clung to her head, shaped to perfection. The cut was certainly well worth the money spent on it. He had been upset when he first saw her without her long locks but now he congratulated her. 'That's a nice haircut you have.'

'I like it. It's easy to keep tidy.'

She started to set the table and Davey was on his feet in a flash. 'Here, let me do that.'

'OK. Everything should be ready by now. I'll strain the spuds before I waken Danny and then I'll serve the dinner.'

During the course of the meal, Davey covertly examined his daughter. She looked quite drawn and he felt heartsore at her pale countenance. If only she had listened to him in the first place! Or . . . He was ashamed to admit this now, at this late stage, but if he had welcomed Adam Brady into his home, everything would have probably worked out all right in the end. His chest tightened with sadness as he remembered practically throwing his pregnant daughter out of the house. For a long time his friends had tried to persuade him to change his mind but he had been an arrogant, cantankerous auld git and wouldn't budge one inch. He cringed with shame; he'd always been so self-righteous. Cassie had made him aware that one couldn't always be immune to temptations of the flesh. Was it too late to mend bridges, put things right between father and daughter? Had he ruined his daughter's chance of happiness? Adam Brady certainly loathed the sight of him, and who could blame him?

He was meeting Cassie later in McVeigh's pub. Should he suggest that he bring Cassie here and they could keep Maura company instead? Perhaps over a bottle of wine and some cans of lager the women would thaw towards each other.

Without further thought, he broached the subject. 'Maura, I've been thinking.'

'So I've noticed.'

His brows climbed his forehead. 'What do you mean?'

'Da, I can read you like a book. You've been

sitting there muttering to yourself and pitying me and wondering if I'll be all right on my own with just Danny for company. Well, don't! I want you to behave as if I'm not here. Go out and enjoy yourself when the fancy takes you. If I was at home, Adam would be working and there'd be only Danny and me in the house, so why should it be any different here?'

He smiled at her intuition. 'Ah, but Adam wouldn't be working all evening. I was thinking that I could fetch Cassie back here and keep you company. We'd be glad to sit in and Cassie's a nice person once you get to know her.'

At the thought of what the evening would be like tiptoeing round each other's feelings, Maura actually shuddered at the very idea. Davey was quick to take offence. Scraping his chair away from the table, he crossed the kitchen and jerked his jacket from the rack. 'If that's the way you feel about it, I'll not bother my ass inviting her back.' Avoiding his daughter's gaze, he bent over the child. 'Here, Danny, give Granda a big kiss before I go.'

The child looked from one to the other of them as if wondering what was going on, but dutifully lifted his face. 'Bye, Grandad.'

Davey walked slowly the short distance to McVeigh's. He was riddled with guilt. Should he cool things with Cassie? Heaven knew, he didn't want to. He looked forward with eager anticipation to his meetings with her, loved her company. Not once since the death of his wife thirteen years ago had he felt alive like this. Others had tried to get him interested but he had never encouraged their advances, never been tempted, until Cassie came along with her teasing ways and her sense of humour. They got on so well together; she had brought warmth and passion back into his life.

But his daughter . . . He had failed her once and he mustn't fail her again, even at the cost of his budding romance. The snag was that Cassie didn't want to let him go either and he dreaded hurting her. He was caught between the proverbial rock and a hard place.

Maura cleared the table and washed the dishes in glum silence. Danny sat on the kitchen floor and played with his cars, furtively glancing at her from time to time with big haunted eyes. He wished they could go home to Daddy and then everything would be all right, and his mummy would be happy. Suddenly becoming aware that the child was too quiet and was watching her, Maura swept him up in her arms and clutched him fiercely to her breast.

Winter or summer, Davcy always kept the grate set, ready to be lit, and although it was quite a warm evening Maura decided to get a fire going, help things look more cheerful. 'Let's light the fire, eh? I'll give you a bath in front of it. Would you like that?'

Uncomprehending – as, to his knowledge, the child had never been bathed in front of a fire – he nevertheless nodded in agreement. His mother was smiling again so he was happy in his own little mind.

Maura set the dry kindling alight and once the flames caught she brought coal in from the back and soon the fire was blazing away. Pleased that her father had not dumped the fireguard years ago, she now got it out of the shed, put it round the grate, then fetched all the paraphernalia needed to bathe her son. She spread his pyjamas on the fireguard and got the plastic bath ready. She then tested the water temperature before removing the child's clothes.

Danny was all excited and squirmed about as she lifted him into the bath. Never having been bathed like this before, he couldn't comprehend what was about to happen; all he knew was that he loved playing in water. Maura laughed at his excitement as she lowered him in to the tub, kicking his feet and creating a big splash. She told him to sit down and he did so with gusto, sloshing water everywhere with his slapping hands.

'Duck, Mammy, I want my duck.'

His duck was in the bathroom at home. Maura promised to buy him a new one next day and handed him a small plastic car to play with. After many minutes fooling about and spilling water, the child settled down and she shampooed his hair and bathed him. She had just stood him upright and wrapped the towel around him, lifting him protesting from the water and into her arms, when there was a knock on the door. She put a finger to her lips and shushed the child's animated chatter, hoping whoever it was would go away. Her dad had his own key so it wasn't him, and who else would come here at this time of night?

Although she was expecting another knock, she jerked in surprise when it was repeated, louder this time. Going into the hall, she cautiously approached the outer door.

'Who's there?'

'It's me . . . Francie Murphy.'

What on earth . . . Shifting the child on to one hip, she opened the door slightly and asked in a none too friendly tone, 'What do you want?'

Pretending not to notice her antagonism, he clapped a smile on his face and brought his hand into sight, clutching a bottle of Blue Nun wine and some crisps. 'Your dad sent these over. He said this is your favourite wine.'

Danny held out his hand and yelled, 'Crisps, crisps.'

She stood, firmly holding the door ajar and making no effort to invite him in. He said tersely,

'Well, are you going to ask me in? I can assure you my intentions are most honourable.'

She gave a tut-tut of annoyance but opened the door wide and turned away as he followed her inside. 'I wish me da would do as he's told. I'm not a child any more, I can look after myself,' she muttered ungraciously.

Setting the wine and crisps on an occasional table, Francie sat down without being asked. Danny was squirming to get down and Maura warned him to be still or he wouldn't get any crisps.

She sat down and towelled the child dry, then liberally dusted him with Johnson's baby powder before putting on his pyjamas and brushing his hair. Free from his mother's attentions, Danny ran to Francie and reached for the crisps. 'Crisps.'

'Say please.'

'Please . . .'

Francie held the crisps beyond Danny's reach and looked askance at Maura. When she nodded her consent, he let the child choose which packet he wanted and without further ado lifted him on to his lap.

'Pour yourself a glass of wine and I'll empty that bath before I go.'

Maura hesitated. Where would this end? She was lonely and he was apparently available. He had yet to mention a girlfriend. Reluctantly, she entered the scullery and came back with two glasses. 'Will you join me for one before you go?'

'I'd love to, thank you.'

Maura poured two glasses and handed him one. 'Cheers.'

'Cheers.'

Before the glass reached her lips, there was another knock at the door. Carefully placing the glass on the table, Maura looked at Francie, a question in her eyes. He shook his head and she said, 'It's not likely to be me da and Cassie, then?'

'No! Definitely not. They'll be in the bar till last orders.'

'Good.' The knock was repeated, louder this time, and she headed for the door.

Shock kept her gobsmacked when she saw who was standing there, the last person she would have expected to see tonight. Amazed at her reaction, Adam said quickly, 'Don't look so scared, Maura. You look as if you've seen a ghost. I only want to talk to you.' Fearing that she might close the door in his face, he pleaded, 'Please, I'd also like to see Danny.'

'I . . . it's not the right . . .'

Not wanting to alarm her, he was cautiously edging his way inside and once there was room enough in the hall to pass, he headed for the kitchen door.

'Adam . . . wait.'

Closing the outer door, she quickly followed him in a state of panic. She could imagine how the scene that met his eyes would look to Adam. Francie relaxed, and very much at home, lounging in the armchair, and Danny sprawled on his lap trying to feed him some crisps and giggling delightedly when Francie refused to open his mouth.

Maura sensed that Adam was beside himself with rage at the sight; his features were distorted with growing hatred as he took in the enormity of the happy family scene unfolding before him. Anger gushed up inside him, fighting for release. The sight of Francie Murphy taking his place so soon hurt him terribly.

However, the second the child saw his father, he scrambled down from Francie's lap and rushed to wrap his little arms round Adam's legs, screeching at the top of his voice in delight. 'Daddy . . . Daddy.'

Francie gingerly rose to his feet. In their amazement, both men stood gazing at each other, ready for whatever might develop. Adam was the first to slowly unwind. Scooping Danny up into his arms, he nodded at Francie. He was in control again; fighting must not take place in front of his son at any cost. 'This is nice and cosy. Mind if I join you?'

Francie met Maura's eyes and shrugged. 'That's up to Maura.'

Maura was in a quandary, not knowing which way to turn for the best. Francie saved her from having to say anything that might send them off on a tangent. 'If you're sure you'll be all right, I'll get back to the pub now. Your dad will be wondering what's keeping me.'

'Thanks, Francie. I'll be fine,' she assured him. 'Tell me da thanks for the wine and crisps.'

He nodded towards the bath. 'What about that?'

'Adam will take care of it for me.' She led him to the front door and he mouthed, 'Sure you'll be all right?'

She nodded. 'Goodnight, Francie, and thanks.'

'Night, Maura.'

Nuzzling his cheek in Danny's soft hair, Adam scrutinised his wife through hooded lids. He was obviously waiting for her to break the silence. She tried to outwait him but when she could bear it no longer, she hissed, 'Stop standing there like an eejit. Sit down. I'll put the teapot on.'

His eyes swept over the two glasses of wine. 'Pity to let that wine go to waste,' he said dryly. 'Or is it only reserved for special guests?'

'I assume you're driving, so you can forget all about the wine.'

Adam sat down and Danny snuggled against him, scowling at his mother, as if defying her to send Daddy away again. Adam hugged the child close, delighting at the feel of his body in his arms and the scent of baby talc and shampoo.

He was surprised at Maura moving on so quickly. But then, hadn't she always had warm feelings for Francie Murphy long before he had appeared on the scene? Adam realised that he had never once admitted to Maura that he loved her. Not once since they had first started going out together. No! Love had never entered into it. She had caught Adam on the rebound, become pregnant and they had got married: as simple as that. Everything had seemed to be working fine, that was until Evelyn had come back to the district.

In the scullery, Maura tried to avoid making undue noise as she prepared sandwiches and brewed a pot of tea. Her temper was on hold at the moment, so she treated the Delft and cutlery with the respect it deserved. She would not give Adam the satisfaction of knowing how upset she was by banging cups, plates and utensils about in anger. Why on earth had she offered Francie that glass of wine? She shouldn't have let him inside the house in the first place. Adam would be jumping to conclusions, thinking all sorts of dark thoughts, and she couldn't blame him. It had been such a cosy little scene to trespass on. But she wasn't going to do any apologising. No way! Let him think what he liked. She had done nothing to be ashamed of.

Sitting across the table from him, Maura nodded towards the sandwiches and said, 'I suppose you're hungry as usual, so tuck in. It's only cheese and onion, mind. I wasn't expecting any visitors,' putting emphasis on the 'any'.

Lowering Danny to the floor, he said gently, 'You sit there, son, and finish your crisps while I have something to eat.' He reached across and took a sandwich, catching Maura's eye as he did so. 'So Francie Murphy is now part of the family, is that what you're saying?'

'Don't be so ridiculous! I'm not saying anything of the sort. Francie and me da have always been good friends, as you well know.'

He sighed. 'Aye, I know that all right. That's why Davey never let me get a look in. I spoiled your chances with his bosom buddy, Francie.'

'Now you're talking rubbish.'

Adam raised a quizzical eyebrow. 'Am I?'

He finished the sandwich and reached for another, all the while trying to think how to explain the true reason for his late visit. He had come prepared to do all in his power to persuade Maura into trusting him, but the sight of Francie Murphy with his son soon put paid to that idea. All the eloquent speeches he had lined up in his mind had now flown out the window. 'These sandwiches are lovely,' he muttered.

'I hope you're eating properly.'

'I get enough to do me.'

Maura's eyes ranged over him suspiciously. 'Surely *she* feeds you.'

'You mean Evelyn. Certainly she does. She gives Jackie and me plenty of tea and sweet stuff during the day.'

'And your main meal of the day? Does she cook that?'

'Why should she? Look, for the umpteenth time, there's nothing going on between us.' At her look of scorn he stressed, 'Honestly, Maura. And why should she feed me? It's purely and simply a business relationship between us: her calling the shots and paying the bills and me doing the graft. Nothing more, nothing less.' Still she looked unconvinced. 'Ach, think what you like. There's nothing I can say that will convince you.'

Before he could draw breath for the next word, Maura thumped the table with her fist and almost screamed at him, 'How the hell can you sit there and expect me to believe you? I know how much you loved that woman, so don't try to tell me otherwise. You're so bewitched by her that she's got you wrapped round her little finger.'

Hearing the anger in his mother's raised voice, Danny began whimpering, eyes wide with fear and staring up at her.

Adam was taken aback by her sudden outburst. Patting his son gently on the head and saying, 'There, there, son,' he replied, 'I suppose it salves your conscience to think I'm carrying on, now that you have someone else around to offer comfort.'

Lowering her voice to a menacing hiss, she stabbed her finger in his direction. 'Listen, you . . . Francie and I are friends from way back. I have no designs on him, nor him on me, so get that into your thick skull.'

His head tilted back, with that arrogant look of disdain she so hated on his face. 'Why are you so angry then, hmm?'

'I . . .' She stopped in her tracks, her tongue stilled. A puzzled look crossed her face. 'Do you know something? I don't know why I'm angry. I've done nothing to be ashamed of.'

'There you go then. In that case, no need to lose your cool.' He dusted crumbs from his hands on to the empty plate and reached for the mug of tea, cradling it in his palms.

She scowled. 'Can I get you anything else?'

He drained the mug and tousled Danny's hair. 'No thank you. That was lovely, so it was. This wee fellow can't keep his eyes open. All that crying has made him sleepy. Can I take him up to bed?'

'Sure.' She led the way and watched him lay his son gently in his cot and cover him with the blanket. 'He's asleep already, so he is, God love him.'

Adam reluctantly turned from the cot. 'He's starting to stretch, isn't he? It won't be long before he needs a bed.'

Maura faced her husband, and although dreading his reply, she had to ask, 'Why did you come here tonight? I'll have the devil of a job explaining to your son why you're not here in the morning.'

His eyes scanned the single bed. 'It would be a bit of a crush, but it could be arranged for me to be here in the morning.'

Her jaw dropped. She snapped it shut. 'You're right. It would be too much of a crush.' How dare he think he could use her at the drop of a hat?

She moved out on to the landing. Adam followed her and gripped her arm. 'Look, Maura, we can't go on like this. I miss Danny something awful.'

No mention of missing her, she noted, but then how could he with the beautiful Evelyn Matthews in tow? 'I know. I do realise that you must miss him.'

He deserved to see his son. At the bottom of the stairs she turned and faced him. 'If you like you can pick him up on your way home on Friday and bring him back Saturday teatime.'

To say Adam was surprised was putting it mildly. She wanted her son out of the way. The very thought of her with Francie Murphy filled him with revulsion.

Face like granite, lips in a straight line, he grabbed his coat, shrugging his arms into it as he headed for the door. 'That'll be fine. I'll see you on Friday evening then. Goodnight.'

Mindful of the sleeping child, Adam closed the outer door gently and strode to where his van was parked. He'd had many persuasive plans prepared to encourage her to give him another chance, but obviously she wasn't interested any more. She had already moved on. Had she ever really cared for him? His thoughts were bleak as he drove home to an empty house.

Maura stood in a daze staring at the door. She had expected Adam to be overjoyed and jump at the chance of having Danny overnight. What was wrong with the man? Perhaps it would interfere with plans he had already made with Evelyn in mind. Well, he would just have to go with the flow this weekend and decide what he wanted to do for the future. He was right! They couldn't go on like this.

Her eye fell on the bath, the water now cold with a scum on top. So much for chivalry. She would have to empty it herself. In spite of the care she took when she started to lift the bath, it tipped over, drenching the rug and floor around it. Falling to her knees she wept long and hard, but she knew it wasn't because of the spilled water. No! It went deeper than that, much deeper. It was the sound of revellers leaving the pub that brought her to her senses. She quickly cleared up and had just reached the sanctuary of her bedroom when she heard her father returning.

12

Davey crept stealthily about the scullery as he prepared his breakfast and got ready for work. He had been surprised to find that Maura had retired to bed when he got back the previous night, especially since Francie had told him that Adam had called at the house, at which Francie had excused himself and left them to it. Davey had hoped that a reconciliation was about to take place and had worked himself up to eat humble pie if necessary. However, it didn't look as if a reconciliation was on the cards. If only it did, he'd do all in his power to encourage it.

He could feel the depth of Maura's anguish and would do his utmost to make Adam welcome this time round; that is, if he would only let him. Given the circumstances, Adam was quite justified to distance himself from Davey; how he must despise him. He had every right to walk away in disgust from such an obnoxious creature as himself. He paused in thought: maybe Adam was up there with her now. Wouldn't that be great? He listened anxiously for some seconds before recalling that the van had not been parked outside last night. In case, in his inebriated state, he hadn't noticed it, he went to the window and looked out, confirming that there was no sign of it.

He also found dirty dishes in the sink, something he couldn't remember Maura ever doing. She must be really upset to be so neglectful. Still, if she didn't broach the subject about what was upsetting her, he wouldn't mention it. He nodded smugly in agreement with himself. He wouldn't say a dicky bird, leave the two of them to sort it out between themselves, in case he put his big foot in it . . . again.

The night before, Maura had stood for ages gazing out over the dark lough from her bedroom window. She had been trying to distinguish that part of the County Down coastline that was now a string of lights reflected in the calm water, where their house stood over in Holywood, hoping that Adam was at home and as downhearted as she was at this moment and not indulging himself with Evelyn Matthews. She had stood trying to make up her troubled mind as to what she must do for the best.

If only she had stayed put and let things take their course, before making a move. But oh no! Not the headstrong Mrs Maura Brady! Impetuous as ever, she had to rush straight over here and into the spotlight where everybody felt sorry for her. She was beginning to despair at the few options now open to her. Tired in body and soul, she had eventually thrown herself on top of the bed exhausted, without troubling herself to turn back the sheets, and fell into a shallow, fitful sleep.

She awoke none the wiser and lay quietly listening to the muted sounds coming from the scullery below as her father busied himself getting ready for work. At last she heard the metallic click of the Yale lock as he closed the front door on his way out. As soon as he had gone, Maura descended the stairs to prepare breakfast for Danny and examine the rug. In her haste to get upstairs last night she had been unable to do much about the damage caused by the spilled bathwater. To her relief, the rug wasn't as bad as she had anticipated and she thought it would probably dry out all right. As she made to roll it up to hang outside, a cry of distress brought her racing back upstairs to find Danny standing in his cot, great sobs shaking his slight frame.

Lifting him into her arms, Maura shushed and hugged him in an effort to quell his tears. 'Don't, love. Please don't cry. It'll be all right.' As if she didn't know his wee heart was breaking.

Sobs were making his words incoherent, but she understood what he was saying, over and over again. 'I want my daddy. Where's my daddy?'

'Listen, Danny, your daddy will be coming on Friday to take you home for a day or two. Won't that be nice?'

Arms and legs were flailing as he fought to escape her hold while she lowered him to the ground, and still he kicked out, catching her across the shin. Holding him at arm's length she chastised him. 'That hurt, Danny. There'll be no more tantrums from you, my boy, if you know what's good for you. Do you hear me? If you don't stop this instant, I'll put you back in your cot and you'll stay there till you behave yourself.'

At this threat he slumped to the floor in defeat, but continued to wail, 'I want my daddy. Please, Mammy, take me home. I want to go home,' his words punctuated with hiccups.

Tears and snot ran down the child's face and as she wiped them away Maura felt as if her heart would burst. What on earth was she going to do? Her nerves were shattered. If this goes on any longer, she thought, both of us will be ill. It took some time to pacify him before she could bring him downstairs for his breakfast and get him ready for the road. Perhaps being outside away from the strange environment of the house would settle him down. Soon his tantrums had taken their toll on him and he crept wearily on to the sofa where he dozed off.

Taking advantage of the lull, Maura had a wash and got dressed. She spent a long time in front of her dressing table, trying to camouflage the dark shadows under her eyes with make-up, without much success. Downstairs she tidied up the kitchen and scullery. Hanging the damp rug on the outside clothes line to dry in the sunshine, she turned and was surprised to see Danny watching her from the back door. He still looked weepy and downcast. She said gaily, 'How's about us going over to the shop and buying you that duck I promised?'

He thought about it for some moments, then shook his head. 'Will Daddy come for us soon?'

Taking him by the hand, she led him back to the sofa and sat beside him to explain. 'Your daddy has to work away from home for a while and it's better if we stay here with Grandad until he's finished the job he's working on. He will come here every Friday and take you home with him and then he'll bring you back to me on Saturday. You'll have a great time with your daddy every weekend.'

But what about herself? How would she fill in the void, she silently lamented, while Danny was with his father?

The ever-ready tears welled up in Danny's eyes again and he wailed, 'No, I want to go home now.'

Maura raised her eyes. 'Sweet Jesus, give me patience,' she prayed.

Maura knew it would be fruitless taking her son to the local shops as he would attract too much attention, the state he was in. So to avoid running into anyone she knew, Maura decided to go into town and do a bit of shopping there. She had little money left and was reluctant to approach her father for the cash she had already spent on food for the house, but she would have to, eventually. And she would need to come to some kind of financial arrangement with Adam. If only he hadn't run off in a huff last night, they could have at least sorted out her financial situation. After all, he was still her husband and therefore duty bound to support her and their son.

A knock on the door sent her to the window to look out through the net curtains. Her Aunt Hilda was standing there. What on earth had brought her to the house?

Maura practised a welcoming smile in the hall mirror before opening the door. 'Hello, Aunt Hilda. Nice to see you. And to what do we owe this surprise?'

'I heard you were back and thought I'd drop in to see how you're keeping.'

Maura smiled wryly. 'Not as well as I'd like to, but I'll survive. Take off your coat and sit down. I'll make us a nice wee cuppa tea.'

She headed for the scullery while Hilda removed her coat and hung it on the rack in the hall before going into the kitchen.

Danny didn't recognise her. Seeing how he looked, she approached him cautiously. 'Hello, Danny.' Noting that the child was dressed for outdoors and that he had obviously been crying, she hailed Maura. 'No need to make tea if you're on your way out, Maura.'

Maura responded straight away. 'No, stay there, please. I want to have a wee chat with you. You just might be able to wash my blues away.'

Hilda hoped so, and sat down on the sofa to wait and see what her niece had on her mind.

Removing Danny's coat, Maura settled him down with a couple of Marie biscuits and a plastic beaker of milk to pacify him, while she spoke to her aunt. Sitting beside Hilda, she said, 'I'm glad you called. I need someone to talk to, someone I can trust and who won't discuss my affairs with anyone.' She stressed the word 'anyone' and Hilda rose to the bait.

'If you mean my Dennis, I promise not to repeat a word you say, not even to him.'

Maura cleared her throat and her voice trembled. 'Good! It looks as if I'll be staying here for some time to come. Adam will of course support us but I'll go round the bend if I have to stay here day in and day out. It'll be like being locked up in

252

Armagh jail. I don't suppose you know of any jobs on the go?'

When Maura had left school at fourteen, she had worked in a clothes shop in the city centre, refusing her father's pleas to further her education by going to St Dominic's College. However, Davey had been adamant that she should at least go to evening classes at Belfast College of Technology to learn typing and bookkeeping, so she had enrolled in the college for a business study course and attended three evenings a week. She soon discovered that she liked going there and without much bother had passed her exams. Apparently she was cleverer than she thought. Eventually she had obtained a job as a shorthand typist in a firm of solicitors on High Street. There she remained until she fell pregnant to Adam Brady. When her condition became too apparent she had left and had not worked since.

Hilda was sceptical. She pursed her lips and said, 'I think you'll find it hard to get an office job, Maura. You were a foolish girl, you know. You could have been a private secretary by now. You had all the qualifications. You certainly won't walk into an office job, that's for sure.' She paused for thought. 'You might be lucky enough to find something to suit your talents in that building firm down near Doagh Road. You know . . .'

Maura threw back her head and laughed out

loud. 'Oh, no. I don't expect anything as grand as that. Far from it. I meant in a shop or even a wee cleaning job. You see, I'll need someone to look after Danny, so I could only take on part-time work, that is, until he's up a bit and starting school.'

Cleaning! All that talent wasted. Hilda prayed that her two daughters had more sense. 'It's as bad as that, then?' she said.

'Exactly! As bad as that.' Maura bowed her head. Guessing what her aunt was thinking and not wanting a lecture on her morals, she said, 'I'd rather not talk about it if you don't mind.'

'OK, if that's what you want. But by a strange coincidence, I'm on the lookout for a job myself. You know, now the girls are at Stella Maris School I'm at a bit of a loose end.' Hilda paused, her brow furrowed in deep thought, and Maura sat quiet, sensing something was coming. She wasn't disappointed. Hilda continued in a diffident tone, 'Why don't we share?'

'I don't understand, share what?' Maura had heard of married women sharing jobs, but as far as she knew they already worked for the company and when their maternity leave was up they were offered part-time employment, sharing with someone who wanted shorter hours. Where would she fit in? She was utterly confused. 'Where would we get that kind of work, Aunt Hilda?'

Hilda gripped her hand. 'I don't mean that. I

mean you get a job and I'll look after Danny for you. Mind, I wouldn't ask a lot, just a little pin money.'

Maura's eyes widened as she mulled over the implications. It would be the ideal solution. She could trust Hilda to look after Danny, not worry about leaving him with a stranger. Now she returned Hilda's grasp. 'Thanks, Hilda. That's a brilliant idea. Now let's see if we can find me a job.'

Hilda smiled her pleasure and confided, 'Well, I hear Stewart's are looking for a Saturday worker if that's any good to you?'

Maura's eyes widened. 'As in Stewart's Cash Stores across the road?'

'The very same.'

Maura drained her cup and reached for Hilda's empty one.

'What are we waiting for? Let's see if I can get fixed up for this weekend.'

Maura was in luck. She had worked in Stewart's when she was studying at Belfast Tech in her teen days and the manager remembered her. He said the job was hers and she could start next Saturday morning, eight-thirty sharp.

Her visit into the city centre did nothing to raise her spirits. With very little money to spend, she had to watch the pennies. A yellow plastic duck was at the top of her list of priorities. A milk shake and a gingerbread man for Danny, and a cup of coffee and a doughnut for herself were next on the list. This treat usually made her day, but at the moment nothing could lift the gloom that had settled on her.

Not wanting to go back to an empty house, she spent some time window-shopping along Royal Avenue, then going through to Smithfield Market and meandering round the stalls for an hour or so. Normally she enjoyed this, stopping here to examine bits of jewellery, then browsing through the second-hand records and books, going there to ask the price of a certain piece of china and in the end buying nothing. All good fun, which on better days she gained a certain buzz from and put her in a better frame of mind, but not today; today she was too depressed. Even the fact that she had got the Saturday job in Stewart's had not helped matters.

At last she headed along Gresham Street towards Shepherd's Dairies at the bottom of North Street, but couldn't pass the pet shop without Danny wanting to look in at all the rabbits and tortoises, canaries and budgies, puppies and kittens and of course the aquarium full of brightly coloured tropical fish. She had to practically drag him out of the pet shop and along to Shepherd's Dairies where she bought some groceries. Careful to keep enough money for her bus fare, she then boarded a number ten bus outside the public library on Royal Avenue and headed back to Greencastle, still in the doldrums.

That evening as they sat round the table eating dinner, Maura related all the day's events to her father, starting with the visit from Aunt Hilda, the new job in Stewart's, and finishing with her exped-ition into town, but she couldn't bring herself round to discuss the subject of housekeeping money. She found it too embarrassing, not wanting to sound as if she was begging for money from her father.

'I suppose you'll want me to look after the wee fellah while you're at work, eh?' he said, in a matter-of-fact way.

'Oh no, Da. I wouldn't impose on you like that, especially on a Saturday. Aunt Hilda has already agreed to do that. You still follow Glentoran, don't you?'

'I sure do. Hail, rain or snow, me and Francie will be at the Oval shouting on the Glens.' He smiled as if remembering something amusing. 'But the football season's finished till August. Mind you, they'll be playing some friendlies in the run-up to the start of the new season. But if I can help out in any way, be sure you let me know, OK? Anyway, enough said about me, what does Adam have to say about you going out to work again?'

'He doesn't know yet, but I'll tell him when he comes to pick up Danny. Somehow or other I don't think he'll be best pleased, Da, but that's the least of my worries right now.'

'Well, if you want me to stay in on Friday, I'll be too happy to oblige, until he goes away,' he said with a little chuckle. 'As a kind of arbitrator, that is.'

Maura had to smile at the idea of her father's intentions. 'I don't think there'll be any need for that. He might do a bit of sounding off, but he wouldn't raise a hand to me.'

'I hope not! But there's always a first time for everything. And if he does get rough with you, I'll make sure he'll regret ever meeting you,' her father replied, his words dripping with menace.

On Friday, Danny was subdued as he waited for his dad to come for him. Maura had tried to explain to the bewildered child why she wasn't going with them but of course he couldn't understand. Davey had made himself scarce, hoping that if he wasn't around Adam might persuade Maura to go home with them. It broke his heart to see his daughter so unhappy.

Adam cringed with shame when he saw the state of Maura. To say she looked haggard was putting it mildly. This would never do. He would have to spell it out to Benny and get him to take him off that job. That is, if his wife agreed to come home. He scooped Danny up into his arms and the child huddled close. Before Adam could open his mouth to speak, Maura beat him to the punch.

She had seen the look in his eyes when he came in and to his surprise she said, 'Don't you dare pity me, Adam Brady.'

'There you go again, jumping the gun as usual, letting your pride get the better of you. And what makes you so sure I pity you?'

She straightened to her full height. 'And don't you patronise me either. I'm sick, sore and tired of being on the receiving end of all this pity. It's like getting condolence cards.'

Bidding his son to remain quiet, Adam set him down on the sofa and tentatively approached his wife. Head bowed, Maura waited, fiercely willing him to take her in his arms and tell her that he loved her and wanted to take her home, that he needed her.

Adam, afraid of outright rejection, hovered near but made no effort to reach out to her. He didn't want to antagonise her. 'Listen, Maura. This can't go on, we have to sort it out once and for all. You're becoming paranoid. Tell me, how will you manage?'

Maura's heart bled. He couldn't even bear to touch her; Evelyn Matthews must be really in control. Raising her chin she bellowed, 'Don't you kid yourself for one minute that I can't manage without you. I've already got myself a Saturday job in Stewart's across the road and I've no doubt that I'll get proper employment in time. I'm not thick, you know.'

'You're going out to work?' Adam sounded aghast.

'And why not?'

'What about Danny? Who's going to look after him?'

'You'll have him on Saturdays for a start. When I get a part-time job Aunt Hilda is going to look after him during the week.'

'You're not wasting any time. I forbid you to go out to work. Do you hear me? The boy's upset enough as it is without you leaving him for hours on end with someone he hardly knows.'

'This might come as a surprise to you, Adam Brady . . . You might have green fingers, but even you can't make money grow on trees round here. I haven't any cash left and I have no intentions of sponging on my da indefinitely.'

He looked horrified. 'Good God, I never thought. Why didn't you say? Do you think I'm a bloody mind-reader? But don't you worry, I'll look after you and Danny financially.'

'Even you must have known that I would be short of money. Your mind's so preoccupied with *her* that you can't think straight any more.'

'You'll have no need to work. What kind of a man do you take me for?'

As their voices rose, Danny started to whimper. Frustrated, Adam turned to the child. 'It's all right, love. Come on. Let's get you out of this madhouse.'

The child scrambled down from the sofa and ran to him. Lifting him up in his arms, Adam threw a contemptuous glance at his wife. 'I'll bring him back tomorrow around teatime. We'll sort this out then. It'll be better if your father isn't here . . . but that's up to you.'

Without a further glance he left the house. Maura watched him strap Danny into the passenger seat of the van. The child's face was crumpled with bewilderment as he gazed back at the window. Lifting the nets, Maura gave him a smile and a big wave as the van pulled away from the door; the tears that flowed so easily these days threatened to fall yet again. She fought them back and grabbing her coat left the house. She must not wallow in self-pity and start weeping or her face would be puffed up and red-eyed. She would soon be so ugly that she'd be ashamed to go out altogether.

Davey was talking to Tommy Stewart outside the newsagent, waiting until Adam had left before going back over. Davey saw him eventually go and could see that all was not well with his son-in-law. There was no sign of Maura and Adam's face was like thunder as he strapped Danny in the van and drove off.

Then Maura came out and, bidding Tommy a hasty goodbye, Davey hurried across the road.

In her despair Maura didn't notice him and would have passed him by had he not gripped her arm to get her attention. 'Here, now. What's the big hurry, love?'

She looked blindly at him, then shook her head as if to clear it. 'Sorry, Da, I forgot all about you. Your dinner's in the oven. I'll be back soon.' And pulling free from his restraining hand she blundered off down the road in the direction of Whitehouse.

Davey watched her go, debating whether or not to follow. He decided against it. His daughter obviously didn't want any company at the moment. With a weary sigh he headed home to his belated dinner.

Maura's headlong gallop brought her past Barbour's mill and on into Merville Garden Village. She found herself gazing blindly into the shop windows, wondering how on earth she had got there. A gentle pat on her arm startled her, jolting her out of her reverie, and she turned to look into the concerned face of Annie Devlin.

'I've been down to see Dr Canavan and I've arranged for Sean to pick me up outside the chemist here. Are you all right, Maura?'

'I think so. I just need some time to think.'

Annie thought she looked far from being all right. In fact, if the truth be told, she'd say Maura was very ill, but she respected Maura's privacy. 'Are you waiting till it's time for your appointment at the doctor's?' she probed in an effort to get Maura talking.

'No. No, I've just been out for a wee walk along the road.'

Annie hid her bemusement and, as a car drew up to the kerb, said, 'Here's Sean now. Can we give you a lift back?'

Maura had now regained her senses and answered gratefully, 'That would be nice, if you're sure Sean won't mind.'

Sean assured her it was no trouble. Maura climbed into the back seat and in no time at all the car pulled up outside her father's house.

'Thanks very much for the lift, Sean. I'm obliged to you.'

Before she got out of the car Annie caught her eye and said earnestly, 'If you ever need an ear, Maura, pop up any time you feel like it. Mine is always available . . . and I know how to keep my mouth shut.'

'I'll remember that, Annie, thanks.'

Her father had finished his dinner and had washed the dishes and put them away. Maura stared round the clean scullery and tidy kitchen. 'You must have been busy, Da. Thanks, but you shouldn't have. I'd have been only too happy to clear up.'

'What happened, Maura? You looked terribly upset.'

'All my own fault, Da. Self-inflicted! Adam couldn't get a good word in edgeways with all my ranting and raving, so he just took off with the child to get away from me. But we had already arranged it anyway. He's bringing him back tomorrow evening. Meanwhile, I must get ready for my new job.'

'I'd forgotten that you were starting across the road tomorrow. What are you doing tonight?'

'Like I said, getting ready.'

'Come along to the pub with me and Cassie.'

'No, Da, I don't feel like talking to anyone at the moment.'

'Well, I'm not going to leave you here on your own to mope. I'll bring Cassie down.'

'No, Da. If I'm going anywhere, I'll go up and see Aunt Hilda. Will that satisfy you?'

Still unsure, Davey dithered. 'Well then, I'll not be late.'

'Be as late as you like, Da. I'm a big girl now and I can be trusted on my own.'

13

Determined there would be no more tears, and to take her mind off her husband and son and what they might be getting up to, Maura shampooed her hair. Half filling the plastic bath with warm water from the immersion heater and adding a substantial sprinkling of bath salts, she had a good wash down in the locked scullery. She had never known any difference while growing up, had never minded scraping her elbows on the scullery wall or trying not to splash too much water on the floor. Now she knew what she was missing out on and longed for the luxury of a proper bathroom. Just to lie soaking for a half-hour in hot perfumed water would be divine.

She brushed her hair until it shone, and put on a little make-up to add colour to her pale complexion, which made her feel more confident to face whatever the outside world threw her way. Although she could find plenty to do in the house, she couldn't bring herself round to start cleaning bedrooms or washing out cupboards. She was too restless to stay in to do these mundane chores. On the spur of the moment she decided she would get ready and go for a dander. It was a lovely evening and a leisurely walk up Gray's Lane and along the Antrim Road would be just the job to blow away the cobwebs. It would be nice viewing the big houses on a fine evening like this, give her an idea of what she was up against. Dressed for comfort in a pair of slacks that were still respectable for outside wear, but not for socialising in, a fine wool sweater and flat shoes, all topped with a lightweight jacket, she was ready for the off. She was locking the front door when she became aware of another presence. Looking over her shoulder she saw Francie Murphy, who had come up the road and was standing a short distance away watching her.

Before she could speak he approached and held out a small twig that looked as if it had been cut from a laurel bush or similar, offering it to her. A puzzled expression crept over her face as she gazed at it. Her eyes met his.

'What's this and what am I supposed to do with it?' She giggled.

'Receive it in the manner it's given. It's a poor

man's olive branch. I apologise for hanging around too long the other night. If I'd just minded my own business and left when it was obvious that you didn't want me to stay, you and Adam might have made up your differences and you would be safely home in Holywood by now.' His shoulders rose in a resigned shrug. 'My intentions were good but, with hindsight, bloody stupid, if you'll pardon my French. I should have given you the wine and crisps, and gone straight back to the pub.'

She handled the twig and said dryly, 'I accept this olive branch, although there's absolutely no need for it. You did nothing wrong. Who would have dreamed that my husband would decide to visit? Certainly not me.' She emitted a sigh and dropped the twig into her handbag. 'I suppose my da has sent you on yet another errand of mercy?'

He laughed. 'You know him only too well. He did, as a matter of fact, say that maybe I could persuade you to come down to the pub for a couple of hours. You can't sit in on your own on a Friday night, Maura,' he cajoled, looking hopefully at her. 'Your da's very worried about you, you know.'

'Just tell him that you met me on my way out, and I didn't say where I was going. That should intrigue him and stave off any more questions. What you don't know you can't tell.'

A quick glance at her attire made him curious. 'If I may be so cheeky to ask, where are you going?'

'For a walk, Nosy.'

'Alone?'

She laughed without humour. 'Do you see anyone else about?'

He smiled in return. 'No, but you might be meeting someone. Are you?'

'No, I'm not. Do you remember Greta Garbo's famous quote in *Grand Hotel*? Well, that's me. *I want to be alone. I just want to be alone.*'

'Very funny! You can't really want to be alone. It's not natural. Come down to the pub, Maura. At least you'll have plenty of company there and the craic's good.'

'No, thank you. I'm not dressed for the pub, as you have already noticed. And for goodness' sake stop worrying about me. I can look after myself and I can do without company at the moment, thank you. Forget about me! Good evening to you, Francie. Away back to McVeigh's and enjoy yourself.'

As she turned to go, he said on impulse, 'At least let me come with you.' She hesitated, and he immediately moved closer. 'Please.'

For a moment she had considered letting him tag along but at his nearness she had second thoughts. It would be too risky. 'No, my life is complicated enough right now, Francie, without you getting involved. Even so, you'd be bored stiff, I don't feel like talking to anybody just now.'

She started to walk and he fell into step with her. From the corner of his eye he saw the sad droop to her mouth and muttered, 'I wish I could do something to cheer you up, Maura. I feel so useless not being able to help.'

'Why? I'm no concern of yours. I've made my bed and now I must lie on it. I'll get it sorted out eventually, one way or other.'

'I don't like the idea of you walking on your own.'

A short sharp bark that was supposed to be a laugh escaped her lips. 'I've walked alone many a time when I lived here. I know this district like the back of my hand and I know most people around here.'

'Look, why not let me take you to the Troxy?'

This gave her pause for thought and she hesitated as she mulled over his invitation. It was a good idea. She didn't really want to walk, especially on her own, and they wouldn't have to talk much in the cinema. 'Why not! I'd enjoy that. It's a long time since I've been to the pictures. Is there anything good on?'

'A musical, with one of your favourite actresses, if I remember rightly.' A grin creased his face and he quickened his step; the Troxy was a short distance along the Shore Road. He glanced at his watch. 'We had better hurry or we'll miss the start of the big picture.'

A look in each direction showed that the road was clear. Taking her by the arm, he raced her across. Still holding her arm, he hurried her along Shore Road to the Troxy cinema and up the steps into the foyer, congratulating himself on coming up with such a brilliant idea.

They got in just as the lights were dimming for the start of the film. There weren't many patrons in the back stalls, probably because of the good weather, and they chose two seats near the back. Francie helped her off with her jacket and she settled in her seat and relaxed. It was a musical. *By the Light of the Silvery Moon* starring Doris Day and Gordon MacRae. They had both seen it when it had first been released some years ago but Maura was glad just to sit in the peaceful, dark surroundings and let the pleasant music wash over her. The tension of the long day ebbed from her body and she had difficulty keeping her eyes open. She closed them, just for a minute or two, to rest them.

Next thing she knew, Francie was gently shaking her by the shoulder, whispering in her ear that the film was almost over. She glanced around her in confusion, aware that his arm was around her and she was close against his body.

Digging her elbow viciously into his side brought a wince of pain from him as she shrugged herself free, exclaiming in high-pitched tones, 'What on earth do you think you're doing?'

People were struggling into their coats, and some of those in front of them were glancing over their shoulders to see what the commotion was about. Francie was glad the darkness hid his blushes. He must look as guilty as sin as he fumed with indignation; he certainly felt so.

'I wasn't doing anything, Maura,' he hissed. 'You fell asleep and laid your head on my shoulder. I just made you comfortable. That's all there was to it. Now I wish I hadn't bothered.' The credits started rolling on the screen and he said abruptly, 'Come on, let's get out of here before the lights go up. I hope no one recognises me.'

There was every chance that someone they knew would be there, and he didn't want people to think that he was a fly man chasing after a married woman.

The walk back was conducted in a stony silence. Maura knew she had offended him, but couldn't find the right words to fit an apology. Francie sulked, resentful that Maura didn't trust him. What on earth did she think he was doing? Worse still, what would those around them in the cinema think he was up to? They'd think he was chancing his arm. He cringed inwardly at the idea.

Tentatively, Maura tried to make amends. 'I'm sorry, Francie. It was just waking up like that. For a while back there I couldn't remember where I was. I felt a bit frightened.'

271

He smiled grimly. 'Did you see those heads in front of us crane round? They'll think I was up to no good to deserve an outburst like that.'

She hung her head in shame. 'I know it sounded bad. I'm sorry. What else can I say?'

'Did you see anyone there you knew?'

'No.' She was bemused. 'Why, would it matter if I did?'

He shrugged. 'I don't want Adam Brady coming after me with a pickaxe handle, should he somehow get wind of it. You know damned well he's not too keen on me.'

'Yes, I certainly do.'

She could now understand Francie's concern. Adam could work himself into a right old temper at times, especially if Francie Murphy was involved, no matter how innocent the situation might be.

'I really am sorry, Francie. Is there anything I can do to make amends?'

They had arrived at her father's house. Francie warmed to her again. 'If I ask you to go to the pub for last orders, would you think that I was pressurising you?'

Glad he wasn't going to hold a grudge, she smiled. 'Well now . . . I don't know about that.' She glanced down at her clothes. 'I'm not really dressed for socialising, as you are aware. But maybe if you twist my arm, who knows?'

'You'd look lovely in rags.'

His eyes were appreciative and she said, 'All right, let's go.'

He refrained from touching her as he urged her along the short distance to the pub. 'I hope we haven't missed last orders.'

Inside McVeigh's, Maura was hesitant, wishing she had not allowed herself to be coerced into coming, especially in her old clothes. However, it was too late for second thoughts. She would just have to grin and bear it.

Still feeling nervous, she climbed the stairs ahead of Francie in silence. The instant they came through the door of the lounge, Davey was on his feet and beckoning them over. A great big grin spreading over his face, he said, 'Glad you could make it, Maura.' He pulled a spare chair from another table and motioned Francie to do likewise.

As she crossed the room Maura returned a smile here, a nod there. No one stopped her to pry into her affairs and she suddenly realised how stupid she was being to keep these friendly people at bay. She was being stupid with herself. It was all in her mind. She had known most of them all her life and they were just that: friendly and obliging. Bar the odd few who couldn't find a nice word to say about anyone, even if they tried. Cassie looked a bit apprehensive as Maura approached but willingly moved to make room for the extra chairs.

Last orders had already been called and her da and Francie went to the bar.

Maura still had the olive branch in her handbag and considered offering it to Cassie but her courage failed her. She broke the silence between them by asking her if she liked Doris Day and they were still gabbling away about films when the men came back from the bar.

Davey and Francie had each bought a round of drinks and Maura resigned herself to being at least an hour in the pub by the time her da finished two and a half pints of Guinness, maybe longer. The drink Cassie had already consumed had mellowed her defences and she was easygoing, but Maura found she had little in common with her and conversation became strained. Davey still had a full pint of Guinness on the table and Cassie a half of lager when Maura downed the dregs of her second Pernod. To her surprise, Francie gulped down the last of his lager and rose to his feet.

'If you don't mind, I'll see Maura home now. She has to prepare for her stint in Stewart's tomorrow. So we'll leave you to it. Goodnight.'

He was holding out Maura's jacket. Thankfully she rose and slipped her arms into the sleeves. 'Goodnight, Cassie. Thanks for asking me to join you. I'll see you in the morning, Da.'

Outside the pub Maura turned to Francie. 'Thanks. That was very thoughtful of you.'

'Well, your father will linger another hour over that pint, and I thought you wouldn't want that.'

'No, we were running out of things to talk about. Thank you for a lovely evening. It was kind of you. Goodnight, Francie.'

'I'll walk you to the door.'

'There's no need.'

He raised his hands, palms out defensively. 'OK. I get the message, I promise to behave, but I'll still walk you to the door.'

Her steps were reluctant as they approached the house. She hoped he wouldn't prove awkward. Just in case, she had no intention of asking him in. At the door he took hold of her by the shoulders. 'Goodnight, Maura.'

He meant to give her a peck on the cheek, but big haunted eyes gazed at him and he thought he saw longing there. Throwing caution to the winds, his lips met hers and were accepted; the kiss was long and satisfying.

At last she pushed him away and muttered, 'No . . . I can't . . .'

He released her slowly. 'I understand, goodnight, love.'

Saturday morning began with a drizzle, but there were blue patches visible between pewter clouds and that was promising. Maura was glad that she just had to scoot across the road to her place of work and shortly before half past eight she was in the shop ready for business. She was met by the store manager, Mr Johnston, who welcomed her with a smile and a comment on the weather. She already knew the other girls by sight and they were friendly towards her. The young man who did the donkey work – like hauling sacks of potatoes and boxes of fruit and vegetables outside, and setting up the stalls under the awnings to display a large variety of soft goods – was pleasant enough.

At first business was slow, but once the rain had eased off they were kept on the go. They staggered their tea breaks at mid-morning and then at lunch-time so that the customer service was continuous, and the time flew.

When Mr Johnston handed Maura her pay packet at the end of the working day he congratulated her on her work rate and asked her whether she could work on Wednesday as one of the other girls was going to a wedding. Wednesday being only a half-day opening, Maura was only too happy to oblige. She crossed the road tired but relatively contented; at last she had money in her purse.

There was no sign of her father but an envelope with her name on was propped in front of the clock on the mantelpiece. Inside was more money and a note apologising for not giving her the housekeeping money sooner. It never rains but it pours, she mused. He also wrote that he would stay out till late and not to worry about making him any supper.

Maura went to great lengths over her general appearance for Adam coming while scorning herself for doing so. She could never reach Evelyn Matthews' standards of beauty, but she would at least be presentable. She watched for the van and when it drew up outside she was out on the pavement to greet her son. Adam gave her a curt nod and when he lifted Danny down from the van the child gave a delighted whoop and raced to his mother.

Maura lifted him up in her arms and he buried his face in her neck. Over the top of his head she eyed Adam. 'How did he do?'

'As well as can be expected, I suppose. He kept asking for you.'

Maura was glad to hear that Danny had missed her. 'But he did settle down?'

'Oh, yes. I bathed him and he tried to tell me about the small bath Grandad had.' Adam smiled fondly at the recollection. 'He's coming on well at the talking. He slept in bed with me last night. I hope you don't mind?'

'No, but don't make a habit of it. I want him to be independent.'

Adam nodded his agreement. 'I know. But I sure

as hell miss him. He ate all his dinner but I promised him an ice cream. Have you time for a run out somewhere?'

Pleased at the idea, Maura said, 'Yes! I'll just fetch my jacket.'

Adam was hopeful. He could see that his wife had taken care with her hair and make-up for him coming and had on her best clothes. That was a good sign. Perhaps he would at last get through to her, persuade her to trust him for another month or two. 'Shall we take a drive up to the Floral Hall? There's an ice-cream van parked there every day.'

She nodded. 'Danny would like that.' Inwardly she was wondering how Adam knew an ice-cream van was there every day.

After a short drive up to Bellevue, Adam parked his van and suggested that they take a walk round the zoo first before it closed.

'I suppose you've already brought Danny up here?'

Maura shook her head. Why did she get the feeling that she was being neglectful, not having taken Danny to see the wild animals? They had only been in Greencastle a few days, for God's sake. 'No, this will be his first time, but he'll soon get fed up looking at them, now we're living here,' she retorted with a toss of the head.

Adam grimaced but didn't rise to the bait. Why

did Maura always have to say the wrong things at the wrong time? He hadn't meant any malice, just an innocent bit of talk for something to say. He couldn't seem to do right for doing wrong these days, where she was concerned. Tight-lipped, he led the way towards the turnstile, paid for their entrance tickets and they filed into the zoo, Danny literally jumping with excitement.

The child was fascinated with the animals as they walked along in front of rows of cages holding panthers and cheetahs, leopards and lions, bears and tigers. Then they strolled around fenced enclosures containing less dangerous herbivores, such as bison and goats, zebras, various deer and antelopes, and a pair of giraffes. By then they had reached the monkey house where Danny could hardly contain himself at the antics of the smaller monkeys. Some of the braver ones reached through the cage for pieces of fruit or nuts or whatever the visitor chose to toss to them, ignoring the 'Don't feed the animals' signs. There wasn't much to see in the reptile house as the inhabitants were hiding behind logs and small boulders, or lying, coiled up, on the floor. The next port of call was the elephant pen, passing the birds of prey and the polar-bear pit on the way.

A short time later a uniformed zookeeper advised them to start heading out, as the gates would be locked in ten minutes. They appeared to be the last visitors to leave and, much later than they had intended, they sought out the ice-cream vendor, who was packing up for the day. Recognising Adam from the previous week, he greeted him like an old friend, bringing yet more doubts to Maura's troubled mind. Did her husband really frequent this place? Had Joe Moon genuinely seen him up here with Evelyn?

Adam led them to the grassy mound opposite the Floral Hall from where they had a clear view across the lough. Belfast shipyard sprawled out to their right, with the County Down coastline straight ahead and to the left the Carnmoney hills, Carrickfergus and Whitehead. After some moments of deep thinking, Adam turned to Maura. Now was the ideal time to talk things through, while Maura was relaxed and at ease and Danny was busy torturing his ice-cream cone. The opening address died on his lips.

Maura was concentrating on her ice-cream cone as if she had never seen one before, a frown furrowing her brow. Her thoughts were in a whirl. Did Adam really come here with that woman? Sensing his eyes on her, she met them square on.

'It's nice here, isn't it? Do you come up here often?' What a corny thing to say. It was like making conversation with a stranger in the Fiesta dance hall, she thought. 'Is that how the ice-cream man knows you?'

Seeing the accusation in her eyes and the tightness of her lips, Adam had no difficulty guessing what she was insinuating. His nostrils flared with contempt. 'You think I bring Evelyn up here!'

'Well, don't you?'

'Believe it or not, I've never been here with her. As a matter of fact, I've never been anywhere with her.'

'Why can't you be truthful for once in your life?' she hissed. 'You were seen, in case you didn't know.'

At a loss, Adam just gawked in disbelief. Then the penny dropped. 'Ah, now I see. It was Joe Moon, wasn't it? His gossip mill has been working overtime again, and he's been grinding out malicious rumours without any substantiation whatsoever. Just what did Mary tell you?'

'That Joe saw you and Evelyn Matthews up here.'

Adam was on his feet glaring down at her. 'He's a liar!' he spat out. 'He saw me, but I was *alone*. A-l-o-n-e!' He enunciated each letter slowly through clenched teeth. 'Do you hear me?'

Taken aback by his sudden outburst, Maura thought back and recalled that Mary had told her that Joe had *assumed* that Evelyn must have been in the vicinity. She was quick to apologise. 'I'm sorry, it seems I've got the wrong end of the stick again, but the way you've been behaving lately, you can hardly blame me, now, can you?'

281

'Why change the habit of a lifetime? I can't win where you're concerned. You'll believe anyone but me.'

'That's not fair! My mind's all mixed up these days. I don't know what to believe any more.'

'Then try listening to me for a change. The truth won't hurt. I'll tell you, I can't take much more of all this bickering, so we'd better start talking . . . and soon, before I go round the bend.'

Maura sat up straight and eyed him defiantly. 'Why not now? You first.'

Danny had been listening to this volley of angry words, frightened eyes darting from one to the other, as if he was watching a game of tennis. He knew in his innocent little mind that, from the harshness of their exchanges, all was not well. He turned to his mother and buried his head in her lap. Seeing his son's reaction, sadness overwhelmed Adam. To think his son should be caught up in the middle of all this turmoil. Poor wee soul.

Maura cradled Danny in her arms and looked up at Adam. 'It's past his bedtime, he's tired.'

Adam gently prised the ice-cream cone from the child's limp grasp and reaching down scooped him up into his arms. 'Let's go. I'll take you home. The talking will have to wait for another day.' Leaving Maura to scramble to her feet unaided, he took off with deliberate strides towards the car park.

* * *

At the house Adam lifted his son from Maura's lap.

'Where's the key?'

He waited impatiently while she searched her pockets. Taking it from her, he carried the sleeping child inside and gently placed him on the sofa. Maura had hopped down from the van and was waiting outside on the pavement, apologies quivering on her lips. Anxious to make amends, she opened her mouth ready to urge him to stay and thrash the matter out, but Adam had had enough for one day. With an abrupt goodnight he swung himself into the van and with a grinding of gears drove off. Hurt and bewildered, Maura watched him out of sight, tears pouring down her face and resentment in her heart. At this rate they would never get things sorted out. What did he expect from her? She was coping as best she could.

She felt as if Adam had slapped her on the face and glanced round to see whether anyone had been observing them. To leave her standing there like an idiot was bad enough, but to drive off without so much as a wave was downright insulting. He would never get the chance to slight her again. Especially in public, like this. Not that anyone seemed interested in her predicament, but then who knew who was watching them from behind their curtains?

She'd had more than her fill of Adam's antics. Tomorrow she would go into town and see a solicitor to seek advice on how she stood with regard to a legal separation.

14

Adam's hands shook so much that he felt he was in the throes of a fit. Fearing an accident, the first opportunity he got he indicated and, carefully drawing the van to the side of the road, switched off the engine. He pressed his brow to the steering wheel. He felt exhausted, as if he had just climbed Ben Nevis instead of walking on the Cave Hill for a short time.

He felt a surge of guilt wash over him at having left his wife standing on the pavement gazing after him. As he watched her receding figure in the rear-view mirror, she had looked so lost, so forlorn. God forgive him. It was a cruel thing to do and most uncharacteristic of him, but he just couldn't take any more. They were tearing each other apart and the one to suffer most was their darling son,

Danny. It couldn't go on any longer. Should he go back and beg her forgiveness? No . . . she might not answer the door if she saw the van parked outside and, given the state they both were in, God knows what the outcome of that would be.

He couldn't see himself just walking away again. Something would have to be done and quickly. He would make arrangements to see her somewhere alone, soon, so that they could thrash their out differences once and for all.

Thinking she must be ill, as they hadn't seen her about lately, Benny and his staff had been asking after Maura whilst she was away. Adam had told them that she was fine. The excuse he made for her absence was that she had taken Danny to see his grandfather, and finding Davey poorly she had decided to stay a few days to look after him.

Adam had something else to worry about now. When Benny had seen young Danny in the van the night before and no sign of Maura, Adam had volunteered no information, just eyed him balefully, silently daring Benny to start prying into his private affairs. Bewildered, Benny had respected Adam's privacy and, taking the worksheets from him, with an abrupt goodnight had waved him off. Later, however, whilst he and his wife Beth were eating their evening meal, he had shared the suspicions he harboured that something wasn't quite right between Adam and Maura. He was met with a barrage of questions and, raising his arms in a defensive gesture, explained that he didn't *know* anything. It was just an uneasy feeling he had that all was not as it should be in the Brady camp.

Without more ado, and very much against her husband's wishes, that very Saturday morning Beth had landed herself at Adam's door, determined to find out just what was going on. Benny had tried to reason with her, to respect the couple's privacy, but Beth had pooh-poohed that idea. Maura was like a daughter to her and she owed it to her to enquire after her welfare, to make sure she was all right, or needed any help.

Danny had been trailing his father around the house like a shadow, as if afraid that he might suddenly disappear at any moment. When Adam opened the door and Danny saw it was Beth, a figure of normality in his mixed-up world, he flew to her, clutching at her skirt. Concerned, she crouched down before him.

'Hello, sweetheart. What's the matter with you?' she asked, pulling him close into a hug.

Danny just swung his head from side to side and cuddled closer. At a loss, Beth eyed Adam over the child's head.

With a resigned sigh he said, 'You had best come in, Beth. It's a long story.'

When she was inside and the door had closed behind them, he said, 'Sit down.' He nodded towards the settee. 'I'll make us a cup of coffee. Or would you prefer tea?'

Leading Danny by the hand, Beth ignored the settee and followed Adam into the kitchen. 'Coffee will be fine, thank you.'

She pulled a chair away from the table and lifted Danny on to it. Sitting close beside him, she draped her arm along the back of Danny's chair, running her fingers lightly through his hair while he opened the bag of chocolate buttons she had brought for him.

'What on earth is the matter?' she cried indignantly. 'I can't believe the change in this child. He's usually such a cheerful wee soul.'

'He misses his mum,' Adam reluctantly admitted.

'And where is she? Benny tells me that her father isn't too well. What exactly is wrong with him? Is it terminal?' Struck by a terrible thought, her face crumpled up. 'Don't tell me he's—'

Adam quickly interrupted her. 'No! He's doing fine.' He was in a dilemma, wondering how much he should reveal to Beth without upsetting his wife even further.

Deciding it would be best to avoid the issue, he explained, 'It's a long story, Beth. Maura will tell you all about it when she comes home.'

'And when will that be?'

He shrugged and confessed, 'I'm afraid I don't know.'

'Hmm. I want her father's address. I'm going to pay her a visit,' she demanded in no uncertain terms.

Taken aback, Adam said, 'I don't think that's a good idea, Beth. Believe me, she'll not thank you for interfering.'

'Interfering? That girl is like a daughter to me and I think she needs a friend at the moment, someone to confide in, so I'm going to see her, no matter what you think. I want her father's address now . . . please.'

Placing a cup of coffee in front of her, he gave in. 'All right. You win, but I'll leave all the explanations to her. OK?'

'If that's how you want it,' she grunted.

With them both, in their own way, thinking about Maura, and Adam reluctant to explain her absence, there seemed little else to talk about and the conversation petered out. Adam was glad when Beth at last got up to go. Without further prompting, he wrote Davey's address on a sheet of paper, adding directions on how to get there, and handed it to Beth as she left the house. Danny had scrambled down from the chair and was clinging to her hand. She looked at Adam defiantly. 'Can I take the child with me?'

'No. He'll be fine here with me.' He lifted Danny

into his arms. 'This is my day for access and I want to make the most of it.' Beth's eyes widened at the word *access* – a legal term for separated spouses fighting for custody – but when she opened her mouth to question him further, he forestalled her. 'Yes, it's come to that,' he sighed. 'Access to my own son. Can you believe it? I can't talk sense into Maura. I've tried and tried till I was blue in the face, but to no avail. Maybe you'll be able to do better. Goodbye, Beth.'

Beth stared at him in consternation for some moments, then murmured, 'Oh, my God.' With a concerned glance at the child, she turned and headed for her car. The sooner she saw Maura Brady the better.

Adam bumped his forehead again and again on the steering wheel in despair. To crown it all he had forgotten to tell his wife to expect a visit from Beth Gallagher. Another black mark against him. He had intended telling Maura that Beth would surely visit her tomorrow morning, but the way things had panned out, he didn't get the chance.

For the first time he regretted not having a phone installed at home. If he had, he could have phoned the pub and asked to speak to Davey, who was always there on a Saturday night. Then he could have asked Davey to get Maura to ring him from the public phone box across the road. He straightened up in his seat and prepared to drive home, thinking philosophically that things could hardly get any worse. He was wrong.

Maura walked down the driveway from St Mary's Church, holding Danny by the hand, on Sunday morning after Mass. Mary Moon's daughter, Jenny, held his other hand. Skipping and swinging along between his mother and his friend, for the moment he was happy.

'Children are very adaptable, aren't they?' Maura mused, a hopeful glance in Mary's direction begging her agreement. 'I mean to say, if Adam and I do separate, Danny will be able to cope . . . won't he?'

Mary gave a frustrated shrug. 'I don't know, Maura. Some children do, but some don't. I mean, if one parent dies or goes off to America or somewhere like that, the child will, hopefully, in time forget about them. It's when the parents are living in the same neighbourhood, trying to influence their offspring's future, that's when the trouble starts. They tear the children apart when they try to make them choose. When all's said and done, the children more than likely love both parents and don't want to disagree with any of their suggestions. Of course it's much better if the parents can agree to stay together for the sake of the poor children. They're always the ones to suffer. So, you're a fool if you let Evelyn Matthews waltz back into your life and steal Adam from you. I can't understand you at times, Maura Brady.' She threw Maura a sympathetic smile. 'I'm sorry, Maura, but you did ask and as I see it that's my tuppence worth.'

'Well, the ball's in Adam's court now and whatever will be will be.' Maura stopped to make her farewells, then paused on the footpath before crossing the road. 'Fancy coming over for a cup of tea?'

Just then Danny started jumping up and down with excitement and pointing. 'Mammy, Mammy, it's Auntie Beth.'

Only then did Maura glance across the Shore Road. She immediately recognised Beth's car and was in time to see her friend disappearing into the house. Her father caught her eye before closing the door behind Beth and gave an open-handed shrug as if to say, what else could I do? He also mouthed the words 'Hurry up!'

'Look, Mary, a friend of mine has just gone into our house. I'm afraid we'll have to forget that cup of tea for now. I'll see you tomorrow some time.' The road was clear, and holding Danny tightly by the hand Maura proceeded to cross, saying over her shoulder, 'Sorry about that, Mary.'

Mary shouted, 'Not to worry. Another time then,' and continued on her journey home.

* * *

Maura opened the door with her own key and her father met her in the hall. Grabbing a jacket from the coat rack, he said softly, 'I'm off, Maura. I'll leave you to entertain your friend. If you want to go out for the day or anything, don't worry about me. I'll get a sandwich later.' He raised his voice. 'Glad to have met you, Mrs Gallagher.'

'You too, Davey,' Beth answered, thanking God that Danny looked much happier as he stepped ahead of his mother into the room. She spoke softly to him and handed him a pear, which he turned over and over in his hands as he examined it. He cautiously started nibbling it, leaving a small bunch of grapes to one side for later.

Unable to comprehend why Beth was there, Maura was in a fluster. Surely Adam hadn't told her the whole unsavoury story and she had come to plead his case? Maura brushed a hand through her hair, composed herself and went into the kitchen. 'This is a surprise, Beth. What brings you here?'

'My, but aren't we rather formal today? No nice to see you, Beth, how are you? Just, what brings you here! Now, Maura, that's not a nice way to greet an old friend.'

Beth had risen to her feet and going to her Maura clasped her hands in her own. 'Forgive me, Beth. I don't know whether I'm coming or going these days. Would you like a cup of coffee?'

'Yes, please.'

Maura nodded in her son's direction. He was sat, tentatively nibbling away at his pear and examining the Corgi car that Beth had brought him along with the fruit. 'I see you still have the magic touch. I don't think he's eaten any fruit since he last saw you.'

'I imagine that's the least of your worries at the moment. Away and make the coffee and then you can tell me all about it.'

As she boiled water for the coffee, Maura tried to gather her wits about her. She wished she knew what had prompted Beth to see her. It had to be something very important to bring her here on a Sunday morning. Had Adam confided in her and, if so, how much? Somehow, Maura couldn't see Adam discussing their personal affairs with anyone. He certainly wouldn't dwell on intimate details, that much she was sure of. She would have to play it by ear and see how it went.

Beth sat cup in hand and examined Maura over its rim. Seeing that her young friend was as taut as a fiddle string, she didn't know where to start. She sipped at her coffee and let the silence hang between them a long time, then putting her cup back on the saucer she leaned forward. 'Now, Maura, tell me all about it. You know what they say about a problem shared.'

'Beth . . . I don't want to offend you . . . but

294

this is a very private matter between Adam and me.'

'Look, I promise you that not one word you tell me here this day will pass my lips. I won't even tell Benny, cross my heart and hope to die. And mind you, Benny's worried about the two of you. He keeps telling me he's got great things planned for Adam.'

'Ah, Beth, you're a lovely person, but I'm too ashamed to tell you. You'd be scandalised, so you would.'

'I don't, for one minute, think I'll be scandalised by anything you feel like telling me, Maura. I'm more than twice your age, remember, and I've had more than my fair share of temptations along the way. I could write a book about them if I had the inclination. But I'd much rather forget some of the experiences I've encountered in my past. Oh yes, I've had my ups and downs all right, but I learned from my mistakes, and I'm more than contented with my lot today, thank you . . . and so will you be.'

Danny, who had finished the pear and, unobserved while they talked, had ignored the grapes, was on the floor playing with his new car.

Seeing Maura eyeing her son, Beth urged her, 'Come on, he's wrapped up in his own little world; he's not listening. Get it off your chest.'

Her face suffused with embarrassment, Maura

cleared her throat. 'I don't even know where to begin.'

'Try at the beginning,' Beth urged. 'Or maybe once upon a time, if you like.' She beamed, trying to ease Maura's obvious distress.

Maura's lips twitched with the scarcest trace of a smile in return. Throwing caution to the wind, she hesitantly started relating her tale of woe. Once started, the little hesitant sobs evaporated and the words poured out, from the time she first met Adam until the present day. She left nothing out: she told Beth about Adam's engagement to Evelyn Matthews; how Evelyn had jilted him and he had started dating her. How she had become pregnant, and he had had to marry her, and how Evelyn had come back and everything had gone haywire.

Beth interrupted her once. 'Is this the same Mrs Matthews whose gardens Adam is working on?'

Maura kept her head bent as she finally lost control. The tears rolled unheeded down her face and dripped on to her hands, tightly clasped on the table. 'The very same. Beautiful, wealthy and very available.'

Beth heard her out in silence, her own throat choking back tears. Then she went round the table and gathered Maura close. 'You poor, poor dear. Bottling all that up inside you. You should have confided in me.' She tilted Maura's head up and waited until she met her eye. 'And you have nothing to be ashamed of. If we were all like you the world would be a better place. The shame's on your father for putting you out. I'm surprised he found that necessary in this day and age.' She thrust a tissue into Maura's hand.

'That hurt, but it didn't really matter. I could understand his shame. I was ashamed too. You see, he's very old fashioned.' Cassie crossed her mind and she added bitterly, 'At least, he used to be. What matters is that Adam *had* to marry me and I think he now regrets it.'

'No! He didn't have to marry you. He *wanted* to marry you. It's obvious to anyone with eyes in their head that Adam is devoted to you. How did he take the news of your pregnancy?'

A faint smile flitted across Maura's face as she recalled his kindness. 'Actually he was very supportive. I remember his every word as if he'd said them only yesterday. He hugged me and said, "Oh dear, we'd best get married right away then." Those were his exact words.'

Beth was bewildered and showed it. 'There you are then! What are you worried about? Has he said he wants this other woman back?'

'No, quite the contrary, but he won't ask Benny to send Steve over to finish the work, and I won't live under the same roof as him while he works alongside Evelyn Matthews, day in, day out. He shouldn't expect me to. It's not fair.' She eyed Beth closely. 'Have you seen her?'

'No. No, I haven't,' Beth admitted.

'She really is beautiful, you know.'

'Listen to me, Maura. Why can't you believe me? There are different kinds of beauty. For instance, there's the film-star type or the glossy-magazine type who look absolutely ravishing. I am thinking that this is how you see this Mrs Matthews. But if you were to see some of these ladies first thing in the morning, without all that make-up on and their beautiful hairdos looking as if they'd been pulled through a bramble bush backwards, you'd soon change your mind about calling them beautiful. And then, there's your kind of beauty: great bone structure, wonderful wide-spaced eyes, which is a natural beauty and requires the minimum enhancement. If you had all the beauty treatment these glamour girls get you'd be right up there with them. Believe me when I say this, Maura, you'd be top of their league in the glamour stakes. In your own way you're a natural beauty and don't you dare let anyone tell you otherwise.'

A loud derisive snort greeted these words. 'Huh! If you say so. I certainly haven't noticed any sign of it lately when I've looked in the mirror.'

'That's because you're letting yourself go to the dogs. You're not taking care of your appearance.'

'I can't be bothered. I'll not be going anywhere that's important.'

'Well, we're going to change all that, my dear. First thing tomorrow morning I'll book an appointment with your hairdresser to get your hair trimmed. Who cut it last time?'

'Rosemary. But it was only a few weeks ago.

'So I'll book you in with her then and I'll arrange a facial and a cosmetic hour.'

'Oh my God, no, I couldn't afford that.'

'My treat.'

'No! I can't allow it. Besides, who'll look after Danny?'

'It will be my pleasure to do that, as you well know. Meanwhile, I'll have to rush off; I've to meet Benny in town. We're going over to Roselawn Cemetery to tidy up my parents' grave. Can I persuade you to come along for the ride and maybe afterwards to The Old Inn at Crawfordsburn for lunch?'

Maura's eyes widened in horror. 'Oh no, Beth, I couldn't face Benny right now, the state I'm in. Besides, I have a roast to put on and a dinner to prepare.'

'That's OK, love.' Before Maura could argue any more about the beauty treat, Beth bent down and taking Danny's face in her hands said, 'I'll see you in the morning, love. Won't that be nice? Give us a big kiss.'

Danny beamed from ear to ear and pouted his lips for her kiss.

'And make sure you eat those grapes, you hear me?'

Another cheeky grin, and with a final hug Beth was out the door before Maura could raise any further objections.

The smell of roast pork permeating the air greeted Davey's nostrils as he entered the house. Danny was having his afternoon nap on the sofa and Maura was busy in the scullery. He joined her there.

'That smells lovely, Maura.' Covertly eyeing his daughter, he could see that she had been crying. He hesitated, not knowing what to say for the best. 'Did that woman upset you, love?'

'On the contrary, she cheered me up no end. That was Beth Gallagher. You know? Adam's boss's wife. And she's also my best friend in Holywood. Tomorrow we're going to spend the day together. We had a good old heart-to-heart and, thank God, I feel much better for it.'

'That's good. What about Danny?'

'He's coming with us, Da. Isn't that great? Will you set the table and give Danny a shake? Dinner's almost ready.'

Adam picked up young Jackie Flynn on Monday morning as usual and headed for work. He felt betwixt and between. During a night when sleep had eluded him, he had decided that the only way to save his marriage was to hand in his notice. However, he must finish the job first; he owed that to Benny. Then he planned to get a job away from Gallagher's Nursery. Move house, because he had at last faced up to the facts. He knew Evelyn would conjure up more and more jobs for him and he had admitted to himself that perhaps Maura was right. It was a temptation that he should and must avoid at all costs. He had at last decided to take a stand. He had made up his mind not to let Evelyn ruin what Maura and he had going for them. Evelyn had already approached Benny and got his permission for Adam to work on her gardens. She had the upper hand. He had no choice but to change his place of employment. Hadn't McCartney's of Lisburn approached him in the past with the offer of a good job, so he shouldn't be too bothered at being unemployed. And Lisburn was a fair distance from Belfast . . . and Evelyn.

Instead of going via Carlisle Circus as usual, Adam took the Shore Road route to work. The previous night he had written a note and intended putting it through Davey Craig's letter box, asking Maura to please come out with him tonight. He'd pick her up at seven and would be taking her somewhere special, where maybe they could talk. He signed the note with love and kisses – as if it was a little billet-doux. Once the note was delivered he felt as if a weight had been lifted from his shoulders.

He had just pulled into the Matthewses' driveway and was going around the back when the urgent sound of an ambulance caused him to pause and look towards the Antrim Road. To his amazement it turned in through the Matthewses' gateway. Adam jumped from the van with dread in his heart, while Jackie remained seated. When the ambulance men reached the front door, it was wrenched open by Linda Morrison, who stood talking earnestly to the paramedics. They took a couple of medical holdalls from the back of the ambulance and quickly followed Linda inside the house.

With a sinking heart Adam climbed the steps to the house. Although the door was still wide open, he hesitated before going inside. The ground floor was silent but he could hear urgent voices coming from upstairs. It sounded as if there was a panic on. Evelyn cried out in anguish and he heard Linda remonstrate with her, but couldn't catch what was said. Unable to bear not knowing what was going on, he went outside again and moved the van round the back. Between them, he and Jackie unloaded it. Then he set the lad some work to do and, leaving him to it, went back to the house. He had decided that he must find out what the emergency was.

Evelyn would be beside herself with worry. She would need his support.

Charles looked as if he were already dead. What Adam could see of his face was chalky white as they carried him down the stairs. An oxygen mask covered his mouth and nose, and his eyes were closed. Adam looked on helplessly, feeling utterly useless. Linda helped Evelyn down the stairs and was obviously glad to see Adam. At the foot of the stairs Evelyn passed him without as much as a glance but the nurse released her elbow and approached him.

'What's going on, Nurse?'

'Mr Matthews has suffered a heart attack and he's in a bad way. I've telephoned his son and he's meeting Mrs Matthews at the hospital. I hope she'll be all right for a while on her own.'

'Aren't you going in the ambulance with them?'

'No. I'd only be in the way. Besides, I've other patients to attend to.'

'Then I'll go with them and keep Mrs Matthews company till her stepson arrives.'

'That would be great. She is very distraught and needs someone with her.'

'Will Mr Matthews pull through?'

'I don't know.' Linda sadly shook her head. 'I honestly don't know.'

'Which hospital are they taking him to?'

'The Royal.'

'I'll let my mate Jackie know the score and then I'll be on my way.'

The Royal Victoria Hospital was, as was usual for a Monday morning, crowded. George Gallagher had had a heart attack some years back and Adam had visited him there in the coronary unit, so he remembered the layout. Now he piloted himself through the visitors' waiting room towards the lifts. When he stepped from the lift at his designated floor, he went straight to the sister's office at the entrance to the ward. A nurse sat behind a desk poring over some official-looking papers.

He knocked lightly on the door. 'Excuse me, Sister. Sorry to disturb you, but I'm enquiring after a patient who was admitted a short time ago with a heart attack.'

She glanced up at him. 'Name?'

'Charles Matthews.'

She singled out a sheet of paper from those she was reading and said quietly, 'I was expecting him, but he was taken directly to intensive care. Try the intensive care unit.' She gave him instructions how to get there and with a 'Thank you for your help' Adam set out to find the ward.

He found Evelyn sitting on a bench seat in the corridor outside the ward. She was hunched over, her arms clasping her body as if for comfort. As Adam approached, a nurse pushed through the swing doors of the ward and sat beside her, caressing her arm as she spoke quietly to her for some moments. Evelyn thanked her and some more words were exchanged. As the nurse turned away, her gaze met Adam's and she looked askance at him.

'I'm a friend of Mr Matthews and I came to make sure his wife's all right.'

'That's good news. She could be doing with a bit of company right now. I'm fetching her a cup of tea. Would you like one?'

'Yes, please. Milk only.'

Adam kneeled in front of Evelyn and reached for her hand. 'How is he?'

'They're still working on him.' She leaned towards him and buried her face against his chest. 'Oh, Adam, what will I do if anything happens to Charles?'

'He's in good hands, with the best of care, Evelyn. You have to think positive.'

Her face was blotched and her eyes red-rimmed from crying, but her beauty still shone through. In her vulnerable state he wished he could soothe away her fears. Suddenly she pushed away from him and, bunching his lapels in her fists, gazed intently at him. 'Promise me you won't leave me here, Adam.'

'Listen, Evelyn, I've no right to be here. When David comes he won't want to see me around.'

'It doesn't matter what David wants.'

'Oh, but it does matter. I'm only an employee of your father's. David can dismiss me out of hand.'

She clung more tightly still. 'What will I do if Charles dies?'

'Your solicitor will look after you. Leave everything in his capable hands.'

They were unaware of company until David Matthews spoke. 'My, my, what a cosy little scene.' A scowl on his face, he glared at Adam. 'What are you doing here? Why aren't you working on my father's gardens? It's what you're being paid to do.'

Evelyn slowly let go of Adam's jacket and he rose to his feet. 'I was keeping Mrs Matthews company. The nurse thought she shouldn't be alone at a time like this.'

'Well, you can go back to work now. I'll look after Evelyn.'

Adam leaned over her. 'Remember what I said and you'll be all right. OK? I'll see you tomorrow.'

David watched him walk down the corridor and out of sight before taking the space on the bench beside Evelyn. She squirmed away from him but he pretended not to notice and inched closer. 'How is my father?'

'I thought you'd never ask. He's at death's door, if you must know.'

David looked at her in disbelief, and for a

moment she detected a glint of fear in his eyes. 'Surely not,' he muttered. 'Surely not.'

Evelyn glared at him. 'Hindsight is a wonderful thing. I wish now I had gone along with my own instincts and persuaded Charles not to ring you. But he was so insistent and in such good form, I thought it would be OK. What on earth did you say to upset him so much?'

'Nothing! We just talked about the business.'

'Well, that wee business talk almost killed him.'

'I assure you it was nothing that I said. Is he really that bad?'

'Here's the doctor. Ask him yourself.'

Evelyn stood to face the physician in charge of intensive care patients; David followed suit.

'How is my husband, Mr Monaghan?'

'He is in a stable condition at the moment. Tomorrow we will decide what to do, but until then he needs plenty of rest.'

'Will my father recover?'

The surgeon eyed David for some moments. 'I can't answer that in all honesty. Only time will tell. We will do our best and I'm inclined to think he will pull through, but we'll know more of his condition tomorrow when we examine him again.' He turned his attention to Evelyn. 'You can see your husband now, Mrs Matthews, but just for a few minutes. He's been sedated and won't know you're there. As I said, he needs to rest.'

David had listened in silence and now he stepped forward. 'Can I see him?'

'I would prefer you to wait until tomorrow, Mr Matthews.' Not giving David a chance to respond, the doctor wished them both good-day and strode off.

Evelyn said, 'I don't want to see you here when I come out, David. Stay away from me, do you hear? And I don't want you near Charles until he is well enough to stand up to you.'

The ward door closed behind her and he gazed at it in dumb fury. Who the hell does she think she is, he raged inwardly. Should he ignore her and charge in regardless? He made towards the ward but hesitated. It'll only make matters worse if I barge in on them. It would be best if I left now and came back tomorrow when I'm in a better frame of mind, he thought to himself as he turned and headed for the exit. He didn't want to make a scene by hanging about waiting for Evelyn to reappear.

15

Beth Gallagher called at ten o'clock on Monday morning to take Maura to the hairdresser. She was pleasantly surprised at the change in her friend; an aura of suppressed excitement seemed to hover in the air around her. Maura greeted her with a tentative smile and handed her the note Adam had put through the door sometime earlier that morning on his way to work. She said in a hushed voice, 'What do you think of that, then?'

Opening the folded page, Beth silently scanned the contents. Still looking at the note, she paused to gather her thoughts together. Maura so obviously wanted to comply with Adam's wishes but Beth was somewhat sceptical. Looking her friend in the eye, she volunteered, 'You know something? I think you should keep him guessing for a while.

String him along as if you couldn't care less.' Maura's face drooped slightly and sadness settled there, but Beth continued, 'It wouldn't do any harm, you know, but I can see from your expression that you wouldn't like to chance it in case it backfires on you.'

An embarrassed flush suffused Maura's cheeks and she shrugged her shoulders, not knowing what to do for the best. 'I suppose so. Do you think I'm getting on like a wimp?'

'No, of course not. I'd probably do the same if I were in your shoes, but what you say goes. Whatever you think is best for you is all that matters.' She paused again to give Maura a chance to change her mind but she remained silent. 'Well then, all I can say is that Adam has certainly chosen the right time to wine and dine you. Tonight you'll be able to hold up your head and face him with confidence. He won't be able to resist. In fact you'll have him drooling over you.'

'I do need to get this matter settled once and for all, Beth, or I'll finish up in the laughing house.'

'Take my word for it, tonight you'll be so beautiful and alluring he'll be falling over himself to please you. As I said, his timing couldn't be better.'

Beth hoped she was proved right and things would live up to her friend's expectations, but she doubted whether it would be that simple, not after hearing about Adam Brady's shenanigans. She found it hard to believe that he could be so callous and was inclined to think this other woman must have got her claws into him good and proper.

Without breaking any confidences, the previous night Beth had tried to sound out Benny about his employee, but her husband was adamant that he knew nothing about Adam outside of his work. What he did when he went through the gates at night was his own business, he said. In fact, his very words had been 'Good God, Beth, if I pried into all our employees' private lives I'd go round the bend in no time at all.'

Now she continued gaily, 'Adam won't be able to resist the gorgeous creature he'll find waiting for him tonight. The ball will be in your court, girl, so make the most of it. It could be your last opportunity at a reconciliation, so, if you're sure you want to win him back, don't blow it.'

She was dismayed at the despicable creature Adam Brady had turned into. She wouldn't have believed it possible, having always looked on him as a fine, upstanding young gentleman, a man of integrity. But then, she cautioned herself, there were always two sides to every story, and she had yet to hear his.

Danny was dancing around and tugging at Beth's skirt, seeking attention. She gripped him by the shoulders and bent to look into his eyes. 'Hello, young fellah. We're going to have an exciting day,

311

so we are,' she informed him, then turned to Maura. 'I've booked you in with Rosemary for eleven o'clock. You won't be too long in there, so I'll hang about and drive you to Ralph's beauty salon. It's in Bangor, the one I sometimes go to for a massage when I'm feeling a bit under the weather, and the staff are very good. You'll have to be there by one o'clock. Everything's already paid for.' She raised her hand to wave away the protest when Maura opened her mouth to object. 'If we hurry we'll have time for a coffee before we part.'

Maura headed for the scullery. 'I'll put the kettle on.'

'No! I mean we'll have coffee in Brannigan's café, you know, the one near the hairdresser. So get a move on, love.'

Maura motioned Danny towards the pushchair but Beth intervened. 'Let him walk. It'll do him good to exercise his little legs. And, anyway, we'll be in and out of places where the pushchair will only be a hindrance. Ready?'

Maura picked up her coat and handbag and nodded.

'Right then, let's hit the road.'

The day went according to plan. Rosemary was very efficient and Maura could feel her excitement rising as she watched the girl's every move in the mirror. She liked the way Rosemary confidently

312

clipped and trimmed without hesitation, until her hair clung to her head in a perfect bob. The blow-dry finished it off to perfection.

When she asked how much she owed, Rosemary shook her head. 'Mrs Gallagher has already settled everything.'

'Well, at least accept this.' A blush tinged Maura's cheeks and, seeing her embarrassment, Rosemary accepted the tip she offered.

Beth had had a second cup of coffee to while away the time as she waited in Brannigan's. Danny was behaving himself and sat at the table entertaining himself with a colouring-in book and crayons.

When she saw Maura enter the café, Beth said urgently, 'Look, Danny, do you recognise that lovely lady over there?'

Danny swung around to face the door and with a surprised glance at Beth cried in a loud voice, 'That's my mammy,' causing bursts of laughter from nearby customers.

Beth rose to her feet. 'Your hair is gorgeous, Maura, but I'm afraid you haven't time for coffee. We're cutting it fine as it is.'

Maura was happier than she had been for a long time and replied in a sing-song voice, 'I'm ready, willing and able.'

Someone muttered, 'Don't give up the day job.'

Maura grinned at the surly man, evoking a

reluctant smile from him. She assured him she wouldn't and they left the café in high spirits. In the car Maura tried to convey her thanks to Beth, only to be told to behave herself.

'I'm having the time of my life,' Beth assured her.

In the massage parlour with subdued lighting, and Handel's *Largo* playing softly in the background, Maura unwound in the soothing atmosphere, determined to enjoy the expert treatment of Shirley, the beautician who would be attending her. Her hair was protected by a wide band, and lotions of various colours, as well as perfumes and creams, were spread out on a handy table. Making sure that her client was fully relaxed and comfortable, Shirley began massaging Maura's shoulders and neck with aromatic oils, slowly working her way down to her waist. Maura breathed in the fragrance and submitted herself to the sensual feel of Shirley's expert hands, kneading and probing, and relieving the tension from her aching muscles and joints. The massage continued for some time, and when Shirley had finished she asked Maura if she would like a break before the next treatment. When Maura said no, Shirley started on her face, explaining as she went along what each lotion and cream was for as well as the essential ingredients they contained and their benefits: a deep cleanser, a toner and moisturising lotions to soften her skin. Then the area around her eyes was cleansed and special oil applied. Finally some kind of mask was applied that completely covered her face. It was of a fine gossamer texture and clung to her skin. Maura thought she would find it cloying, and maybe make her feel claustrophobic, but it was so light it didn't bother her in the slightest.

Shirley touched her gently on the hand to get her attention. 'I'll be away for a few minutes but I'll bring you back a nice cold drink if that's OK?'

Maura inclined her head to let her know she understood and some moments later she heard the door open and close.

She must have dozed off, for the next thing she was aware of was the mask being gently removed from her face and yet more lotions applied. Removing the protective cover from around Maura's shoulders, Shirley said, 'You can sit up now and take a short break and enjoy your drink. You'll find it most refreshing. When you've finished we'll move into the make-up studio and Ralph will take over.'

Maura sat on the easy chair Shirley had indicated and sipped gratefully at the long glass of multicoloured liquid. It looked like a non-alcoholic Tequila Sunrise. She nodded her approval, 'Lovely, thank you,' then queried, 'Ralph? I thought you would be doing the whole works.'

'Well, normally I would, but today, Ralph – he's the owner, by the way – has called in. He has three salons. The other two are in Belfast and Antrim. He likes to keep his hand in and must have a new product to try out. That's probably why he's here today, to do a demonstration, so you're the lucky one.'

Feeling a bit uneasy now, Maura thought that Ralph was treating her as a guinea pig for his new lines. Beginning to fret that all might not go to her liking and that she mightn't be satisfied with the final result of his experiment, she asked apprehensively, 'What if I don't like it, Shirley? Will he be mad at me?'

'Of course not! Rest assured, Mrs Brady, if you're not completely satisfied with the finished article it will be cleaned off and I'll take over. Ralph's motto is that the customer is always right, and we've got a regular clientele to prove it. Ask Mrs Gallagher if you don't believe me, she's one of our regulars. Trust me, I know you won't be disappointed. Ralph is one of the best in the business. No, let me rephrase that, Ralph *is* the best.'

Ralph turned out to be George Nesbit from Jordanstown, an old acquaintance of Maura's and originally from Whitehouse.

They gazed at each other for a moment or two and Maura, her brows puckered in a frown, enquired tentatively, 'Ralph?'

A wide grin on his face, the tall, elegant man said, 'I've been caught out, Shirley. This young lady is an old neighbour of mine.'

Maura made a quick mental calculation that George Nesbit must be almost thirty years old now, but he looked older. His hairline had inched quite a distance back from his forehead. He had let it grow long at the back and tied it in a ponytail, but his face had a haughty, proud kind of look, a far cry from the gauche, pimple-faced youth Maura remembered from her teens. It was obvious Shirley had a shine on him; her eyes sparkled as she hung on his every word.

'You probably remember me as a bit of a scallywag, Maura, but worry not, I promise you I'll have you looking beautiful before you walk out that door. I always did admire your bone structure, you know. Even back then I had this urge to make girls aware of their potential.'

'I'm glad to hear that, George, sorry, Ralph. It seems that, for better or worse, I'm in your hands.'

'And what capable hands they are. You'll be fine, Maura. And I swear if there is anything you don't like, we'll start over again. I have a new line in blusher and lipstick to try out. Is it all right if I test them on you? If you're not delighted with them when I've finished, I'll go back to the original plan.'

Maura nodded her consent and the transformation

began. As it turned out she was not disappointed. First her eyebrows were plucked; hastily she told Ralph that she just wanted a slight trim, and he took her at her word. With each hair he pulled out he asked for her approval.

'Is that enough?'

'That's fine.'

She suddenly realised that he was doing this, tongue in the cheek, to tease her, and with a wry smile she said, 'All right, I'll leave everything to you.'

He smiled at her reflection in the mirror and she had to admit he was an attractive man. As he went along, Ralph gave her some tips on how to apply make-up to suit the contours of her face and eyes. Shade here, highlight there. Remember to do this and remember never to do that, but whatever you do never do . . . She thought her head would explode as she tried to remember everything he said.

At last she couldn't hold her tongue any longer. 'That's easy for you to say, George, you're the expert. Look, I'm sorry, I just can't get used to calling you Ralph. Is that OK, George?'

'Of course it is. Feel free to call me anything you like, so long as it's not too early in the morning.' He laughed. 'I'm having you on, Maura. It's quite easy when you get used to it. Just don't overdo it.'

With clever strokes and various kinds of creams, Ralph explained what was best for her skin and natural colouring, and kept asking her whether she understood. Job finished, he at last stepped back and stood with arms folded across his chest, looking smugly at her in the mirror.

'Who's a pretty girl, then?'

Maura raised herself up in the chair for a clearer view. Even to her own eyes she looked beautiful. Her eyes appeared enormous and she found it hard to believe that her lashes were so long or her cheeks so prominent. She very much resembled Audrey Hepburn whom she had long admired. Shirley saw her reaction and said, 'I told you you would be pleased, didn't I?'

'I look lovely.' Her glance held Ralph's and her voice was humble. 'I can't believe that's me. Thank you very much, Geor— I mean Ralph.'

'I'm only doing my job,' he replied, but she could see that he was delighted by her enthusiasm.

Shirley removed the band protecting Maura's hair from the make-up and brushed it so that it fell into place around her face. A fitting finish to the new Maura Brady. 'There you are, Mrs Brady.'

'Thank you both, very much.' She gave a little giggle. 'I just hope my son recognises me.'

'I see you're married. Anyone I know, Maura?'

'I don't think so, but you might. Adam Brady? We live in Holywood now.'

He slowly shook his head. 'The name rings a bell but I can't put a face to it.'

Shirley was helping Maura into her jacket and with a final farewell she turned to leave. Ralph's voice stopped her. 'Hold on a minute, Maura. Shirley, give the lady one of those gift pouches. The latest one in. They are samples of the lotions and new-line cosmetics I have been using on you today, Maura. If you like them you can order them from any of my salons, any time. Just mention that you're a friend of mine and they'll give you a good discount.'

Opening a cupboard, Shirley took a black pouch from within and, putting it in one of the salon's black carrier bags with the device *Ralph* emblazoned across it in gold letters, brought it to her.

Although convinced that the cosmetics, even with the discount deducted, would be well beyond her pocket, Maura nevertheless thanked them both and headed out the door.

Outside she paused to check that she had all her belongings. A peek in the Ralph bag containing the pouch of free samples intrigued her, and spying a bench she sat down and examined the contents. It contained unusually big samples of six lotions and creams, eyeshadow, blusher and lipstick. Pleased, she continued on her way with a smile on her face, thinking the samples would last her a long time. She arrived at the previously arranged spot along the marina where she was to meet Beth and Danny, flustered and ten minutes late.

'Oh, I am sorry, Beth. I'm sure you're fed up hanging about all day for me.'

'On the contrary, I've had a wonderful time. Danny and I went to the beach and walked along the water's edge in our bare feet. Then we had a hot dog and ice-cream cones and Danny had a ride on the amusements. I haven't enjoyed myself so much in a long time. It was great . . . wasn't it, Danny?'

There was no response from the child and they both looked down at him. He was staring in confusion at Maura, with a comical expression. 'Mammy's face is different.'

Beth laughed. 'It sure is. It has surpassed all my expectations. Are you pleased with the result, Maura?'

'Pleased? I'm over the moon. I couldn't believe it was me in the mirror when he had finished.'

'He?'

'Yes, he. The top man himself. My, but that man is gifted. And wait till I tell you this, I recognised him. He's originally from Whitehouse. My da, before his accident, played golf with his father at Fortwilliam. His real name is George Nesbit. It's a small world, isn't it?'

'Is this *the* Ralph you're talking about?'

'The very same.'

'I've never had the pleasure of meeting him, but really you do look beautiful, Maura. But then, I'm not surprised, he had a good bone structure to work on.' She took Danny by the hand. 'Shall we tell your mammy the good news, Danny?'

The child's eyes lit up and he shouted, 'Yes, yes . . .'

'I've got a black Labrador puppy and Danny is coming home with me. He will help me to get it settled in because it will miss its mummy. Excuse me, I should be saying he, as it is a boy, but we haven't decided on a name for him yet. Danny would like to spend the night with us, if you will let him, that is.'

Danny had been listening to her every word and now his eyes implored Maura to agree.

'Of course you can stay, sweetheart.' She was rewarded with a big hug. She peeked into the car. 'Where is this new puppy then, Danny? Are you hiding him?'

'No, Mammy, the man has him.'

'We have to collect him from a friend's house on the way home.'

Above her son's head, Maura mouthed, 'Thank you so much.' Beth was making the way clear for Maura to be free for whatever happened that night.

'Let's get you home, so you can relax before your big night out, Maura.'

*　　*　　*

Disappointed at not being able to stay with Evelyn and face up to David, Adam returned to work in the garden. After all, that was what he was supposed to do, as David had so rudely pointed out to him. He was met by a barrage of questions from Jackie Flynn about Mr Matthews' condition. After he had brought him up to date, he suggested that they finish what Jackie was working on before lunch, as it looked as if rain was on the way. The rain didn't materialise and a hour later they were sitting on the steps of the veranda eating their sandwiches.

They were finishing their lunch when a taxi drove into the driveway. Evelyn stepped out, glancing about her. Catching Adam's eye, she beckoned him over and greeted him with relief. 'Adam, am I glad to see you. I forgot to bring my purse with me. Could you do the needful and then come into the house, please.' She thanked the driver for his kindness and headed for the front door.

Adam nodded and, hoping he would have enough money to cover the taxi fare, he fetched his jacket, relieved to find enough change in one of the pockets.

Apologising to Jackie for leaving him on his own again, he set him more tasks and, promising to be quick, strode off towards the house, removing his work boots before entering.

Evelyn lay prone on the couch, her eyes closed.

Adam approached her quietly and whispered, 'Are you asleep?'

Her eyes flew open and she reached out a hand. 'I've been waiting for you before I try to nod off.'

'How is Charles?'

'Holding his own. The doctor says things are looking favourable, but that the next forty-eight hours will be crucial. He told me to go home and get some rest. I hated leaving him there on his own but the doctor said there was nothing I could do. I asked him, what if he wakes up and asks for me? The doctor assured me there was little chance of him wakening before morning. So here I am. How much do I owe you?'

'Forget it.'

'No. Please, humour me.'

'No rush. Some other time. Can I make you something to eat?'

'I'm not hungry.'

'You have to eat something to keep up your strength,' he admonished her. 'How about some tea and a slice of toast?'

She made dissenting gestures, but he continued to stare at her. Throwing her hands in the air in surrender, she said, 'Oh, all right then, if you insist.'

When he returned with the tea and toast she was fast asleep. Leaving the cup and plate on a table close by, he threw a cover from the back of another chair over her slight form and quietly withdrew from the house. He and Jackie worked hard the rest of the afternoon and when the rain eventually came he felt it was better to call it a day. Making sure Evelyn was still asleep, he locked up. If he had to come back, she had told him where the spare key was hidden.

He dropped Jackie off at the nursery as usual with the day's worksheet. Seeing Benny coming towards the van, he pretended not to notice him and sped off.

Benny gestured for Jackie to leave the paperwork in the office and gazed after the fast-receding van in frustration. He had wanted to warn Adam that something was afoot concerning his wife and Maura. He hadn't a clue what the two women were up to, but he would dearly have liked to tell Adam to be careful, not to put his foot in it. To be forewarned and all that, but he never got a chance.

After a quick shower and shave, Adam put on his best suit with the shirt and tie that Maura liked him to wear. He decided that he had sufficient time to call in at the hospital and check on Charles, then go and see whether Evelyn was all right. That would set his mind at ease and he should have plenty of time to pick up his wife for their date. He had booked a table at the Chimney Corner Inn.

How he wished things were back to normal. Would they ever be? He just had to make her see reason, he resolved. Hopefully, tonight he would find the right words to convince her that he had been a silly, mixed-up fool and that he now realised Evelyn meant nothing to him.

16

Back home there was no sign of her father. Maura spent longer than usual examining her image in the hall mirror, turning her head this way and that. She had been too embarrassed to take a proper look at her reflection in the hairdresser's with others present and now she couldn't believe how well she looked. However, now that the excitement had worn off somewhat, she wasn't foolish enough to think that this transformation would last. Tonight at bedtime when she creamed off the make-up she would be back to normal and, she hoped, so would her relationship with Adam. Perhaps with the tips she had picked up at Ralph's she would in time learn how to make the most of her good points. For the moment she felt beautiful. Roll on tonight when she would see what reaction her glamorous looks had on Adam. She couldn't wait.

She was preparing her father's evening meal when he came in. He stood in the kitchen watching her through the open scullery door for some time, then slowly approached for a closer look.

Knowing his opinion of *painted hussies*, she stood shaking, head tilted, waiting for some sarky remark as his eyes roamed over her face. Thankfully there were no snide remarks. In fact Davey actually seemed pleased with what he saw. 'Amazing. For a minute there I couldn't believe it was you. You look beautiful. What brought all this on? Are you thinking of going in for one of those beauty competitions or something?'

She sensed a shyness at his frank appraisal. 'Adam is taking me out to dinner tonight and to talk things over: a make or break decision. Maybe the Last Supper.' She gave a tremulous smile at the pun. 'You know how it is.'

'Good! I'm glad to hear it. To tell you the truth, I'll be glad when all this is over and done with.'

Her lips trembled and she turned aside to hide the hurt that gripped her. 'Am I such a nuisance, Da? I didn't realise you felt so bad about it. Still, I don't suppose I can blame you for getting fed up with me and the child.'

Seeing her shoulders slump, he was quick to exclaim, 'Here now, don't go on like that. I'm not trying to get rid of you. And you're not a nuisance at all. Not at all! Do you hear me? I just want to see you happy again, is all,' he stressed, floundering about for some soothing words to say to cover his gaffe. Realising that it was too quiet, he changed tack. 'Anyway, where is the wee boy?'

'He's stopping over with Beth Gallagher tonight, so that I can be free to have it out with Adam.'

'That's a good friend you have there, lass.'

Her hands waved up towards her new look. 'I know. Beth is a very generous person, she paid for all this.'

'In my eyes you always look great, love. But you'll certainly bowl that husband of yours over. He won't be able to resist you. What time's he coming?'

'Seven. Do sit down, Da, your dinner's ready now.'

'Aren't you having anything?'

She smiled, a wonderful happy smile, as Davey passed her to wash his hands at the sink. His heart lurched in his breast at her obvious happiness. If Adam Brady lets her down, he'd kill him with his own bare hands. He'd strangle him, he vowed.

'I'm saving myself for the meal tonight.'

Davey ate his meal in silence. He was trying to figure out how he could make himself scarce and give his daughter the free run of the house. Maura wasn't eating anything because she didn't want to spoil her appetite for tonight but she sat at the table sipping a cup of tea and covertly watching her father.

'I've been thinking, Maura.'

'I know.'

He glanced up in surprise, then laughed. 'You know me too well. I'm taking Cassie to the pictures tonight and I'll be home late.'

'Don't stay out because of me, Da.'

He gave an exasperated sigh. 'I'm not, but Cassie and I need some time alone . . . to talk. When the film's over we'll take a stroll up to the Grove Tavern and have a few bevvies.'

Her face clouded. 'I really am spoiling things for you, Da, aren't I? Are you and her . . . you know?'

'No, we're not!' His fingers were crossed out of sight under the table. 'Besides, what if we were? Eh? We wouldn't be doing anybody any harm. We are both adults, in case you didn't know.'

'I just don't want to interfere with any future plans you might have. I'd be better off knowing how I stand if things don't work out tonight between Adam and me.'

'You'll stay here. That's what you'll do. Don't you go worrying yourself on that score. We'll sort this out between us, Maura. You go on and get ready and I'll clear up here when I'm finished.'

'Thanks, Da.'

She was on the bottom stair when his voice

reached her again. 'And by the way, I've decided I won't be home tonight.'

She hesitated, foot poised on the second tread, but decided not to question his change of mind. After all, he had made it quite plain that it was none of her business what went on between him and Cassie.

Davey sat slumped in his chair when Maura was gone. He hoped to God that that big eejit of a son-in-law of his would see some sense. Cassie was putting pressure on him and he could understand her point of view. He wasn't the only one interested in her, not by a long shot. Harry McCoy from the Mill Road, for one, was making a fuss of her every chance he got in McVeigh's. Sidling over to her table to have a cosy wee word in her ear when Davey went to the bar for the drinks, leaving her pink-cheeked and smiling at him. And then there was Kenny Patterson, another widower who was showing more than a casual interest in Cassie. Davey couldn't believe the jealousy that built up inside him when these two rivals were skulking around.

Sometimes he felt like laughing at the very idea of it. Imagine three auld lads like them, striving over the attentions of a middle-aged woman. Who would have thought it possible at his time of life to have feelings of jealousy? He would never have believed he would ever find himself in such a position. But he was, and he had, and, furthermore, he liked it. She made him feel young again, put a spring in his step. He had discovered that there was plenty of life in the old dog yet and he would like to cement his relationship with Cassie by putting a ring on her finger. He didn't want to be pipped at the post by two old fogies like Harry and Kenny, or by his own seeming lack of interest in marriage. But at the moment his hands were tied. His daughter and grandson must come first . . . this time.

Maura plumped up the cushions with unnecessary vigour for what seemed the hundredth time to try to diffuse some of her tension. She was a bundle of nerves. After much thought and consideration she had made up her mind to agree to whatever Adam suggested, putting her faith in his hands and trusting him to stand by his every word.

On the low table near the hearth she had set a tray with two wineglasses, for the bottle of rosé chilling in the fridge. Perhaps they would have a small drink before leaving. It might help settle her, give her enough Dutch courage to face up to what-ever lay ahead.

God, but this waiting was killing her. It was like watching paint drying. Her eyes drifted to the clock again. Adam was now ten minutes late. She moved to the window to peer through the nets; not too close, as she didn't want Adam to catch her on and know she was anxiously watching out for him.

When half past seven came and went, she sat with her elbows on the table, head in her hands, debating what to do. She was managing to keep the tears in check, just, as she tortured herself with the idea that Adam might not be coming. One moment she was hoping to be proved wrong; the next she was scorning herself for not wanting to ruin her make-up in case he did show up. Eight o'clock: she would wait until eight, then . . .

Then what, her mind screamed. At eight o'clock was she going to bawl and cry, let all the expense Beth had lavished on her get washed away in a flood of tears? Not if she could help it. But what else could she do? Go out on her own?

Another glance at the clock. She had twelve minutes left on the countdown, then she would have to think of something. Meanwhile she prayed that Adam would walk through the door. Surely he couldn't be so heartless as to leave her sitting alone like this? Something must have happened to delay him. She continued to pray.

At the hospital Adam was allowed in to see Charles. He lay, his upper body raised slightly and supported by pillows. His eyes were closed as if he were in a deep sleep or unconscious, with barely a rise and fall of his chest to indicate that he was still in the land of the living. Sensors were stuck to his bare chest, leading to a cardiac monitor unit on an adjacent shelf. The sister who had allowed Adam in to see his employer paused at the bedside and Adam questioned her.

'How is he, Sister? Will he pull through?'

'Holding his own. We'll keep him sedated for another twelve hours and then we'll do some tests. We'll know more about his condition then. Now remember, don't stay too long, just a few minutes.' She gave him a warning look.

'It's all right, I'll go now. Thanks for letting me see him. Goodnight, Sister. I'll call in and let his wife know the latest.'

'Goodnight.'

A glance at his watch told Adam it was a quarter past six. He should have time to call in and let Evelyn know that Charles was still sedated and would remain so until tomorrow morning. She could, without feeling any guilt, spend the night at home and get a much deserved rest. Then he would go down and pick up his wife, wine and dine her and beg her to give him a little leeway. He'd get down on bended knee, if necessary, and promise that he would never be unfaithful to her. If that didn't work, he would hand in his notice to Benny. He had made up his mind. He couldn't go on like this. His marriage must come before all else.

He had completely forgotten to take into account the rush-hour traffic. It was heavy going down the Falls Road to Northumberland Street, then crossing over the Shankill Road into Agnes Street towards Crumlin Road. At the junction he made a right turn, passing HM Prison and the Mater Hospital on the left as he headed for Carlisle Circus. Why couldn't they have taken Charles to the Mater, he fumed, and save all this hassle? At Carlisle Circus he turned left on to Antrim Road, about fifteen minutes from his destination, providing there were no hold-ups.

He was not so sure now that he would still be in time for his date. Fingers impatiently tapping the steering wheel as he crawled along in the traffic, he pictured Maura working herself into a right old state. They certainly were going to get off to a bad start if he arrived late.

Halfway along the Antrim Road it suddenly dawned on him that he must be running low on petrol. A glance at the gauge confirmed this and soon he pulled into Fortwilliam petrol station, exiting from one queue and joining another at the pumps. Adam was really getting anxious now. Everything was going against him and it was fast approaching seven o'clock. Still, with a bit of luck he should be able to nip in, set Evelyn's mind at rest and then drive down Whitewell Road and arrive, if not at seven, at least shortly thereafter.

Raring to go, when his turn came he quickly filled up, paid for the petrol and nudged his way back into the main flow. The traffic seemed to have eased somewhat, enabling him to make better progress along the Antrim Road. With a sigh of relief he at last turned into Evelyn's driveway, only to stop in consternation. David's car was parked outside, close to the front door. Did this let him off the hook, Adam mused?

Could he just go on, now he knew she had company? In a quandary, he debated what to do for the best. He was fast running out of time; even now he would be a bit late. But . . . what if David was harassing Evelyn? Reluctantly, he swung down out of the van. There was nothing else for it: he would have to go inside and find out how the land lay.

He climbed the steps, but before he reached the door, Evelyn, who was crossing the hall on her way to the kitchen, saw him through the side window, hurried to the door and pulled it open. Putting a warning finger to her lips, a frightened look in her eyes, she beckoned him in.

'Thank God you're here,' she whispered. 'David's inside.' As if he could fail to see the big saloon car taking up half the driveway. Adam hung back, but gripping him by the arm she tugged at his sleeve until he followed her into the hall and she closed the door.

Adam reluctantly let himself be led until they were in the kitchen, plagued with the thought that he was definitely going to be late now to pick up Maura.

Distracted, Evelyn clasped him close. 'What am I going to do, Adam?'

He tried in vain to release himself from her arms. 'Listen, Evelyn, you'll be all right! I . . .'

The kitchen door was thrown open with such abandon that it banged hard against the wall, causing Evelyn and Adam to jump apart as if caught out in some guilty act.

David surged in, his face livid with rage as he glared at Evelyn. 'So this is where you are.' She cringed backwards and his gaze turned viciously on Adam. 'What are *you* doing here?'

Adam drew himself up to his full height. 'That's none of your business. But since you ask, I'm here to see Mrs Matthews on a private matter.'

'I can see you're not dressed for work and I'm sure you're not going for a job interview at this time of day.' His voice dripped with sarcasm. 'Is there something going on here behind my father's back?'

Adam's fists clenched at his sides but he controlled his voice. 'You know something? You've got a dirty mind, mister. I have been up to see your father in hospital and then called in here to find out how Mrs Matthews is fending—' He was rudely interrupted.

'And do you embrace all your employers with a kiss and a cuddle every time you meet them? Your wife must love that. Does she know anything about the carry-on here between you two?'

Adam continued as if he hadn't heard him, 'And let her know her husband is holding his own, but still in a deep sleep. There's no need for you to go back to the Royal, so you can spend the night at home, Evelyn.' Adam could have cut off his tongue for letting her name slip out, but he went on, 'And see your husband in the morning. Now if you'll excuse me, I'll be on my way. I've an appointment to keep,' he glanced at his watch, 'and I'm already late.'

'Ah! So it's Evelyn, now, is it?'

Evelyn intervened. 'I asked Adam to address me by my first name; it makes our talks less formal. Not that it's any business of yours,' she added defiantly.

'How cosy. So that's why you're dressed to kill. You thought you could spend the night here with Evelyn. Maybe coax her into bed. Isn't that it? But unfortunately for you, I got here first and spoiled your lecherous plan. You can be on your way now. I'll look after her.'

'Don't go!' Evelyn was obviously agitated. She gripped Adam's arm. 'Please stay.'

Without taking his eyes off David, Adam gently prised her hand from his arm. 'I have to go, Evelyn.

338

I'm picking up Maura from her father's house and I'm already late.'

A sob caught in Evelyn's throat. 'Please stay. I don't want to be alone with him.'

She was trembling. Aware that she was a very good actress, Adam examined her closely for a moment but was unable to tell whether she was putting on one of her acts. He decided to delay no more. After all, what harm could David do without incriminating himself? He wouldn't dare hit her. He couldn't afford to risk it, of that he was sure. Too much depended on what Evelyn told his father should he make a full recovery.

Adam moved hesitantly into the hall. David followed him and with a flourish, gallantly opened the front door, practically pushing him out. Without another word, he slammed the heavy door on him with a resounding thud.

Undecided, Adam hovered outside on the veranda for some moments, uncertain what to do. Then, retracing his steps, he peered through the side window of the door. The hall was empty. Making his way along the veranda, he cautiously looked through the lounge window; the room was also empty. Changing direction, he went along the veranda to the back of the house and gingerly tried the door. It was unlocked and he quietly let himself into the back hall. He could hear heated voices coming from the kitchen and paused to listen.

David's voice was gruff with passion. 'Listen to me, Evelyn. Please! I only want to convince you that I care for you. I really do care.'

'No, you listen to me! I don't want you to care for me. Your father's hanging on to life by a thread and you're worried in case he's changed his will. Isn't that what's prompting you to suddenly declare your feelings for me? I can read you like a book. It's his estate you're so worried about. You're worried that Charles will leave everything to me. Well, I don't know anything about the will. Charles never discusses business with me.'

'No, you're wrong. I'm honestly not interested in the will.'

The catch on the kitchen door wasn't caught properly. Adam had softly pushed it open a crack and could see the couple. Evelyn had been backed into a corner near the cooker and David stood squarely in front of her, blocking her escape. He was leaning close, speaking earnestly.

'I've loved you from the very start, Evelyn. I was devastated when you went off to live in Cork. If my father should die, I'll take care of you. Surely you must have guessed my feelings for you?'

'What?' Evelyn was flabbergasted. 'You actually expect me to believe that? Why, you've always treated me like a piece of dirt. You and Rose put me down at every opportunity. Your father had to warn you off, remember? He even told you to watch your mouth, or else.'

'That was because I couldn't let my wife know how I felt about you. My life wouldn't have been worth living if she had even guessed the truth.'

Her shoulders slumped in defeat. 'I don't want to hear any more of this drivel. Just shut your mouth and crawl back to your wife. But before you go, listen to this. Strange as it may seem to you and a lot of others, I care a great deal for your father and I pray he'll pull through this latest scrape. Charles is a fighter and I'm sure he will.'

'And you expect me to believe that?' David's voice had risen an octave and little flecks of froth shot from his mouth as he ranted. 'Why, it must be obvious to all and sundry that you're carrying on with that . . . that slimy git of a gardener. Surely you can do better than that contemptible pig. You know you can.'

Without more ado, Adam burst into the kitchen. 'One thing is obvious. She certainly doesn't want you, so why don't you go and leave her in peace?'

David swung round and with a howl of anger propelled himself in a headlong rush towards Adam. Unprepared, Adam tried to ward off the blow but wasn't quick enough. David's fist caught him on the side of the head, knocking him off balance and sending him crashing against the wall. Before he could recover, another blow landed squarely on his nose and blood spurted everywhere.

Evelyn stood mesmerised, unable to believe her eyes. Then she surged forward and, grabbing David's arm, she hung on, forcefully insinuating her body between the two brawlers. When Adam would have retaliated, she urged him, 'No, Adam . . . don't! David is leaving. Aren't you, David?'

He stood, arms swinging by his sides, a tight smirk of satisfaction spreading over his face at the sight of Adam's blood dripping from his nose and splattering down the front of his shirt and tie.

Pleased at his handiwork, he nodded his agreement but leered into Adam's face. 'All right, I'll go for now. But don't let me find you inside this house ever again. Right? Stay where you're supposed to be, out there in the gardens. And I'll tell you something for nothing: if my father should die, you really will be out on your sorry ass.'

Adam couldn't hold his tongue. 'Only if you're still mentioned in the will.'

'Why you cheeky—'

This time Adam was ready for him and a hard, straight left jab smacked into David's mouth, stopping him dead in his tracks as if he had run into a brick wall, followed by a right haymaker that landed flush on his chin, jerking his head back and sending him sprawling down on the carpet. He howled with pain as the blood ran down his chin from his split lips.

'Let that be a lesson to you, big head. Never lower your defence until you're clear of the enemy. I hope I've loosened a couple of those expensive-looking gold fillings. Now get the hell out of here before I really lose my temper and give you a good hiding.'

'Go! Please, David. I'll speak with you tomorrow,' Evelyn pleaded.

Scrambling groggily to his feet, he backed reluctantly away and reached for his jacket. When the door closed on him Evelyn turned to Adam with a heartfelt 'Thank God.'

Motioning him to sit down, she went into the downstairs bathroom and returned with a towel, a wet flannel and a box of plasters. Cupping his face in her hands, she examined his features intently and murmured, 'Poor dear,' gently kissing him on his mouth, which was starting to puff up from the blow to his nose. He drew back with a wince and she apologised. 'I'm sorry, so sorry. I didn't mean to hurt you. You've already suffered enough because of me.'

'He took me unawares. If he ever tries it on again he'll finish up next to his dad in the Royal.'

Guessing his pride was hurt, she assured him, 'I know he did, but he suffered for it. And it was all my fault, so it was.'

The bleeding had stopped. She cleaned his face with the flannel and gently patted it dry. 'You'll look the worse for wear in the morning, but for now you're not too bad. You'll pass.'

When he examined himself in the mirror he laughed outright, a bitter, hoarse sound that caused him pain. His nose looked out of shape and he gingerly tweaked it, thinking it might be broken. His eye where the first blow to his head had landed was starting to swell. He looked a right sorry sight, as if he had been in a bar-room brawl. Imagine arriving at Davey Craig's door in this state. He couldn't do it. He'd have to go straight home.

She made to put a plaster on his injured eye, but hesitated. 'That might need a stitch or two.'

He waved her away and rose shakily to his feet.

'I'm glad you came back, Adam, thanks. Sit down. I'll make you a cup of sweet tea.'

He declined the offer. 'No thanks. I should have cleared off when I had the opportunity. You'd have been all right with him. The guy's besotted with you. He wouldn't have dared touch you, at least not to hurt you. I just happened to be there.'

'I had no intention of letting him paw and slobber all over me, if that's what you mean. Then what would he have done? We don't know what he's capable of when he doesn't get his own way. He's a spoiled brat and I'm glad you came back.'

'You'd have been able to control him.' Adam

nodded towards the clock and wailed, 'Look at the time.' It was almost eight o'clock. 'I was supposed to pick Maura up at seven. I'll have to go. I'll see you in the morning.'

Evelyn was startled. 'You can't leave me here alone. What if David comes back? What will I do?'

'What you do best,' he growled. 'Use your charm on him. Or, better still, lock up and go to bed and don't answer the door to anyone.'

With these words of wisdom and not giving her a chance to protest, Adam was out the door.

Before climbing into the van he examined his clothes. What a mess! He groaned in frustration. It was his best suit too and blood was so hard to remove. Maura would kill him. He laughed at the foolhardy idea. He was an hour late. She probably wouldn't even speak to him. He'd have to go on home.

Tomorrow he would see his wife and try to explain away the situation. No! He'd better go down there now, he decided. The bloodstained clothing would be evidence enough of the cause of his being late: that he'd been in a fight. Maura would certainly not appreciate him receiving the wounds through protecting Evelyn, but he would have to chance it: throw himself on her mercy and hope that she would take pity on him.

The blood from his nose had dripped mostly on to his tie and jacket. He removed them and examined his shirt as best he could in the wing mirror of the van. Not too bad. He would go and see Maura, lay his cards on the table and hope for the best.

Taking his time driving down Whitewell Road, he went over in his mind how best to explain to his wife what had happened to delay him and had to admit that even to his ears it didn't sound too good. He could imagine her response: why did you go to see Evelyn in the first place; why put her first when we had a date? She would go on and on, and although he could see her point of view he'd probably protest at the unfairness of it all, and nothing would be gained. He could but try.

The clock on the mantelpiece struck eight. The chimes trespassing into the quietness of the house startled Maura from her reverie. What to do? She examined her options. There weren't many. Monday night was a bad night for socialising. Most people would remain indoors, relaxing after the weekend, and wouldn't appreciate unexpected visitors. Her father and Cassie were at the pictures so she needn't go to McVeigh's. Monday night was a slow night with only the few, old, regular diehards sitting over a pint on their usual seats in the bar; the lounge would be empty, so that was out. Her Aunt Hilda would be at home, but Dennis and the girls would be there as well. Where on earth could she go? She had to get out of the house before she drowned in self-pity. Then Maura recalled a chance remark Francie Murphy had made.

He had actually made it to her father in Maura's presence: 'I'll be in Conway's early on Monday night if you're at a loose end, Davey. Me ma wants a bit of decorating done and I'm meeting Billy McDowell there to go over what's wanted, so I'll be there till about half eight.'

Before her courage failed her, Maura was on her feet, grabbing her bag and her jacket. She must not let pride stand in the way. A glance at the clock showed it was after eight o'clock. She had better hurry or she might miss him.

A glance into Conway's bar showed no sign of Francie. She was too late. As she paused, a voice hailed her from inside the bar.

'Are you looking for your da, Maura?'

'No. No, actually I thought I'd catch Francie Murphy in here, Peter.'

'He hasn't been in tonight, Maura.' He asked the company he was in, 'Anyone see Francie tonight?'

Heads shook, and thanking them Maura moved further into the hall. Eyeing the foot of the stairs that led to the lounge, she listened for sounds. It was very quiet up there. Was it worth while going up? She was of the opinion that the lounge didn't open on a Monday night. Well, she was here now,

347

so might as well make sure. The lounge was indeed open for business, and Francie was sat there huddled deep in conversation with Billy McDowell.

He had his back to the door, so it was the barmaid, Marie, greeting her that made him aware of her presence. With a glance over his shoulder, he quickly rose to his feet. Saying something to Billy, he came over to join Maura as she was ordering a fruit juice.

'I'll get that, Marie.' He gestured to an empty table. 'Would you like to sit over there, Maura? I'll join you in a minute.'

He paid for the drink and brought it over to her table, his eyes taking in her appearance. He nodded as if in approval and said, 'I've almost finished my wee bit of business. I'll only be a couple of minutes.' He coloured slightly. 'Perhaps I'm being too presumptuous. I take it you want to talk to me?'

She laughed. 'I can't see anyone else here. I hope you don't mind me seeking you out?'

'No. Not at all.' It was getting more intriguing by the minute. With a smile he hurried back to his table.

Not many minutes later he was back. As Billy passed her table Maura acknowledged his nod of farewell with a 'Hi, Billy, how's Sue these days?'

'Fine, fine. She's probably up in Grace McLaughlin's now, putting the world to rights. You know what these women are like when they get together,' he replied with a wink as he moved on.

'Tell me about it,' she called after him.

Francie wished him goodnight and sat down at the table.

He raised his glass to Maura. 'Cheers. You look fabulous. Does this new look mean that you and Adam are back together?'

'Far from it, I'm sorry to say.' Feeling her emotions were getting too close to the edge for conversation, she said, 'I don't want to talk about Adam. I needed to get out for a while and I remembered you saying you'd be in here tonight.' Her glance swept the empty room. 'Look, I don't want to stay here. I'm hoping you'll take me somewhere. Somewhere nobody will recognise me. That is . . . if you're not otherwise committed?'

He shook his head; he had nothing on tonight. 'That won't be too hard to do. I hardly recognised you myself. The car's parked outside. I've only had this half-pint, so drink up and we'll set off into the unknown.'

They made desultory conversation as they finished their drinks. He kept gazing at her and Maura knew he was longing to ask her what was wrong, but he kept the conversation neutral. Soon, with a shout of farewell to Marie, they left the lounge and descended the stairs. Outside on the pavement Francie faced her.

'Where would you like to go?'

'Anywhere! I just don't want to spend the next couple of hours alone in that house. I need some company.'

At the bottom of Whitewell Road, Adam halted the van to let a bus pass along the Shore Road. From his position he could see that there was no sign of life in Davey Craig's house. Surely Maura wasn't waiting in the dark? The bus passed and he glanced to the left to see whether the road was clear. He noticed Francie Murphy's Austin Cambridge parked on the road outside Conway's and was just in time to see Francie exiting the bar and heading over to his car. Adam was about to move off when Maura stepped out on to the pavement. He couldn't believe his eyes. *The bitch!* She couldn't wait. He could have crashed the van and been lying badly injured somewhere, and she couldn't sit at home waiting and wondering what had happened to him. Oh no! There she was, dolled up to the eyeballs and climbing into the car with her old flame, Murphy.

At least now he knew where he stood: Maura didn't care whether or not she came back to live with him. In fact, he was making it easier for her to leave him. He'd have to see a solicitor and make sure he had access to his son before that budding romance took off. Grief wracked him as he sat in abject misery.

The blast of a horn from the car behind made Adam aware that he was holding up the traffic. He had been so consumed with anger that he had forgotten where he was. A glance again to the left showed him he had missed which direction Murphy had taken. With an apologetic wave at the driver behind, he indicated and, turning right, headed towards town.

At Fortwilliam Park he came to a decision. Why go home to an empty house when Evelyn would welcome him with open arms? Why indeed? With a defiant thrust of his chin he indicated to the right and turned the car up Fortwilliam Park towards Antrim Road. He might as well enjoy himself too.

17

Dazzling sunrays streaming through fine curtains lit up the bed, enveloping Maura in a warm comfortable glow. Still in the throes of a very pleasant dream she lay snug and contented. Throwing an arm across her eyes to shield them, she turned on her side away from the glare. She had settled down again into an easy doze when a loud thumping noise invaded the tranquillity of the bedroom. Who on earth was hammering at this time of morning, she wondered, pulling the blanket over her head to lessen the din. Just what time was it anyway? They'll waken Danny. Thoughts of her son brought her upright, causing her to fall back again with a groan as a sharp, stabbing pain pierced her head. She peered at the bedside clock with sleep-filled eyes but couldn't focus on the hands.

She slumped back on the pillows, holding her head tightly between her palms, trying to squeeze out the pain until reality sank in. She must be suffering from a hangover! That was the only time she felt this sick. The night before flashed before her eyes and soon the reason for the hangover became apparent. At the same time it registered in her mind that the hammering outside was on her own front door and Danny wasn't in his cot. Who could it be, she wondered?

Completely disoriented, she staggered out of the room as quickly as she could muster under the circumstances and, grabbing the banister firmly, gingerly descended the stairs. As she crossed the hall the insistent knocking continued and she growled angrily, 'All right! Hold your horses, I'm coming.' She unlocked the front door, pulled the bar off and, throwing the door wide, squinted at the figure standing on the pavement.

A bewildered Francie Murphy gazed back at her in amazement, making tutting sounds. 'Did you sleep in?' His eyes took in the dishevelled state of her clothes and he exclaimed in disbelief, 'Did you go to bed at all?'

She scowled at him. 'What's it to you?'

He was very aware of her pale drawn face and smeared make-up. Her usually well-groomed hair was in spiky disarray, as if she had been dragged backwards through a bramble bush. He pushed roughly past her.

'Close the door before someone sees you in that state. You look a right mess.'

'OK, there's no need to make a song and dance about it.' She shut the door and stamped after him into the kitchen. 'Anyway,' a frown bunched her brow, 'what do you think you're doing here? Eh?'

He was angry now and it showed in his tight-lipped expression. Placing his bag of work tools on the floor, he turned on her. 'Look at yourself. You're a disgrace, so you are.'

For the first time Maura glanced down, took stock of herself and whimpered, obviously in dismay. He was right. She was still in the clothes she had worn the night before. Her skirt was a mass of wrinkles and hanging awry: her top was only half secured and her new tights were laddered. She was indeed a complete mess.

He gazed intently at her for some moments. 'You're not with it, are you? Anyone looking at you would think you had been on drugs last night instead of Pernods. That's what I would have thought, only I was with you.'

It was her turn to look bewildered, and then pictures started to filter through the fogged layers of her mind. Images of sitting across from Francie Murphy, trying to eat a steak that kept sticking in her throat and washing it down with rosé wine.

She must have drunk the full bottle. Oh, surely not! Sinking down on the settee, with her elbows resting on her knees, she clasped her head in her hands. 'Give me a chance to think,' she pleaded and blinked up at him with bleary eyes. 'We were out last night, weren't we? Together?'

'That's right. We went to the Steak House but you ate practically nothing. And you didn't have all that many Pernods. I can't believe you're in this state.'

He really couldn't. When he'd left her at the front door the night before she had appeared a bit tipsy but otherwise fine. He had declined her offer of a coffee and shooed her off to bed, all with the best intentions. Aware of how vulnerable she was, and not knowing how things were between her and Adam, he had been afraid he would be tempted to give in to the emotions that were surging within him, demanding release. If she did indeed split with Adam, that would be a different matter entirely. He would be there to pick up the pieces, that was for sure, but until then he would avoid being alone with her again. It might make him try to manipulate things to his advantage.

'Look, the reason I called this morning was because when I passed the house on my way to the bus stop there was no sign of life. I knew Davey wasn't at home last night and—'

She was suddenly all attention. 'How did you know? Who told you?'

'For heaven's sake . . .' What on earth was the matter with her this morning, he wondered? '*You* told me, last night! Don't you remember?' A slight shake of the head was his answer, plummeting him into more confusion. 'You also told me that your friend was keeping Danny overnight and was bringing him back this morning.'

At the mention of her friend, Maura jumped to her feet, wincing with the pain it caused. 'What time is it?'

'Half past nine. I should be in work by now.'

'Oh my God! Beth will be here soon, and look at me.' She gazed wildly around the kitchen.

'Listen to me, Maura. The place is spotless.' His eyes noted the wineglasses sitting ready and put two and two together. Adam had let her down. 'Go and have a wash with cold water to waken yourself up and make yourself more presentable. I'll stay here in case this Beth comes before you're ready. Who is she anyway?'

'My good friend from Holywood. What about your work?'

'I'll go in late.'

'Thanks, Francie. I owe you.'

'We'll talk about that later. Away you go and tidy yourself up before anyone else comes.'

She climbed the stairs and in her bedroom mirror examined her face with distaste. All that money wasted; she creamed the make-up off. It saddened her to think that Adam hadn't seen her looking so glamorous and now he never would. But Francie had, and what an awakening he must have got, seeing her in this state a mere few hours later – such a difference.

From what she could recall of the previous night, they'd had a pleasant time. She hadn't drunk much, just wine with the meal, but could she possibly have drunk a full bottle? She doubted it. A couple of Pernods and limes in a bar afterwards. Francie was drinking non-alcoholic lager because he was driving, so she *had* probably finished the wine. What a foolish thing to do. And Francie had let her! What had he hoped to gain? Another thought filtered through in her bemused state, making her more alert.

Ah! There lay the answer to her sorry, painful state. Mixing her drinks, on top of the two sleeping tablets she had taken from her father's medicine cabinet, wouldn't have helped; she was probably lucky to be alive this morning.

Francie had been so kind that she had gradually relaxed and, pushing her hurt and frustration to the back of her mind, she had managed to give a good impression of enjoying herself. When he had left her, she had taken the tablets to ensure she got a good night's sleep, to be ready to face the barrage of questions Beth would fire at her this morning. Adam hadn't been mentioned, not once while she was out with Francie, and for that she was grateful.

Pleased to have sorted out the reason for her memory block, she felt much better. Grabbing her washbag and fresh clothes, she descended the stairs. Francie had his head stuck in the *Daily Mirror* and didn't even glance in her direction as she passed him and locked herself in the scullery.

When at last Maura was as ready as she'd ever be for Francie's inspection, he rose slowly to his feet and ran a critical eye over her. 'That's much better,' he smiled. 'Now you can go out and face the world.'

She was pale-faced but composed. He was glad that she obviously hadn't spent the night crying over Adam Brady; her eyes were like green emeralds, clear and shining in a colourless, wan face. To his eyes she still looked beautiful, even without all that extra make-up.

'I'll be off then. Is it all right if I call back tonight?'

'Please do.'

Beth's car pulled up to the kerb as he left the house and she glanced at Francie, a frown furrowing her brow. When she opened the car door, Danny scrambled out and ran to throw his arms around Francie's legs. Dropping his tool bag to the pavement, he scooped him up and tossed him in the air. 'How's my best wee boy?'

Danny whooped with delight and gasped,

'Auntie Beth has a new puppy. Haven't you, Auntie Beth?'

'I certainly have. Tell this gentleman what you named him.'

But Maura had come to the door and Danny struggled down from Francie's arms and ran to her. Francie thrust out his hand towards Beth.

'You must be Beth.'

'And you must be Francie. I'm pleased to meet you.'

'Likewise. Here's my bus coming, I'd better run. Bye for now.'

Grabbing his bag from the ground he ran up the road. Beth watched him climb on the bus and then went to greet Maura, her mind in turmoil. Had that young man spent the night here? It looked very much like it.

Maura must have read her mind, as she gave her a wry grimace. 'It's not what you're thinking. He just called in on his way to work. Come inside, I'll make us some coffee.'

Danny was full of chatter about the new puppy. The women were seated facing each other with elbows resting on the table as if preparing for an arm-wrestling contest, before he quietened down long enough to eat some biscuits and afford them a chance to talk.

Even then, having been stood up by Adam, Maura was loath to tell Beth about her experiences

359

of the previous night and kept the talk on a general level.

'Danny certainly enjoyed himself by the sound of it.'

Fed up with the small talk and anxious to know what had gone wrong, Beth asked, 'And what about you? Did you enjoy yourself last night? Where did Adam take you?'

Taking a deep breath to steady her voice, Maura said, 'He didn't take me anywhere.'

'Oh-h-h.' Beth paused for a moment to let Maura elaborate. When she didn't, she probed further. 'So you just had a quiet evening at home, then?'

'No. Adam didn't bother his backside to turn up.'

Beth gasped in amazement. This was so unbelievable. She slumped back in her chair. 'You're having me on, aren't you?'

'Would I fib about something as serious as that? I only wish I could.' Maura's voice was low and sad. 'I sat here in all my finery until eight o'clock, but he didn't bother showing his face.'

'So you were alone? Poor dear, you must have felt awful. Why didn't you go across to that public phone and ring me? I'd have come over.'

Maura hated the pity she felt radiating from her friend. 'Thanks, Beth. I would have, but I didn't intend letting all the money you spent on me go to waste. I waited until after eight, then I went over to Conway's bar where I knew Francie

360

Murphy would be. He took me into town and wined and dined me. We had a marvellous time but . . . he didn't stay the night, and no matter what you might otherwise think, it's the God's honest truth.'

'I see.' Beth didn't see anything of the kind and her doubt showed.

'He didn't! Honestly! Did you see what he was wearing? Do you think for one minute he would have taken me out in his old work clothes?'

'Maybe not,' Beth agreed none too confidently, thinking that he could have nipped home and changed. 'But were you right to go out with him? Surely Adam came eventually and made his excuses?'

'Afraid not.'

'How do you know if you were away out with that lad?'

Maura shrugged her shoulders in exasperation. 'I just know.'

'He didn't put a note through the letter box later on explaining why he was held up?'

Maura mutely shook her head and her face crumpled as she fought back the tears. Beth was wearing her down and she didn't want to break down in front of her or Danny. If she started blubbering now, God knows when she would stop.

Beth reached for her coffee and sipped at it to give her friend time to gain control of her emotions. She didn't mean to badger Maura, but she intended getting to the bottom of this affair and finding out what really happened last night.

After a short pause, during which Maura reached for a tissue and gave her nose a good blow, Beth continued. 'Adam must have had a very good reason to let you down,' she said with conviction.

'Oh, I'm sure of that, and I can guess the very good reason. Her name is Evelyn Matthews,' she answered sarcastically.

'No.' Beth was decidedly shaking her head. 'It must have been something very serious. He would never have left you sitting here, waiting. He cares too much, so he does.' Ignoring a derisive snort from Maura she went on, 'With hindsight I can't believe Adam is as bad as you're making him out. I'd trust him with my life. Are you maybe letting jealousy cloud your mind?'

'Huh! You're entitled to your opinion. I know him better than you do and I never want to see him again. As soon as I can arrange it I'll move all my belongings over here to me da's house and I'll never speak to Adam Brady ever again. I'll make a fresh start here.'

Beth stretched forward, gripping her friend's hand. 'Listen, Maura, please don't do anything foolish until you've heard Adam's side of the story. He could have been involved in an accident, for all you know. At this minute he could be even lying at death's door in the Royal or somewhere. Have you thought of that?'

Maura's chin dropped. 'No! Oh, no.' It had never entered her mind.

'I don't want to frighten you, but accidents do happen, you know.' Beth picked up her handbag and headed for the door. 'I'll go over and call the police and ask if there were any accidents reported last night and, if so, who they were.'

Maura stood at the window to watch Beth cross the road and enter the phone booth. She was gone a while and Maura guessed that the police had her friend on hold. What would she do if Adam was injured, or even dead? How could she live with herself for doubting him? After what seemed a lifetime to Maura, Beth left the booth and returned.

Maura met her at the door. 'Well, what did they say?'

'They were kind enough to check their records for me and no young man of Adam's description was involved in an accident.'

Relieved, but not willing to show how much she cared, Maura shrugged. 'See? I told you so.'

'That doesn't mean he's safe and sound.'

'I think I'd have heard by now, don't you? Now, I don't want to see or hear tell of him ever again.'

Adam drove up Fortwilliam Park still fuming. He couldn't believe what he'd just seen with his own eyes: Maura dolled up to the eyeballs, looking great he had to admit, but stepping into Francie Murphy's car. Of course, he had been very late. Would he have given her the benefit of the doubt if the boot had been on the other foot? On reflection he didn't think so. Was he doing the right thing coming up here to cry on Evelyn's shoulder?

Of course he was, he argued with himself. Maura was expecting him. She should have waited; anything could have happened to delay him. He could be dead for all she knew. In the circumstances he felt justified to seek other company.

When he turned into Evelyn's driveway, there was still a light burning downstairs in the house and he sat debating what to do. He longed for someone to talk to. He didn't want to be alone at this moment but he was aware that he might get more from Evelyn than he bargained for. They were both in fragile states: she worrying about her husband and him all cut up over the shenanigans of his wife. They would be crying on each other's shoulders and, with neither of them in control of their feelings, anything could happen. And wasn't that what he was secretly hoping for?

He dithered so long that Evelyn became aware that a car was outside. Peering out to make sure it wasn't David, she saw Adam's van. Opening the front door of the house, she looked anxiously across at him. When he remained seated in the van, she came out and approached it.

'What on earth are you sitting out here for, Adam? Come inside for heaven's sake. For a minute there when I heard the engine I thought it might be David back, but I don't think he will return now. Is anything wrong?'

She thought he was here to protect her from David Matthews; how wrong she was. He was here because he had been rejected. 'Maura stood me up.'

'I find that hard to believe. Come inside and tell me all about it.'

'Why? Why would she not reject me? I was over a hour late. I was just in time to see her get into an old flame's car and take off, and it hurt; it hurt badly. I'm in need of some company, Evelyn.'

Evelyn was dumbfounded. She couldn't comprehend the idea of Maura rejecting Adam. 'Did Maura see you? Like, I mean . . . was she putting on an act for your benefit? Rubbing your nose in it?'

'No. They were too busy looking at each other to notice me. I could have been lying dead somewhere for all she cared.'

'Ah, now, you don't know that. She was probably putting on a big act for this guy, whoever he is.'

'Well if she was, it was an Oscar-winning performance. It was one hell of a good act, I can tell you. She was beautiful. She was all aglow. I've never seen her look so lovely. She must really fancy Francie Murphy to go to all that trouble.'

'Please come inside, Adam. I'll make us something to eat and we'll chew the fat, see what we can make of it. I still think you're wrong about Maura.'

Evelyn busied herself in the kitchen, wondering what was wrong with her, that she wanted to convince Adam that he still loved his wife. If Charles died she would find it hard not to turn her attention to Adam, but it would be a different matter entirely if Charles survived. Some people simply would not believe that she truly loved her husband and found it more convenient to brand her a gold-digger. She shut her eyes and offered up a prayer. Please, God, let Charles live and bring him back safely to me.

Adam sat nursing his hurt pride. His eyes had been opened, and he had to admit that he deserved all he got. He had been treating Maura rather shabbily. He had expected her to believe everything he said and follow his lead blindly. He was surprised that she had put up with him for so long. Had he ever told her how much he loved her? No! They had been married almost four years and he hadn't uttered a single word of endearment to her. He had never taken her on holiday or made a really big fuss over her. It had always been nose to the grindstone, pulling his weight at the nursery and working on the house at weekends. He had had no time for socialising. He cringed with shame as he realised how isolated and neglected Maura must have felt.

Evelyn's voice jarred him awake. 'Come in here, Adam, I've made a couple of omelettes and a small salad. We can eat at the kitchen table.'

Adam joined her and took his place at the table. He didn't particularly like omelettes and, with a slight grimace at the plate she set before him, said, 'What's in it?'

'Chopped ham, mushrooms and tomatoes. It's all I could rustle up at such short notice. I've heated up those bread rolls and made a pot of tea, so take it or leave it.'

Adam was ravenous. Once he sampled it and found out how tasty the omelette was, he cleared his plate in record time and devoured three of the warm crusty rolls, dripping with butter. A far cry from the planned slap-up meal at the Chimney Corner Inn, but delicious nevertheless. Leaning back in his chair and nursing a second cup of tea in his hand, he complimented her. 'That was very tasty indeed, Evelyn, thanks. I didn't imagine you could cook.'

'Don't be so insulting! Who do you think feeds Charles?'

'Sorry. Sorry. I enjoyed it. It was very kind of you.'

'You're welcome. Now tell me why you're so down on Maura?'

He shrugged. 'I just think we've reached the end of the road as far as our marriage is concerned.'

'Is it because of me?'

'Yes, that and other things.'

'Look, much as I care for you, Adam, I want my husband to live. I admit that I was toying with the selfish idea that I might have you on the side as well. But I would never leave Charles. Never. I don't expect you to believe this, but in my own way I do love him and I feel safe and comfortable with him. His brush with death has made me realise how much I would miss him. You see, Adam, I really do love Charles.'

He scowled. 'I'm pleased to hear it. To be truthful, I was very attracted to you when you returned. I imagined that I still loved you, but it must have been an echo of the past that blinded me from my responsibilities. I suppose I did give Maura cause for concern. Now that I know how much she means to me, I'm terrified I've driven her into Francie Murphy's arms for ever. It would serve me right. I imagine it was the sight of the two of them together that brought me to my senses and made me realise how much I love Maura. Now I don't know what I'm going to do.'

'Well, we'll just have to see how it goes and we most certainly will not give Maura any more reason to doubt you. When Charles gets better . . .' She paused and blinked back a tear. Dabbing at her eyes with a lace hankie she said, 'I've got to be positive about this, Adam, or I'll go off my rocker. When he is well enough I'll wait on him hand and foot. Who knows, maybe we'll go on that cruise he's always talking about. Meanwhile, you can tell your boss to send someone else over to finish the gardens. I'll vouch for you if he has any doubts.'

Adam reached for her hand and gripped it tightly. 'Thank you. I really think Charles will pull through, Evelyn. I really do. And I'll keep him in my prayers.'

'Only time will tell. Now let's go to bed.' She laughed at his start of surprise. 'Don't worry, it's not a proposition. I'll make up the bed in the guest room for you.' He followed her slowly up the stairs as he pondered on how things had changed. Was he too late to win Maura back?

Adam awoke late next morning. He had a shower and, feeling refreshed and more at peace than he had done for a long time, he dressed and made his way downstairs. Evelyn was in the kitchen and the aromatic smell of coffee filled the air.

'Good morning, sir,' she said gaily. 'I feel much more hopeful after our talk last night.'

'Do you know something? So do I, and I think we could be friends.'

He took the cup of coffee she held out to him

and their fingers touched. Startled, he glanced up to catch her reaction. She had obviously felt the tingle. Or maybe not, he thought. Maybe it was all his imagination.

Becoming more businesslike, he said, 'When I finish this coffee, I'll have to rush off. I need to go home and change, then collect Jackie Flynn and some shrubs and plants from the nursery. I'll see you later.' Draining the cup, he left it on the table. 'Bye for now.'

Evelyn stared after him for some seconds. She had sounded so convincing the night before and she had meant every word of it, but the attraction was still there. They had both felt it. They would just have to put a damper on it, kill it stone dead. She didn't want to ruin what she had going with Charles. Nor did she want to separate Adam and Maura. In her heart she knew that he truly loved his wife and she didn't want to spoil that, for lustful gratification. Oh, God, please let Charles make a good recovery.

Adam was in a more settled frame of mind after his conversation with Evelyn. True, there had been a small spark of electricity between them this morning, which they had managed to ignore, but that could be contended with. They would see very little of each other once Steve was put on the job and he would crawl all he had to, to make Maura understand.

As he approached the bottom of Whitewell Road, he pondered whether or not he should call in now and start grovelling. Maura would want her pound of flesh and the sooner he gave it to her the better.

He changed his mind, however, when he saw Beth's car draw up to the kerb. At the same time the front door of the house opened and Francie Murphy stepped out. Adam could see that Beth was surprised and not too pleased to see Francie. They exchanged words, then Danny jumped from the car and ran to Francie. Adam seethed with rage as the other man lifted *his* son in the air and Danny squealed with delight. Then Maura came to the door, and Danny ran to her.

Adam glanced right and left and, seeing the road was clear, he turned to the right and with a screech of tyres roared past them. To his great chagrin no one paid him any attention.

18

Davey Craig was whistling as he stepped into Grogan's shop to collect his morning paper. He felt happy and contented but still a little apprehensive. Surely Adam and Maura had resolved their differences last night, which would leave him free to make his own plans. He'd had a lovely evening with Cassie, a long, uninterrupted discussion away from the distractions of the auld lads in McVeigh's sticking their nebs in. They had talked about the future – something he had always shied away from before – and furthermore she had agreed to wait . . . but not indefinitely. Fingers crossed that Maura would be preparing to return to Holywood when he got home, then it would be full steam ahead.

'Top o' the morning to you, Annie,' he greeted the girl behind the counter, a big smile on his face.

Annie Moore had always thought him a very dour person and was surprised at his show of exuberance. She answered him merrily, 'And the same to you, Davey.' She reached him his *Daily Mirror* and continued, 'What have you got to be so cheerful about this fine morning?'

'Why not?' He held his hands wide in supplication. 'It's a beautiful sunny day. The birds are chirping and the future looks bright. What more can I say?'

Still amazed at the difference in his demeanour, she said, 'Nothing apparently. Lucky you. I saw your Maura last night and she sure looked a treat. Oh, to look like that.' A long envious sigh accompanied the words. 'Have you won the pools or something?'

In the act of paying for his newspaper, Davey paused. 'Oh, and where might I ask did you see Maura?'

Annie was eyeing him strangely and he realised he was still holding on to his money. With a smile of apology he relinquished the cash.

Annie said as she took it, 'I thought you didn't want to part with it there. What were we talking about? Ah, I remember, your Maura. I stayed behind last night to help Mrs Grogan do a bit of stocktaking and as I was leaving the shop I saw Maura come out of Conway's.'

'You sure? What time was this? I thought she was going to the Chimney Corner Inn for a meal.'

'About half past eight.'

Davey frowned. What on earth was Adam playing at? He was supposed to be taking Maura out to wine and dine her, not take her to the pub for a drink. In fact, Maura wouldn't have settled for less. She'd want her due in all ways. He tilted his head and chided her, 'I think you're seeing things, Annie.'

Annie's slim frame straightened indignantly. 'Oh no I'm not! I saw her with my own two eyes. Her and Francie Murphy came out of Conway's and got into his car and they headed towards the town centre, not in the direction of the Chimney Corner. So there!'

Hiding his alarm, Davey edged towards the door. 'You're probably right, they must have changed their minds.' No need to whet her appetite for gossip by mentioning that anything was out of place. Annie obviously wasn't too bothered about Maura going out with Francie Murphy. Less said soonest mended. He conjured up a smile and said, 'See you later, Annie.'

Davey wasn't whistling now. In fact he was gutted. All his happiness wiped away with a few innocent words. What on earth was his daughter playing at? She had looked so beautiful and happy, and Adam had put a note through the letter box, saying he would pick her up at seven. How had he resisted her? What could possibly have gone wrong between them? Had Adam said something to needle her and had Maura jumped on her high horse and sent him packing again? Davey couldn't believe that. In his heart he knew Maura wanted her husband back. Deep in gloom now he approached his home on reluctant feet, dreading the news that surely awaited him there.

Beth pleaded earnestly, but in vain, for Maura to seek Adam out and give him a final chance to explain himself.

'There's always two sides to every story,' she had insisted, but Maura was adamant that she would never speak to Adam Brady again. From now on they would correspond through their respective solicitors. She was so cold and emotionless, Beth couldn't get through to her. What on earth was Adam thinking of to have let his marriage crumble like this without making an effort to save it?

Hearing a key rattling in the lock, Maura rose resolutely to her feet. Throwing Beth a warning glance to remain silent, she prepared to face her father. She feared that, between them, Beth and Davey would wear her down and make her seek Adam out for an explanation. She was determined this must not happen. What excuse could he possibly offer? There was no way that she would ever submit to him, because that was what she would be doing. She had given him every chance, every opportunity to make amends. But no more. Enough was enough! She would never willingly see her husband again if she could help it. His betrayal had been long drawn out and painful. She ached to the very core. Then to crown it all, to have let her down as he had last night, when everybody was waiting with bated breath to see the outcome . . . Ah, no, the hurt went far too deep for forgiveness and reconciliation.

Staring her father straight in the eye she greeted him with her rehearsed speech.

'Da, before you say anything . . . Adam didn't come here last night. Nevertheless, Francie Murphy kindly took me to the Steak House to show off the new me and we had a marvellous evening, but we didn't spend the night together. We are just good friends. I want to make that crystal clear from the beginning so you will understand why I don't want to hear Adam's name mentioned in my presence in this house again. So please bear with me while I make a new life for Danny and myself. I'll get out from under your feet as quickly as I can.'

Davey stood open mouthed. He had prepared himself for bad news, but this was disastrous. Damn Adam Brady! He had done it again. He had let his wife down. By God, he would gladly strangle the bastard with his bare hands, given half a chance.

He stared at her in confusion, unable to drag

up words of comfort. Before he could think of any kind of reply, Maura went into the scullery and closed the door.

Bewildered, Davey turned and made a face to Beth. 'What was all that about? What happened?'

Beth shrugged and sent a glance in Danny's direction. The boy had sat quiet while his mammy had been bringing Grandad up to date. Beth realised that the boy was bright enough to know something was wrong and that it involved his father. There was a worried pucker on the child's wee face.

Quick on the uptake for a change, Davey went to the boy and hunkering down in front of him said, 'How are you today, Danny? Did you enjoy your stay with Beth?'

Danny scrambled to his feet, distracted for the moment from his worries. 'Yes, Grandad. Beth has a lovely new puppy and she let me name him.'

Lifting him up into his arms, Davey ruffled the child's hair. 'That was very kind of her. What name did you give him?'

The child giggled, obviously proud of the name he had chosen. 'Frisky, because he's always running around my feet trying to trip me.'

'That's a grand name. Shall we go down to Grogan's and buy some sweets and you can tell me all about Frisky?'

'Yes, Grandad.'

'See you later, Beth. Say goodbye to Beth, Danny.'

'Bye-bye.'

There were no sounds from the scullery, and after tapping lightly on the door Beth opened it. The room was empty but the back door was wide open, like an invitation, and she continued on out to the back garden. A fist seemed to grab her heart and she felt like crying at the sight before her. Maura was sitting hunched over on a wooden bench, tightly hugging herself as if for warmth and swaying slowly from side to side. Her face was pale and drawn and Beth wished she would cry, releasing some of the tension that was engulfing her. Such a difference from the happy, beautiful girl of yesterday. Adam Brady had a lot to answer for. Still, she couldn't believe he would deliberately do something like this, not without just cause.

'Mind if I join you?' she asked tentatively.

Maura mutely nodded agreement and Beth sat down beside her. Maura turned and faced her.

'I apologise for wasting all that money you spent on me yesterday, Beth. I was really so hopeful and proud, but you know what they say . . . Pride comes before a fall. I really thought deep inside that it was going to work out for the best last night, but Adam had to spoil it all as usual. I just don't understand the man any more, but it's the last time he'll let me down, I promise you that. I'll pay all that money back some time in, I hope, the not-too-distant future.'

Putting her arm across Maura's shoulders, Beth drew her close and heard her out. 'Now you listen to me, girl. I'm not bothered about the money. I told you that was my treat. I don't want anything from you.' She paused a moment then continued, 'Unless of course I can persuade you to talk to Adam. That would please me no end. I'm sure in my heart that he didn't deliberately let you down.'

Her arm was shrugged roughly away. 'I'm sorry, Beth, but I can't do that. I'm dead inside and I don't want him to make a fool of me ever again. I think at this moment I actually hate him.'

'Don't you know that hate is akin to love?' her friend said gently.

'No, you're wrong there. The hate I feel inside me now makes me want to drive a knife into his cheating heart, again and again and again. That's how much I hate him.' She tossed her head and faced Beth. 'Would you mind very much if I ask you to leave? I need time to think, to sort out what I'm going to do.'

Beth readily agreed. 'I understand that you want to be alone, but will you let me take Danny back with me? He senses that all is not well here, and if I take him home with me, the puppy will distract him. Will you do that?'

Maura gave this some thought. She knew that

she would lose all her composure if Danny was with her. She'd break down and be crying all over him and the child would get upset.

'I think that's a good idea. That's if you're sure you don't mind? What about Benny? Won't he object?'

'Away with you. You know Benny loves that child. It'll be a pleasure to have him overnight again and also give you a chance to sort out your problems. I'll keep Danny as long as need be, Maura, remember that.'

'Thanks, Beth, I appreciate everything you're doing and I'm so sorry for being so curt with you. I'll go and pack some of his things and a few toys.'

'Good, and there's no need to apologise; I understand fully the strain you're under.'

When Davey came back and heard about this arrangement, he was far from pleased. He waited until Beth took Danny out to the toilet. 'I think you're doing the wrong thing, Maura. Adam is sure to want to see his son, then what'll you do?'

'Tough! Adam will see his son when I say so and not before.'

'He won't take this lying down, you know,' Davey cautioned. 'You mark my words. You'd better prepare yourself for one hell of a fight.'

'Don't worry. After all he's put me through, I'll fight him tooth and nail. There'll be no holds barred. He'll not know what hit him.'

Davey saw not only his daughter's chances of happiness, but his own, going down the drain. If this wasn't resolved now, it never would be. And then what would become of him?

Hating himself for putting his own needs before his daughter's, Davey said, 'Ah, now, Maura, you know you don't mean that.'

'Don't I? Just watch me.'

When Beth came back with Danny, Maura went to him and took him in her arms, hugging him close and whispering in his ear. 'You're going back with Beth, love, to help walk the puppy.'

'But, Mammy . . .'

'Not for long, love, I promise. I have things to do here but I'll come for you soon.' The child continued to look bewildered and she didn't blame him. Sending Beth an imploring look, she said, 'I've Danny's clothes ready, Beth. If you'll grab that box, I'll see you out to the car.'

Danny's anxiety returned and he twisted round to look at Beth. 'I don't want to go. I want to stay with you, Mammy,' he cried, a sob catching in his throat.

Hugging him close, Maura explained, 'Listen, love, Frisky will be looking for you. You have to go and look after him.' Still he dithered, not knowing what to do. 'Please, love?'

Eventually with a farewell hug and kiss for Grandad he let Maura lead him out to the car.

Beth nodded across to the phone booth. 'Thank God that's handy. You'll ring if you need me?'

'Yes, I will.'

'Any time, day or night. Promise?'

'I promise. Away you go, and thanks for everything, Beth.'

She waved the car out of sight, then straightening her shoulders she went indoors to face her father.

Adam was now running late for work. He drove the van past Gallagher's, hoping no one would notice, and went home to change into his work clothes before going back to the nursery. When Benny Gallagher saw the van turn in and drive as far past the office as space would allow, he went out and dandered over to meet Adam. Jackie Flynn followed him and they waited as Adam climbed out and slowly turned to face them.

Jackie's jaw dropped and Benny exhaled a hiss of dismay when he saw Adam's face.

Adam smiled wryly and said, 'You should see the other guy.'

'What happened?'

'Let me show Jackie what we require today and he can start loading the van, OK? Then I'll bring you up to date.'

Benny nodded affably and headed back towards the office. He sat at his desk in deep thought until Adam entered, then gestured for him to sit down.

He waited in silence for an explanation from his employee.

Adam took in his grim expression and started his monologue. 'Has Jackie told you what happened when we arrived at work yesterday morning?' A slight shake of the head from Benny brought a frown to Adam's brow. 'That's strange. I thought he would have filled you in.'

'Why should he? He wasn't in charge. He headed straight home as usual when you dropped him off. You were the one who should have "filled me in" as you so nicely put it. Why didn't you? Instead you took off as if the devil himself were after you. Was it because of the state of your face?'

'No. No, this . . .' He gingerly fingered his swollen nose. 'This happened much later. Let me start at the beginning.'

'I think that would be a good idea.' Benny nodded and settled back in his comfortable chair to listen.

'When we arrived at work yesterday morning there was an ambulance in the driveway. A few minutes later Mr Matthews was carried out on a stretcher. He looked awful.' Adam met Benny's stern gaze. 'To tell you the truth I thought he was a goner, Boss.'

'Why didn't you phone me? I'm sure Mrs Matthews would have allowed you the use of her phone, had you asked.'

'Everything happened so fast, I didn't have time to think. Evelyn was devastated, didn't know whether she was coming or going.'

'Evelyn?' Benny's eyebrows lifted in query. Although he already knew who Evelyn was, he asked, 'Who may I ask is Evelyn?'

'Mrs Matthews.' The anger Adam had dampened down and thought he was in control of raised its ugly head again and his guard slipped. His words were clipped and cold. 'Why the interrogation?'

'This is not an interrogation, so keep a civil tongue in your head, young man. If you had had the decency to stop and report to me yesterday, I wouldn't have had to ask all these questions. I do pay your wages after all and am certainly entitled to know about anything that interferes with my workers doing their job satisfactorily.'

Inwardly, Adam had to agree with him; he hadn't been thinking straight. 'I'm sorry. I should have kept you in the loop. You see, the nurse knows that Evelyn and I are friends from way back and she asked me if I would be able to follow the ambulance to the hospital and make sure Evelyn was all right.'

Benny frowned. 'The nurse asked *you*, a complete stranger, to follow the ambulance?' He sounded incredulous and Adam didn't blame him.

'No, no, not the nurse from the ambulance. Linda Morrison, the district nurse who attends to

Mr Matthews every morning. She had to go on to another patient. I gave Jackie enough work to keep him busy and did as Linda asked.'

George Gallagher came into the office and looked from one to the other of them in silent bewilderment. Benny canted his head, indicating that he leave, and with a puzzled expression on his face he backed out the door.

Uneasy now, Adam thought he must really have blown it. He kept silent for some moments until Benny prompted, 'And?'

Adam had never seen Benny in this light before; he had never known he could be so distant and calculating. He had always found him easygoing, ready to see the other person's point of view: the complete optimist. He licked lips that had now gone dry. He knew he was in the wrong, having broken every rule in the book. His job could be on the line here.

Cautioning himself to be careful what he said, he straightened in his chair, and once again apologised. 'I'm sorry, Boss. I was way out of order.'

In his heart he didn't really think he was out of order. He had only done what had to be done, what any decent person would have done under similar circumstances, but it was vital that he pacify his boss.

Benny was no doser. Sensing that Adam thought that he was making a mountain out of a molehill, he decided to give him something to worry about.

'You know, Adam, up till now I had great faith in you, thought you could be trusted to put your job first. But you've let me down. You actually left your post with an apprentice in charge. What if a neighbour was watching the antics of you? What if someone was waiting to see how you did the job before approaching you for an estimate for his garden, eh? I imagine that request would go to another nursery. I certainly wouldn't give the job to someone who was flying his kite instead of getting stuck in. I was just saying to George the other day that you were ready for advancement but you've knocked that on the head, good and proper.' He turned away in disgust and rose to his feet to show the interview was over. 'Away you go and get that job on the Antrim Road finished. I'll have to think what I intend doing about you. And don't think to leave the job again without my say-so.'

Jackie Flynn resigned himself to another miserable day. He had always liked working alongside Adam in the days before he was made up to site manager. Then Adam had been light-hearted and happy, always singing to himself or cracking jokes. Nowadays he was morose and hardly spoke a word to him.

He had been unconsciously giving Adam covert looks to try to ascertain his mood when Adam suddenly turned and snapped at him, 'What the hell are you looking at?'

'Sorry, sorry, no need to bite off my head. I know the boss gave you a rough time back there and I was just trying to think of something comforting to say.'

Adam grimaced and confessed, 'You're right! He did give me a rough time, but I deserved it. There's no need to take it out on you, Jackie. Sorry.'

Turning into the Matthewses' driveway, he wondered what today had in store for him. Surely it couldn't be any worse than yesterday . . . or could it?

19

There was no sign of her father when Maura returned inside. She guessed he would be out the back smoking. Tempted though she was to go on upstairs and avoid the inevitable confrontation, she squared her shoulders, deciding to face the music and get it over with. On reluctant feet she passed through the scullery to join him.

Davey was standing on the sturdy box conveniently placed against the garden fence, from where he could see the football pitch behind the houses where the local team, Castle Rovers, played. Distant shouting proclaimed that the local lads who were out of work had gathered there and a five-a-side match was in progress. He glanced round when he heard her come through the back door and, with an abrupt nod towards the bench, gestured for her to sit down, then turning his attention back to the football he ignored her completely.

An uneasy silence reigned for a while, her da puffing angrily at his Woodbine as if smoking was going out of fashion, refusing to look in her direction and avoiding her eyes, which were fixed firmly on his back, urging him to look at her. Maura sat, mentally trying to string words together in a bid to explain her feelings in such a way to her father that she could still manage to keep a roof over her head without losing face; she couldn't afford to alienate him now.

At last she cleared her throat and broke the silence. 'Da, I'm sorry if I have upset you.'

She hesitated, a puzzled frown bunching her brows as she was struck by a sudden thought and pondered on it for some moments. The revelation brought her to her feet, all apologies forgotten as she found herself glaring at him in anger.

'Actually, I'm surprised at your attitude,' she accused him. 'Just what gives you the right to judge me, eh? Not so long ago you were ridiculing me for turning a blind eye to Adam's carry-on up in that house, as you so politely put it. As if you thought it was a den of iniquity. How dare you? And do you know something else? At that time I really didn't know Adam was working there. I was still in the dark. In fact I'd just heard from Mary Moon the day before that Evelyn Matthews was back. So how could I have possibly known that Adam was playing away? Eh? Tell me that.'

She shook her head at the enormity of it. How had she been so blind, letting her da speak to her like that in Conway's?

'You, however, knew Evelyn was back. Why didn't you let me know if you were so worried what Adam might get up to? Instead of which, you sat in a corner of the bar and derided me for being an eejit. Fine father you turned out to be, letting me find out from Mary Moon when the talk of Evelyn Matthews' return must have been all over the village. You bastard. You knew and had obviously already made up your mind that he was having an affair, whereas I was completely in the dark. I still don't, for that matter, know whether he is or ever was carrying on. But you've the gall to be upset because I won't admit defeat and try to win back Adam's affection. Why? Has he suddenly sprouted wings, or been canonised lately?'

She sighed and turned away in disgust. 'I still don't know whether Adam is up to no good, or what people expect of me. But one thing you can be sure of: I will never give in to Adam Brady. I'm the victim of the piece here.'

Match forgotten, Davey had stumbled in startled dismay from the box in the face of her hostile assault. He tried in vain to interrupt her tirade from time to time, gesturing at the fences dividing the gardens, miming a warning of what his neighbours might hear, but she shouted over his endeavours.

'Do you know something, Da? I don't give a damn about the neighbours. I want an apology from you.'

Admitting that he had been in the wrong was humble pie that Davey Craig was loath to swallow, but he made an attempt and said gruffly, 'Things have changed since then, Maura. I'm not as sanctimonious as I used to be.'

To his surprise, instead of being pacified she hissed back at him, 'Is that supposed to be an apology? If it is, then you can stuff it.'

Davey spread his hands wide, palms down, patting the air in a placating motion. 'All right, I was wrong. I admit it, but as I've pointed out, it's all a different ball game now.'

'Do you think I don't know about that? You and your secret love affair. You're behaving like a wee schoolboy with a crush on his teacher. I'd have thought you were above that kind of nonsense by now.'

Davey recoiled with embarrassment. His face flooded with colour and he spluttered angrily, 'How dare you! How dare you speak to me like that, you young upstart? If you had behaved yourself and not let Adam Brady have his way with you in the first place, none of this would have happened. I was ashamed of you. But remember this. In spite of it all, if it hadn't been for me, you wouldn't have a roof over your head now. Who else would have taken you in, I ask you? You with your wounded pride, and your sarcastic tongue. Let me tell you something, my girl, you can't afford to be proud with a child to care for.'

Maura was mortified; she had let her temper rule her tongue. It was her turn to flush deeply. They faced each other like bare-knuckle fighters waiting for the bell. Dear God, to think it had come to this. She hadn't meant to antagonise her father. What would she do without him? Where would she go with a young child to look after?

With great difficulty and a lot of gulping for breath she gained control of her voice.

'Da, I'm sorry. I shouldn't have said all that. I really don't begrudge you your happiness. In other circumstances I'd be delighted for you. It hurts that I've come between you and Cassie. But that's your fault again, so it is,' she accused him. 'You played your cards so close to your chest that no one knew anything about your involvement with Cassie. Not even Mary Moon, and you know what she's like. So it came as a shock to me. You should have been honest with me at the start. I never meant to upset your routine, your plans for the future. I promise, Da, I'll work something out and get out from under your feet as soon as I possibly can. If you'll just bear with me in the meantime. OK?'

She turned to leave, then turned back to gaze at him bleakly. 'I don't suppose you know anybody who has a couple of rooms to rent?'

He reared back on his heels and glared at her with such indignation that she recoiled in fear. Then, head hanging in shame, he said, 'Don't you dare think of looking elsewhere for rooms. Do you hear me? This is your home. I won't let you down again. I promise you that.'

She was silent so long that he glanced at her for her reaction. Tears, long denied, poured silently down her cheeks. With an exclamation of concern, in three strides Davey was beside her, gathering her close, nestling her face against his chest, patting her sympathetically on the back. 'Ah, there now, daughter, don't let it get to you like this. We'll work something out between us. Even if it means me pushing Mr bloody Adam Brady under a bus.'

She snuggled closer, smelling the familiar cigarette scent on his cardigan, the long-remembered musky fragrance of Burley aftershave he used daily. She was glad of the comfort, needing to feel wanted. This was the closest she had ever felt to her father in many a long year. It was heartwarming to know that in spite of their differences she had family who cared for her and Danny's well-being.

'No, Da, that would never do. In spite of everything, you see, I still love him,' she wailed. 'Poor silly old me. In fact I've never stopped loving him and I always will, no matter what.'

'Ah, love, I know. I know you do. And do you know something? I think he still loves you too.'

Davey wished with all his heart he hadn't interfered at the beginning. Perhaps he and Adam would have got over their grievances by now. Even if they hadn't, the big galoot had made Maura happy and he knew now that was all that mattered.

Silently Maura took these words to heart. Could it possibly be true? She didn't think so.

'What about the child's birthday? You'll have to let him see Danny then, so you will.'

Maura pushed back from her father's arms and gaped wide-eyed into his face. She had forgotten completely all about her son's birthday. Quickly she mentally counted the days. He would be three this Sunday. 'Good Lord, I'd forgotten his birthday. Completely forgotten all about it. I'll have to go and get him.'

Davey moved between her and the door. 'Not today, you won't. Tomorrow. You can fetch him home tomorrow. Today you're going to rest. OK?'

Glad to find that Evelyn had already left for the hospital, Adam set about trying to make amends with Benny for his negligence. His boss had sounded so disappointed in him. He didn't think that he had much hope of making him change his mind, but he could try. But what if Maura were to apply for a legal separation? What would he do then? He would need to have a job.

He shook his head in exasperation. For heaven's sake, it was only a matter of weeks since all this nonsense started, he reminded himself. He would have no bother getting another job. Maybe not as good a position as he had at Gallagher's but enough to live on until he found something better. He didn't know personally any couple who had separated and fought for custody of their children, so had no idea just what was in store for him.

Still, if they couldn't come to an agreeable arrangement about sharing Danny, he'd have to file for custody. He couldn't afford to sit back and let Francie Murphy get too comfortable with his wife and son. What if Danny learned to care more for Francie than himself? How had it come to this? What exactly had he done to deserve all this aggravation?

Suddenly he stopped in his tracks, questioning his thoughts and causing Jackie to bump into him with the wheelbarrow loaded with compost. Adam let out a yelp of pain and almost toppled over backwards into the wheelbarrow.

Jackie quickly steadied the barrow. 'Sorry, Boss, I didn't know you were going to stop so suddenly,' he wailed, frightened of Adam's likely reaction.

'It's all right, son. How could you? I didn't know I was going to stop.'

Jackie looked stupefied. 'Huh?'

'Forget it. It was my fault entirely, Jackie. Let's get on with the job.'

As he dug a trench Adam was thinking. He hadn't done anything wrong. A few kisses were no grounds for a separation, let alone a divorce. Whereas on the other hand Maura appeared to be getting on quite nicely with Francie Murphy. Hadn't he seen him on Tuesday morning leaving her da's house where he had obviously spent Monday night? Had it been so innocent? How could it be? They must be having an affair. It would be the obvious assumption of anyone watching them. Adam knew now how much he loved his wife and he hoped he hadn't pushed her into doing something foolish. If she had, then Church or no Church, it was the divorce courts that they'd be facing.

Then again, Maura was no mug, he consoled himself. She wouldn't jump out of the frying pan into the fire. There had to be an innocent explanation for seeing Francie Murphy leave the house so early in the day. In a happier frame of mind, he set to work. He and Jackie gave it their all and laboured non-stop, taking only a half-hour break for lunch. Here, at least, everything was beginning to come together and Adam was able to envision how the back garden would look when they were finished. All the major tasks were taking shape; in his mind it would be like paradise. He sincerely hoped Charles Matthews lived to enjoy it.

Late in the afternoon, wiping the sweat from his brow with a rag, Adam said fervently, 'That was a grand day's work, eh, Jackie?'

'It sure was, Boss. I'm exhausted. Job satisfaction is a wonderful thing, isn't it? If we hadn't had so many interruptions, this garden would be finished by now. The front garden won't take half as long.'

'I agree with you there, Jackie, but for heaven's sake don't let Benny hear you say that.'

'I won't.' Glancing over Adam's shoulder, Jackie said, 'Here's Mrs Matthews now. I'll start packing the van. All right, Boss?'

'Yes, you do that, while I enquire after Mr Matthews.'

Evelyn unlocked the door and, gesturing for him to follow, entered the house. Adam felt obliged to obey, though he had hoped never to set foot in it again. He was ashamed at how often he had wanted to be alone with Evelyn here. He had lusted after her. What on earth had possessed him? If he lost his wife, he had no one to blame but himself.

In the hall she turned to him. 'Charles was in surgery for such a long time today it seemed as if he had been in there for ever.'

'Were you on your own in the Royal?'

'No, David was there most of the time. The surgeon says they can't of course be certain, but the operation went well and Charles should make a good recovery. Isn't that great news, Adam?'

'Thanks be to God! That is indeed great news.'

She looked at him, lips trembling and tears glistening in her eyes, the blue of her fine wool twinset turning them to sapphire. She looked beautiful and fragile and lost. He longed to take her in his arms and comfort her, but he acknowledged the danger and kept his distance. They were tears of relief and in spite of her declaration of love for her husband it would be tempting fate. That spark might just take them unawares and explode into a raging inferno.

Still keeping his distance, he gestured outside. 'Come out and see how well the garden's looking. It's beginning to take shape at long last. Charles will be pleased when he comes home and sees it. It'll help his recovery.'

Dabbing at her eyes she followed him and stood gazing about her in surprise. 'You're right, it certainly is beginning to take shape.'

He walked her around the garden pointing out different plants and shrubs, explaining how they would all complement one another when they bloomed. Tour over, he stopped and fixed his gaze on her and held out his hand. She took it hesitantly. 'Is this what I think?' she asked.

'Yes, I won't be back, Evelyn. Steve will probably take over here from now on.'

'Are you all right where Maura is concerned?'

'I'll have to work on that, but I hope so. Goodbye, Evelyn. I'll clear up here and be on my way . . . And by the way, don't take any nonsense from that David fellah. Sure you won't?'

The tears were dropping fast and furiously down her cheeks and he knew he must go – and quickly.

'Listen, Evelyn, talk everything over with your solicitor before you commit yourself to anything, no matter how trivial it may seem to you. Confide in him and take his advice at all times. That's what you're paying him for. To look after your interests. OK?'

She nodded and he gave her a quick peck on the cheek, then hastened to where Jackie had finished loading the van. The sooner he was away from her the safer it would be for him.

When they arrived back at the nursery there was no sign of Benny. Leaving Jackie to put away the tools and get rid of the rubbish before he went home, Adam went looking for his boss.

He found Benny in the greenhouse where the tropical plants that required expert attention were kept. Adam watched him, as with gentle hands he examined the delicate plants for any sign of disease, then fed them from bottles that lined the shelf above. He glanced up at the sound of Adam clearing his throat.

'I was just thinking about you.'

Heart thumping in his breast, Adam asked fearfully, 'Not all bad, I hope?'

Benny threw him a slight smile. 'I need to talk to you in private, somewhere we won't be overheard.' He glanced at his watch. 'I'm just about finished in here. Everybody should be away by now, so we can sit uninterrupted in the office.' Taking a final check of the temperature he led the way out.

Adam trailed behind him, trying to sort out in his mind how to put his excuses across without appearing a complete idiot or a crawler. Seated across the well-worn desk from him, holding a whiskey cupped in his hands, he consoled himself that all must not be lost. Surely Benny wouldn't be giving him a whiskey if he was planning on sacking him? Adam wasn't very partial to spirits but he needed some Dutch courage, so he sipped the pleasant-smelling liquid, surprised at how smoothly it passed down into his stomach. Unconsciously he licked his lips and Benny nodded approvingly.

'That's Jameson's! Warms the cockles of your heart, it does.' It was his turn to clear his throat. 'As I'm sure you're aware, we've always wanted to branch out, and lately with Steve and Desi Keenan showing so much potential I thought the

400

time was right. Well, these past few months George and I have been looking at some properties that would be suitable for converting into nursery grounds.'

Adam straightened in his chair, giving Benny his full attention and realising that he was being warned that he now had competition in the form of Steve and Desi.

'Mind you, it was harder than I thought trying to find anywhere suitable within a given radius that would be acceptable all round. The workers don't want to spend too much time travelling. Then, just by chance I was speaking to a friend in the club one night and he was telling me about a cousin of his who was selling his smallholding. It sounded just what I was looking for. A couple of arable fields, but with one big drawback. He is also selling the house that sits on the land. My friend advised me to go see him and see whether maybe I would be able to change his mind and get him to sell the house separately, but in spite of my persuasions, he declined the temptation, more's the pity.'

Benny reached for his glass and sipped at it. His wife had arrived home the day before with Danny still in tow and Benny had at last heard all the ins and outs of Adam's alleged affair. The whole sorry tale about the possible separation was related in hushed tones when Danny was in bed. It had come as a shock to Benny, this happening just when he was preparing to set the lad up to manage the new nursery.

'Seems this man's wife died some months ago and he is going to live with his only daughter and her family in Canada. He wants everything sold, lock, stock and barrel, as soon as possible, so that he won't be going out empty-handed, expecting charity from his daughter. He wants the luxury of being able to pay his own way. I can understand his point of course. I'd feel exactly the same.'

'Yes, yes,' Adam agreed with him and took another sip of his whiskey. He sat on the edge of the chair tensed, afraid of saying the wrong thing.

'It's a lovely spot on the outskirts of south Belfast. I asked Beth whether she would fancy moving there but she wasn't in the least interested. She loves where we live and we have the house the way we want it, so why move? I had to agree with her.'

Adam thought it safe enough to back him on this. 'Beth's right. Your house is beautiful and in a lovely elevated spot. You'd be daft to move.' He tentatively asked, 'What about George? Would he not sell his flat and move there?'

A real genuine laugh answered his words. 'Come off it, Adam. You know our George wouldn't move for all the tea in China. Leave his flat? That flat's his whole life. And living so close to his beloved golf club? No chance. So you can forget about George moving. Wild horses couldn't budge him.'

'You seem set on this piece of land. Would you not consider putting a manager in charge?' Adam winced at the scornful look Benny bestowed on him.

'A manager?' he bellowed. 'I had you in mind for the job. I couldn't believe my ears when I heard of the capers you got up to. Chasing a married woman, indeed. Have you no sense at all, lad? Maura is a lovely girl and a great housekeeper. And, take my word for it, they're all the same under the blankets.'

The imp in Adam that popped up at inconvenient times prompted him to retort, 'How would you know?' However, he quickly stifled the desire and defended himself. 'I wasn't chasing her. I sent Steve over there right at the beginning, remember? But you overruled me. I was between a rock and a hard place, so I carried on and hoped for the best.'

'Why didn't you confide in Maura? Surely she would have understood.'

'That's where you're wrong. You see, I was once engaged to Evelyn Matthews and she dumped me for a man old enough to be her grandfather.'

'Did Maura know this?'

'She was the one who helped me out of a deep depression and eventually we married. She always feared that Evelyn would return one day.'

'Seems she was right then to worry.'

'No, listen . . . please. I love Maura, but I think she might have turned to an old flame for comfort. From experience I know where that can lead.' He leaned forward in his chair. 'Are you still thinking of offering me the job?'

'Only if you sort out your problems and quickly. If not, I might consider Steve for the position. It's up to you. The ball's in your court. And I don't want anyone getting a whiff of my intentions until I'm sure just who I will be promoting.'

'Can I have a few days off to see Maura and try to sort things out?'

'Better still, you can take five days off without pay. You're suspended for breach of company rules.'

Adam sat gobsmacked but couldn't argue the point as he knew he was in the wrong. Instead all he could utter was, 'I've already suggested to Mrs Matthews that Steve will probably take over from me.'

'Well, you shouldn't have. I'll see to all that.'

Adam rose to his feet but Benny waved him down again. 'Finish your whiskey and then go get your wife back.'

Adam left the office, his mind swimming. Benny had made his intentions crystal clear. The die had been cast. It was obvious that he meant to buy the land, house and all. All that remained now was who would be asked to manage it.

Adam knew he had hurt Maura badly and he'd be a very lucky man if she took him back. It was Danny's birthday on Sunday. She must be persuaded to let him see his son. He would bring the child a present and grovel to Maura if necessary, while he was there, or say goodbye to promotion.

He considered this for a long time. Was promotion all he was interested in, he asked himself? No! Not if he couldn't win back his wife. Without her and Danny he would have nothing but an empty life to look forward to. But on the other hand, promotion would provide an excellent platform from which to work in an effort to win Maura back.

20

The front door banging shut brought Davey at a trot through the scullery into the kitchen. There was no sign of his daughter. He regretted being unable to ease her pain much, but at least now she knew he was on her side, come what may. He arrived outside in time to see her running to catch a bus. She must have heard his shout but chose to ignore it, because when she was safely out of reach on the bus platform she turned to give him a cheery smile and a wave. Where on earth was she off to, he wondered? Probably to fetch Danny back home with her. God go with her, he prayed. She was living on the edge these past few days. The state she was in, anything could happen. He hoped Beth Gallagher would be able to talk more sense into her than he had.

*　　*　　*

Maura climbed the stairs to the upper deck of the bus and was glad to find it empty. She was devastated, and didn't know where to turn for the best. This space was what she needed. No distractions. Time to sort out her muddled thoughts, tear out her hair if need be. Imagine her forgetting Danny's coming birthday. How could she have been so neglectful?

Before all this nonsense began, Adam and she had already been discussing what to buy their son; it had been top of their priorities. Then unknown to her Evelyn Matthews had returned. Still beautiful, but now very rich as well. And married! Was Adam so wrapped up in her that it didn't matter any more the havoc he was causing?

She paused. Was that all it was: nonsense? Was she being stupid? No, she was kidding herself, Adam *had* betrayed her and, worse still, everybody knew about it. She closed her eyes tightly and, drawing in deep breaths, fought for self-control. She mustn't go down that road or she would lose her sanity. Still, no matter what had taken place, she couldn't believe she had forgotten Danny's birthday. What kind of mother was she? Would Adam remember?

She admitted the fact that her father was right. Adam had every right to see his son on his birthday. She would just have to make herself scarce and make sure she didn't have to talk to him, thereby causing a possible confrontation between them in front of the party guests. She would use her father as a go-between.

Although Maura was torn by all kinds of dark thoughts, she was none the wiser when she got off the bus than she had been when she got on. She wasn't so fortunate when she caught the next bus for the final leg of her journey to Holywood. The single-decker was packed and she sat crushed in her seat gazing soulfully out the window. Still in a miserable mood when she arrived at her destination, she trudged to the cul-de-sac at the end of the avenue where her friend lived.

Some rain had fallen during the night, quenching the thirsty earth, and Beth, taking advantage of the soft soil, was on her knees weeding the borders, which were a profusion of multicoloured flowers. A credit to her hard work. She couldn't believe her eyes when she looked up and saw Maura walking up the driveway towards the door of her bungalow. Just then Frisky came bounding round the side of the house from the back garden, followed by an excited Danny. Catching sight of his mother he let out a whoop of delight and rushed to meet her, the puppy at his heels.

Beth rose stiffly from her aching knees and slowly made her way across the lawn to greet her friend. 'This is a surprise. I left you only a couple of hours ago,' she stated unnecessarily. Kissing Maura on the cheek, she eyed her in bewilderment.

Embarrassed, Maura's words came in a rush. 'You've every right to look at me like that. You must think I'm daft. But do you know what? I had completely forgotten all about Danny's birthday on Sunday. I need to keep him with me till then. Take him into the city centre and let him choose his own present.'

'It's no wonder you forgot. You've had too much on your mind lately to think straight. But don't worry, I remembered. I'd have reminded you eventually. Come inside and we can talk about it over a coffee.'

Danny was clinging to Maura's skirt. Cupping his face in her hands, she bent down and kissed him soundly on the mouth, whispering, 'I love you, Danny,' for his ears only. Then, her arm around his shoulders, they followed Beth round to the back of the house and into the conservatory.

'Actually, it was me da who mentioned it. He says Adam must be allowed to see his son on his birthday. Da's very upset about all this, you know. I think Cassie's putting some pressure on him.'

'I have to say that I agree with Davey on that score. It would be cruel if you denied Adam his parental rights. But I don't think Davey would be the type to let Cassie influence him where his family

409

is concerned. He'll be behind you all the way without anyone else's advice.'

'You really think so? You believe that?'

'Yes, I do. And so am I, for that matter. You're not on your own, and don't you think for one minute you are. Sit down. I won't be a minute.' She removed her gardening shoes and knee pads and, taking them with her, said, 'I'll get rid of these and wash my hands.' She moved off but suddenly realised that the dog had followed them inside. 'Danny, take Frisky outside and stay with him, please. You know he's not house-trained yet.'

The child cowered closer to his mother, probably afraid she would leave without him. Maura rose to her feet and with an apologetic wink at her friend said, 'Come on, love. I'd like to take another look at Beth's lovely flowers. I haven't seen them for a while. You can show me round the gardens.'

'And whose fault's that, madam?' Beth shouted after her.

Maura envied Beth her wonderful home. The Gallaghers had had the big sprawling bungalow built to their own specification and it was beautifully laid out and surrounded by gardens. At the bottom of the rear garden stood a gazebo where you could sit and view the lough.

Constantly glancing over his shoulder to make sure that his mother was still following, Danny made a beeline for the gazebo with the faithful

Frisky romping at his heels. It was a peaceful haven. Danny sat, the dog on one side of him, his mother on the other. Suddenly out of the blue he said, 'Mammy, Daddy not love us?'

Aghast, Maura slid to her knees in front of her son and gripping him by the shoulders gave him a gentle shake. 'Listen, Danny. Your daddy loves us very much. It's just that at the moment he is very busy and he can't get to see you as often as he would like.' She paused and offered a quick prayer to God, begging His forgiveness for the lies she was telling her son.

Big blue eyes searched her face. 'Daddy coming to my party?'

This was something she could make sure of, and she solemnly promised him, 'Yes, sweetheart, he'll be at your party.' *She* just needn't be there all the time.

To Maura's relief further questions were shelved as Beth called them back to the conservatory. She had the small table set with a coffee pot, cups, a drink for Danny and a plate of sandwiches. 'Come on, you pour the coffee while I get the milk and something for the child to eat.'

Once seated, Beth was pleased to notice that her friend was more relaxed and questioned her. 'What are you planning for Danny? Are you having a party?'

'I'm not sure. He doesn't know any kids in

Greencastle, just Mary Moon's two, but I'll have to arrange something.'

Beth clapped her hands. 'I know what. Let me throw a party for him, here in my home.' She was full of enthusiasm at the idea. 'Then all his young playmates from around here can be invited. And we'll invite Mary and her two girls over as well. How about that?'

'Ah, no, Beth. You've done too much for us already. Besides, you won't want a lot of youngsters running wild over your lovely home. Heavens, no!' She shook her head determinedly. 'No! I won't hear tell of it.'

'There won't be that many and we can confine them to the conservatory. If the weather is good they can have the run of the gardens. Does that suit you?'

'I can't let you go to all that trouble, Beth.' Her friend's continued goodness had brought tears to Maura's eyes and she strove to contain them.

'Here now, we'll have none of that auld nonsense. That's what friends are for, to be there in times of need. Let's finish our coffee and we'll make out a list of who to invite. Then we'll take Danny down to the shops to help choose the invitation cards.' She smiled at Danny. 'Won't that be great, love?'

'Will Daddy come to my party?' he asked again.

With a sad look at Maura, it was Beth who

answered him. 'Of course he will. He wouldn't miss your birthday for the world.'

Pacified, the child nodded solemnly and settled down but still stayed close to his mother, pressed against Maura's knees. Frisky was whining outside the door but for once Danny ignored his yelps. It was as if he was afraid that his mother would disappear if he left her side even for one second.

Beth coaxed him to sit on a cushion and placed his drink on the floor beside him, next to a plate with his favourite iced finger on it. He fell for the tempting morsel and polished it off in record time.

They decided to go into Bangor where there were more shops and a bigger selections of cards and toys than here in Holywood.

'Adam was talking about us buying him a two-wheeler bicycle. You know, the type that has stabilisers attached. I wonder if he'll remember. I don't know what to do. I don't want to be saddled with two bikes.'

In Bangor town centre, Beth canted her head towards a shop across the road whose window was displaying all sizes and colours of bicycles. 'Let's go over there and see if they have anything to suit a three-year-old.'

There were quite a few bikes to suit Danny's age and height. He fell in love with all of them.

After a lot of mind-changing he chose a blue bike with a bell.

Maura was pleased at his show of happiness. She put down a deposit and arranged with the assistant for the boy's father to pay the rest when he collected the bike on Saturday. Feeling in a much happier frame of mind, she insisted on treating Beth to lunch. Knowing it would please Maura, Beth bit back the refusal to let her spend her money that lurked on the tip of her tongue. They went to an upstairs café and spent an enjoyable hour there.

Maura paid the bill, then with a shamefaced look said, 'I know I told you you could have Danny overnight, but would you be very disappointed if I take him back with me?'

Beth sighed. 'I'd a feeling that's why you came. I enjoy the child's company tremendously, but I can understand your need for his presence. I'll send out the invitations for you and make arrangements for the party. Meanwhile you must get in touch with Adam and let him know what you are planning. Promise?'

'I'll get my father to act as go-between. There's no way I'm going to speak to Adam again.'

It hurt Beth to hear this and she cautioned her, 'Don't be so stubborn, love. Don't do something you might regret the rest of your life. Talk to Adam. Hear what he has to say and then decide what to do.'

'You don't understand how much he's hurt me, Beth. No matter what he says, I won't be able to take him back.' She shook her head. 'Who am I kidding, eh? He won't want to come back. I suppose I'm just putting off the inevitable.'

'Well then, you've nothing to lose. Listen to what he has to say.'

'My pride. It's all I have left to lose.'

'Pride won't keep you warm on a winter's night, mind,' Beth reminded her.

Tired of being pressurised, Maura rose to her feet. 'I'll catch the bus home, Beth. I've taken up too much of your day as it is.'

'Catch yourself on, girl. I'll run you home. Besides, I've a couple of things to get in Belfast. I'll make the one run do.'

'Then you could drop me off at High Street, Beth, I want to take a look around the shops.' She reached for her friend and hugged her close. 'Thanks again for everything.'

Adam felt at a loss without the use of the van. Maura had pleaded with him time and time again to buy a small second-hand car, so they could be independent. He remembered her reply when he had argued with her that they didn't need a car, so why waste money; when did they ever go anywhere special that required owning a car? There was a cynical look in her eye as she retorted,

'Exactly!' Knowing that she would bend to his will in the long run, he'd waved her sarky remark thoughtlessly aside.

He now realised how wrong he had been. Maura had been confined to the house with no phone and no car. And with no children for Danny to mix with. Their nearest neighbours were a good distance away. She had nevertheless made sure Danny met other children of his age; it wasn't only imaginary play friends he had, Maura had seen to that. So why hadn't he pulled his weight and made life a bit more comfortable for her?

Especially as he was on a decent wage, and with a bit of care they could easily afford a small car. No wonder she had become restless, cut off as she was from all her close friends. Evelyn coming back, and him hiding the fact from his wife, must have been the last straw. And to crown it all, her old flame Francie Murphy was there, ever ready to step into Adam's shoes and salve her pain. If Adam won her back and got the management job, the world would be their oyster.

Well, he had five days to woo his way back into Maura's affections. And no van to get about in. Tough! Now he would learn the hard way the frustration of waiting for buses. Benny's ultimatum was still ringing in his ears as he quickened his pace and was home in a few minutes. He had a quick wash and shave, then changed into his best clothes before heading out to catch the bus into Belfast.

He was just in time to see the rear end of one disappearing up the road and had to wait fifteen minutes for the next. Once in the city centre he caught another bus to the Royal Victoria Hospital, intent on explaining to Charles Matthews his reason for not finishing the gardens. He wouldn't be able to tell him too much, of course, just enough to let him know that he had no say in the matter and it was inevitable that he must move on.

Charles, although still wired up to the monitor, was propped up in bed and looking much better. He had a bit of colour on his face. Evelyn was at her husband's bedside holding his hand. She greeted Adam warily.

'Hello, Adam, I didn't expect to see you here. I've been explaining to Charles that you won't be finishing the work on our gardens.'

Adam moved forward and clasped the other hand Charles weakly lifted towards him. 'It's not because I don't want to see it finished, sir, but due to things beyond my control I am unable to do so.'

Charles's voice was faint and Adam had to lean closer. 'What if I spoke to Mr Gallagher?' His eyes were roaming over Adam's face, but before he could comment on his bruises, Adam rushed on.

'No, sir, please don't do that. It's complicated.

I'm needed elsewhere and it's in my best interests that I go. When the work is completed I'd like to come back and inspect it and if you are pleased, as I'm sure you will be, perhaps you'll offer me a celebratory drink.'

'Don't you forget to come and see me,' Charles whispered in a weak halting voice.

'I won't. Look, don't tire yourself. Mrs Matthews wants you back home as soon as possible, so she can indulge you.'

'Hi, Dad. I'm glad to see you looking so much better today.'

Only when David spoke did Adam become aware that the other man had come up behind him. He swung around and, straightening to his full height, greeted him. 'Hello, David.'

'Did you run into someone's fist?' David taunted.

'Aye, but you should see the other guy.' Adam smirked. David's face was a damned sight more bruised than his own. Adam didn't envy him having to explain everything when Charles had fully recovered and was ready to listen to his excuses. He leaned over Charles again. 'I'll leave you now, Mr Matthews. You take care.'

Evelyn walked out to the lift with him. 'Thanks for everything, Adam. How's Maura?' Her voice was tentative.

'I'm on my way to try to see her now. She's refusing to have anything to do with me.'

'I hope things work out for you. I feel so guilty. I've brought you nothing but trouble since I came back.'

'Would you listen to yourself! You've got nothing to feel guilty about. All right, we did kiss on impulse. Surely you're not feeling guilty about that? And thank God it went no further than a kiss. So don't you go blaming yourself over me, do you hear? You just watch out for yourself and don't let that git David get too close.'

'Never fear, Charles knows just what his son is capable of. Actually we are waiting for his solicitor. He's due here any minute now.'

The lift door slid quietly open and Evelyn warmly greeted a tall gentleman who stepped out, before giving Adam a farewell kiss on the cheek. Adam suspected the stranger to be the very person they were waiting for.

A short wait for a bus down Grosvenor Road, and a brisk walk to Wellington Place where he joined yet another queue for the number ten bus to Greencastle, set off a line of thought that shamed Adam. He could picture his wife struggling on and off buses with a child and pushchair. Perhaps Francie Murphy was just helping her after all, the day he saw them at the bus stop? And rewarded himself by kissing her like that? Adam didn't think so, but then again, Maura would have been on the defensive, had the kiss meant anything. Or would she?

Now he could understand why Maura was so angry at his audacity in leaving her to catch two buses home. He also realised why she kept plaguing him to buy a car. If he was lucky enough to win her back it would be the first thing he would set in motion.

Lost in thought, he was startled when suddenly something thumped against his legs. He looked down with a scowl, preparing to retaliate. Then he joyfully recognised his son's smiling face and heard his voice shouting, 'Daddy!' Stooping down he scooped the child up into his arms and hugging him close glanced about, looking for his wife. The queue had grown and she was at the end of it, calling for Danny to come back to her. Under the wide grins of other would-be passengers and without thinking twice Adam left his place in the queue and went to join her.

He had forgotten about his swollen nose until Danny touched it and asked if he had fallen down. Maura also gazed at his face in astonishment but didn't comment on it. 'You've lost your place,' she admonished him. 'Go back. People will understand; they'll let you back in again.'

'I'll go back if you'll come with me.'

'I'm afraid people won't be all that accommodating,' she said wryly. 'Besides, it's true what they say, these buses are like bananas: they come in bunches, so we won't have all that long to wait. Where are you off to anyhow?'

'Where do you think? To visit you, believe it or not.'

'Where's the van?' She wasn't taking any chances by presuming that he was really on his way to Greencastle. The number ten bus would also take him on up Whitewell Road on to the Antrim Road to Evelyn.

He drew her out of the queue and to a shop doorway where they would have some privacy. 'Look, let's find somewhere we can get a cup of tea and have a chat and I'll explain everything.'

Flustered at being so close to him, she opened her mouth to refuse but he forestalled her.

'Please, Maura. It's wonderful seeing Danny like this. I've missed him something awful.'

Maura's heart was thumping so hard she thought he must surely hear it. However, at these words sadness engulfed her. He missed Danny! No mention of missing her. In spite of this, she still wanted to be in his company, to hear his voice. What kind of a fool was she? She found herself nodding in agreement.

'There's a café in College Street. Let's go there,' she suggested.

Adam kept glancing sideways at her as they walked along Queen Street, Danny gripped tightly in his arms. She was pale and there were dark rings around her eyes. That was his fault. This was what he missed most: being with his wife and child.

In the café he couldn't take his eyes off her as she poured the tea. Cheeks now pink at the intensity of his gaze, she motioned for him to pour Danny's drink.

Silence reigned for some seconds and not knowing how to break it, she challenged him. 'You wanted to talk, so talk.'

He held her eye and smiled. 'I can't believe I'm here with you and Danny. Let me savour this wonderful moment for a while longer.'

She frowned suspiciously. 'Here . . . hold on a minute, why aren't you at work today?'

The lovely happy feeling quickly dispersed, like the butter melting on their toasted muffins. Now for the reckoning. He bowed his head in shame as he confessed, 'I've been suspended.'

Her eyes widened in surprise. Was this something else she would be blamed for? 'How come?' she asked fearfully.

'Because I wasn't doing my job properly.'

'What on earth do you mean? You could do your job blindfolded.'

'Well, when Charles Matthews had a heart attack Evelyn was in an awful state,' Adam started to explain.

Maura quickly interrupted him. 'Evelyn's husband had a heart attack?'

'Yes, I thought perhaps you would have heard.' She shook her head and he continued. 'Yesterday morning. After I put the note through your letter box saying I would pick you up at seven, I went on to work. I'm sorry about standing you up, Maura, but I couldn't get away.'

Another abrupt nod. Had Adam a genuine excuse for standing her up after all? Was she the one in the wrong for going out with Francie Murphy?

'It was a horrendous day, Maura, truly. I couldn't leave Evelyn's side.'

'Why? Had she no one else to turn to?' Here it was, his limp excuse. Caught up in his sorry tale of woe, Adam failed to notice the sarcasm in her voice.

Completely unaware of the change in his wife's attitude, Adam explained, 'Yes. Charles's son was there, but he has feelings for Evelyn . . . which, by the way, she doesn't return.'

'And you of course were afraid that she might change her mind. Is that it?'

Adam blinked in confusion. 'No. Not at all. But, you see, she was afraid to be alone with him. As it turned out she was right. David came to the house and started mouthing off and we had a bit of fisticuffs.' He gestured towards his face. 'That's how I received these bruises. What else could I do? I had to stay. I couldn't leave her. Could I?'

How wonderful for Evelyn. Two men fighting for her affections, while Maura had sat at home alone, betrayed and rejected. She sat, head bowed, taking this in. The pain was still too fresh in her mind and it was easy to recall the depth of her misery as she had sat in all her finery the night before, patiently waiting for Adam to come and take her out to wine and dine her. The very thought of it overwhelmed her. All the time he had only one thing on his mind: he had been taking care of Evelyn, the love of his life.

'Maura?' Confident that she understood, he was unprepared for her reaction.

She lifted her head. When he saw the hurt etched so deeply in her eyes, now blurring with tears, he drew back in dismay.

A sickly smile wavered across her face, as she blinked furiously to prevent the tears falling. She wouldn't give him the satisfaction of the humiliation of her weeping in public. 'Of course you couldn't leave her. I for one can understand that. I wouldn't expect you to.' She started to gather up her belongings, then helping a bewildered, complaining Danny from his chair, she put on his coat and rose to her feet.

Adam sat dumbfounded, unable to comprehend what she was up to. What had he done now to create such a change in her? The fact that Danny was crying, and Adam wanted to lift him and run away with him while he had the chance, didn't help any.

'What are you doing?' he growled and reached for her arm.

'Don't you touch me ever again,' she hissed in his face. 'Do you hear me?'

Heads were turning in their direction. 'So does everybody else by the looks of it. Sit down and finish your tea.'

'It would choke me. I'm going home to my father's house and I don't want you to bother me ever again. You are invited to Danny's birthday party at Beth's on Sunday.'

He was hurrying to pay the bill before she could leave the café, when her voice reached him.

'By the way, I've ordered a bike in Bangor for the child. You have to collect it on Saturday. Beth will tell you the name of the shop if you phone her.'

Under the curious stare of other customers Maura hastened out the door, dragging a confused Danny behind her.

The queue to the till was short but the woman in charge talked a lot to each customer as if they were old friends. Adam's patience was stretched to breaking point. At last in exasperation, throwing some coins on the counter to cover the bill, he charged from the café. Looking up and down the street he could see no sign of Maura. Neither was she at the bus stop on Wellington Place. Grim-faced, he headed for the bus station to catch yet another bus back to Holywood. His resolve to win her over was more consuming than ever. He vowed he wouldn't give up the fight. What would he do without Maura?

21

Maura had no recollection of how she got home that day. On the bus Danny cried himself into an exhausted sleep in her arms and she clutched his precious body closely to her, rocking him gently. Poor wee soul. God forgive them for upsetting him like this. They should be cherishing him. And she would! With God's help, given the chance she would devote her life to him. Aware that some of the other travellers were eyeing them, she stared blindly out the window until the bus at last reached Greencastle, afraid someone might approach her and ask whether they could be of any help. Pity from strangers was the last thing she wanted just now.

Her father had chopped up a cabbage and was peeling potatoes when he heard her entering the kitchen. Placing the peeler on the draining board he popped his head round the kitchen door. Seeing her expression, with a distraught gasp he hurried from the scullery and relieved her of Danny's weight. He gave her a worried look as he laid the sleeping child on the settee, then taking his daughter in his arms and patting her on the back, he gently chastised her.

'Here now. Nothing is all that bad,' he said soothingly.

'Well, I'll tell you this, Da. I hope it doesn't get any worse or I don't know what I'll do. I'm at my wits' end.'

He led her to the chair close by her son. 'You don't mean that, love. Sit there and I'll make us a nice strong pot of tea.'

The cure for all ails, she thought. What on earth did people do in the olden days when nobody had as yet heard of tea?

Davey turned to go to the scullery but with a motion of her hand she quickly stopped him. 'No tea, thank you, Da. But I do need a big favour of you. Can we talk?'

'You're sure? A cup of tea might help you relax. Or I have some whiskey, what about a wee tot?'

A very definite shake of the head brought him to sit down facing her.

'Of course. Anything! Anything you need, if I possibly can, I will get it for you.'

A wry smile briefly touched her lips. 'Don't commit yourself so readily, Da. You mightn't think so when you hear what I have to say. Let me explain, try to sort things out in my own mind as I go along.'

Davey nudged his chair closer and leaning forward, arms on thighs, gazed intently at his daughter and prepared to listen. He could see that she was at the end of her tether. God grant that he'd be able to help her.

Haltingly, Maura began her tale of woe. How she had gone to Beth's to bring Danny back, and had accidentally met Adam at the bus stop in town. She explained about the state of her husband's face where David Matthews had roughed him up.

This name was new to Davey and he queried, 'David Matthews?'

Maura grimaced and explained. 'Evelyn's stepson . . . I've never met him but he must be in his forties, at least.'

Davey nodded in understanding and his daughter went on.

'Adam looked a sorry sight, so when he asked me to join him for a cup of tea somewhere, I let my pity overrule my heart and foolishly agreed. We went to that café in College Street and Danny was beside himself with excitement. To be truthful, so was I,' she admitted shamefaced.

Davey was confused. Why was she so upset? All

this sounded promising. Indeed it sounded like good news to him. Surely Adam had taken this opportunity to plead his case? Maura went on to tell him that Mr Matthews had suffered a heart attack on Monday morning and that Evelyn was in such a state that Adam had felt compelled to stay with her.

He quirked a brow at her. 'Well now, Maura, maybe he really couldn't get away. Have you thought of that?'

She flashed a pale, strained smile at him. 'No, as I already told you, Adam dotes on that woman. You see, he had every right to stand me up. I told you, Evelyn comes first with him . . . every time.'

Davey immediately interrupted her. 'No, he hadn't any right to disappoint you. You should have been his sole concern no matter what. Was this David fellow not with her?'

'I don't know.' Maura's mind shied away from the implications of this remark. Was that the reason for Adam's excuse? Was he afraid to leave Evelyn alone with David in case he seduced her?

'What did you do?'

'Oh, I tried to be cool about it. I didn't want to let myself down in public. I let him rant on about not being able to leave his great love. After all, I was already aware that she always came first, so it came as no surprise to me. But still, I was disappointed and hurt that he thought so little of me. Then when he had the audacity to expect my understanding and co-operation . . . well, I completely lost it.'

Inwardly Davey groaned. He knew what his daughter's temper was like when she got wound up. He asked fearfully, 'What happened?'

'It was awful.' She blew her nose and tears poured down her face. Davey reached across and gripped her hands tightly. She sniffed and tried to smile but failed miserably. 'Terrible. I was trying to get Danny into his coat and he was wailing and struggling against me. Every head in the café must have turned our way to see what the racket was about and it pleased me no end to see Adam actually squirming with embarrassment. His face was red as beetroot and he didn't know where to look.

'He was over at the till queueing to pay the bill when I eventually reached the door. And my final words to him were, he was to collect a bike for Danny and bring it to his birthday party on Sunday.'

Davey slumped back in his chair. Maybe there was hope yet. 'So he's coming here on Sunday to the child's party?'

'No. The party will be at Beth's. She has invited you also, and anyone else who cares to come along.'

'Does Adam know that?'

'I think I told him to phone Beth to find out the details.'

'And how can I be of help?'

'I want you to act as a go-between. Help me pass myself. I don't want to speak to Adam face to face if I can possibly help it. Anything I might have to say to him, I want to say it through you. A kind of intermediary, if you like. I don't want to spoil the child's party by my absence, but I'm not sure I can be brave enough any longer to pretend in public that everything is all right between us. I'll be hovering about somewhere in the background and I'll need you there to keep things running smoothly. Will you do that for me, Da?'

'Of course I will, love. I'll make sure there are no scenes,' he promised. Inwardly he added, but I'll do my best to get you two back together again or my name's not Davey Craig.

As they cleared up after dinner on Tuesday night, Benny told his wife about suspending Adam that afternoon.

She was appalled. 'You what?'

'You heard. I was just stamping my authority on him. He was making excuses about his treatment of Maura.'

'Oh, dear God, you didn't say that I told you, did you?'

'Of course not. I didn't have to, he started talking off his own bat.'

'But to suspend him? Ah, Benny. For how long?'

432

'Only till next Monday.'

'But I've offered to have Danny's birthday party here on Sunday. Adam is coming. If you're here it will make things a bit awkward for both of you.'

'Don't worry, I'll be well out of the way before anybody arrives. I'm playing golf on Sunday, remember?'

She breathed a sigh of relief. 'Thank God for that, Benny. I'd forgotten all about your golf.'

On Wednesday a worried Adam trekked over to Greencastle to see his wife but the house was empty. He assumed Davey was at work. But where was his Maura? How on earth could he make his peace if he couldn't find her?

Crossing over to Stewart's he asked her work-mates when she would be next working there and was told she wouldn't be in that weekend as her son's birthday party was on Sunday. As he left the shop his eye lit on the phone booth and he thought of Beth. She might know where Maura was.

His heart thumped in his breast with surprise when it was Maura who answered the phone although she immediately hung up when she heard his voice. Hands shaking, he tried again and again, but the phone was engaged each time he rang. She obviously had no intention of speaking to him and had left the receiver off the hook. Well then, he would go to her. He'd call a taxi. There were numbers of many taxi firms beside the phone and he dialled one. To his frustration, when he got through he discovered he hadn't enough change to connect the line and hung up in disgust.

Deciding to come back around teatime when he would at least see Davey Craig and find out what he knew, Adam headed across the road to the bus stop. He would stay in the city centre and while away the next few hours window-shopping. Easier said than done when he was raring to go. Time dragged. Sitting outside a pub eating a pork pie for his lunch with a pint to wash it down, Adam watched cars of all shapes and sizes pass by. Hastily he finished his pie and drank the rest of his beer. What was he thinking of, sitting here wasting time? He could be at least looking at second-hand cars, seeing what was available and what he could afford.

The rest of the afternoon was spent walking round motor showrooms doing just that. He couldn't see anything that he thought Maura would like. After all, once she learned to drive, Maura would be using the car more than him. If it all panned out he would have the use of the van. This gave him pause for thought. Was he being too hasty? Was there a real chance of winning Maura back?

Sensing that Adam was really interested in the car he was walking around and examining with such care, a salesman who was hovering near by closed in for the kill.

'She's a wee beauty, isn't she? And a bargain at the price.'

'I'm just looking today.'

Adam didn't want to be rushed into something he might later regret. He wished he could get big Reggie, who serviced all the works vehicles, to give it the once-over, but time was of the essence. He nodded to the salesman and walked away, only to swing round on his heel and turn around. Ah, what the hell. If he lost his job he'd need a car anyway. He went back inside. Sensing a change of mind, the salesman hurriedly approached him.

With a wave of his hand Adam said, 'Sell me that car. By that, I mean I want to know all about it, warts and all.'

Under Adam's amused gaze, the man straightened to attention and started into his sales patter.

Adam listened in silence. When he stopped Adam said, 'That's all its good points. Now tell me, if it's so good, why's it still here?'

'Believe me, it has only been on show a week and it won't be here for long. There's been plenty of interest in it this past few days.'

Adam was becoming suspicious now. 'Then why haven't you sold it? What's the snag?'

The man sensed a sale fading away and sighed. 'This is what I call a young person's car. Older folk think it too fast and flashy. Have you got a job?' Adam nodded. 'Well, some young people have come in and looked it over and would dearly love to buy it but being on the dole at the moment, they can't afford it.'

Adam could well believe that. He quickly made up his mind. 'What's the least you'll take for it?'

He watched as the man debated on how much of his commission he could forfeit. 'Tell you what, I'll let you have another fifty off. That's the best I can do. Is that all right?'

Adam held out his hand to shake on it. 'Done. Can I drive it away now?'

'If I can have proof of identity and you have a current driving licence, it's all yours.' He paused. 'How do you intend paying for it?'

Adam took a chequebook from his inside pocket. 'I'll pay a deposit and the rest on those easy terms you've been quoting to me, OK?'

'That'll be fine. I'll need ten per cent deposit. Follow me, sir, and I'll make out the paperwork. I'll also need to phone your bank, if that's all right with you?'

'Be my guest.'

A short time later Adam drove the dark green Mini Cooper from the salesroom straight to a petrol station and filled the tank. A glance at his watch told him he would probably catch Maura at home now or, failing that, Davey would be there by now preparing his evening meal.

When the shiny, new-looking car pulled up outside Davey's door, curiosity brought him to peer from behind the net curtains, wondering who was in it. When Adam stepped from the car, surprise sent Davey rushing into the hall to open the door.

Stepping out on to the pavement, he exclaimed, 'Have you won the pools or something, lad?'

'No such luck. It's second-hand; one careful owner, so I've been told. And I can well believe it. It looks as if I've got a bargain there. I'm trying to win myself back into favour with your daughter. What do you think my chances are?'

'She's not here. Come inside and let's have a chat.'

They sat each side of the hearth and it was Davey who broke the silence. 'Maura's staying at Beth's until after the party on Sunday.'

Alarmed, Adam gasped out, 'She can't! I need to talk to her before that.'

'I'm afraid she can and she will. She wants nothing more to do with you and I can't say I blame her after all the torture you've put her through.'

'Torture? What are you on about?'

'Don't you think it torture to leave her all dolled up and sitting alone for a hour or more waiting for you? And believe you me, she went to a lot of trouble for her big night out and she did look beautiful.'

Maura stepping out in Francie Murphy's wake

437

flashed across Adam's mind. He had assumed that she was trying to impress Francie, but it was him she was all dolled up for.

Overcome by his stupidity, he whispered, 'I know she looked beautiful. I saw her, Davey.'

Davey stiffened and his face became stern. 'What do you mean, you saw her?'

'I arrived at the bottom of Whitewell Road in time to see her climb into Francie Murphy's car outside Conway's bar.'

'And you didn't stop and explain why you were late?'

'I had been in a fight with Charles Matthews' son and I was in a right mess. Blood everywhere. I couldn't bear to have her compare me with Francie, the state I was in. He seems to be worming his way into her heart, doesn't he?'

'Here now, don't you go putting the blame at Francie's door. You're responsible for all that has happened, nobody else. I'd be only too glad to see her and Francie make a go of it. But it's you she loves.'

Mouth open, Adam stared at Davey. 'Do you honestly think so?'

'I don't think so . . . I *know* so.'

Adam pondered over this for some moments, then said humbly, 'I know you're not too keen on me, Davey, but will you help me? Otherwise I'll never be able to get Maura to speak to me.'

'I don't really dislike you, son. I just wish you'd married Maura decent like, ye know. But I will admit that you've made her happy . . . till now, that is. Beth arrived in a fluster last night and took Maura and the child back with her until after the party.'

'Did she say why?'

'I wasn't here. But I am grateful that Maura will be in good company for the next few days at least, so I wouldn't have questioned it anyway.'

Adam put his head in his hands and groaned. 'How can I ever put things right if she won't see me?'

Davey studied him for some moments and came to a decision. 'All is not lost yet. So let's put our heads together and see what we can come up with.'

Maura hovered nervously near the phone until she was sure that Adam would have given up in his endeavours to reach her, then she replaced the receiver on the cradle. Beth and Danny had taken Frisky for a walk. She had completely forgotten that Adam was supposed to phone Beth and get the information from her about the party or she wouldn't have answered the phone.

When Beth had learned about Adam being suspended, she had gone post-haste to Greencastle to tell Maura the bad news, only to find out that she already knew as well as how she had come to know. Sensing that Maura must be hurting something awful, Beth persuaded her to come to Holywood and stay with her, her excuse being she needed help to arrange the party for Sunday. Glad of the pretext that she could be of assistance, Maura left a note for her father, telling him about Beth's flying visit. Gathering together some clothes and belongings for their stay, and carrying her son, still dressed in his pyjamas, she went home with Beth.

She had been apprehensive at intruding into their privacy but Benny was his usual affable self and made her feel most welcome. He felt a bit of a traitor, knowing he was making it harder for Adam to gain access to Maura, but in the face of Beth's determination there was nothing else he could do.

The rest of the week passed in a whirl of activity. A birthday cake was baked along with small fairy cakes. Sweets and potato crisps and candles for the cake were purchased as well as plenty of fruit juice and lemonade. There were also balloons and small novelty packs for each child. At last everything was ready for the party as far as the children were concerned. Sandwiches and savouries would be prepared next morning for the adults. Happy that everything was going according to plan, Maura and Beth retired with easy minds for the night.

Danny had the household awake bright and early on Sunday morning and after breakfast Benny presented him with a Lego set from Beth and himself. Overjoyed with his present, Danny hugged and kissed them both and, while Maura explained to her son how the Lego worked, Beth put away all her good china and cleared the conservatory of anything that was breakable. She also set a couple of tables along one side of the conservatory to hold the food and drinks. The young guests were due to arrive at two o'clock. Shortly beforehand Benny excused himself and went off for his day of golf, glad that he wouldn't have to listen to screaming children or face Adam Brady until Monday morning.

The first guests to arrive were Davey Craig and Mary Moon with her two children. Francie Murphy had driven them over and though he would have done a hasty retreat, Beth insisted that he was more than welcome to stay if he wanted to. He glanced at Maura. She felt that it would be downright rude of her to disagree with Beth and send him packing, although she would give him a friendly word of warning to be on his behaviour with Adam. Giving this some thought she nodded her approval. Francie quickly removed his jacket and prepared to make himself useful.

Danny was excitedly ripping the wrapping paper off the presents Jenny and Emma had brought for him. Maura admonished her friend, 'You shouldn't have, Mary. One present would have been enough.'

'Oh, you know what they're like. Each had to have a parcel of their own to carry. Besides, it's what I wanted to do.'

Squeals of delight brought everybody running outside, but Maura, guessing what the cause of all the excitement was likely to be, locked herself in the bathroom.

She was right! Adam was soon surrounded by laughing children as he tried to teach Danny how to conquer his new bike. He kept an eye out for Maura but there was no sign of her about the place. She was probably avoiding him. He hoped Davey would keep his promise to help him. Eventually, as more guests arrived, he managed to join Francie in the garden where they made desultory conversation over glasses of beer.

After beating about the bush for some minutes and getting nowhere fast Adam said, 'Is Maura not here?'

Francie genuinely had no idea where she had got to and he answered truthfully, 'I really don't know, Adam. She was here earlier on and I didn't see her leave, so I imagine she's still around somewhere, probably inside the house.'

It was obvious Adam didn't believe him and it showed. 'Is Davey here or don't you know that either?'

'Yes, he's here all right. I drove him and Mary Moon and her two girls over.' He glanced around.

'I see smoke coming from the gazebo so I imagine you'll find him there. Where there's smoke there's Davey.'

'Smoke signals! It's the Indians calling me. If you'll excuse me, I'll go see what they want.'

He didn't invite Francie to accompany him, just strode across the lawn in a purposeful manner. Francie watched him until he disappeared into the gazebo, wondering whether Davey and his son-in-law had finally made up their differences.

Maura stood out of sight at the corner of the street waiting for a bus. She wanted to visit the house that she had shared with Adam for almost four years. In the meantime, her father had promised to ward off any questions about her disappearance from the celebrations until she returned. She didn't want to miss any of her son's party but felt the need to say a final goodbye to the home that had held so many happy memories for her.

Eventually she was wandering around the house she held so dear but must surely now leave. Beth might be a close friend but even she couldn't expect her husband to let Maura continue to rent it if it was meant to encourage one of Benny's workers to stay put at the nursery. Good horticulturists are hard to come by these days, he would remind her.

Maura went from room to room, running her fingers lovingly along a piece of furniture or lifting an ornament, reminiscing and wiping away a tear at the memory. The rooms were in an untidy state and the kitchen could do with a good wash down. Her fingers itched to get stuck in and clean everything but she controlled the urge. This was Adam's mess, let him clean it up.

Standing outside the back door, she decided she had time to take a last walk down to the water's edge. Near the beach there was a cut that led up to a rocky knoll prominent with signposts warning of its dangers. Choosing this route, Maura climbed to the highest point. Except for the sheer drop, today it didn't look so dangerous. She stood on the edge of the rocks and gazed out over the lough to the distant Antrim coastline. What a wonderful panoramic view it was, the lough a gently heaving mass under a cloudless azure sky. She looked over the water towards Greencastle, where she would probably spend the rest of her life, and sighed. If she could just get over this wild deep love she had for Adam, she imagined that she'd be quite happy there once all the fuss and gossip died down. She hoped so, for where else could she go?

Davey greeted Adam warmly, surprised how taken he now was with this young man. Why hadn't he listened to friends and neighbours when Maura had confessed that she was pregnant? Pride! Silly stupid pride had made him spurn the daughter he loved. Even when Adam had made overtures to try to get to know him for Maura's sake, he had remained an obnoxious, distant old goat. Was he about to get a chance to make amends? He sincerely hoped so.

'Sit down, son, I'm glad you're here.'

Adam sat down beside him and prepared to listen. After their talk on Wednesday evening, he had trusted Davey's word that he would be able to point him in the direction of Maura today. Davey sat puffing away on his Woodbine, watching his son-in-law covertly. The lad's bruises were fading and he was strung as tight as a drum. A right bundle of nerves, he thought.

Becoming impatient, Adam said tersely, 'Did you manage to find out anything about Maura?'

'I did. I did indeed.'

Adam was on his feet in an instant. 'Well, tell me, man. I'm running out of time and patience here. Where is she?'

'She's in the perfect place for you to throw yourself on her mercy and make your peace with her without interruption,' Davey said proudly, as if he himself had set the stage for a reunion. As indeed he might have, fingers crossed.

Adam was shuffling with impatience. 'Ah, come on, Davey. Out with it. I can't afford to hang about any longer.'

'She's at your house. Saying her last farewells,

no doubt. And for God's sake, Adam, make her listen to what you have to say. This will probably be your last chance. Slip away now, son. Don't let anybody know where you're going in case they invite themselves along.'

He was talking to thin air. Adam was already on his way.

Ten minutes later Adam was parked outside his own front door. It was unlocked and he quietly entered the hall. Not a sound. Had Davey got his wires crossed? Maybe his wife was upstairs. He climbed the stairs two at a time, dashing from room to room, but there was no sign of Maura. Puzzled, he gazed out the window and was startled when he saw her in the distance, standing motionless on the edge of the rocks.

He knew how dangerous a spot that was. Over the years a few suicides had thrown themselves from that very place. There was a sheer drop down to more rocks hidden in the water below. In this sheltered cove, the tide never went out. Since the birth of their son they didn't dare go there as it was far too dangerous for the unwary. They didn't want Danny to know of its existence until he was old enough to understand the dangers, in case he ever wandered off there on his own. What was Maura thinking about, standing so close to the edge?

In a panic now, Adam thundered downstairs, out the back door and down to the cut. Clambering over the rocks as fast as he could, he remembered that Davey had said Maura was at the end of her tether and how he feared for her state of mind. Surely he wasn't hinting that Maura was distressed enough to take her own life? Please, God, no. Please, God, help me.

When he was close enough he paused for breath. Maura was standing perfectly still, gazing across the lough. She was so near the edge that he approached as quietly as he possibly could, afraid of startling her and causing her to topple over to an inevitable death. At last he felt safe enough to say her name. 'Maura,' he said in little more than a whisper.

Lost in thoughts of regret of what might have been, Maura was completely unaware of his presence until he spoke. She twirled around, almost losing her footing. For a split second Adam thought she would go over the edge, but she regained her balance and gaped at him in amazement. He leaned forward and, grabbing her by the arms, pulled her away from danger and gave her a good shake.

'That won't solve anything,' he yelled at her. She tried to break his hold on her but he only tightened his grip. 'How could you even contemplate something as desperate as that?'

Still struggling, she gasped, 'I don't know what

you're talking about. How did you know I was here?'

'Your da told me.'

Her eyes stretched wide in disbelief. 'Hah, surprise, surprise. Is there anyone I can trust now?' She pushed against his chest. 'Let me go.'

'Promise you won't do anything foolish.' He slowly released his grip but kept his eyes on her for any sudden movement.

She brushed grim-faced past him and headed back towards the house. 'I haven't got a death wish and have no intention of doing anything foolish if that's what you're ranting on about. Never had, never will.'

She couldn't believe what she was hearing. Adam had the audacity to think she was contemplating suicide.

He was right on her heels at the door. Inside she rounded on him. 'You're an arrogant swine. How dare you think you could drive me to take my own life? Do you really think I'm that desperate? I love my son too much to leave him in your sole custody, so you can prepare yourself for a fight.'

'Maura, listen. I don't want to share Danny with you. I want us to be a family again. I love you and—'

She interrupted him. 'Say that again,' she said softly.

Taken aback, he hesitated. Surely she knew he

loved her . . . 'What?' he asked, needing confirmation of her words.

She sniffed. 'You heard!'

He moved towards her but was afraid to break the spell. Without touching her, he said earnestly, 'I love you, Maura. How can you doubt it? I love you more than you'll ever know.'

'How can you expect me to believe you? After all you've done to hurt me and humiliate me, I'd be a fool to trust you ever again. No, Adam, I'm afraid it's too little too late.'

He was so close now that his breath fanned her face and she backed away from him, thinking, he mustn't touch me at all costs or I'll be lost.

'Please, Maura . . .'

Cautiously he inched forward, then throwing caution to the wind, he gently pulled her into his arms. She stiffened, then relaxed, but still stared balefully at him.

'Look, Maura, all I want is the chance to explain how this whole debacle came about and then you can make up your mind what you want to do. I never meant to deceive you, but we were each so suspicious of what the other was up to that everything went haywire. Before I could get up the courage to tell you the truth, you left me. I was gobsmacked. Couldn't understand why. I'd done nothing wrong, you know. This is the first chance I've had to explain my side of this sorry saga and

I don't want to mess it up, so please listen to what I have to say.'

He was gently edging her towards the settee. When she was seated, he sat down beside her and, putting an arm round her shoulders and holding her close, he explained from start to finish how things had spiralled out of control. He held nothing back – except that he thought it would be more prudent not to mention his hugs and kisses with Evelyn – as he explained in detail all that had happened. How he had been confused about his feelings for Evelyn but put it down to past memories when they had been together and adding that he really loved Maura more than anything. How he had come to be late that night and saw her looking like a film star and getting into Francie Murphy's car. The jealousy that had consumed him.

Listening in silence to his version of events, Maura realised how all her suspicions had swayed her to the wrong conclusions and she now believed him. When he had finished his narrative, she gave a long-drawn-out sigh and sat in deep thought for some time before starting her own.

When she had finished, her voice was trembling. He cupped her face in his hands and whispered against her lips, 'How could we have been so foolish, so blind?' She stared at him, her heart in her eyes, and tentatively offered her lips. Never were lips so passionately received. When they came up for air, gazing at her flushed, happy face, he said, 'Unfortunately our reunion will have to be postponed for a short while. I know a young fellow who will be wondering where we are. You will come back home with me today, won't you?'

'Just try and stop me,' she sighed and snuggled closer.

A wide smile split his face and her heart surged with joy at the love shining in his eyes. She nodded and smiled wryly. 'There'll be more than Danny wondering where we've got to. Me da will be over the moon for more reasons than us when he sees us back together, and Beth will be delighted. I owe them both so much for all they've done for me; I couldn't have lasted this long without them. I'll never be able to repay their kindness.'

'Aye, your dad's not such a bad auld git after all,' he replied with a smile. 'I think we'll get on all right together. And what did you mean about him being over the moon?'

She smiled inwardly, thinking of how Cassie would receive the news. 'Oh, it's a long story, love. I'll tell you all about it when we've nothing better to talk about,' she replied with a giggle.

He locked up and turned to see her gazing at the car. 'Who lent you the car? It's a beauty.'

'Now that's another thing I forgot to mention. You're going to have to learn how to drive, Maura. I bought that car for you. If we have another baby you won't be able to manage two children on and off the buses.'

Her eyes glowed for a second as he held open the door for her, then fixed on his and a frown gathered on her brow. 'You were that sure of me?'

He reached for her hand and clasped it in his. 'Now, Maura, we agreed there would be no more suspicious thoughts niggling at our minds, that we'd trust each other totally. And no, I wasn't in the least bit sure of you, but I did need to think positive or I'd risk losing everything I hold so dearly.'

She gave a contented sigh. 'Thank God. Now let's go back to Beth's and give everybody a surprise.'

PAINFUL DECISIONS

Mary Larkin

Life in 1920s Belfast is tough for the McGuigans.
Tommy, a man traumatised by action in the Somme,
exerts a powerful influence over his family with bouts
of drunken violence and cruelty. Son Johnny must deal
with the shameful consequence of young love, while his
sister Louise, a beautiful and hard-working mill girl, has
fallen for the educated and handsome Conor O'Rourke
– against the wishes of his manipulative mother. But it is
Nora, wife to Tommy and mother of Johnny and Louise,
whose actions threaten to destroy the very foundation
of the McGuigan family when she embarks on a secret
relationship of her own.

978-0-7515-3986-8

SWORN TO SECRECY

Mary Larkin

1971. With the troubles in Belfast at their height, a happy domestic life is something that Tess Maguire yearns for. Although her dressmaking business is successful, her partner's boyfriend Bob always seems to be nearby. Near enough, one night, to declare his true feelings for her . . . Tess, in confusion, has to confront her own mixed up emotions concerning Bob. And to address her feelings for her own ever-faithful boyfriend Tony. Especially when he asks her to marry him . . .

Another marriage seems, at first, to bring some stability into their lives. Tess's widowed mother Alice is finally to wed Dan, her long-standing partner. Free at last from his troublesome wife Anne, he can spend the rest of his years with Alice and his beloved grandson Jackie. Jackie is almost an orphan: his father Jack died in a motorcycle accident. His mother Colette may as well be dead – she decamped to Canada shortly after his birth.

And then, when Colette suddenly shows up to reclaim her son, the cracks in every relationship start to widen. Colette's arrival in Belfast opens old wounds, triggers a bitter custody battle – and unearths secrets that will change everyone's lives for ever.

978-0-7515-3718-5

Other bestselling titles available by mail:

☐	For Better, For Worse	Mary Larkin	£6.99
☐	Ties of Love and Hate	Mary Larkin	£7.99
☐	Best Laid Plans	Mary Larkin	£7.99
☐	Sworn to Secrecy	Mary Larkin	£7.99
☐	Painful Decisions	Mary Larkin	£6.99
☐	The Wasted Years	Mary Larkin	£7.99
☐	Playing With Fire	Mary Larkin	£7.99

The prices shown above are correct at time of going to press. However, the publishers reserve the right to increase prices on covers from those previously advertised, without further notice.

───────────── sphere ─────────────

Please allow for postage and packing: **Free UK delivery.**
Europe; add 25% of retail price; Rest of World; 45% of retail price.

To order any of the above or any other Sphere titles, please call our credit card orderline or fill in this coupon and send/fax it to:

Sphere, P.O. Box 121, Kettering, Northants NN14 4ZQ
Fax: 01832 733076   Tel: 01832 737526
Email: aspenhouse@FSBDial.co.uk

☐ I enclose a UK bank cheque made payable to Sphere for £ . . . .
☐ Please charge £ . . . . . . to my Visa, Delta, Maestro.

☐☐☐☐☐☐☐☐☐☐☐☐☐☐☐☐☐☐

Expiry Date ☐☐☐☐   Maestro Issue No. ☐☐

NAME (BLOCK LETTERS please) . . . .

ADDRESS . . . .

. . . .

. . . .

Postcode . . . . Telephone . . . .

Signature . . . .

Please allow 28 days for delivery within the UK. Offer subject to price and availability.